Katherine Greyle is the author of four historical romances and a RITA Award finalist for her first novel, *Oracle*. She is half Chinese-American and lives in the Chicago area with her husband and two daughters.

Karen Harbaugh is the author of several paranormal Regency romances. Born in Japan (and half Japanese-American), she was a navy brat and lived a gypsy childhood up and down the U.S. West Coast. She currently lives with her husband and son in Washington state.

Sabeeha Johnson is the author of Harlequin Temptation's *The Better Man,* under the pseudonym Sabrina Johnson. An immigrant from India who got her master's degree in journalism from Northwestern University, she lives in Flint Hill, Virginia, with her American husband.

Cathy Yardley, half Vietnamese-American, half Irish-American, is the author of three Harlequin Blaze novels and *L.A. Woman,* a Red Dress Ink novel. She lives in California.

Playing with Matches

Katherine Greyle
Karen Harbaugh
Sabeeha Johnson
Cathy Yardley

A SIGNET BOOK

SIGNET
Published by New American Library, a division of
Penguin Putnam Inc., 375 Hudson Street,
New York, New York 10014, U.S.A.
Penguin Books Ltd, 80 Strand,
London WC2R ORL, England
Penguin Books Australia Ltd, 250 Camberwell Road,
Camberwell, Victoria 3124, Australia
Penguin Books Canada Ltd, 10 Alcorn Avenue,
Toronto, Ontario, Canada M4V 3B2
Penguin Books (N.Z.) Ltd, Cnr Rosedale and Airborne Roads,
Albany, Auckland 1310, New Zealand

Penguin Books Ltd, Registered Offices:
Harmondsworth, Middlesex, England

First published by Signet, an imprint of New American Library,
a division of Penguin Putnam Inc.

First Printing, April 2003
10 9 8 7 6 5 4 3 2 1

Contents

Romancing Rose

BY

CATHY YARDLEY

Rose Parker stepped into the lobby of the Au Co Vietnamese Cultural Center with a sense of wariness. She hadn't been in anything remotely like this in . . . God, more years than she could remember. Probably since she was four, and that was about twenty-five years ago. She had the same impressions then: people speaking in a language she didn't recognize, the colorful posters and slogans hung on the walls in words she couldn't read. Smiling faces that looked at her curiously, obviously unable to place her, all with the same sort of expression: *What are you doing here?*

She took a deep breath. She couldn't blame them. A big part of her wondered what she was doing here, as well.

You're here because it's the only thing that's going to stop your grandmother from trying to set you up with every eligible Vietnamese bachelor in New York State. And you're going to learn about the Vietnamese culture, or die trying.

She smiled as she walked into the main office. Okay, so that was a little dramatic. Her grandmother had that effect on her.

"Can I help you?" a dark-haired woman said.

"I hope so," Rose said, smiling. "I spoke on the phone with a Paul, er, Young?"

The woman smiled. "Duong. Yes, he's the head of the center."

"I'm supposed to meet him."

"Certainly." The woman stood up and led Rose to a small office. "Paul? You've got an appointment."

"Send her in."

Rose took a deep breath, then stepped into the office. It was small, but scrupulously clean. There were attractive pictures in frames, a bamboo plant in the corner. And behind the desk was one really, really cute guy.

"Ms. Parker. It's nice to meet you." He stood up, his dark eyes flashing with humor. He was taller than she was, but not overwhelmingly so, and he was wearing a white cable-knit sweater and khakis. He looked about as old as she was, maybe late twenties or early thirties. His hair was pure black, cut short, emphasizing the sharp angles of his cheekbones and the line of his jaw. Dark eyes surveyed her curiously. He looked relaxed, she thought, admiring his easy smile. That would help. He gestured for her to sit in the chair opposite him. "I'm sorry we couldn't speak longer on the phone, but I had a class to teach. I'm glad you could make it this weekend, though. What can we do for you?"

She sat down, noticing that her knuckles were tight on her purse. *Silly to be nervous,* she thought. "It's sort of complicated, but in a nutshell, I want to learn about Vietnamese culture."

His smile turned puzzled. "Then you've come to the right place." He paused. "Any particular part of the culture? What interests you?"

"Oh, anything is fine. I'm interested in, well, all of it."

He leaned back, his arms crossing slightly as his smile moved to his eyes, making them twinkle. "All of it? That could take a while."

She shrugged. "Well, I'm not on a deadline." She frowned,

thinking of her grandmother's ultimatum. "Not exactly, anyway."

"If you don't mind my asking . . . is this for personal edification, or for an article?" His tone was still gentle, but she could tell he was trying to pin down why this half-Asian woman was asking to be immersed in "all the culture," all at once. "I am guessing you're Vietnamese."

She sighed. "Half-Vietnamese, half-white."

He nodded, but made no other comment.

She fidgeted with her purse. "I sort of made a promise to my grandmother that I would learn more about my Vietnamese half." She laughed nervously. "Well, more like struck a bargain."

"A bargain?" Paul's eyebrows went up. "How so?"

"It's stupid," she said. "My grandmother . . . don't get me wrong, I love her a lot. But she's making me nuts."

Paul actually laughed at that one, and Rose smiled.

"She's always trying to set me up," she continued, heartened. Maybe this wouldn't be as difficult as she thought. "First it was just giving me the phone numbers of guys she knew from her friends in New York City. Then she would have my mother and me over for dinner— and one of said men would just *happen* to be there. How she kept persuading them to drive a couple of hours out of the city just to have dinner with me, I have no idea." She smirked, shaking her head. "I finally stopped showing up to those dinners. Now she actually gave one guy my *address,* and he showed up on my doorstep with flowers!"

Paul chuckled. "So . . . how do you think we can help you with something like that?"

She leaned back in the chair. "I finally hit the roof and got into a big fight with my grandmother. She said that she's afraid I'm going to marry some non-Vietnamese guy, and my kids will never know the Vietnamese culture because I don't know anything about it. When I asked her if it would be different if I were more in touch with my Vietnamese roots, if she'd stop setting me up, she said yes . . . so here I am."

He leaned onto his desk with both arms, his eyes still friendly. "So . . . you want to learn about the Vietnamese culture . . . so your grandmother will stop setting you up with blind dates."

"Exactly," she said. That wasn't half as complicated as she had thought it was going to be.

"Because it's unlikely you're going to marry a Vietnamese man?" he asked, and his voice was deceptively mild. "Just curious."

"I hadn't thought about it," she said. "I've never dated any Asian men." That comment hung in the air for a moment, and she thought about how that would sound . . . especially to an Asian man. She quickly corrected her statement. "There aren't a lot of Vietnamese men where I live. I mean, upstate New York isn't exactly Asian central." She realized her voice was defensive, and modulated it. "I'm not saying that it's not a possibility."

"Just a slim one."

She narrowed her eyes. "Is there a reason for this line of questioning?"

He stood up. "You're welcome to participate in any of the programs or festivities we've got coming up," he said, and his voice was a shade cooler than when she had first come into the office. "But I really can't help you, Ms. Parker."

"Can't, or won't?"

He looked at her, his dark eyes intense. "I help people who have a real love for their background, who want to learn. My time is limited. If you've got an interest, that's one thing." He opened the door. "If you're just looking to stay single or keep your grandmother quiet, that's another entirely."

She stood up, totally off balance. "I didn't mean any offense," she said. "And I could really use your help here. Is there anyplace else I could go?"

He shrugged. "Maybe the city. And there are lots of books. The Internet is a wonderful resource."

She looked at him. "You're really insulted, aren't you?"

"Not insulted," he said, still staring at her. "Disappointed. Drive carefully, Ms. Parker."

"Hey there, Paul." Long, one of the organizers of the yearly Spring Festival, had stayed late with his committee, and was still there as Paul shut down the center for the night. He smiled. "Who was the fox who came in earlier? A volunteer?"

"You're not that lucky," Paul replied, causing the other man to laugh. Neither of them was that lucky, Paul thought. *I've never dated any Asian men.* Her words had repeated themselves in his head all afternoon. "She was here for some . . . information. That's all."

"Great body," Long said, then shook his head. "Something a little weird about her face. Is she Vietnamese?"

"Half. Half-white."

"I thought so. What kind of information did she want, anyway?"

Paul shook his head. He wasn't even about to explain it. "Just background . . . wanted to get in touch with her roots, that kind of thing." He shrugged.

"Uh-huh." Long rolled his eyes. "Banana, huh?"

Paul looked sharply at Long. "We don't use terms like that here."

Long put up his hands in a defensive gesture. "Sorry. Just . . . you know." He paused, fidgeting under the intensity of Paul's gaze. "I didn't mean anything."

"I won't have racial slurs in this center," Paul said, then sighed. He'd heard the names before, when he was in college, used often by his friends. *Banana. Twinkie.* They all boiled down to the same thing: yellow on the outside, white on the inside.

Paul might not like Rose's reasons for coming to the center, but after growing up in rural upstate New York as the only Asian in a twenty-mile radius, he understood the pressure to blend in. And he wasn't going to have those kinds of terms used at the center. It was a place for broadening your mind, not shutting it closed.

Long cleared his throat, obviously intent on getting away from the hot-button topic. "So . . . we're making some real progress on the festival. We've got people coming in all the way from Connecticut."

Paul smiled. "You're doing a hell of a job, really. If it's anything like last year, we're going to be in for a treat."

"You gonna bring a date this year?" Long said, winking.

Paul shrugged. "When I get the time."

"You work too hard," Long said. "You need to find yourself a nice girl to make sure you go home more often!"

He laughed loudly at his own joke, and Paul smiled. The older contingent of volunteers was perpetually ribbing him about his single state as well. He'd been single since he'd opened the center two years ago. Most of the people here didn't know about his life when he was in San Jose—when he'd been engaged, when he'd still been in the computer business. He'd get around to finding a "nice girl" one of these days, he assured them. But for now, the center was more important.

He thought of Rose again, the way a dimple appeared when she smiled, the way her eyes warmed up.

It was a pity she wasn't looking for more from him than a dodge from her grandmother. And at the same time, it was just as well . . . since he really, really wasn't interested in finding a "nice girl" who didn't date Asian guys.

"Rose!"

Rose groaned into her soup. Her grandmother was sitting at one end of her mother's kitchen table, her mother at the other. "Yes, Grandma?"

"You'll come to my house for dinner." Like most of her grandmother's announcements, this wasn't an invitation—it was an order.

"I thought we talked about this, Grandma," Rose said, ignoring her mother's pleading look. "Who have you dug up to meet me this time?"

Her grandmother looked affronted; then she shrugged. "I may be having some friends over."

Rose looked at her mother, who was shaking her head. "Mom, isn't there something you can do about this?"

Her mother sighed. "Mom, you know how Rose feels. . . ."

Her grandmother suddenly let out a flurry of Vietnamese, staccato, like machine-gun fire. Her voice pitched higher. Rose's mother's face set in a stern expression, and her answers, also in Vietnamese, were low and serious.

Rose watched the conversation volley back and forth like a tennis match. *I hate it when they speak in Vietnamese,* she thought miserably. Her grandmother was angrier than usual. Worse, her mother was looking more tired, for which Rose felt guilty. Still, her grandmother had been pulling this "you'll come over to dinner" business even more regularly in the past year. If Rose was going to have any peace in the family, this had to stop. And she hated to see her mother stuck in the middle of this generational clash.

Finally her grandmother threw her hands in the air and pushed away from the table, aiming some last jibe in Vietnamese at Rose's mother. Her mom rubbed at her temples.

"Mom, I'm sorry," Rose said. "But she's making me crazy. You know she sent some guy to my house, right? I had on sweats and a T-shirt, and I opened the door to a forty-year-old businessman in a suit with an armful of roses."

"I already told her to stop that," her mother said, her faint accent slightly more pronounced after her argument. "But she's worried."

"Worried about what?" Rose sighed. "Not the kid thing again. I really think that's just a cop-out."

"Not as much as you'd think," her mother said, and she pushed her hair back from her face. Rose was struck by how pretty her mother was—even at fifty-six, she looked no older than forty . . . unless you counted the tiredness and sadness in her eyes. "Still, she's got a point."

"What was she yelling at you about?"

"She blames me for the way you turned out," she answered, then held up a hand before Rose could counter. "Now, it's not that bad, Rose. She's just jealous of your Grandma Irene."

Rose sighed. "You and Dad lived in Grandma Irene's house for three years when you first had me. She . . ." She thought of her father's mother, tall, heavyset, with a strong matriarchal streak. "She was a strong influence, granted. . . ."

"She was more than that, and you know it. My mother still hasn't forgiven me for giving you only American names. She thinks you're too American. And right now she thinks you're too old to be unmarried—and too likely to make the same mistake I did and marry somebody outside the culture."

"That's just racist, Mom."

Her mother shrugged. "She throws divorce in your face, it's hard to argue with."

Rose looked down at her half-empty soup bowl, pushing the swirls of egg around in the clear chicken broth. "It's not your fault . . . not the divorce, not the way I am. "

"I know that," her mother said, with a grateful smile, reaching over and patting Rose's hand. "Still . . . she's got a point. If there's one thing I regret, it's not teaching you how to speak

Vietnamese. Not teaching you anything about your culture. I just wanted you to fit in."

Rose smiled, squeezing her mother's hand in return. "And I did. Captain of the cheerleading squad and head of the math club, remember?"

Her mother smiled back. "Still, if I had it to do over again, it would be nice . . ." She gave Rose's hand one last squeeze, then stood up and got out the cha gio, the meat-laden egg rolls that she'd made from scratch. She also pulled out a salad that she'd made for Rose, knowing that she didn't eat the traditional food—it was hell on her daughter's diet, and she saved it for special occasions. "She's just trying to preserve her family. And she really does love you. It's a different culture. You can forgive her for that, can't you?"

Rose nodded.

"If you could just try . . ."

Her grandmother walked back in. "Are you going to cook that, or just sit talking all night?" she said with a touch of asperity.

Her mother shook her head, making a comment in Vietnamese before sliding the plump rolls into the hot oil.

Her grandmother sat down next to her, and Rose fought against the stiffening of her spine.

"This one is a businessman," her grandmother said without preamble.

"Grandma, they're *all* businessmen."

"Good-looking. He's younger, too. Thirty-five." Her grandmother nodded. "He liked your picture."

"You sent him my *picture*?" Rose suddenly got a picture of herself on a Web site, with a *seeking single Vietnamese male, apply in person* tag beneath it. Thank God her grandmother wasn't comfortable with the computer! "Grandma Mai—"

"I know. You think you know best. You think that you want to find some tall blond American who will sweep you off your feet. Ha." Her grandmother wagged a finger at her. "Believe me, I know who would be good for you. Someone stable, someone Vietnamese."

Rose saw her mother glance over her shoulder, mouthing the words *be nice,* and sighed.

"Grandma, I know that you're worried because I don't know about my culture . . . and that I'm not going to raise my kids to know they're Vietnamese," Rose answered slowly, ignoring her grandmother's snort of disbelief. "I will. I'll do research. There are plenty of books, and plenty of research on the Web—"

"Ha!" her grandmother said, jabbing her finger on the tabletop. "There are some things you can't learn from *books.* You can't just read a book and know about your history!"

"Actually," Rose said through gritted teeth, "that's how we learn about history *here.*"

"No Vietnamese person would believe you know anything about your culture," her grandmother countered. "The head of my Vietnamese Women's Society is a perfect example. Her name is Lailu, and while I've never met the woman, we've written back and forth a good deal. She lives in New York City. She still goes to Saigon once a year, even though she's lived in the United States for twenty-five! Even when she had to sneak through Thailand, she visited!" Her grandmother's voice rose slightly. "If I introduced you to her, in her home, you wouldn't dress like a Vietnamese woman, you wouldn't eat like a Vietnamese woman, you wouldn't even know how to talk to her!"

Rose felt a stab of anger. "So what you're saying is . . . you're ashamed of me?"

Her grandmother's eyes widened, and her face softened. "I am saying you don't know about your culture. A husband could show you," she said, her voice a little gentler. "A husband could teach your children."

"I don't even know if I'm having children," Rose said, then at the anxiety in her grandmother's face she added, "but I'll be able to show them."

"I'll tell you what. Remember our bargain?" her grandmother said, her dark eyes glinting. "I suggest we change it a little."

Uh-oh. Rose knew that glint. Her grandmother was up to something.

"What's the deal?" Rose answered warily.

"You come with me. Lailu is having a party at the end of this month. You come with me and talk to her. If she agrees with me, you'll marry a Vietnamese man."

"Grandma!" Rose said.

"Mom!" her mother said sharply.

"Oh, all right." Her grandmother obviously tossed that out, expecting it to get turned down. She was a champion haggler. She'd helped Rose buy her car—Rose had paled during the exchange. Rose felt her guard go up. "So you'll go out with a Vietnamese man for a month."

"Grandma . . ." Rose said warningly. "What is this woman going to do? Test me? And how do I know you're not just going to make a deal with her and guarantee I'll fail? No way."

Her grandmother was silent for a few minutes, her brows almost knitting together with her intense frown of concentration. Finally, she smiled, her eyes lighting up with an obvious brainstorm. "You just need to go dressed formally, you have to eat traditional food and know what it is, and you have to answer a few questions." Her grandmother's smile was crafty. "If she says you're traditional enough, well, I will leave you alone."

"Forever?" Rose said. She wasn't a slouch, either.

Her grandmother made a face. "For a while."

"A year."

Her grandmother started to protest, but when Rose's mother

made a sharp noise, she consented. "A year. But I'm an old woman; I don't know how long I have left."

"You'll bury us all," Rose said dryly. "So. I go to dinner, dress up, name my food, and answer a few questions correctly, and I'm off the hook for the next year?"

Her grandmother nodded.

Rose sighed. "And you leave Mom alone, too."

Both her mother and her grandmother stared at her for that one.

"I don't want you bothering Mom to get me to date Vietnamese guys, either. I don't want you telling her that she went wrong with how she raised me," Rose said sternly. "Promise me that you won't bug Mom on either of those points, and I'll agree to it."

"Rose, that's not—"

"Mom, you know how I feel about this."

Her grandmother let out a sharp huff of breath. "Fine. It's a deal."

Rose smiled. She hadn't been a slouch in school, either. She had a month. Plenty of time to get a dress or whatever, learn about Vietnamese food, and learn some details about Vietnamese history. How hard could it be?

"Mom, I think I'll have some imperial rolls, too," Rose said, her smile widening. If her grandmother was going to be off her back for a year, she'd have reason to celebrate.

"Wonderful," her mother said, setting out an extra plate.

Her grandmother looked her over. "Aren't you gaining a little weight?"

Rose sighed as her grandmother and her mother got into conversation again. *Family.* Vietnamese or not, they were enough to drive you nuts.

Paul looked up and felt a jolt through his system as he recognized Rose. She was dressed in another suit, with a slightly shorter skirt—she had the legs for it, he noted. "Ms. Parker," he said, leaning back in his chair. "Gotta say, I didn't expect to see you here. Did the research suggestions not help?"

She sighed. "Well, to start off with, I'd like to apologize."

His eyes widened. He didn't expect her—and he was still wary of her. She seemed pretty driven, and she had her own agenda. He wanted to help her—that is, he wanted to help anybody who wanted to learn about the culture, he corrected himself. But it didn't seem like she wanted to learn. She just wanted to shut her family up. She could figure out how to do that on her own.

And that was exactly what he'd tell her, as soon as he was sure that was what she was up to.

"What would you like to apologize for?" he asked. "Wanting to use the center to stop your grandmother's dating service?"

"Actually, I was going to apologize for the not-dating-Asian-guys statement," Rose said, and he noticed the pink rising in her cheeks. "I still feel bad about that. But you're probably right about using the center, as well."

"Probably?"

"Well . . . I still think I've got some valid points. You don't know my grandmother."

He smiled at that. He had two of his own. He knew quite well what kind of pressure a Vietnamese family could bring when it came to dating and marriage—but that still didn't necessarily justify her approach.

And the Asian-guy crack *had* stung, now that she brought it up. Not that that was the point of this exercise.

"Okay. Apology accepted," he said, and stared at her.

She bit the corner of her full lower lip. "Um, since I'm forgiven, I don't suppose you'd reconsider helping me out?"

She was persistent, but he wasn't falling for her cuteness for an instant. "Same reasons, I assume?" He didn't even wait for a response. "You get the same answer. There are plenty of resources—"

"I don't learn that way," she interrupted. "I need more visual clues. I was always better in classes that had a lot of presentations than the ones that made me plow through textbooks."

He stared at her for a second, then played a hunch. "But you were still an excellent student, right?"

She paused. "Well, I got pretty good grades. But I knew how to counteract my weakness, and I got a tutor when I hit crunch time."

He took that in. "And it's crunch time now?"

"In a manner of speaking," she said. "I've got a . . . well, let's say I'm taking a cultural test, and it's in my best interest to pass."

"A cultural . . . test?" He frowned. She was interesting; he'd give her that. Weird, yeah, but interesting. "Okay. And what do you get out of it?"

She paused. "You won't like the answer, so why ask?"

"And why should I help you?"

She smiled impishly. "Because you're a good, kind man, and I'll be in your debt?"

He grinned at that one—he couldn't help it. "Besides my altruistic nature, why should I?"

"Well," she said, sighing slightly and starting to reach for her purse, "I could pay you—"

"That's not the point here." He waved a hand at her, gesturing to her to put her money away. "The point is, you're still basically trying to use the cultural center not to learn about your background, but to get out of a dating scheme. That's not really what we're here for."

"Then what are you here for? Honestly, what are you, the cultural police?" Rose's sharp impatience grew. "I want to learn. Isn't that enough?"

He didn't know why, but it wasn't. Maybe he was still holding her prejudices against her. Maybe it was because he knew, once she jumped through the hurdle her grandmother had put before her, she'd just go back to her blissful ignorance.

Hell, maybe it was still about the Asian-guy thing.

"We have people who come here who want their children to know the country and the traditions of their homeland. I have adults who come here from Vietnam to learn English, who drive clear across the county because this is one of the few centers in upstate New York that will help them. Now, tell me why I should use my time to help a completely assimilated young woman fake being Vietnamese so her family will let her off the hook?"

Rose reacted as if she'd been slapped. She stood up.

"You've never known what it's like, have you?" The question was quiet but cold as the North Atlantic. "I'm not Vietnamese. And I'm obviously not white. Ever known what that felt like—that you don't fit in either place?"

He stopped. This wasn't the funny, self-assured woman who had walked into his office a week ago. He'd hit a nerve. No, he'd hit a raw, open wound.

"So you think it's funny and frivolous that I'm trying to show my grandmother that I'm Vietnamese enough to stay single. It's stupid, I know. But what's my alternative, Paul? Tell her, 'I'm not Vietnamese, I'm not *anything,* so shove off'? If you've got a better solution, I'd *love* to hear it!"

He stood up, his hands out in a calming gesture. This was more serious than he'd realized. His self-righteous temper fizzled out completely. "I'm sorry. I was out of line, questioning your motives like that."

Her eyes still flared, but she clamped down on her statement and picked up her coat. "I shouldn't have come here. There are places in the city, if it comes to that."

"That's a few hours' drive at least. When is your, er, test?"

Paul asked, standing between her and the door as she struggled to tug her coat on. "Maybe I can help."

"Maybe I don't need your help," she said. "If I wanted my life dissected, I could just go see my grandmother."

Ouch. He leaned back against the door, steeling himself against her frown. "I apologized. I won't do it again. And I really do think I could help you. Really. I'm really, really sorry."

Two could play the cute thing. He smiled his most winning smile, putting a hand out. "Come on. Friends?"

She looked like she might bat his hand away, but she stood silently for a moment before sighing heavily. "Well, all right." She reached out and took his hand, giving him a firm shake.

He didn't let go immediately. *Soft hands,* he thought. A firm shake, but hands that were silky as rose petals.

He let go a moment later, letting his fingers trail against hers. He practically felt a shock between them. Maybe it was static electricity. Yeah, that was probably it.

But he continued to stare at her. "So what do you need to learn?"

She sighed. "Well, I need to get a formal Vietnamese dress, I need to learn about Vietnamese food, and I need to learn some cultural historical background."

He blinked. "What, are you applying for citizenship or something?"

"It's not as bad as it sounds," she said, allowing a reluctant smile to creep into her expression. "Well, it's probably just as strange as it sounds, but I don't think it'll be that tough."

"How long do you have?"

She pulled out her organizer and glanced it over. "A month."

"A month, huh?" He went over to his desk. "That's four weekends. I get the feeling that works better into your schedule. Tell you what. Other than the Spring Festival in two weeks, I can take the time to teach you as best I can. Private lessons, if you will. How does that sound?"

She nodded. He thought she looked relieved. "Here at the center?"

He shrugged. "If you like."

"Okay."

"I'll see if I can ask one of the ladies where you could get a traditional dress," he said, jotting down the note on his calendar, "and maybe, if you're very good, I'll make you some food."

Her smile was more real now, and warm. "You can cook?"

"I'm a man of many talents." *And boy, would I love to show you one or two of them.* He shook his head—in a way she was a student now, and those thoughts were hardly appropriate. "So. Three o'clock Saturday? With any luck this will cut into your unwanted dating plans." Or any other dating plans, he realized. He couldn't really bring himself to feel bad about curtailing her social life, for some reason. *After all, she came to me.*

She frowned, glancing over her calendar again, then nodded. "I guess that's okay." She paused. "That's only basically three weekends. Is that going to be enough time?"

He thought about it. "It'll be enough for an overview. I am going to assign you some reading, and then we'll go over the high points. You'll pass your little test, I'm sure."

She smiled again. A man could get used to that smile. "Fantastic," she said.

He stepped out from the door. He didn't want her to rush off. "Did you want to, er, take a look around?" He thought about it, then took a deep breath. "Maybe we could start the lessons tonight." *Say, over dinner?* But he didn't want to go there. The "I don't date Asian guys" response reared its ugly head in his memory.

She shook her head. "I've got to do some stuff for work—

I'm a freelance writer. I need to do some brainstorming for a Web site, and write up a newsletter. But I will be here next Saturday, definitely."

For a moment he thought she was going to hug him. Instead her eyes grew bright. "I really appreciate this, Paul. Here's hoping we get off to a better start than this, huh?"

"Here's hoping," he echoed.

He watched her walk out of the office and down the hallway, her hips swaying gently.

Here's hoping I don't regret this decision, he thought, and shut the door.

Rose sat at a desk at the community center. She'd gotten there at three o'clock in the afternoon. It was now eight o'clock, and her brain felt like tapioca.

"Let me get this straight," Rose said, rubbing her temples. "This prince guy—"

"Lac Long Quan," Paul supplied.

"Right. Anyway, he came from . . . the sea?"

Paul nodded.

"And he married a princess from the mountains."

"Right." Paul smiled. "Her name was Au Co. She may or may not have been married to a Chinese intruder. The legend isn't really clear."

"So she gets together with good old Lac Long Quan, and then she"—Rose squinted at her notes—"lays *eggs?*"

"One hundred eggs." Paul grinned at her. "And each egg turned into a son."

Rose looked over the story again. "And then the father separated from the mother, saying that because he was a water guy and she was a mountain girl, it wasn't going to work out." She paused, then looked at Paul. "Shouldn't that have been something he thought of *before* he slept with her?"

Paul laughed. "Well, I'm sure it seemed like a good idea at the time."

"So why do her kids go with her and become the Muong, and then *his* kids get all the glory and become the ancestors of the Vietnamese?"

He shrugged. "I just retell the tale; I don't write it."

"Hmm. All sons, split family, no visitation rights. Yeah, I can remember this." She rubbed her eyes, feeling the muscles in her neck, stiff as boards. "What next?"

"Next, I think, is you getting some rest."

Rose had already cracked open another book, groaning at its weight, before his words sank in. "Huh?"

"You're exhausted." He shut the book, smiling at her. "Do you always approach things this way?"

She rubbed awkwardly at her shoulders. Now that he mentioned it, she was pretty tired. "When I was in school, I would go into subjects like this. College especially."

"Oh?"

She had leaned back in the chair and had closed her eyes, vaguely noting the sound of him rustling around. He'd been walking around the table all night, talking. He apparently wasn't a sit-still sort of man, despite his laid-back appearance. When she felt his hands on her shoulders, she started, her eyes flying open.

"Shh. I'm not trying anything here," he said, his voice soothing, his hands still. "But I couldn't help but notice that you look like your shoulders and your neck are killing you. May I?"

She felt a disturbing sensation of warmth in the pit of her stomach, but still managed to shrug, wincing as she did so. "Whatever floats your boat."

He chuckled. "So . . . you would cram in college? What did you study?"

"Sociology . . . Ugh, " she said as he started working on a

particularly tension-filled knot. "It wasn't tough to study for the tests. Retention wasn't really my strong suit, though."

"Hmm. So how much of this do you think you'll remember after this 'test' of yours is over?"

His hands felt like heaven, working the sore muscles until she felt her tension melting away. His palms were warm—she could feel the heat through her sweater. "I don't know. I don't think I'll forget that last story. It's too poetic and weird. But the other details we went over? Probably not. This is just another class for me at the moment. A history class."

"But it's your history," Paul said quietly, his voice near her ear. "Doesn't that make a difference?"

She closed her eyes a little more tightly, and sighed. "How much does your history influence *your* life, Paul?" she asked instead. "I mean, do you think about Au Co and Lac Long Quan on a daily basis?"

He laughed. He had a nice laugh, she noticed. "It's hard to be in America and retain a sense of history, I suppose. I know—I grew up here, in Pleasant Valley."

Her eyes opened at that, and she leaned back. She saw his face upside down, noted the amused smile. "Really?"

"Then I moved to California with my family. They're still over in San Jose," he said. "Talk about culture shock. I went from a mostly white school in upstate New York to being surrounded by Vietnamese people. We always spoke Vietnamese at home, but this . . . this was different."

She noticed the way the cadence of his voice changed, the gentleness of his touch—he hadn't stopped touching her, even though his massage was lighter now, less intent. It was still comforting, and, mixed with the soothing quality of his words, it was drugging. She closed her eyes again, just listening to him.

"I just dove into it. I ate all this food that my mother had only *told* me about. I hung out with Vietnamese kids. Lunar

New Year was suddenly a *huge* deal. I felt . . . I don't know. Like I belonged. And knowing my history and being with people who understood it . . . all that helped. "

He moved his hands off of her shoulders, and she let out a little sound of protest before she realized what she was doing and stopped herself. Her eyes opened to see him pulling out the chair next to her and scooting near her. He leaned over, smiling into her eyes.

"That's why I want to know if maybe you can get something more from this than just answers to your 'test,'" Paul said. "Knowing my history, being around people like me, all made me feel like, for the first time, I was *home*."

Maybe she was tired, but suddenly her throat tightened and she felt her eyes misting slightly.

"Hey," he said. "You okay?"

"Yeah. Just tired," she said, rubbing at her eyes in order to get the tears away. She *was* tired. That was the problem—it made emotions come to the fore way too strongly. "It sounds like you had a great childhood."

"It had its ups and downs, but yeah, for the most part it was great," he said, but his eyes never left her face. "How about you?"

She thought about it. "My family loved me," she said slowly. "My parents didn't get divorced until I went to college."

He nodded, but his eyes turned sympathetic.

"I never really felt like that," she said. "I never felt like I fit in. I didn't even meet my grandmother until I was eighteen, when she came over. She didn't speak much English, but she was always sort of yelling at me. It was easier to be with my father's family. As far as they were concerned, I was American, and white. That first year my Vietnamese grandmother came, she and my mother took me to a Lunar New Year celebration in the city."

"What did you think?"

She thought about it — about the noise, the crowd. The staring. "I hated it," she said honestly. "I didn't understand what anyone was saying, and nobody spoke to me. Everybody stared. One guy asked me what I was, and he was dead serious — he wanted to know what my racial mix was." She shook her head. "So I wound up going to McDonald's afterward and telling my mom that I wouldn't do that again. And up till now, I haven't."

"I understand."

To her surprise, it sounded like he really did.

Then he reached out and stroked her cheek. It was a gentle motion, a delicate caress.

"Paul?" Her voice broke slightly.

"You've been alone a lot, haven't you?" he mused, and his eyes were dark, hypnotizing.

They must've stayed that way awhile, but then he shook himself and leaned back, smiling as if nothing had happened. "So. Same time next week?"

She nodded, gathering up the books and resources she'd collected into an awkward mess. He helped her. She was careful not to touch him.

"You know," he said, helping her put her coat on, "if you want to meet with me more, I'm okay with that. Or maybe, you know, call."

"I don't want to take up too much of your time," she hedged.

He looked at her, and his eyes were warm. "Believe me, it's no sacrifice."

They stood like that for a long while.

"Um, I'll see you tomorrow," she said, then blinked. "I mean next week! Next week," she reiterated, buttoning her coat. "Good night."

As she walked out the door, she could still feel his hands on her.

An hour later Paul was pacing around his kitchen like a tiger in a zoo. He couldn't seem to settle down. Ever since he'd spent time with Rose, *calm* was hardly the word he'd use to describe himself.

She'd looked so lost. Lonely. Homesick. He wanted to take her into his arms and comfort her, wipe the tears from her eyes.

He wanted to do a hell of a lot more than that, but he wasn't sure if it was all on his side or not.

He poured himself a glass of iced tea from the fridge. The house seemed emptier tonight, as well. It had been almost two years since he'd thought about it. He hadn't lived with anyone since he broke his engagement to Phoung. In fact, he'd dated only casually for the past two years, and any liaisons had been short-term at best. He claimed it was the center—the long hours necessary to get it started up, the dedication—but he also knew that part of it was a lack of connection.

She just looked so lonely.

He sighed, staring at the phone.

It's been a while since I called family, he thought. He picked up the phone and dialed.

"Hello?" his mother answered in Vietnamese.

"Mom? It's Paul."

"Paul!" He heard a rumbling in the background. "It's so nice to hear from you! I was just telling your father you don't call enough. You're too busy. Are you well?"

He smiled. This was familiar. "I'm fine, Mom. Just busy, with the Spring Festival coming up and all. Are you having dinner?"

"Yes, but don't worry about it. Your brother is here with his wife and little Michael, and your sister will be by soon—she's nine months along already; can you believe it? But she's doing fine, the doctor says. When will you be home for a visit?"

"I'll be out by the time the baby gets there; don't worry," Paul assured her. "How's Dad?"

"Oh, you know. Doctor complains of his cholesterol, and mine, tells us to stop eating so much red meat. We went to the herbalist, though, and got something." She sounded smugly pleased. "Tastes awful, yes, but your father is feeling better daily."

This was one thing he and his mother never agreed on. "You are still going to the regular doctor, though, right?"

She snorted. "Yes, Paul. We're not stupid."

He laughed at that one. She hated it when he bugged her about the "conventional" doctor. "Say, do you think I could talk to Mike for a minute?"

"All right. Hold on a second." He could hear her covering the phone, heard the muffled shout for his brother. Soon his brother was on the phone.

"Hey, Paul. How is it in New York? Still cold, huh?"

"You get used to it," Paul said. His brother had been eight or so when they moved to San Jose, and he'd never been back to New York—had had no desire to go back, other than to maybe visit Paul. "I've got a sort of weird question. Have you ever dated a half-Vietnamese girl?"

"Huh?"

Paul knew that Mike had been far more outgoing and far more social than Paul had been at that age—although it galled him a little to ask his little brother for advice. "I was just wondering. Have you met girls who wouldn't date Asian guys?"

He could almost hear Mike shrug over the phone. "Well, since I'm Asian, yes, I've met them, no I haven't dated any, and I haven't dated anybody who was half. What's going on? You seeing somebody?"

This caused a flurry in the background that Paul half heard:

"Paul's seeing somebody?" "Is she half? Half what?" And little Michael yelling, just in general.

Paul rubbed his forehead. Okay, maybe calling wasn't such a good idea.

"Hold on a second," Mike said, then passed the phone over, and Paul heard his sister's voice. "Hello, Paul?"

"Nala," Paul said, smiling. He was closest to his sister, who was only a year younger than himself. "I hear you're as big as a house."

"And happy," she said. "I just walked in. So you're finally seeing someone? Good." Before Paul could correct her, she plowed forward. "You've been living like a hermit since you broke up with Phoung. Nobody blames you for that, except maybe you."

Phoung. "She's a great girl. How's she doing?"

"Mom says that she's getting married in a few months. Some guy who owns a restaurant. Sounds pretty successful." She paused. "That doesn't hurt to hear, does it?"

"No. I love Phoung; you know that. She was one of my best friends since we were kids," he said, and meant it. He wanted her to be happy. He just knew that there was no passion between them—and that he certainly wasn't the one to make Phoung happy in the long run. "Of course I want her to be happy."

"Good," his sister repeated. "I'd hate to cast that shadow on your new relationship. So you're dating a half-Vietnamese girl? Did I hear that correctly?"

He shook his head. The other reason he moved to New York—he loved his family, but living in and out of each other's lives had gotten on his nerves—especially after he broke up with Phoung. He could respect Rose's desire for privacy and independence from that standpoint—and he knew what matchmaking was like. "I'm not seeing her," he said slowly, then sighed. Nala he could talk to openly. "But I want to. But she says she doesn't date Asian guys."

"Hmm. I know women like that. Even pure Vietnamese," she said. "Do you know why?"

He thought about it. "I don't know. I get the feeling it's because she wasn't attracted to any—sounded like it had never happened, rather than a conscious choice on her part."

"Do you think she's attracted to you?"

"I don't know." He paused. "I think so . . . but we haven't seen each other a lot yet."

"Are you dating?"

"No. I'm teaching her about Vietnam—the culture, a little language, stuff like that." Before his sister could interrupt, he said firmly, "Don't even ask why. It's too complicated. Well, I will say this: If she gets what she wants, her grandmother will stop fixing her up with Vietnamese guys."

"Ouch. You're going to have to tell me the story of that someday," Nala replied, then stayed quiet for a second, thinking about it. "Well . . . how does *she* feel about being Vietnamese?"

The question caught Paul off guard. "I don't know. I don't know that she considers herself as such." He remembered her face—the sadness. "Nala, if you could've seen her . . . She just looked lost. She said she felt so . . . I don't know. *Other*. She felt like an outsider. I didn't know what to say."

"You don't have to say anything," Nala said. "You have to show her that she's not an outsider."

"Oh?" Paul smiled. A year younger, and she lectured like an old auntie. "And how do I do that?"

"Accept her," Nala counseled. "Help other people to accept her. Show her that you're not so different."

Paul thought about it. "I could take her to the Spring Festival," he muttered, thinking aloud.

"Sounds like you've got it." He could hear Nala's grin. "Tell me how it turns out, okay?"

Could I fit in a little less?

Rose stood awkwardly off to one side of the crowded center. There were bodies everywhere, dressed in a level of formality from what she'd classify as nice interview wear to heavily embroidered silk outfits, obviously traditional. She had to admit, the little girls running around in their fitted long-sleeved outfits were really cute to see.

And that's what I'm doing. Watching. The part of spectator will be played by Rose Parker.

"What are you doing over here?" a low voice murmured near her ear.

She spun and met Paul eye to eye. "Um, nothing."

"My point exactly." He smiled, warming her down to her toes. "Why aren't you participating in anything?"

She winced at this one. "You know I don't speak the language, Paul," she said.

"You don't need to," he replied. She looked at him dubiously, then started laughing nervously when he took her hands. "C'mon. Over here."

He took her over to where a variety of food was piled on a folding table. There was a short older woman standing guard over it, her face like a prune, tanned and wrinkled. Her eyes were deep-set and seemed, to Rose, fairly suspicious.

Paul said something to her in Vietnamese, and in response the woman smiled—a very sweet smile. "Try this, try this," she said, pointing to a plate of what looked like rice cakes. Maybe. Rose wasn't actually sure. She picked one up gingerly, not wanting to offend the older woman, and took a bite. It was sticky, and the red stuff inside was sweet and soft. She smiled around the mouthful.

"Thank you," she said when she was finally able.

Paul set up a plate of various tidbits—"part of your education"—and set her down on a seat.

"The kids are going to be putting on a presentation," he said. "I figured, being the visual person you are, you'd get a kick out of this."

She smirked as he sat down next to her. Other people spoke with him, and he introduced her to everyone. She smiled for the most part, but at least she wasn't pulling a wallflower act. He made sure that she felt included.

It was nice, she thought. Weird, a bit like being a blind date at a family gathering, but still sort of nice.

The kids were adorable—little girls and boys in formal Vietnamese dress, acting as only little kids could—getting constant prompts from the teachers on the sidelines and being reminded of where they were and what they were doing. They were acting out the story of Au Co and Lac Long Quan, she noticed. She leaned over to Paul.

"I know this one," she whispered into his ear, and was warmed by his answering smile.

It wasn't that long a skit, and it was followed by the kids' singing a song in Vietnamese. To her surprise, Paul and some of the other adults joined in. It was complicated and involved clapping at various points, which Rose was able to join in with. After the kids did their presentations, the adults wound up circling around, getting more food, talking more as the kids wove their way among the throngs of people. Rose found herself in conversation with a young Vietnamese couple from nearby Wappingers Falls.

"It's so wonderful that Paul started this center," the woman, Daphne Nguyen, gushed. "It's a little bit of a drive, but before we could only take the kids to the city for Tet Festival or any other cultural events. Now we've got a summer camp where they can speak Vietnamese with other kids, and they don't feel so . . ." She motioned with her hands.

"Left out?" Rose supplied. "Alone? Like an outsider?"

Daphne nodded. "You understand. Dutchess County needed something like this."

Rose looked over to where Paul was involved in some game in which the kids were chasing him around the hall, and smiled. "He's certainly done something wonderful here."

"He mentioned that you're looking into studying more about your culture," Daphne said, regaining Rose's attention. "I think that's wonderful."

"You do?"

Daphne's husband, Tan, nodded. "I grew up trying to assimilate—basically I wanted to be a six-foot blond-haired football player." Daphne chuckled at this one, and he put his arm around her shoulders. "It wasn't until college that I started embracing my culture. Like Paul."

"Really?" Everyone seemed to know Paul well—he was the hub that the center revolved around. "How so?"

"Paul went to college in Berkeley, joined the Vietnamese student union, and just immersed himself," Tan said. "It's easier in California especially, when there are so many Asian groups. But he decided it was more important for him to come back to the East Coast and set up the center than keep doing what he's doing."

"Can you believe it?" Daphne said conspiratorially. "He was making a ton of money in real estate—I think he's still got apartment buildings and all sorts of land there—and now he's working a nonprofit in a little town in New York."

Rose couldn't believe it. But at the same time, knowing Paul's easy, laid-back attitude, she found it hard to believe he was some sort of land baron, either.

There was a lot she didn't know about Paul, obviously.

Paul walked up. "You aren't telling a lot of tales about me, are you?" he asked Daphne and Tan, standing close to Rose. For a brief moment she thought he might put his arm around

her, much as Tan had around Daphne. Of course he didn't—
she wasn't there on a date; she didn't know him that well. Still,
some part of her realized that would have been nice.

"Of course not," Daphne said. "Just common knowledge."

A traditional piece of music came on, and some people
started to push chairs aside and clear the center floor. Old people and young people got together to dance, something they all
knew, a dance that seemed complicated to Rose. Paul tugged
at her.

"I don't know this," she protested, resisting him.

He smiled warmly. "I'll help you."

With encouragement like that she gave in, letting him lead,
trying to follow the footsteps he showed her. She didn't do
very well, but after a minute it didn't matter that she wasn't
doing the same thing as everybody else. The people around her
smiled with good humor, and little kids laughed but not with
any insult. And most of all, Paul was continually encouraging.
When the dance ended and everyone clapped, Rose felt warm
from the exertion, and breathless from laughing.

"You want to get a breath of fresh air?" Paul asked.

She nodded, letting him lead her by the arm to the door.
They stepped out into the spring air, off to the small park that
adjoined the center. She leaned against the slide and he stood
next to her. The cool air felt heavenly against her skin.

"You looked great out there," Paul said in a low voice.

She smiled. "I looked like a spastic chicken out there," she
corrected, giggling, "but you're sweet to say so."

"Well, you still need to get the hang of the dancing," he
admitted, stepping a little closer, "but I wasn't really talking
about that. You looked beautiful. You still do."

She felt her chest constrict; it was suddenly hard to breathe.
The cold evening vanished in a haze of warmth. "Mr. Duong,"
she said, trying for a playful tone, "are you hitting on me?"

"Depends," he murmured back, and his smile was like warmed honey. "Is it working?"

She laughed. "Maybe," she said.

"I thought you don't date Asian guys," he said softly.

She looked away. "I said I *hadn't* dated Asian guys," she corrected, her own voice soft. "There's a difference."

"I see."

When she turned back, he was close to her . . . much closer than he had been.

"Maybe I could change your mind," he whispered, then leaned down and kissed her.

She didn't know what she was expecting—she'd never been with a really good kisser before. And Paul seemed like a virtuoso. He didn't rush, didn't push, didn't overwhelm. His mouth coaxed hers, brushing against her lips gently, teasing her with warmth and the hint of pressure.

Then she sighed with pleasure and gratitude, and the kiss changed.

He leaned into her, his lips parting slightly as his tongue traced the insides of her lips and one hand stroked her ribcage while the other braced him against the swing set. She barely noticed her own arms coming up, looping around his neck . . . pulling him in closer.

She didn't know how long they stood like that, mouths mated, bodies pressed together in the cold air that neither paid attention to. But eventually Rose registered giggling. She pulled back from Paul, reluctantly, and looked over.

There was a group of children, obviously evading their parents' care for a few minutes to step outside and maybe play . . . only to see one of their favorite teachers kissing the strange lady he'd brought to the festival.

Paul said something to them in Vietnamese, and they laughed again and ran, arms flailing, back into the building. He looked at her, his eyes still low-lidded.

"Now. Where were we?"

Rose shivered . . . she wasn't sure if it was with the cold or not. "I think we'd better go back inside," she said, feeling cowardly but not caring.

He smiled, a warm smile, and took a step back, although when she turned toward the building he put an arm around her. She liked how it felt . . . how he felt, next to her. Sort of protective.

They walked in, and Rose could have sworn she saw grins on the faces of several people there—Daphne, for one. The older woman who'd given her food, for another. Rose blushed a little.

All we did was kiss, she argued to herself, then felt the heat in her cheeks increase.

The fact is, if that was "just kissing," she'd be amazed to see what more than just kissing was.

Actually, I'd sort of look forward to it.

She turned to Paul. "It's been really fun, but I've kind of got a drive ahead of me."

He didn't say anything, just stared at her, and for a moment she wanted to stay as long as she could, just to be by him. "Your 'test' is in two weeks, right?"

She blinked. She'd almost forgotten the whole point behind this exercise—to learn, to pass muster, to get her grandmother off of her back. She nodded.

"Okay. Well, I think I can take care of the clothes, and you've got a good background overall, but I think we'll need to go into food more."

"Whatever you say." She grinned. "You're the teacher."

"Great. Come here a second."

She followed him back to his darkened office, wondering if he was going to treat her to another one of those mind-blowing kisses. But instead he scribbled something on a piece of paper, and handed it to her.

They were directions. She looked at him questioningly.

"Well, I can't cook here at the center," he said in a matter-of-fact tone, although his eyes gleamed. "I thought I'd cook for you. At my house."

Her heart picked up its tempo. "Your house?"

"I want to cook for you." And his eyes finished the thought: *I want to spend some time with you. Alone.*

She swallowed hard. What was going on here? She'd come to him to teach her . . . not to get involved with him. But he was very sweet. And those kisses—wow. They were no joke.

So why not?

"What time do you want me there?" she said, and felt warmth in her chest when he smiled in response.

Paul spent the rest of that week in a half daze. Kissing Rose had been everything he'd hoped it would be—and more than he'd expected. If they hadn't been at the cultural center, he got the feeling they wouldn't have stopped at one kiss.

In fact, he wondered if they would have stopped at all.

"Paul?" He blinked at Mrs. Nguyen, his assistant. "Yes. Sorry. What?"

"Call on line one."

"Thanks." He smiled at her as she shut the door to his office behind her, then picked up the phone. "Paul Duong."

"Hey, you. It's Nala."

He sat up in his chair. "Is everything okay? Did you have the baby?"

"No. It's any day now, but I'm fine." He heard her laughing at his concern. "Everybody's on pins and needles. I just wanted to see how things were going with you and the half-Vietnamese girl," she said, and he could tell there was an underlying current of tension in her voice.

"Pretty well," he said, remembering that kiss. "Pretty well, indeed. I'm cooking for her this weekend. Why? Something wrong?"

"No." Nala sounded hesitant. "Well, not really."

Paul paused. "Okay. Something's making you nervous. Spill."

"Well, I did a lot of thinking since the last time we talked, and I wonder . . . is she really the right girl for you, Paul?"

"Why wouldn't she be?" Paul responded, trying not to be defensive. "This isn't because she's only half-Vietnamese, is it?"

"Of course not," Nala scoffed. "Honestly, Paul, what do you take me for?"

"Sorry." And he was. "I really like her. She's so open, and so . . . I don't know. Homesick, I guess."

"That's just it," Nala said. "You said she came to you because she wanted to learn more about the culture. That's sort of a teacher-student relationship."

"Well, not officially," Paul said, frowning. "I mean, she's not paying me; we're not in a formal class setting. . . ."

"But you see what I mean," Nala insisted. "If she's as homesick as you say, then she's looking for something. Validation, a sense of connection. She's lonely. But loneliness isn't love."

"It's a little early for love anyway, don't you think?" Paul countered, but even the words caused a pang in his chest. "I mean, I'll give her plenty of time to figure out what she wants. But I'm not going to hang back just because I'm afraid she doesn't know what she's doing."

Nala sighed. "You've decided, then. I can hear it in your voice. You're going after this girl."

"Yes," Paul said, realizing just how serious he was. "Rose is special. I want to see where we could go with it."

"All right," Nala said. "But just . . . be careful, okay? Somebody who's never dated Asian guys, then suddenly goes on a cultural roots–finding expedition and starts dating the first Vietnamese man she's in close contact with . . ."

Her voice trailed off, and Paul gritted his teeth.

"I'll be careful," he responded.

They exchanged news for the next five minutes, before Nala had to go, but all Paul could think of was her warning.

Dating the first Vietnamese man she's in close contact with.

It had nothing to do with that, he thought after he hung up. He wasn't just an experiment or a cultural lesson for her. He felt sure of that.

He closed his eyes. Fairly sure, anyway.

"Mom, I need to talk to you."

It was Saturday, and Rose was about to drive over to Paul's house. Suddenly, unaccountably, she'd been struck with nerves.

I really like this guy. It had been a long time since she'd felt this sort of attraction. Not since Sean. She frowned. Maybe not even then.

She needed to talk this out, but didn't feel comfortable discussing it with any of her girlfriends—her white girlfriends. They wouldn't understand.

Her mother would.

Her mother looked up from the kitchen table, concern in her eyes. "What is it? Is something wrong?"

"What's wrong?" Rose's grandmother said, walking in.

Rose took a breath. She should've called. But sometimes seeing her mother's face helped. "Nothing's wrong," she said. "Grandma, I just need to talk to Mom. Nothing serious. Is that okay?"

"Why can't I listen?"

Rose took a deep breath. *Because you're going to just push me, and I hate being pushed.* "Because it has to do with stuff you're not interested in."

Her grandmother's eyes narrowed suspiciously. "Like what?"

Rose paused, thinking it over. "Grandma Irene's birthday is coming up, and I wanted to talk about plans for that."

As she'd suspected, her grandmother's expression turned sour. "I'll be watching television in my room, she replied, moving slowly out of the room.

Rose waited until she heard her grandmother's footsteps up the stairs, and the door of her room closing, before turning back to her mother. Her mother, she noticed, was grinning.

"That was slick," her mother said, fixing herself a cup of tea and then fixing one for Rose. "Irene's birthday isn't until December, and you know it. But it's the one thing that's guaranteed to get your grandmother out of the room. So . . . what's so important that you need to talk to me without your grandmother being here?"

"I'm . . ." Rose took a deep breath. "I'm going on a date. And I'm really nervous."

"Why?" Her mother put the steaming mug of green tea down in front of her.

"That's just it. I don't know why."

Her mother looked at her shrewdly. "Ah. I see." Her eyes sparkled. "Anyone I know?"

Rose hadn't told her about the cultural center—she didn't know why. Maybe because she was afraid of her grandmother expanding her matchmaking schemes. "No. He's not even someone I know very well," she said. "I was wondering something, though."

"Yes?"

"You lived in Saigon all those years," Rose said slowly. "Why Dad? When did you know he was the one? And why not somebody, you know . . ." She let the words trail off.

Her mother smiled gently. "You mean, why didn't I marry a Vietnamese man?"

Rose nodded.

Her mother looked off at the cupboards for a moment, as if remembering something, then smiled. "Your father was like nobody I'd ever met before. So different from anything I'd expected from an American. He was kind and gentle, and he didn't mind that I had my own aspirations. Different from the man your grandmother wanted me to marry."

"Grandma wanted you to marry somebody else? I mean, somebody specific?"

Her mother nodded. "Old friend of the family. He was nice enough, but he . . . how do I say this? He wanted things his way. He wanted things the traditional way. He had . . ." She motioned with her hands. "I think that you'd say he had *issues.*"

Rose laughed.

"Most of the Vietnamese men I knew were like that. Even your grandfather," her mother said. "They weren't bad. That just wasn't what I was looking for. When I met your father, I thought I'd found what I was looking for."

"But then it didn't work."

Her mother patted her hand. "It's not that. It's just . . . I think that I was different from any woman that he'd ever met. We focused on those differences without making sure we had enough things the same. We grew apart, Rose."

Rose processed that for a minute, then looked at her watch. "I have to go. He'll be expecting me."

"All right."

"But thanks for talking to me." Rose gave her mother a hug. "That helped."

When Rose turned to the door, her grandmother was standing there, arms crossed, a determined look in her eye. Rose groaned.

"Your grandmother Irene, hmm?" Her tone was smug. Rose figured the woman must have crept down the stairs to catch the tail end of that conversation. "You're going out on a date. And you asked your mother for advice."

Rose sighed. "I have to go, Grandma."

"After she married the wrong man, you're asking her for advice?" Her grandmother shook her head. "She didn't marry someone from her culture either, and look how *that* turned out! And you want her advice for another American?"

Rose felt anger burn in her stomach. "I have to go," she repeated, walking past her grandmother, who was now speaking hurriedly in Vietnamese with her mother.

"Be careful," her mother admonished before going out the door.

Rose got into her car and closed her eyes, leaning her head against the steering wheel for a moment.

She loved her grandmother—and at the same time, the woman knew how to push her buttons, make her angrier than anyone she knew.

What would my grandmother say if she knew I was dating a Vietnamese man tonight?

She'd probably start hounding, and relentlessly at that, Rose thought with a groan. She'd keep Paul a secret a little while longer. Maybe he'd be what her mother had mentioned—possessive, overly traditional, somewhat domineering. Maybe they just wouldn't have enough in common. There were too many "maybes" to justify telling her family, anyway.

Still, Rose thought as she started her car, she got the feeling she wasn't going to be very good company tonight.

Paul had only burned himself slightly on the cha gio, and now he was cleaning up the kitchen. He had several dishes, and even had some bean cakes and lychee fruit for dessert. Rose would be getting a crash course gastronomically, since there were only some traditional dishes he could cook. She wasn't coming over to get his bachelor's specials of baked potatoes and microwave dinners. He'd made several frantic calls to his mother about some of it, all the while trying to fend off her intensifying questions about who he was having over who required such a fuss.

He'd tell her about Rose eventually, he thought, stirring the soup and glancing yet again at the clock. He wasn't even sure if Rose was interested in a relationship. But after his conversation with Nala, he was going to be extra careful.

If she's more interested in "learning" so she can get her grandmother off of her back, would she go so far as to date a guy just to get her grandmother's silence?

He put the lid back on the pot. It sounded awful, but it *was* something he could relate to. Not that he hadn't cared about Phoung, the woman he'd been engaged to. He had, deeply. But he hadn't been in love with her, and suspected he had known that deep down when he'd proposed to her. His parents and her parents had thrown them together at every opportunity— even their respective grandparents approved of the match. However, no matter how perfect she was for his family, every day showed that she wasn't the perfect woman for him—and he hated to admit it, but his parents' disappointment over the broken engagement was almost worse than Phoung's was.

Maybe that was why he could understand Rose's desire for peace from relentless matchmaking. It wasn't that he had anything against Vietnamese women—in fact, he thought they were some of the most beautiful, intelligent women on the face of the earth. But being introduced to so-called "perfect" women, day after day, by his eager family, and feeling unable to connect with *any* of them in any sort of lasting way, had been terribly depressing.

Funny how the one woman he finally *could* connect with was out in New York, away from his family, away from most Vietnamese people, period . . . and he'd found her when she asked for his help because she didn't want to date Asian men!

I said I hadn't *dated Asian guys,* he remembered her saying. *There's a difference.*

The doorbell rang, and he shook himself out of his thoughts. He walked to the door, opening it. It was a chilly night—Rose had a jacket on, and her cheeks were pink and her hair mussed from the rising wind. He quickly shuttled her in, shutting and locking the door.

"Can I get your coat?" he asked, studying her. She looked great, as usual, but something was wrong—she looked a little tired or sad around the eyes. She handed her coat and purse to him wordlessly, and he put them in his bedroom, trying to think of how best to broach the subject.

When he came back out, she still had that look . . . faint, but still there. "Something smells good," she said with a small note of forced cheer. "What is all that?"

"Let me give you the tour," he said, walking her over to the kitchen and resisting the impulse to put his arm around her shoulders. There was nothing he'd like more than to kiss her like he had in the small playground by the center, but he didn't want to rush. They had plenty of time, and he didn't want her to think that was all she was here for. Also, there was that lingering sadness—that would *definitely* need to be addressed before he jumped the gun and went for the kiss.

"Well, this is the kitchen, where all the magic happens," he said, glad to see a little smile on her face. "On second thought, why don't you sit down at the table, and I'll serve you?"

"I've been waiting to hear that from a man all my life," she said with a low laugh.

"Maybe I've been what you're waiting for," he said wryly, and her gaze darted to him as the laugh turned nervous. He didn't press it, just led her to the small dining room table. At Nala's suggestion, he'd gotten a single rose in a vase, and had set the table with two candles.

"Wow," she said, and the nervous laugh was still there. "Sort of went all-out, didn't you?"

He shifted. Maybe he'd gone heavy-handed on the romance. Perhaps he should've tried to surprise her with it. Still, she smelled the rose and turned to him. "It's nice," she said with a small smile.

"Well, you'll remember things this way," he said. "Besides, this is a special occasion."

"It is?"

He pulled out a chair for her, and watched as she settled herself.

"Why?"

"Other than the fact that you're here?" He grinned. "Well, to be honest, I don't really cook."

"That's okay," she said, and the smile was a little warmer now, the sadness slowly receding from her face. "Heck, I won't know any of these dishes, anyway. So you could make them completely wrong and I'd have no idea."

"Sort of makes you the perfect audience," he said with a laugh. "Okay, wait here; I'll be right back."

He brought the food out in serving dishes, and finished with bringing two bowls of soup, one for her, one for him, "This is the starter," he said. "It's sort of special. In Vietnam, it's really fancy. My mom only served it at the really ritziest of parties, or when she was trying to impress someone."

Rose put her napkin on her lap, and quirked an eyebrow at him. "You trying to impress me?"

He wiggled his eyebrows. "Is it working?"

She stirred it, and bit her lip. "I hate to ask, but . . . what is it?"

"Crab-and-asparagus soup," he said. "Sort of in an egg-drop base, if that's more familiar."

She dipped her spoon in and took a few tentative bites. "It's not bad," she said slowly; then she must have realized how lackluster that sounded, because she hastily added, "I mean, it's really good."

"You don't have to like all of this," he said. "I'm just giving you an overview. It's not like you're really going to need to name stuff, I'm assuming?"

Rose took a deep breath and slowly stirred the soup in her bowl, making no effort to eat it. "I have no idea how she's going to do this," she answered. "I'm sort of starting not to care anymore, honestly."

Paul felt a prickle of alarm at the back of his neck. "What happened?"

"Nothing, really." Rose pushed the soup around in her bowl. "Well, not exactly nothing. I think I'm just sick of her pressuring me into doing things I don't like to do."

Paul took a sip of his wine. "Like studying history again, or eating food you don't like . . . that kind of thing?"

"Yes." She took a deep breath.

"Like coming here?"

She put her spoon down and stared at him. "It's not that," she said, and her dark eyes were sincere. "I've appreciated all the time you've spent with me. I enjoyed spending time down at the center. I just hate feeling like I can't just do something and *enjoy* it. I hate feeling forced into anything, even if it's something I have fun with, or something that winds up being good for me. And it's like I'm not making the right choices anyway, and I probably won't ever be Vietnamese enough for her . . . or good enough."

Paul nodded heavily. It was a tough position to be in. "But if she hadn't pressured you, you wouldn't have learned about this side of your family. Or your life."

"That doesn't lessen the resentment." Rose's eyes flashed. "I know she's family. But I don't take orders well."

He took a deep breath, then pushed his soup bowl to one side. He noticed that, although her bowl was still half-full,

Rose did the same. "Well, I take orders very well," he said, hoping to coax a smile out of her. "What would you like to eat?"

She goggled at the choice he laid out before her. "What *is* all this stuff? All I can recognize are the imperial rolls . . . oh, wait, I mean cha gio."

He pointed to the dark brown, crispy-fried Vietnamese-style egg rolls. "They're a standard—they always were my favorite when I was little. This is beef pho . . . I know, it's another soup, but it's got a lot of rice noodles and cilantro, and some crushed peanuts, and you can put this hot sauce in"—he pointed to a bottle of bright red chili sauce with a picture of a rooster—"but be careful. If you're not used to spicy stuff you might want to avoid it." He went on to explain the bean crepe and the crab legs with green onions.

She tried things, a few tentative forkfuls at a time, until she found what she liked. He hadn't gotten the pho quite right, but the rolls and the crab legs he'd nailed. His mother would've been proud.

"Ready for dessert?" he asked when they'd finally finished the meal. "I've got bean cake and lychee fruit."

She looked hesitant and uncomfortable. "I was wondering . . . I don't mean to sound ungrateful, because it's all been quite wonderful. . . ."

He smiled gently. "What's up?"

"Do you have anything American?" She closed her eyes when he laughed out loud. "That sounds so awful! But . . . I think I'm having a little sensory overload."

"Wait right here." He cleared off the table, then returned with his hands behind his back. "How's this?" he said, presenting her with a Dove bar.

"Perfect," she said, and he laughed again. "I'm sorry. . . ."

"Don't be," he said. "You're just trying to learn a little here. You're not trying to be brainwashed, for pity's sake. And I don't even eat like this every day. I appreciate Vietnamese food, but I also like Mexican, Indian, French. . . ."

She smiled, her lips rimmed with dark chocolate. "Sounds cosmopolitan."

"And nothing beats a hamburger and a beer on a hot summer day."

Now she laughed, the last traces of sadness finally clearing from her face. "I like you, Paul."

He felt his chest warm at that. "I like you, too. Rather a lot, actually."

They finished their ice cream and threw the sticks away. Then they looked at each other.

"I suppose we ought to hit the books," Rose said with a sigh. "I'm going to pick up a traditional dress from that woman you recommended tomorrow, and I've got the food notes down, so . . ."

He took her hand, and she looked at him, her breathing going shallow.

"I've got a better idea," he said, leading her to his living room. "I think you've got enough studying done for three weeks. Don't want to burn out, do you?"

She smiled, and she didn't release his hand. It felt nice in his, she noticed. "Nope. What would you recommend?"

"Well, when I had finals in Berkeley, I'd always wind up watching movies during finals week, just for a break. Everybody I knew would be stressed out and spending every waking hour in the library, and they'd stare as I made my way to the latest matinee. Drove 'em nuts." He was gratified to hear Rose laugh.

"So you want to go to the movies?"

"Better." He opened a cabinet. "A video. All the enjoyment of the movies, and you don't have to worry about parking or tickets or anything."

"So . . . you're having me over for a home-cooked dinner and a video?" she said, her smile somewhat sly.

He nodded. "What? Too lame?"

"No," she said, releasing his hand and flopping onto the couch. She stretched out and made his eyes pop as she worked out the kinks of tension on his sofa. "Just nice. Comfy. I haven't done this in a long time."

He smiled and forced himself to focus back in on the task at hand. "Do you have a preference?" he said, muttering a curse as he fumbled with the DVD cases. "I've got comedies, action stuff . . . a few dramas . . ." He shot her a glance, hoping she wouldn't pick one of those. His original plan had been to get her talking about herself, but although she was relaxing, she still hadn't quite unwound enough to talk comfortably to him. This might set him back a little, time-wise, but he thought it was the wiser plan.

"A comedy, I think," she said. "All right if I take my shoes off?"

Take whatever you want off, he thought. "Sure. Like I said, make yourself comfortable."

She slipped her shoes off, tucking her legs beneath her. They settled on a comedy and he put it in the machine, working the remote until the picture came up. He settled next to her on the couch—close enough to touch if he wanted to, far enough away to give her a sense of her own space. He didn't want to crowd or rush her, but he did want her to get used to his proximity.

Later, he'd see just how close that could be.

"Rose," he said, thinking of broaching the subject and wondering if she'd mind if he put an arm around her.

"Shhh," she said with a smile. "I haven't seen this one before."

So she watched the screen, and since he *had* seen the movie before, he contented himself with sneaking frequent glances at her face . . . her large brown eyes, her high cheekbones, the full curve of her lips.

This isn't going quite the way I'd planned, he thought ruefully.

Still, the important part was, she was *there.* He hadn't quite romanced her, and they hadn't talked about a possible relationship . . . *yet.* But the evening was still pretty young. He had time.

More important, he thought, smiling as he watched her laugh, he had patience. She was worth waiting for.

The credits rolled, and Rose sighed to herself. The unpleasantness of her little tiff with her grandmother had melted away. She felt comfortable to the point of sleepiness. Paul had been more than a gentleman—he'd been a friend. He picked up on the fact that she'd been upset, and rather than pushing her about the dinner he'd obviously spent a lot of time preparing, like some men she'd known, he'd switched gears and done everything in his power to make her happier. He hadn't even so much as touched her as they sat side-by-side on the couch, enjoying the movie.

She frowned a little. Okay, so maybe he was being a bit *too* much of a gentleman.

"So, did you enjoy the movie?" he asked as he shut off the TV.

"Very much. Thanks, Paul."

His smile turned puzzled. "For what?"

"For being considerate." She shrugged as he sat back down on the couch. "For being, you know . . ."

His grin was wicked. "A devastatingly sexy host?"

She grinned in response. "I was thinking nice."

She laughed when he winced. "Oh. *Nice.* Just what every guy wants to hear."

"Now, now," she said, leaning forward and putting a hand

on his shoulder. She could feel the heat of him coming through his shirt, and she thought of the kiss he'd initiated on the playground . . . the gentleness and the heat. She'd thought of that as she drove over. Even with all the confusion and the upset, she knew that he could comfort her in more ways than just making her dinner and watching a movie.

The bottom line was, she *wanted* more from him than that. She wasn't sure how far she wanted to go with it, or how far *he* wanted to go with it. Kissing was one thing — getting into a relationship was something else.

Something she might want to try.

"You don't have to go home right away, do you?"

She glanced at the clock. It was nine . . . not too late, but considering her drive home . . .

"I've got some time," she said instead.

"Great." His eyes were intense. "I thought we could talk."

She suddenly didn't want to talk. She wanted to *feel*.

"What did you want to talk about?" She noticed her breathing had shallowed a little, and she felt her heart start to increase its tempo. She leaned forward, stroking his sleeve lightly.

His gaze darted to her hand, and perhaps unconsciously he leaned forward as well. "I wanted you to know how much I've enjoyed spending time with you," he said with a slight stammer.

"Same here." She stared at his hands. Nice, long-fingered artist's hands. She wondered what they'd feel like on her.

"I know you've got your 'test' or whatever you want to call it coming up soon," he said slowly. "And I know that you initially only wanted my help in getting you past that. . . ."

She frowned. She didn't want to think of the "test" or of her grandmother. She only wanted to think about him. "It's not that important, as I said."

"It was very important to you before," he countered, his

eyes so dark they were almost black. His face was set solemnly. "I want you to know that I respect that."

She nodded, staring at his lips . . . the way his bottom lip was full, the way his strong chin seemed to make his face almost militantly stern when he wasn't smiling. He smiled so often; she hadn't noticed before.

"Rose, are you listening to me?"

She blinked, looking at hlm. Now a half smile was on his face. "I am listening," she responded.

"Because if you're tired . . . if this is a bad time . . ."

She sighed. Men. Sometimes they complicated things so much.

"Well, it *is* a bad time," she said softly.

He paused. "I'm sorry. We don't have to talk now," he said, and she could have sworn that was disappointment lacing his voice. Then another pause. "Why is it a bad time? If you don't mind my asking."

She smiled and leaned forward. "Because I'd rather you were kissing me now," she whispered.

She watched as his eyes warmed. "Oh." He started laughing. "Well. I guess I could—"

She didn't even wait for him to finish. She simply leaned forward and kissed him, as she'd been fantasizing about for the past hour. *Hell.* For the past *week.*

His lips were full, firm, and warm, and he responded with heat and hunger. She wasn't the aggressor for long. He pressed against her, and to her surprise his tongue traced the outline of her mouth, tickling it in invitation. She parted her lips for him, moaning low in her throat as he put a hand on her waist and his other hand against her face, holding it steady against his gentle onslaught. His tongue twined with her own as his mobile mouth moved against hers with sensual intensity, causing her to shiver. After a long period of time, they broke apart, panting for air.

"This better?" he said unevenly, kissing her neck and causing the shivers to redouble.

"Mmmm." She tilted her head back so he'd have better access, and she felt his hands stroke her rib cage. She leaned back far enough that she tumbled against the plush pillows of the couch. She gasped as he followed her, his weight pressing against her. His hands moved up, tracing the undersides of her breasts. As she'd suspected, his hands felt incredible. *"Paul,"* she murmured.

He paused, his long fingers cupping her, his breath warm on her throat. "If you don't want me to do something, say so."

"I . . ." She took a deep breath and pressed herself harder against his hands. "I don't want you to stop."

She could have sworn she felt his smile against her skin.

It was as if any restraints he'd been putting on himself in deference to her feelings fell away at her statement, and she was thankful for it. He kissed her hungrily, and she met him with equal ardor, putting her arms around him, her fingers lacing in his thick hair. He was half on top of her, and it wasn't quite enough. She made a sound of protest, and he pulled away long enough for her to lie back on the couch, looking at him with invitation.

He stretched out his weight bearing down on top of her. Even with clothes on she felt his heat, especially between her legs as he pressed against the sensitive juncture of her thighs. She could feel how hard he was, and she went damp at the prospect.

"Paul," she whispered, reaching for him.

Instead of kissing her again, his lips moved lower, to the cotton of her shirt. He covered her nipples with his mouth, and heated them through the cloth. She could feel his tongue teasing the material, rubbing against her in slow circles. She went taut and arched her back, trying for more of the delicious sensation. Her legs instinctively clenched and she heard him groan before he returned to her mouth. She kissed him crazily, clutching him to her with arms and legs.

She hadn't done this on a first date with *anyone*. There might be some casual kisses, some conversation, hints of later liaisons. But this . . . She closed her eyes and moaned as he kissed the sensitive hollow behind her earlobe. It was stronger than anything she'd ever felt with anyone. She hadn't intended things to go this far . . . not this quickly.

Now she wanted them to go even farther.

"Paul," she whispered. "I want—"

"I do, too," he said, propping himself on one elbow and pressing against her with his hips, making her almost whimper with desire. "Are you sure?"

She bit her lip. "It seems crazy, but I've never wanted anyone this way. I want to make love to you."

He closed his eyes at this, his jaw clenching. "And you'll want more than that?"

"What?"

He sat up, and she felt bereft and cold with his absence. She leaned up to follow him. He sat back, and he moved her to straddle his lap, groaning as he did so. She pressed heated kisses against his jaw and neck, until he moved her back to look at him.

"I want you," he said. "Not just tonight. I want there to be more to us than just sex."

She blinked. "I think that's my line."

"Is that how you feel about it?" His voice, taut with desire, sounded harsh. His eyes all but glowed.

"I . . . I hadn't thought about it." She shook her head. "I mean, I *did* think about it. But I'd stopped thinking about it tonight." She put her forehead against his shoulder, feeling desire edged in shame. "I sort of stopped thinking tonight."

He stroked her back, kissing her cheek before nudging her chin so she faced him again.

"I'm glad you did," he said, his voice low and serious. "I would have, too, except I want this too badly. I want to see you, Rose. Exclusively. I think we have something together."

She nodded, squirming slightly and regretting it as she felt his erection brush against her. She clambered off of him, retreating to the other side of the couch.

"Is that such a bad idea?" His eyes looked guarded.

"No." She shook her head, her mind darting frenetically from thought to thought. "I just hate it when I let my body do my thinking for me."

He smiled. "I actually rather liked that part," he said, and she let out a raw half laugh. "But it wouldn't be fair. And as much as I'd love to make love with you, I don't want there to be any regrets later." He stroked her hair, her face, and she half closed her eyes at the warmth of his touch. "And I really don't want to know what you feel like and then never get to touch you again."

She closed her eyes. She'd hate that, too . . . if he could do this to her with just kisses, what would she do when she knew what it felt like to have him inside her, his naked skin sliding against hers?

"I may not seem it," she said, her voice ragged, "but I appreciate you giving me some space."

"Like I said, I want you to be sure." But his voice definitely held regret. Then he paused. "So. Should I give you, like, half an hour to decide? Maybe get you a cup of coffee?" The wicked grin was back. "Then we could pick up where we left off."

"I don't rush into things." She thought about the way she'd all but jumped him on his own couch, and felt the heat of a blush rush from her chest to her face. "All evidence to the contrary."

"Don't do that," he said, his voice firm.

"Don't do what?"

"Beat yourself up for making out with me," he said. "Yeah, it was headed toward something serious, but in this day and age, even sex on the first date is nothing to be ashamed of."

"It's not something I do," she said with an embarrassed shrug. "And it's definitely not something my date stops me from going through with."

"Tell you what," he said, tugging her into the crook of his arm and giving her a comforting hug. "Next time you can do anything to me that you want, and I won't protest at all."

She grinned against his shirt.

"It's okay, all right?" He squeezed her against him. "It wasn't any big deal."

But the problem was that it felt like a big deal to her.

"I have to think about this." She kissed his jaw. "I think I know . . . but I want to be sure."

"And I want you to be." He sighed roughly. "But Rose?"

"Mmm?"

He kissed her gently on the lips, and she could feel the longing . . . probably because she wanted, as well.

"Don't take too long," he said.

Three days later Paul sat on his parents' patio in San Jose, sipping a glass of iced tea.

"How are you feeling, Paul?" his mother said.

"Like an idiot," he muttered.

She stepped out onto the patio. "What was that?"

"Nothing, nothing." The last thing he was going to discuss with his mother was his sex life — or lack thereof.

In another time, forgoing sex would have been seen as a sign of nobility. Chivalry.

He shook his head. *Nope. Stupidity.* Even in the Middle Ages, he felt sure other knights would have laughed at him for telling a woman who obviously wanted him that he wanted to wait until he was surer of their relationship, rather than compliment him on his "chivalry."

What were you thinking?

He took another long draw off the glass of iced tea. The thing of it was, he knew what he was thinking.

He was in love with Rose Parker. And some part of him was afraid that she didn't feel the same way. He'd rather never know what making love with her felt like if she was only going to hurt him and run.

He got up and walked inside the house. His sister, Nala, had had her baby, and now his mother and father were taking care of her for a few days while her husband was out on business. They were feeding Nala every time she let them, usually as an excuse to hold the baby for her. He glanced into the room she was currently staying in.

She held a finger to her lips. "She's sleeping."

He walked over to the crib, taking a look at his new niece. She had a dark sprinkling of black hair, and a tiny rosebud mouth. Everything about her—her nose, her eyelashes, her fingers—was impossibly small.

"She's beautiful, Nala."

"I know." Nala beamed, and she squeezed his hand. "You know, when I got married, I never thought I could love anybody as much as Minh. But now I've got her, and it's like I love both of them even more."

Paul felt a stab of envy. "That's great. I'm happy for you."

"I only wish that you could feel the same thing one day," she said, her voice dreamy.

He sighed. "You and me both."

She turned to him, eyes narrowed, then stood up and tugged him to the other room, leaving the baby monitor on. "All right. What happened with the half-Vietnamese girl?"

"Rose," he said, hating the way the appellation "half-Vietnamese" sounded. "Her name is Rose."

His sister nodded. "I'm sorry. What happened with Rose?"

He closed his eyes for a second. "Nothing, really."

"So why are you so unhappy?"

He shook his head. Nala could be like a bulldog—worse when she was in person than when he spoke to her on the phone. "We're sort of debating what the next step in our relationship is going to be."

"You're both deciding," Nala said slowly, "or *she's* deciding?"

He frowned.

"Never mind. Your face answered my question already." Nala frowned as well, showing the family resemblance. "So what does she need to think about? And are you sure that you want somebody who isn't sure of how she feels about you?"

"It's not like that," Paul quickly defended. "For pity's sake, you said so yourself—I used to be her teacher, kind of. When she met me, it wasn't like we were dating. She was asking for my help. The attraction sort of grew. Now I want to take it to the next step, and she needs to think about it. That's not hard to understand."

Nala chewed this over for a minute; then her eyes flew wide open. "Paul, you're not pressuring the poor girl to have sex with you, are you?"

He felt the slow stain of a blush. "*Nala.* Come on."

She put her hands on her hips. "Well, are you?"

"I am *not* having this conversation with my little sister," he muttered darkly.

"I'm a mother now, remember?" She glared at him. "Honestly, Paul. You can't be—"

"I'm not," he finally said. "Quite the contrary."

Then he wished he'd kept his mouth shut. Nala's expression of disbelief would have been comic if the subject hadn't been so painful.

"If you say a word to *anybody*—"

"Never mind that," Nala said impatiently. "Are you trying to tell me that she wanted to sleep with *you* . . . and you didn't want to?" She bit her lip, obviously trying to keep a laugh in. "Now I might be worried for other reasons."

"I wanted her, believe me," Paul said, letting out a deep breath.

Nala's humor slid away. "You really love her, don't you?"

He thought about it. The way Rose joked as she pushed her way through her "studies." The way she'd been so shy at the cultural center's Spring Festival, and the way she'd laughed as she attempted to dance. The way she felt when he kissed her, the way she told him she wanted him to kiss her.

"Yeah," he said. "I thought I wasn't sure, but I think now there's no question."

"And how does she feel?" Nala asked quietly.

"I don't know," Paul said. "She doesn't know. So I'm giving her time to think."

"Oh." Nala looked at the floor awkwardly. "How long will it take?"

"She's doing this thing in New York City, some party or something with her grandmother." The "test" that he'd worked so hard to prepare her for. Whether she passed or failed, technically she wouldn't really have any more need for him in that area. If they stayed together, it would be for each other. "I'm supposed to pick her up from the train station in Poughkeepsie and take her home. She knew I'd be flying out here in the meantime, to see you and the baby. I figured that giving her a little space to think without me crowding her would be a good idea." And it was torturing him.

Nala studied him, then gave him a hug.

He hugged back, then smiled at her. "What was that for?"

"For a really pain-in-the-butt big brother," Nala said, "you're a really good man, Paul."

He grinned. "As long as you don't call me 'nice,'" he joked. "Now, why don't we get you something to eat?"

Nala groaned as he tugged her toward the kitchen, where his mother was busily cooking. They didn't say another word about Rose. Still, he couldn't help thinking about her.

He wondered if she was thinking about him.

Just hang on for another couple of hours, Rose told herself. *Then you'll get to see Paul, and things will be much better.*

She was wearing a red *ao-dai,* the formal Vietnamese dress-pantsuit thing that Paul had mentioned to her. She'd seen pictures of her grandmother and mother in them before, but tonight both of them were wearing them, her grandmother in silver, her mother in light blue. It was a fitted dress with snaps from neck to shoulder and down the side, with a long "skirt" that split all the way to the waist, worn over long white pants. It wasn't the most comfortable thing in the world—she'd been in a hurry, so the seamstress had gotten one that fit but was a little bit tight—but from her mother's praise and her grandmother's look of reluctant pride, she figured she'd passed that aspect, at least.

Not that it matters anymore.

She'd missed Paul. She knew he had flown to the West Coast to visit his family and to see his sister's new baby, but she'd almost wished he'd called, just so she could hear the sound of his voice. She'd tried focusing on her work, coming up with content for a few more newsletters and submitting some magazine articles. She'd tried hard to keep herself busy.

It hadn't worked.

Now she was looking forward for this evening to be over. They'd arrived about half an hour before, at her grandmother's friend Lailu's house. It was a posh place in the city, easily a few million dollars. They were in the large, opulently decorated living room. Waiters were passing out hors d'oeuvres and champagne. Her grandmother was obviously envious and impressed by turns. Rose was pretty impressed herself.

"Now, you behave yourself," her grandmother said to her in a hissed whisper.

"Count on it," Rose said. "By the way, what do you think of my *ao-dai*?"

Her grandmother made a low huffing noise and turned away in search of her friend. Rose laughed.

Funny that now, after all this effort to get her grandmother to stop pushing her to date Vietnamese men, she would get her wish after all. And Rose would make sure that Paul knew that, as soon as he picked her up from the train station.

Hopefully not long after that, they'd finish up what they'd started on his couch.

She smiled, hugging herself slightly. Not that it was just about sex—he'd proven that when he pulled away from her when she was ready to go pliant and mindless beneath him. In staying away from her for a week, letting her body cool down as it were, he'd showed her that he cared about her—and that he wanted more than just a casual affair. And when she realized how much she missed him, not just for what he made her body feel, but for how he made her feel emotionally, she realized that he was right.

"What are you thinking about, Rose?" her mother said, hugging her, then glancing around. "Are you still thinking about that date you had? How did that go?"

Rose sighed. "It went well, I think. But next time will go better. I just want to get through tonight, so I can see him."

Her mother nodded. "It won't be too much longer."

"So . . . how is this 'test' thing supposed to work out, anyway?" Rose asked. "Her friend's supposed to ask me questions or something, is that it? I've already got the dress, and I have been trying to tell Grandmother I recognize most of the food."

Rose's mother shifted her weight nervously. "I . . . um, I'm not sure. . . ."

"Rose!" her grandmother called, with another woman in tow. The other woman was wearing an obviously expensive *ao-dai,* heavy with embroidery, and huge diamonds on her wrists and at her throat. This had to be Lailu. Rose could see how the woman could afford a place like this. "This is my friend, Lailu Huynh. Lailu, this is my granddaughter."

Lailu nodded. "How do you do?"

Rose shook her hand, feeling slightly nervous. "I'm so glad to meet you. I've heard a lot about you."

"As I have about you. Your grandmother has been writing to me for some time. It's so nice that I could meet her and her granddaughter at the same time." Her English was good, Rose noted, with only a slight accent. She felt the woman's gaze assessing her coolly. She wondered if Lailu was going to start peppering her with questions, or just decide in her grandmother's favor and insist that Rose get a Vietnamese husband for the sake of her kids' cultural inheritance.

"You're half-American, yes?" Lailu said, her voice appraising.

Rose nodded. "But I've been studying Vietnamese culture," Rose said hastily, causing her grandmother to frown. "I don't speak the language yet—"

"Oh, that's all right, dear." Lailu glanced at her gem-encrusted watch. "Where *is* he? It's not like him to be this late," she murmured.

Rose's eyes narrowed. "I'm sorry. Where is who?"

Lailu looked at her, smiling. "Why, my son, John. I can't wait for you to meet him."

Rose turned to her grandmother, betrayal flashing in her eyes. "Grandmother . . ."

Her grandmother shot her a look of complete innocence before accompanying Lailu to another table.

Rose turned to her mother, almost shaking with anger. "She *lied* to me," she said in a low voice. "I jumped through all those hoops, intent on proving to her that my kids had nothing to worry about . . . and it was all a big *sham!* She just wanted to set me up with her rich friend's old, businessman Vietnamese son!"

"Rose," her mother's voice cautioned.

"I am going home," Rose said sharply. "I never should have come here. If she's not going to respect our deal, then I'm certainly not going to care if I embarrass her by leaving—"

"Rose," her mother said more insistently, holding her arm. "She meant well."

"She can't keep doing this, Mom," Rose said, feeling tears well up. "Why can't she love me the way I am? Why can't she just leave me alone?"

Rose headed for the door, veering to the closet, where a maid was taking coats. She bumped into a tall, blond-haired man before she could get there.

"I'm sorry," he said, his voice deep and booming. "Are you all right? Did I hurt you?"

She brushed at the slight sheen of tears in her eyes. "No, I'm fine, I'm fine. . . ."

"John!"

Rose turned to find Lailu bearing down on them, her grandmother and her mother close behind. Rose watched as the tall man gave the tiny Lailu a hug.

"Hello, Mother." He smiled down at her warmly. "I'm sorry I'm late. There were some hangups in getting the contract signed over in New Jersey, and then there was an accident in the tunnel. Traffic was hideous."

"A small excuse," Lailu said, almost sternly, but there was obvious fondness in her eyes. "I see you've already met the granddaughter of one of my dearest friends."

Rose didn't listen to the rest of Lailu's introduction. She

kept staring at the Nordic giant standing in front of her. "You're John?" she said, feeling a bubble of hysterical laughter start to well up in her.

"Can't see the family resemblance, huh?" he said with a wink.

Lailu frowned. "Of course, John is adopted. His parents were some of our very best friends, and business partners of my husband. When they died when John was only eight, we took him in and took care of him."

There was obvious love in the woman's voice; Rose could tell that much.

"But . . . he's *American,*" Rose's grandmother said, incredulous.

Rose couldn't help it. She burst out laughing, even as her grandmother frowned at her.

Lailu frowned at Rose's grandmother. "He's my *son,* dear."

Grandmother, Rose noticed, quickly acquiesced. Still, as Lailu went on to describe John's various business successes and his devotion to the family, Rose couldn't help but notice Grandmother staring at him, obviously aghast. John was everything Rose would have wanted in a man: good-looking, rich, obviously caring with his family. He was well-spoken and not a jerk, from what she could tell. And he seemed to embody everything her grandmother didn't want her going for in a man.

The irony was ridiculous. Rose knew it was probably mean, but she was now having more fun at this party than she ever would have thought she could.

"So what do you do?" John asked her.

Rose saw her grandmother frowning out of the corner of her eye, so she smiled her brightest. "I'm a freelance writer. I develop Web content, work on newsletters, corporate brochures, annual reports, some magazine articles."

"And you're successful, obviously." He nodded. "That's great."

She smiled.

"You know," he said thoughtfully, "you're not what I was expecting at all."

Rose chuckled. "At least they warned you," she murmured.

He laughed, and she realized he'd heard her "I know. Mom can get pretty militant about trying to set me up." He shook his head. "But this time I might thank her. I was wondering . . . would you have dinner with me? Maybe tomorrow night?"

Rose blinked. "Um . . ."

"You live near Pleasant Valley, right? I'll be in that neck of the woods on business. I'd love to take you out."

Rose felt an immediate stabbing pang of panic. What would Paul think? She was going to be getting serious with him. She didn't want to see anybody else. . . .

She looked over to where her grandmother was sitting, wearing an expression of horror. She'd obviously overheard John's invitation—and was not happy about it.

Rose grinned. It was just dinner. And from the horrified look on her grandmother's face, she got the feeling it'd be a long time before she decided to meddle in her love life again.

Paul would understand. He wasn't like her mother had described, one of those stereotypical Vietnamese men who were possessive. He'd given her space to think, hadn't he? He'd understand. She felt sure of it.

"Tomorrow night?" Rose nodded, smiling widely. "Why not?"

Paul sat in his car. It was May, and summer was finally coming on strong after a fairly cool spring. It would be scorching hot soon, and humid.

It's going to be a lot hotter tonight, if things work out well.

He glanced at his watch. He was pretty sure this was her train at the station. In a few minutes she'd be in his car. Not long after that she'd be in his arms.

If everything works out well.

He hadn't spoken with her. She'd have gotten that silly "test" out of the way, and hopefully she'd been thinking about them, about where they were going after this. He hoped that she'd thought along the same lines . . . that there was more to them than just cultural lessons and a really combustible chemistry.

He gripped the steering wheel. After their last session on his couch, he felt pretty sure that she would. He didn't want to rush her, but damn, it was hard to wait.

She rapped on his window, and he smiled at her, feeling his stomach jump. He unlocked her door, and she climbed in. He only had a minute to admire her in her deep red *ao-dai* before she shut the door and the car went dark.

He wanted to kiss her, but he wanted to hear from her first. There would be plenty of time for kissing later—he'd make sure of it. "So," he said carefully. "How'd it go?"

"You wouldn't even believe it." Her voice was ebullient, and her eyes shone as he started the car and pulled it out of the parking lot. "In the first place, my grandmother's friend is incredibly rich. She and her husband are some kind of Asian businesspeople, and they trade or set up stuff or something. . . ."

Paul listened to her as she babbled happily about the house, the woman who owned it, all manner of relatively unimportant things. He wanted to pay attention, but he knew that the only thing he really had any attention span for tonight was whether or not she was going to agree to their relationship or not. He was trying to be patient, but he had a limit.

"So it turns out my grandmother wasn't even bringing me

there to test out my cultural awareness," Rose pointed out, and immediately Paul's ears pricked up.

"Huh? It wasn't?" He glanced over at her in the passenger seat, where she was wearing a smug smirk. "Then what the heck did she want you to do all this studying for?"

"Turns out she didn't care if I studied or not. It was all a big hoax." He was surprised that she didn't sound more upset about it. Instead, she sounded almost triumphant. "It was actually just one big setup."

Paul turned from the interstate to Rose's exit, feeling an inexplicable uneasiness start to crawl up his back. "How do you mean?"

"She didn't want Lailu to test me on Vietnamese trivia. I still can't believe I fell for it." She chuckled. "All she wanted to do was get me to meet Lailu's son. She was still trying to get me a date!"

Paul felt a wave of coldness hit him. "I'm surprised you're not angrier about it," he said neutrally.

"Oh, I was furious," Rose replied, and Paul relaxed a little, until her next statement. "Until I met the guy."

"And then . . . ?" Paul stared at the road ahead of him as if his life depended on it.

"This is too funny. Oh, turn up here," she said, guiding him to her house. "Anyway, turns out the 'son' is adopted . . . and he's not even Vietnamese. He looks like a poster boy for the Vikings or something—tall, blond hair, blue eyes."

Paul let out a reluctant grin. "Bet that surprised your grandmother."

"I thought she'd swallow her dentures." Rose grinned. "That's probably mean of me, but she shouldn't have lied to me, and she shouldn't have tried to set me up."

He pulled up in front of her house, shutting off the engine of his car and turning to her. "So that's all behind you now, huh?"

"Sort of." She grinned, unbuckling her seat belt. "I agreed to have dinner with him tomorrow night. After that, I think that she'll finally get off my back for good, since I'm only doing what she wanted me to do in the first place."

Paul felt anger hit him like a brick. "You *what?*"

Rose glanced over at him, her happy, chirpy voice finally turning serious. "Oh. I'm sorry, Paul, that probably sounds awful. But I figured you'd understand."

"You're going out to dinner with another guy . . . and you want me to *understand* it?" He stared at her, incredulous.

She frowned. "It's not that big a deal, really—"

"If it's not that big a deal," he said sharply, "then you can cancel it."

She stared at him for a minute. "You're not serious."

"Do I look like I'm joking?" he responded.

They sat for a moment in the dark and the silence.

"Maybe I'm not explaining this well enough," Rose said slowly. "It's just dinner. It's nothing serious. There's no commitment here or anything."

"I'm starting to wonder if there's commitment anywhere," Paul muttered darkly. "Rose, I thought we had something going here."

She blinked at him. "We do. What does that—"

"Which means I don't want you going out to dinner with somebody else."

"Paul, you can't be jealous."

"Try me," he said.

"I can't believe this," she said, jerking the car door open. He followed her out of the car and down her darkened walkway. "I just can't believe this."

"How do you think I feel?" he said, catching up to her. "I leave town for a week, giving *you* time to think . . . and you wind up making a *date*? What am I supposed to think?"

"I thought you could trust me," she said. "I thought you'd understand that this isn't anything serious!"

"Are *we* serious, Rose?" he said, feeling anger coil through him like a snake. "I'm serious about you. Serious enough to tell you that if you want to see me, I don't want you seeing *him*."

She paused, and her eyes glittered with fury. "Is that an ultimatum or just a threat?"

"It's a decision," Paul responded. "One you're going to have to make. And I'm not giving you a week on this one."

"Oh, aren't you the paragon of patience," she drawled. "I thought you knew me better than this, Paul."

"I thought I knew you better than this, too."

Her eyes narrowed. "Then I thought you'd know— *I don't like to be crowded, or feel forced into anything.* Not by anybody."

"And I don't like to be played with." He crossed his arms. "So where does that leave us?"

"That leaves me thanking you for the ride," she said in a low voice. "And telling you that I won't be seeing you again."

His chest clenched, and he gritted his teeth. "So that's it, huh? That's all I get?"

"Good night, Paul." She unlocked her door, walked into her house, and shut the door behind her.

He stared at her house dumbly for a moment, stunned. *This was not how I planned this evening to go at all.*

After a long moment, he walked back to his car and started the drive back to his house. He'd planned to make love with her, finally, starting off a long, loving relationship. Now he was driving home alone, furious.

She was seeing someone else. And she couldn't see what was wrong with that! She was obviously the wrong woman for him. She wasn't who he thought she was. She hadn't wanted to date an Asian man. She had simply wanted to get some revenge on her pushy grandmother, and now was going to be dating some tall blond American guy with a clear conscience. But she wanted him to *understand!*

Obviously he was better off without her. He should thank her for clearing things up before he'd made an even bigger mistake.

He shifted gears, his teeth grinding together as he stepped on the accelerator.

So if I'm doing the right thing, he thought, *then why does it hurt so damned much?*

Rose sat at dinner in a small Italian restaurant nestled in some tall trees in Wappingers Falls. She had met John there, and listened to him talk about business through drinks and appetizers.

Unfortunately, she wasn't *really* listening. She was thinking. Of Paul.

If you want to see me, I don't want you seeing him.

She wouldn't have thought he had it in him. Now she wondered why she hadn't picked up on it sooner. The tone, the fury of it, had startled and upset her. He'd asked her to be in a more serious relationship with him, granted, but they hadn't gotten to that stage yet. She had planned to tell him that they were at that stage after she went through the funny story of her grandmother, Lailu, and John. But instead he'd turned on her, becoming possessive, demanding, unreasonable. Demanding they be in an exclusive dating relationship, after he'd so tenderly told her he'd be patient just a week before. He was becoming everything she was afraid of. Everything her mother had told her Vietnamese men were.

How could I have been so blind? He hadn't seemed like that at all.

She missed the man she'd cared so much about. She missed

Paul, the tender teacher, the funny, sensitive, caring guy she'd wound up falling in love with.

She blinked.

In love with Paul.

And now she was out to dinner with a complete stranger, and she didn't know *what* had happened.

"So I told my mother we have to work on increasing relationships with businesses in Saigon now, as boundaries are starting to open up. We'd laid the groundwork out years ago—"

"John, can I ask you a question?"

He smiled. "You can ask me anything you like."

"If you were starting to date a woman, and she told you she wanted to see other men, how would you react?"

He looked puzzled. "Is this a question or a warning?"

She stared at him for a minute. "Oh. A question." It wasn't a warning, because she was sure she wouldn't be dating John again. Even if she'd taken this date on to prove a point, he was definitely not her type.

"Hmmm. It would depend on how much I liked her, I suppose."

Rose thought about it. The way Paul's eyes had gleamed after they'd kissed. The gentle way he brushed her hair out of her face. The effort he'd gone through to cook for her, the time he'd spent helping her with her studies.

"Let's say you liked her a lot," she said. "How would you react?"

"If I liked her a lot, but we weren't exclusive, I'd be upset, of course."

"Would you stop seeing her?"

He laughed. "Well, no. Probably not. I mean, obviously we haven't hit the point where she's my girlfriend or anything."

"That's it, that's it exactly," she said, causing him to look even more confused. "That's just the right way to approach things, don't you think? You wouldn't get angry with her, you wouldn't start tossing around ultimatums or telling her to knock it off."

"Of course not," John said.

Rose smiled . . . until John finished his thought.

"Does she realize I'm going to do the same thing, though?"

Rose blinked. "What?"

"I mean, it's only fair," John said expansively. "If she's going to see other people, what's to stop me from doing it, too? If we're not an official couple, then I'm certainly not going to wait around while she goes out with every guy in town, am I?"

Rose felt her stomach knot into an icy lump.

Paul, going out with other women. Right now, possibly.

Paul had been right. She had been so intent on teaching her grandmother a lesson, and focusing on the fact that he needed to understand *her,* that she hadn't tried to look at it from his point of view.

She was in love with him. If he had told her he was going to take another woman out, for whatever reason, she'd like to think she could be understanding, sure . . . but it would eat away at her like acid. Considering her temperament, chances were she'd have said the same thing to him.

She'd told him she wouldn't see him again. So what would stop him from going out and trying to find a woman who was more understanding?

She felt the blood drain from her face.

"Whoa," John said. "Are you all right?"

"Actually, suddenly I feel very ill," Rose said in a soft voice. "I have to go home."

"All right," John said, obviously nervous. "I guess I'll just take a rain check on dinner."

She shook her head. "You're very nice, John, but I'm afraid I can't have dinner with you again."

He frowned. "Why not?"

"Because I'm in love with somebody else," she said, standing up.

And here's hoping I haven't made the biggest mistake of my life.

Paul sat in his house, nursing a beer and staring blankly at the television. There was a party tonight at the cultural center. This would be the first time in the center's two-year history that he'd missed one of the festivities. He'd even called in sick.

"Are you all right, dear?" Mrs. Nguyen had asked him in Vietnamese.

He'd told her he felt lousy, and he meant it. Even if he didn't have a cold or flu, he was definitely heartsick.

"Feel better soon, then," she had responded.

God, he hoped he *could* feel better soon.

He'd gone over his response to Rose in detail. He'd relived the scene, the pain of her telling him that she was seeing another man for dinner, her request for him to "understand."

How could I have been such an idiot?

He thought they'd been on the same wavelength. He thought she'd cared—that she'd want the same thing he wanted. Obviously he'd been terribly wrong on both counts.

Maybe she had a point.

The thing was, he was still nervous about how she'd respond—and she *hadn't* said yet that she wanted a relationship. So was it all on his side, then? Had he completely misread her, and pushed for something he had no right to? Would she have fallen for him eventually? And had he therefore ruined his chances by leading with his emotions, crowding her, pushing her away?

He didn't know, he thought, drinking more of his beer. And the worst part of it was, now it looked like he'd never find out.

His doorbell rang. He prayed it wasn't somebody from the

center, checking up on him. He'd go back to work, probably tomorrow. He'd be ready for their questions and their good wishes then.

Now, he just wanted to be alone.

He opened the door, and his eyes widened.

It was Rose.

"Hi there," she said, her voice high and nervous. "Mind if I come in?"

He nodded, dumbstruck. "I mean, no. I don't mind. Come in."

"Thanks," she said, and walked in. She was wearing a little black dress that made her legs look long and wonderful.

"I thought you'd be out to dinner," he said, then winced. If he was trying to improve matters, this might not be the best way to start off.

She blushed slightly, looking at the floor. "I was."

"I'm sorry," he said. "I mean, I'll admit, I was still angry. I didn't want you to go. I won't be sorry about that."

She nodded. "Paul, I wanted to tell you—"

"Please, let me finish," he said, taking her hands. "Listen. If it'll take more time for you, then"—he took a deep, fortifying breath, "I can wait. Not forever, and I'm not saying it'll be easy for me. But I care too much about you to lose you, Rose. I think we're right for each other. And I think, given time, you'll agree with me."

He stared at her, and saw that her eyes were misting slightly. "What's wrong?"

"I don't need time," she said softly.

He couldn't have heard that right. Still, hope pounded in his chest. "What do you mean?"

"I was reacting as if you were my grandmother—as if you were being a bully and rushing me," she said. "I didn't look at it the way I ought to. And then it occurred to me . . . if you went out to dinner with another woman, I wouldn't be happy. At all."

"You wouldn't?" he said, finally allowing himself a small grin.

"In fact, I'd be mad as hell," she said, and he chuckled. "So in that light, I can see why you'd react the way you did."

He nodded.

"I still don't like feeling forced, even with good intentions," she said.

"I know," he said. "And I am sorry."

They stood like that for a minute; then she looked at him, her eyes huge, a rich, deep brown edged in tears.

"Could you just hold me now?" she said.

Just that quickly he pulled her into his arms, and they were kissing and holding each other as if they'd been separated for a year rather than one really bad day.

"I'm sorry, I'm so sorry," Paul murmured into her hair.

"Oh, Paul, so am I," she said under her breath. "I love you."

He paused, holding her against his chest. "What was that?"

She sighed. "Maybe it's too soon. But I knew that I cared about you, even before last night. And then tonight I remembered why I cared about you . . . and realized I'd been falling in love with you, and I hadn't even paid attention to it."

She was quiet, waiting.

"Rose," he said, kissing her gently on the lips. "I love you, too."

She burst into fresh tears.

After a long few moments they were kissing again, whispering words of love against each other. And he took her to the bedroom. In between declarations, he helped her take off the dress, and she helped him out of his shirt and jeans. In the next few hours he felt the silky smoothness of her skin beneath his, drinking in her soft gasps as he moved against her, feeling the way her hands bunched into the muscles of his back. When she cried out in climax, he was only a breath behind her, shuddering against her as she wrapped her legs around him.

"I love you," she said, against his damp skin.

"I love you too," he said softly.

Now, as they lay sweat-soaked and twined around each other, he felt happy. Complete. Fulfilled.

There was a thin, tinny ring that he barely registered. He looked over at her, puzzled.

"Oh, damn," she said, leaning over the bed and giving him a great vantage point of her backside. She came back with her purse, pulling out her cell phone. She glanced at the number, winced, then answered it. "Hello, Mom."

She nodded, then closed her eyes. He could hear Rose's mother's voice on the other line, but couldn't make out the words. "I'm sorry I didn't call. I lost track of the time. I didn't want you to worry."

Paul smiled as Rose snuggled against his chest.

"Grandma wants to talk to me?" Rose glanced up at Paul, who shrugged. "Can't it wait until tomorrow? Well . . . okay. But just for a minute. I'm sort of tired."

"Not that tired," Paul whispered, and Rose smirked at him. "I'm not through with you yet."

She stuck her tongue out at him, causing him to laugh.

"Hello, Grandmother. No, I'm not mad at you." He heard the voice on the other end go on at length, and saw Rose smile. "I accept your apology, Grandmother. I know how badly you want me to be with someone you think is right for me. But promise me . . . no more matchmaking, okay?"

The tone of her grandmother's voice sounded grudging, but he could feel Rose's muscles relax. "Thanks, Grandma. That means a lot." She paused. "No, that doesn't mean I'm going to be single forever or only dating tall, ugly Americans."

Paul muffled a laugh.

"Tell you what, Grandma. I'm going to bring somebody by for dinner on Sunday . . . somebody who means a lot to me."

Rose looked up at Paul, her heart shining in her eyes. "Is that okay? It is? Great. I'll talk to you soon. Love you, Grandma."

She clicked off the cell phone, putting it on the nightstand, then turned to Paul, pushing him against the bed.

"Now you're in for it," she said, resting on his chest and straddling him lightly. "You get to meet the woman who put me through all this trouble."

"I like your grandmother," he said. "If it weren't for her, I wouldn't have met you."

She smiled. "Yeah, but now that you're meeting my family, she's not going to ease up on *you* until you do right by me and get me married."

He tugged her down to kiss him, feeling a familiar stirring. He thought about it . . . getting to spend time living and making love with the woman he cared about more than anyone, for the rest of his life.

"I'm counting on it," he replied, and then kissed her again.

Dragon for Dinner

BY
KATHERINE GREYLE

Chapter One

"*I* knew you wouldn't bring a date!" Su Ling's mother firmly pushed her outside the banquet room of Yen Ching's into a hallway filled with the scent of ginger and soy sauce. The elaborately carved paneling in her father's favorite restaurant darkened her mother's face into a forbidding scowl.

"I did bring a date," Su Ling teased, trying to fight the suffocating ambiance. "Me, myself, and I." She lowered her voice in mock seriousness. "It was a little rocky at first, because, between you and me, myself was getting a little uppity. But I got her under control after a swift kick."

Her mother's lips puckered into a tight ball of dark red lipstick. "This is why you do not have a husband. Your sense of humor is too confusing. Me and myself," she muttered as she shook her head. "Such nonsense."

Su Ling pressed her own lips together, unable to give voice to her frustration. She knew better than to speak to her family with anything but total seriousness and respect, but sometimes her irreverent side just got the better of her. Especially lately, when she felt a strange dissatisfaction with her boring accountant's life.

But tonight was her father's birthday party, and she needed to be respectful. So she lowered her gaze and spoke softly. "I'm sorry I didn't bring a date, but Ba Ba knows I'm single.

shocked when his youngest daughter doesn't
with a man." If anything, she thought with a grimace,
father would be stunned if she had brought someone. He'd
thought her a marital lost cause when she turned twenty-
five—three years ago.

Ma Ma threw up her hands, the gesture barely making it to
Su Ling's shoulders. "Ai-yah, Su Ling. It is not for your father
but his mother."

Her grandmother? "But she's in Hong Kong—"

"China, yes. What will she think of your father and me
when her grandchildren have no men?" She didn't wait for Su
Ling to respond, but rushed on without pause. "Never mind,
never mind," she said as she pushed her daughter backward in
the cramped hallway. "I knew you wouldn't bring anyone."
Then she dropped her voice to a mysterious whisper. "I had
another dream."

Su Ling did her best to hold back her groan. The last thing
she needed was another of her mother's dream-inspired
matches.

"Listen to me, Su Ling! You must find a dragon. That is the
man for you."

"A dragon?" Su Ling bit her tongue. She shouldn't have
said anything, shouldn't have encouraged her mother's latest
delusion, but the question had just slipped out.

"Yes, yes," continued Ma Ma. "He must be born in a dragon
year." Then she leaned forward, an excited gleam in her eye.
"I have found him for you, Su Ling. He's waiting in the lobby.
Your father's birthday dinner is the perfect time for everyone
to meet him."

Su Ling stared at her mother with stunned horror. Ma Ma
couldn't possibly expect Su Ling to meet another potential
husband while her entire family sat around and watched? "I
can't meet him now!" she whispered urgently. "Not in front of
everyone." If it were up to her she wouldn't meet him at all,

but then, she'd grown accustomed to doing things just to please her family.

"Do not be rude!" Ma Ma snapped. "Everyone wants to see him. I told them you have been dating for months." Then she lightened her tone to an irritating wheedle. "He is a professional. Very smart. An accountant like you. For taxes."

Su Ling rolled her eyes. She knew accountants. She *was* an accountant. And not one, Chinese or otherwise, had ever been a fun date. The heel of her dark pumps caught in the Chinese restaurant's faded carpet as Ma Ma pushed her toward the lobby. "Please don't make me—" she began, but her mother interrupted.

"He's waiting. Third chair from the right." Then, with a last shove, her mother slipped away back into the banquet room, where all the relatives waited to inspect Su Ling's newest mystery man.

Su Ling just stood there, her anger rising by slow degrees. She'd allowed this to happen, she told herself. She'd been polite to her mother's endless stream of eligible bachelors, and thereby tacitly encouraged her to further excesses. Su Ling moved around a potted plant to look at her mother's dragon choice, involuntarily wincing when she saw him. Another baby-faced Asian man in a boring suit and tie, obviously polite by the way he sat perfectly still in his chair, his hands folded primly in front of him. In short, an uptight mama's boy even though he was probably in his thirties.

That was when she saw the other one. Just now, his ordering take-out food in a whiskey voice sent shivers down her spine. She couldn't see him completely, but her gaze snagged on the bright Chinese dragon embroidered across his black leather jacket. A closer look revealed shaggy hair and a gold dagger dangling from his very Caucasian ear. Normally she wouldn't give this man a second glance, but her intemperate mood still simmered, spawning an evil thought. After all, Ma Ma had said her husband-to-be would be a dragon.

She must have made a sound, a soft whisper of mischief or simple admiration, because this dragon man turned and looked directly at her, one dark slash of an eyebrow raised in surprise. She looked away, pretending to inspect the menu displayed nearby, but out of the corner of her eye she watched a smile curve his lips as he leaned back against the counter. If she hadn't been surreptitiously watching him, she never would have known how slowly and leisurely he inspected her body from the top of her high bun down her trim navy suit to her legs as they extended beneath her short skirt. Nor would her skin have tingled with a sensual awareness she'd never experienced before.

Meanwhile, a few feet away, Ma Ma's dragon man released a soft sigh, obviously bored, but too polite to be irritated. Or even move. Geez, the man looked like a hypnotized statue. Su Ling couldn't imagine the leather-clad hunk waiting on anything or anyone.

What would it be like, she wondered, just for a few hours, to be on the hunk's arm instead of another soft-spoken, weak-gestured man? And wouldn't that just show Ma Ma the ridiculousness of finding a man by a dragon symbol?

Feeling more daring than ever before, Su Ling made her choice. She abruptly spun around, approaching her leather hunk with an uncharacteristically seductive smile. "Excuse me. I need a loud and obnoxious date right now. You get a free meal, fifty bucks cash, and all the relatives you can insult. Interested?" He pulled back, obviously surprised. Then, before he could respond, she fished a fifty-dollar bill out of her purse. She stared at it, stunned by the exorbitant amount and her own rash promise, but one glance at her other date option steeled her spine. She flashed the bill before the leather-clad hunk before tucking it into her jacket pocket. "Deal?"

His smile came slowly, all the more devastating because he took his time. "Always interested." He slowly straightened. God, was he really that tall? "What's your name?"

"Su Ling. And you've got to make this look good."

He grinned. "No problem, Sue. Anything else?"

"Yeah," she commented, her mind working furiously. "You're a lawyer. No, a judge. No, wait. An undercover FBI agent investigating a banking scam. That's why you're pretending to be an accountant."

"You don't do this very often, do you?"

She shot him a startled glance. "You got any better ideas?"

He shook his head. "Nope. A fed is great."

As he canceled his dinner order, Su Ling quickly scribbled a note to Ma Ma's dragon, apologizing in the nicest way possible while sending him on his way. She didn't doubt he would disappear easily. Ma Ma's dates never did anything uncomfortable or impolite, even if it meant they'd just wasted an evening. After giving the note to a waitress to deliver, she turned back to her definitely uncomfortable, impolite revenge date.

"Your name is Dragon, and you were born in 1976."

"Sorry. January 'seventy-seven."

"Suddenly you're interested in the truth?" Then she glanced at him, seeing his fluid gait as they moved down the hallway. Physically he appeared a very powerful man. A tremor of fear slithered down her spine. Just who was she bringing in to meet her parents? "Uh, look," she began, "maybe this isn't such a good idea. . . ."

"Don't chicken out now, princess. Revenge is at hand." Then he paused, obviously reading the concern on her face. "Relax. I'm an old hand at pissing off parents."

But second and third thoughts had begun to assail her. Just outside the party room Su Ling paused, facing off with the monster she'd just created. "Exactly why are you doing this?"

He shrugged, using his white smile to devastating effect. "Fifty bucks buys a lot of Happy Meals." Then, before she could respond, he pushed through the door.

Su Ling had to go up on her toes to peer over his broad

shoulder. At first, all she could see was a large ink brush shrimp painting turning beady eyes her way from over her father's head. Then her dragon moved aside, and she was startled to see their large round table half empty. Right next to her parents, Auntie Wen and Uncle Sammy were greedily eating all the hors d'oeuvres. But the chairs for Su Ling's sister and young niece were conspicuously empty. And that was the last she noticed of the decor as a deafening silence filled the room.

She should have been gratified. She would have been if she were still flush with her rebellious spirit. Unfortunately mortification dominated right now. Her father, as honored guest, sat directly opposite the doorway, his dark eyebrows raised, his jaw clenched as he pulled his head back in horror. Ma Ma and Auntie Wen were even worse, their mouths opening and closing like those of beached fish. But the absolute worst came from not-so-bright Uncle Sammy. He looked up, then snorted with amusement. "Is that Su Ling's date?" He giggled. "No wonder your sister hasn't got many grandchildren!"

But before Su Ling could sink into a perfectly timed faint, Dragon stepped forward to Uncle Sammy, his hand outstretched in a bold Texas howdy. "Why, yes," he bellowed in a voice that echoed off the dark paneling. Gone were the whiskey tones from the other room. Instead he used the thickest, corniest Texas accent Su Ling had ever heard. "Yee-haw, I am the little lady's date," he continued. "But I'm guessing you're not the birthday boy. That must be you, sir." He stepped toward her father, grabbing the smaller man's hand in his and pumping it up and down like a piston. "Why, your little gal's been talking up a storm about how much she admires y'all." He expanded his grin to the room at large. "All y'all."

The silence echoed in Su Ling's head, broken only when her mother leaped up from her chair, grabbed her daughter, and said in a hiss, "Who is he?"

Su Ling blinked, widening her eyes with exaggerated innocence. "He's my dragon." She pointed to the elaborate design on her hunk's jacket. But before she could say anything he stripped it off, revealing the dark stain of a tattooed dragon coiling down his bulging bicep before disappearing beneath his muscle T. Ma Ma nearly choked in horror while Su Ling felt her knees weaken. She never would have credited it, but right then that sinuous Chinese symbol was the sexiest thing she'd ever seen. And all the while her dragon continued to grin and joke like the worst of the B-movie cowboys.

Ma Ma recovered first, hissing another, "Not him!" before disappearing into the hallway, presumably to find the ditched dragon. Su Ling was thankful she knew Ma Ma's wimp had left moments before she and her dragon had entered the party. Then she had no more time to worry, as her dragon snaked his hand around her waist, tugging her close.

"Well, little darlin'," he drawled as he gestured to the specialty food ordered a week in advance. "This here don't look much like meat 'n' potatoes to me." Then he chucked her under the chin as he waggled his eyebrows at her. "But then you, sweet pea, are meat enough for any man."

She felt his hand begin to slide lower, and her face heated, knowing every eye in the room was trained on her rear. She intended to push him away, but as she looked into his rich amber eyes, she felt a shock of warmth course through her. She had no words for what happened, though her mind desperately scrambled to catalog the sensation. She tossed out *thrill of defiance, sexual excitement,* even *simple novelty* as all true and yet none accurate enough. Somewhere inside she knew he wouldn't hurt her, that his act remained for display purposes, and that, in truth, she felt safe with him. No logic could explain the knowledge, and yet she felt it.

And when his eyes widened in surprise, she recognized an echoing intrigue flame within him.

She had no control over what happened next. Instead of

pushing him away, she felt her head lifting, moving toward his lips as if of their own accord. Somewhere in the background her mind registered her father pushing angrily up from his chair, her mother's appalled gasp, even the rush of the door as someone pushed it open, but 98 percent of her body and mind remained fixated on her dragon's full and sensuous mouth.

"Mr. Kurtz? What are you doing here?"

Su Ling felt Dragon's body freeze, the sudden chill translating easily through her clothing. With obvious horror, Dragon turned his head to the latest party attendees: Su Ling's sister, Mei Lu, and her daughter, Amanda. "Mandy?" Dragon asked in a choked voice. "This is *your* family?"

"Yeah," the girl answered as she neatly settled into the chair next to him. "I thought that looked like your motorcycle outside."

Nobody gasped. Su Ling doubted anyone had drawn breath, including herself. Well, nobody except for Uncle Sammy who had started giggling again while Ma Ma's face turned a not-so-festive bright red. Then her father spoke, horror dripping from every syllable. "You're my granddaughter's *teacher?*"

"And volleyball coach," continued Amanda as she reached out and began serving herself a bowl of egg-drop soup. "He's awesome."

Su Ling stared at Dragon, trying to reconcile the man still wrapped around her waist with her niece and middle school. All the teachers she remembered had been prim women with conservative clothing and comfortable shoes. Not one had ever come close to a twenty-something bulked-out, leather-clad, tattooed revenge date with the most hypnotizing amber eyes. "You're a teacher?"

"Social studies," answered Amanda before Dragon could draw breath. "Cool earring. He normally just wears a diamond stud at school."

Suddenly Dragon—a.k.a. Mr. Kurtz, man who shaped

young minds — became a flurry of speed. In one deft movement he sprang away from Su Ling, quickly removed his earring, and grabbed his jacket. Meanwhile he continued to babble, all traces of his fake Texas accent gone, and in its place reigned the flat tones of a Chicago suburb. "Not a real diamond," he stammered. "Cubic zirconium. I couldn't afford a diamond on a teacher's salary." He stumbled slightly as he headed toward the door. "Well, happy birthday, sir. Many happy returns, and all that. Um, gotta go. Lots to do. Christmas break is over tomorrow, you know."

He was out the door before Su Ling could shake off her shock. Then, without conscious intent, she scrambled after him. "Wait a minute!" she cried as he headed for the front door. She caught him outside, snapping his leather jacket against the chill January wind.

He looked up, his eyes heating even as he gave her a self-conscious shrug. "I didn't realize you were Mandy's aunt."

"You're a middle school teacher?" she repeated for what felt like the hundredth time.

"Disappointed?" he challenged. "We can't all be FBI agents."

She didn't know how to answer. Was she disappointed? She'd grabbed a biker bad boy only to find she'd netted a schoolteacher. Except he didn't look so mundane standing beside his motorcycle, his dark hair ruffled by the wind, an intense gleam heating his eyes.

Then he lifted his chin, indicating the restaurant's window, where Ma Ma and Auntie Wen were pressed goggle-eyed against the glass. "We've got an audience."

"They let you wear an earring in school?"

He stepped away from his bike, approaching her with slow, steady steps. There wasn't anything menacing in his movements, merely a focused intensity, but Su Ling shied backward nonetheless. His mesmerizing power remained in full force even as her mind still grappled with the thought of him as a teacher.

"What, teachers aren't wild enough for you?" he challenged, his voice low and throaty.

"Uh . . ." Su Ling didn't know what to say. He'd voiced her thoughts exactly. Except he seemed plenty wild and thoroughly exciting. She couldn't deny the thrill she felt when her back hit the wall and he continued his advance.

"I didn't get the free dinner you promised," he said as he flattened his hands on either side of her head. Then he leaned in slowly, inexorably pressing his thighs, then his pelvis, then his entire massive chest against her, leaving their faces less than a whispered breath of steam apart. "But maybe this will do."

He lowered his lips to hers, and Su Ling felt the blood rush through her body, pulsing too fast. His kiss took control of her, swept into her mouth, and possessed her, taking her, challenging her until she began to fight back—or rather give back, dueling with his tongue as she arched rhythmically against him.

She felt his breath catch, but she didn't relent. And neither did he as one of his hands slid down her shoulder, wrapping around her waist to lift her off the wall, jerking her flush against his hard body. Her hands were busy as well, sliding across his butter-soft jacket until she tangled her fingers in his hair. Luxurious curls flowed over her hands as he broke their kiss to begin tonguing across her face and neck in the most erotic patterns imaginable.

Then she felt it—his hand, sliding up her thin blouse, heating her already flushed skin to flash point as his fingers rose firmly, strongly, inevitably to her breast. She ached for him to touch her, to hold her there. She even released a moan of longing as his fingertips met the underside of her bra, beginning the lift, the caress, the seduction she craved.

But before he made it to her peak, before she could do more than close her eyes, he twisted around, deftly plucking something out of her inside jacket pocket before stepping away. When she opened her eyes, he was pocketing her fifty dollars before donning his helmet and roaring away.

Mitch Kurtz stomped through the school hallway, neatly avoiding the flow of students as nearly three hundred teens scrambled to grab their things before the buses came. Normally the excited chatter about holidays and homework calmed him. Early mornings were filled with preparation for the coming day, but the end of school held the satisfaction of a job well done, a child educated for one more day.

Except today. Today, the Backstreet Boys' latest hairstyle had easily eclipsed Napoleon. Not because the kids were any more difficult than usual, but because Mitch had made one of the most exciting men in history sound like a farm report. Even he'd yawned.

And why? Because last night he'd been propositioned by an exotic Asian temptress, a pinup fantasy who offered him the opportunity—just for one night—to pretend to be someone else. Normally he would have laughed off the chance as too bizarre, but just then, straight from another holiday-in-hell with his repressed family, the opportunity to play a mysterious fed had been too good to resist. Naturally, just as his parents had always predicted, his impulsive nature led him straight into trouble. He'd acted like a jerk in front of a student and her family.

That alone would be bad enough, but then he'd gone and kissed Miss Asian Seductress. Not a simple peck on the check, but an eating-her-whole, can't-get-enough, how-low-can-one-man-go kiss in full view of her family. Then he'd gone on kissing her and doing all sorts of depraved things with her. Not in fact, but all night long as his imagination tormented him.

He still didn't know why he'd done it, much less taken her money. But he knew without a doubt that he'd do it again.

Right now, in fact. In the middle of school even, because for whatever reason, she obsessed him. Everything from her repressed-accountant suit to her subtle ginger-spice scent intrigued him. What woman dressed like a corporate robot but kissed like a wildcat? And why would a woman—one from a very solid and upright family—suddenly want to horrify them with a biker-fed pretend date? The puzzle intrigued him so much that he'd lost an entire school day to the distraction of unwanted fantasies.

Talk about teen flashback. Here he was, back in school, desperately trying to haul his mind off some girl. Maybe his father was right: He'd never outgrown his adolescence.

Then Mitch rounded a corner, heading for the sanctuary of his classroom, only to come face-to-face with his imagination. There she stood—or rather crouched—over her niece, a lost look on her face. Mitch didn't want to interfere. Lord, the last thing he needed was a *higher* profile with Mandy's family, but a second glance revealed the girl in tears.

Mitch stifled a groan. He had ample experience with teen drama—real or imagined—and in this case he probably understood more than Mandy's beleaguered aunt. So, after a stern mental warning to keep his libido firmly in check, Mitch cleared his throat and sauntered forward.

"Are you all right, Mandy?"

The poor girl looked up, stammering in her haste to swallow her tears. "M-Mr. Kurtz!"

He gave Mandy a gentle smile, while beside him he felt more than saw her aunt's lithe body tighten with anxiety. *Down, libido, down!* He forced himself to concentrate on Mandy, settling onto his haunches to look her in the eye.

"One bad grade—even an F—isn't grounds for tears," he began. "Though I am concerned—" He didn't get any farther as, beside them, the seductress exhaled in loud relief.

"Is that what this is about? Lord, Amanda, you scared me half to death."

"No." Mandy hiccuped, her voice a low moan. "It's not that. I mean, it is, but . . ." Her voice slipped away as tears continued to stream down her face.

Mitch tried again, keeping his voice gentle. "I want to help, kiddo, but you gotta talk."

The girl looked up, her eyes tragic. "They'll take me off the team."

Mitch almost laughed, but he'd been teaching teens too long to make that mistake. Still, he couldn't resist smiling. "You're a long way from academic probation. You can still play volley-ball."

Beside him, however, instead of sharing his relief, his myste-rious Sue blew out a soft sigh. "Oh, Amanda, I'm so sorry." Then she opened her arms as Mandy dove into them, the girl's tears darkening Sue's silk blouse to almost black.

Meanwhile Mitch stood up, confusion warring with distrac-tion as he noticed that Mandy's distress had pulled her aunt's top two buttons open. Once again he mentally kicked his libido back into a corner as he quipped, "Honest Injun, she's still okay to play."

Then Sue lifted her dark Asian eyes, meeting his with obvious trepidation, but her voice remained level. "Chinese family, Dra . . . er, Mr. Kurtz." He watched as her olive skin flushed in embarrassment. "If Amanda can't keep up with her studies, then her sports activities go first."

He frowned. "First? Before what?"

"Culture!" Mandy practically spat out the word. "Piano *and* violin."

"Well," he hedged, already recognizing the problem, "music is very valua—"

"I hate them!" the girl cried. "I don't ever want to play again!" Then, before he could respond, Mandy whipped around, her skin blotchy beneath dark eyes suddenly shining with hope. "Wait! Ma Ma's out of town! She left this morning for some training thing, so I'm staying with Auntie Ling." Her gesture definitely indicated his Sue. Then as Mitch sorted that out, Mandy dove into her backpack for her test paper, dragging it out to shove at her aunt.

"Just a minute," he began, but the teen wasn't listening. Since Mitch had graded the test, he knew exactly what it said and what Mandy was doing. Right below the bright red F, he'd stamped a message requiring a parent's signature. It was school policy.

"You can sign," she urged her aunt. "Then Ma Ma never has to know. Oh, please," she begged both of them, "don't make me quit. I love volleyball more than anything!"

Mitch groaned. Not only one siren, but an entire family! First the aunt distracted him in ways he wasn't even allowed to think of in school, and then the niece tempted him to throw away his ethics. If any of his students deserved a break, Mandy certainly qualified. He'd never seen a more studious, more diligent, more repressed child. He also knew Mandy's football-star Caucasian dad had long since skipped town, likely leaving quite a negative impression regarding any sport. Unfortunately the girl came alive only when on the volleyball court, and he would hate to see her give it up.

But if he allowed her to maintain her crushing schedule, he only continued the cycle of oppression.

"Your *mother* has to sign, Mandy," he said, feeling remorse even as he enforced the rules. The girl turned, already opening her mouth to argue, but he held up his hand. "Do you remember what I said the first day of practice? About how sports . . ." He let his voice trail away, hoping she'd answer for him. It took her a long time, but eventually she mumbled her answer.

"Sports test us, teaching us about who we really are." She looked up at him. "But I *love* volleyball."

He nodded. He knew she did, and that made this all that much harder. "Do you really want to discover you're a liar?"

She looked away, refusing to answer. That was when the other siren spoke up. "Maybe there's another way," Sue offered. "Couldn't she do some extra credit? A report or something?" She looked down at her niece. "To bring up your grade before your mother returns. Then she won't be so angry, and maybe you can stay on the team."

Suddenly Mandy was all smiles, and both females turned hopeful eyes to him. Once again he found himself sorely tempted. "But," he said to himself as much as to them, "pouring more work onto an already overburdened schedule is not the solution."

"But I can handle it!" Mandy pressed. "I swear I can!"

Mitch just shook his head. "Why don't you tell your aunt why you failed that test?" Again the girl looked down at her shoes, refusing to answer. Finally Mitch stepped in, answering for her: "She fell asleep."

Mandy cut in, her tone mulish, "There were all those Christmas recitals and stuff. I just got too tired."

Her aunt shrugged, the sight once again pulling Mitch's attention where it definitely should not go. With those top two buttons open, he was hard-pressed to breathe, much less understand what the temptress said. "The holidays are nuts. Everyone gets tired."

Mitch cleared his throat, trying to open up his restricted airway. "She fell asleep *during* the exam." While Sue's eyes widened in shock, Mitch pushed his advantage. He forced himself to look directly into Sue's eyes, seeing her not as a seductress but as Mandy's temporary guardian. "She's trying to manage two instruments, volleyball, and honors classes. She has to cut back."

Sue just shrugged. "Chen family rules, Mr. Kurtz. We all took music."

"But I *hate* it," the girl wailed.

The woman sighed, and the sound pulled at Mitch's thoughts. If it were up to him she wouldn't ever have a reason to sigh. He'd make sure. . . . Then he frowned, ruthlessly refocusing his thoughts. "You need to discuss this with your mother."

"She's out of town," Mandy said with a sniff.

"Any discussion begins with her grades," said her aunt, her voice level and reasonable, yet still sparking unreasonable thoughts in his mind. "Mandy's got to pull them up first before she can change anything." Her tone softened, and Mitch knew he was doomed. The woman obviously wasn't trying to be seductive, but the effect remained the same: he wanted to grant her whatever she asked. "Won't you consider some extra credit?" she coaxed.

He bit his lip, his conscience warring with his need to grant this goddess her every wish. "I don't think it's a good idea," he tried.

"What if I throw in that dinner I promised you? Tonight? At six?"

What could he say to that? She'd just made him an offer he couldn't resist.

Chapter Two

*S*u Ling wiped her mouth with her napkin, feeling pleasantly stuffed as she continued the lively banter that had marked this delightful meal. "Are you going to harangue me about my family all night long?" she asked, feeling much less put-out than she sounded.

"Of course," Mitch responded with a laugh as he polished off the last of his apple pie. He certainly fit right into the Texas Roadhouse — a rootin'-tootin' steakhouse with peanut shells on the floor and food served out of buckets. Truth be told, she loved the atmosphere and was having the "barrels of fun" promised on the billboard, but then that might have more to do with her companion. They'd discussed everything from favorite vacation spots to office politics. Right now they were arguing the merits of high Chinese demands on a child versus the more American "keep it fun" approach. Naturally he supported the more relaxed method.

"It's not just a Chinese tradition, though your family seems to have it in spades," he answered. "My father applied pressure with the delicacy of a sledgehammer." She caught an edge to his voice, but he continued speaking before she could ask for details. "I'm just saying you've got an opportunity with Mandy right now. Try not to waste it."

"Opportunity?" she asked, all the while watching his lips as he spoke. Despite their fascinating conversation, she hadn't been able to keep her mind from replaying last night's kiss. She felt like the worst sort of wanton for constantly focusing on his mouth, his muscled chest, the way he still looked dark and dangerous even though he'd shaved off his three-day beard. She shouldn't be thinking this way, she admonished herself. But no matter how she tried to turn her attention elsewhere, she'd spent most of tonight's dinner being tormented by erotic thoughts.

"You're Mom for the next few weeks," he continued, hopefully unaware of her deviant fantasies. "See if you can lighten up on Mandy. Show her there's more to life than —"

"Being an accountant?" she interrupted, her eyebrow arched in challenge.

He laughed, having the grace to look embarrassed as he stood to retrieve her coat. She stood as well, letting him help her into her outerwear while she relished every moment their bodies accidentally touched. And they had accidentally connected a lot tonight. Their hands. Their arms. Even their feet had played a coy type of footsie beneath the table.

"There's nothing wrong with being an accountant," he continued. "It's just that . . ." He sighed. "She's thirteen. Who ever said, 'I want to be an accountant when I grow up'? She should be thinking rock star or Olympic medalist. What'd you want to be when you were little?"

She didn't even hesitate. "A ballet star. I wanted it so badly."

He bit his lip, and she nearly groaned out loud. What was wrong with her, obsessing about a man's mouth? "So how'd you get from ballet to accounting?"

She frowned, thrown by the question. "I don't know," she said slowly, trying to remember. "Ma Ma refused to even consider ballet, but I was good at math. She signed me up for my first accounting class, and I guess I just fell into it. What about you?"

He grinned. "Teaching. Always and forever, and my parents *hated* the idea. No money in education. But I love my job. I started as a camp counselor when I was fourteen and just kept going. So trust me on this. Forget all that Chinese pressure," he urged, "and let Mandy explore. She'll find something she loves."

Su Ling wanted to argue, but he had a point. She'd seen Amanda's schedule. Didn't normal kids play video games or something? There wasn't time in Amanda's life to listen to the radio, much less turn on a mindless video device. Su Ling greatly feared volleyball was the poor kid's only fun activity. Still, she couldn't quite give up the argument, if only to prevent herself from grabbing him right there and devouring him in a most unladylike way. "You're an educator. Shouldn't you lecture me on responsible parenting and diligent supervision?"

He shrugged as he offered her a helmet before exiting the

restaurant. "How 'bout we settle for responsible motorcycling?"

Su Ling grinned in response, much too eager to climb back on his bike. When Mitch had arrived for their dinner date, she'd expected a respectable, modest teacher's car. She hadn't expected to don a motorcycle helmet and hang on to Dragon's taut belly while he started up his Harley. Neither had she expected the thrill that coursed through her body when the iron beast roared to life between her thighs.

And now she couldn't wait to do it again! What a wanton she was turning out to be, she thought with a giggle, thinking dirty thoughts while once again wrapping her arms around Mitch. She barely waited until they'd left the parking lot before allowing her hands to slip underneath his clothing so she could caress the heated ripples of his abs. He jerked in reaction, taking a corner fast while she pressed her cheek against his leather jacket.

She didn't know what was wrong with her. She'd never acted so impulsively in her life. But something about Mitch just made her feel free: free to express her thoughts, free to challenge his ideas and learn from his opinions. Even free to touch him in the most inappropriate ways. He didn't judge her or dismiss her, but gave her his undivided attention, listening with a focus that went straight to her head. She felt as if he cut the weights that tied her down, the restrictions that made her double think every word, every gesture. She never wanted this night or these feelings to end.

They couldn't speak, not when he was roaring around corners and zipping toward her condo. But as soon as the bike jerked to a thrilling stop in front of her building, he pulled off his helmet and twisted around to look at her. "You're a naughty girl!" he stated firmly, his voice deliciously thick. Then he frowned. "And why are you laughing?"

She gazed into the dark swirls of his gorgeous eyes and smiled. "Just an if-my-mother-saw-me-now thought."

"Got a thing for rebels?" he challenged as he killed the motor.

"Of course not!" she said, stiffening as she tried to pull away, but he grabbed her wrists where they remained beneath his shirt before slowly raising her hands a few inches more. She watched his eyes, seeing his pupils dilate, his nostrils flare as her palms rubbed through the dusting of his chest hairs and her fingers touched the hard, flat disks of his nipples.

"Oh . . ." she whispered, still feeling the residual thrum of the motorcycle between her legs.

"I've been thinking about kissing you all night long," he said as he dismounted, turning around to face her directly. "Then, Miss Naughty Fingers, you started playing with fire."

"My hands were cold," she retorted, but he wasn't listening. Instead he grabbed her head and descended into that soul-devouring kiss she'd been longing for. She pressed into him, wrapping her arms around his broad back as he half lifted, half pushed her off his bike. Thank God the wall support stood just behind her or she would have fallen to the ground, taking him with her so she could feel his weight, hard and hungry on top of her. As it was, the rough wood behind her only accentuated the smooth, living caress of his chest in front.

"My turn," he said hoarsely as he plundered her mouth. Then, before she could ask what he meant, she felt his hands, large and hot, as he slid them beneath her cashmere sweater, first spanning her quivering belly before scaling higher.

She broke from his mouth, gasping out a soft warning. "We're in public."

"I don't care." He caught her lips again while she arched into his hands where they covered her breasts. In one swift move he'd gone from tickling her ribs to completely encircling her breasts, molding them with his hands, rolling his finger across her tight peaks before quickly finding her bra's front clasp.

"Oh, God." She moaned, not knowing what she meant as he deftly clicked open her bra, brushing it away before taking hold of her naked flesh and squeezing her—first one side, then the other—in a rhythm that had her nearly mindless with need. Until her cell phone began ringing. "My pants . ." she whispered. "They're ringing."

"Forget it." He chuckled as he began trailing kisses along her face and neck.

She nearly did. But, as he said before, she was Mom this week. "It might be Amanda." She straightened, dislodging him only slightly. His hands slid to her waist, rubbing the quivering flesh there while he continued to kiss along her collarbone. Meanwhile she grabbed at her phone, flipping it open with shaking hands.

"Amanda?" she said.

"Su Ling?" came her mother's strident tones. "Are you there?"

"Ma Ma?" she asked, mortified at the breathless quality of her voice.

"Are you with him?" Even her mother's demanding tone couldn't quite cool Su Ling's overheated blood. Certainly they had no effect on Dragon as he began to lift up her sweater, exposing her to both him and everyone else in the parking lot.

"Ma Ma?" she said again weakly as her eyes drifted shut. "Is everything all right?"

Fortunately, that caught Mitch's attention enough that he stopped, gently easing her sweater down, though he continued to stroke her belly in mesmerizing circles.

"You must come home. I brought you egg rolls. Homemade. But you're not here, and Amanda's scared, all alone in a strange place."

"Mandy's scared?" Su Ling straightened against the carport wall while Mitch frowned.

"Is she okay?" he asked, his voice filled with concern.

Su Ling nodded as she continued to the receiver. "She knew I had a date."

"You're with that earring-tattoo man!" her mother accused.

Su Ling felt her insides twist. Already overheated from what she'd been doing, she found a ready outlet in attacking her mother. "Yes, Ma Ma, we're at a biker bar right now. He's trying to talk me into doing a wet-T-shirt contest." Then she slapped her hand against her mouth in horror. Had she really just said that?

The explosion of Chinese from her mother told her she had. Meanwhile, even in the shadowy carport, Mitch grinned and waggled his eyebrows at her. Obviously he liked her defiant side. She, on the other hand, didn't know what to think, especially since she knew she didn't dare tell her mother exactly what she *had* been doing.

Then, when Su Ling remained silent, her mother switched to English. "Come home immediately," she ordered. "Amanda needs you here."

"In a moment. Mandy can wait just a bit." Su Ling took absurd pleasure in using her niece's nickname.

"Not alone. Very well. Amanda!" she called, clearly talking to Su Ling's niece. "Go pack your things. You will stay with me. Your aunt is busy." Given her tone, she could just have easily said, "Your aunt is a plague carrier."

"No, no, Ma Ma," Su Ling said with alarm. "Don't make her pack. I'm right downstairs in the carport." To add emphasis to her words, she straightened her top, pushing Mitch's hands away. Then, of course, she had to completely reverse his efforts, awkwardly pinning the phone between her ear and shoulder as she clipped her bra closed before readjusting the rest. And all the while Dragon stood there, his arms folded across his chest, a twinkle of unholy amusement in his eyes.

All she could do was stick her tongue out at him while her mother's voice continued to pound through the phone. "Where are you? I don't see you!"

Su Ling sighed, knowing that her mother would never leave her alone unless she stepped into view. Quickly running her hand through her hair, she moved out from beneath the carport, waving without enthusiasm at the round, Asian face peering through her living room window. "I'll be up in a moment."

"Ai-yah, he is there with that motorcycle."

"I'll just be a moment. Let me just say good-bye." She flipped the phone shut as she turned back to Mitch, feeling her mother's eyes boring into her back even as her blood started to simmer. Lord, she felt sixteen, out on a hot date with a great guy in front of her, and her mother glaring out the window behind.

"Everything okay?" he asked from where he stood, barely covered in shadow.

"Ever have a family who won't leave you alone no matter what you do?"

He shook his head. "Nope. I divorced my parents a long, long time ago."

"Great. Teach me how."

He shrugged. "Get on your motorcycle and ride away."

Watching the way his expression flattened out, Su Ling knew that was exactly how he'd done it. For whatever reason—probably that demanding father he'd mentioned earlier—Mitch'd left home and never looked back, and she didn't know whether to envy him or pity him. In either case, her own family was still watching from a fourth-story window. She needed to say her good-byes quickly before Ma Ma came out and hauled her daughter upstairs.

"I had a really nice time tonight—"

"How long until Mandy goes back to her mother's?" His words came out gratifyingly quickly, the low tone sending shivers of awareness down her skin.

"Two and a half weeks," she said, suddenly feeling shy. He left no doubt as to what they'd be doing now if her condo didn't contain her mother and niece.

He released a low growl as he reached out, snagging her around the waist before pulling her into his arms. "I don't want to wait that long."

"Isn't this inappropriate or something? Kissing a student's relative?"

"I've been inappropriate since the second we met."

"I know the feeling," she returned with a grin. She intended to say more, but he never gave her the chance. He swooped down, kissing her breathless again, bending her backward as he took possession of her mouth, his left hand supporting her back, his right sliding down until he cupped her rear end.

Then, when he was finished and she remained dazed in his arms, he looked up and winked. It took a few seconds before she realized he was winking at her mother, who had no doubt seen the entire thing.

"Oh, God!" she exclaimed, shoving him away from her. "You're taunting her!"

He laughed, clearly unfazed. "I believe, princess, that's what you hired me to do. Just be thankful I didn't lift another fifty bucks."

She stared at him, torn between horror and humor as he climbed onto his bike. "Mitch, I'm not torturing my parents any more."

He turned, challenging her with his focused gaze. "Then send Mama away, and we'll finish what we started."

She hesitated, equal parts excited and terrified by the thought. Terror won. "I . . . I can't. Ma Ma will freak, and Mandy's still here."

He pulled on his helmet. "So you're choosing them over me. Guess I'll just have to visit in your dreams." Then he blew her a kiss before roaring away.

Ma Ma, of course, was waiting at the door when Su Ling finally made it up to her condo. She'd deliberately walked slowly, waiting for the fire in her belly to cool down. Unfortunately the cooling, unfulfilled passion only made her cranky. So when Ma Ma began her attack the moment the elevator doors opened, Su Ling was primed to fight back.

"Su Ling! What were you doing?" Ma Ma demanded.

Su Ling rolled her eyes. "You know exactly what we were doing, Ma Ma. We were making hot banshee noises in the parking lot." Then she bit her own lip, wondering what had gotten into her. She never spoke like that to her parents. Ever.

"With that man!" Ma Ma exploded. "He's not your dragon! He's some busboy at the restaurant!"

Su Ling ground her teeth as she pushed her way into her condo. "He teaches social studies."

"How could you do that? At all hours! And in public! With a child in the house!"

Su Ling slipped past her mother to see Amanda sitting ultra quietly in the kitchen, the crumbs of an egg roll on the plate before her, an open science textbook in her hands. "It's nine-thirty, Ma Ma. And Mandy knows I have dates."

Her mother paused, her eyes narrowing as she stared at her daughter. Meanwhile Su Ling was beginning to feel calmer, more confident. She'd just snapped at her mother, and the roof had not caved in, lightning had not struck her, and the ghosts of her dead ancestors had not reared up to pour shame and guilt upon her.

Then Ma Ma smiled, speaking in a softer, more wheedling voice. "I have found another dragon for you. A better one. A doctor. I will bring him by tomorrow."

"I'm busy tomorrow. Where's Ba Ba?" Su Ling asked, rushing her words as she tried to distract her mother.

"Ah," Ma Ma answered with a dismissive hand gesture. "Some meeting. Very important. You know your father."

Yes, she did. And, more important, she knew her mother. Ma Ma got bored by herself—hence the sudden urge to make egg rolls and interfere in her daughter's life. "Well, he should be home by now," she said as sweetly as she could manage. "Thanks for stopping by. And for the egg rolls."

She dutifully grabbed an egg roll out of the container on the counter and bit into it. God, it was good, and she wasn't even hungry. "These are fabulous." Then she released a sigh, trying to look tired. "You've been very helpful." She pasted on a sincere smile and prayed it would work. Usually Ma Ma just wanted to feel useful and appreciated. The trick was to give her mother warm fuzzies without letting the woman completely take over her life.

Ma Ma hesitated. "I have checked Amanda's homework. She needs help with chemistry. I cannot do those things, but her grandfather—"

"I'm sure Amanda has it under control. Right, Mandy?"

Mandy looked up and blinked as if she hadn't been listening the whole time. Then she gave her grandmother a brilliant smile. "I'll figure it out," she said. "Thank you for quizzing me on the vocabulary. You helped a lot."

Su Ling arched an eyebrow at her niece. Geez, the kid learned fast. She didn't know whether to be impressed or appalled by how easily Amanda buttered up her grandmother. "Hmmm," returned Ma Ma, clearly softening. "Your aunt should help."

"We're going to work on my math now. She's so good at that." Then the girl leaned down and pulled out a math book, dropping the encyclopedia-sized text on the counter. Now, *that* would send Ma Ma scurrying for the hills. Hell, it was enough to send Su Ling running, and she was an accountant.

"Well, then," Ma Ma said as she grabbed her coat. "You should study. Su Ling, I put lunch in the refrigerator. Amanda doesn't like the school's food."

Su Ling canted a glance at her niece, who suddenly took great interest in her math text.

"Make sure she practices her violin," continued Ma Ma.

"No problem." Su Ling began counting as she held open the front door. She figured four steps until her mother made the hallway.

"She'll have to practice her piano at school."

Three steps.

"I could drive her to your sister's home. They have a piano," Ma Ma continued.

Two steps. "No, thanks. We've got it covered."

"Make sure to check her homework every night."

One step. "I know."

"Okay, then. You two study." Ma Ma hovered in the doorway. Su Ling didn't think she could hold her smile much longer. Fortunately all Ma Ma wanted was to kiss her daughter good-bye. "School lunch. Piano practice," she muttered. "You still need me, Su Ling."

"Of course we need you," she answered automatically.

Ma Ma nodded and slipped away while Su Ling finally, blessedly closed the door. Except she didn't quite get it shut. Just before the latch clicked, Ma Ma added her last comment: "We will have the new dragon for dinner on Sunday. Dress nice."

Su Ling sighed, wondering how she'd escape that, toying with the idea of buying a motorcycle and riding off into the sunset with her dragon. But before she could fully enjoy that fantasy, Amanda interrupted her thoughts.

"Did you really kiss Mr. Kurtz?"

Su Ling turned, rapidly pulling her thoughts out of the gutter. "Not answering," she responded quickly. She needed a lot more time to sort through her feelings for Dragon—Mitch—Mr. Kurtz—before she discussed them with her young niece. "Besides," she continued, "we need to set a few ground rules between us. I love having you here, but we can't have any more pity-me calls to your grandmother."

Amanda straightened defensively. "She called me!"

Su Ling folded her arms. "Tell me you didn't sound pathetic. 'Oh, I'm all alone,' " she mocked, " 'studying so hard, and I've only got leftovers to eat after an awful lunch.' "

Her niece had the grace to blush.

"Look, kiddo, all that good home cooking comes with a price: sharing every intimate detail of your life. Right now I don't want my life broadcast to the entire clan. So if you're set on home cooking, then you can stay with your grandparents."

Mandy's eyes widened with horror. "No, Auntie Ling, I'd much rather be here."

"Thought so." Then, keeping Mitch's suggestion in mind about easing up on her niece, Su Ling settled down beside Mandy. "Get Mr. Kurtz's extra-credit paper done; then we'll have some fun. Deal?"

Mandy grinned. "Deal." Then she pushed some math papers forward. "Do you want to check my homework now?"

Su Ling laughed. "Not really. I was thinking of ice cream with chocolate sauce."

Mandy suddenly brightened. "Great. I'm starved."

It wasn't until much later—after two hours of girl talk and chocolate sauce—that Mandy added her last comment. "I think you and Mr. Kurtz would be great together." Then she disappeared into her bedroom for the night.

Su Ling didn't argue. She was too busy fantasizing about just what they'd be great at.

*   *   *

She was here.

Mitch had barely tasted his double espresso mocha when he felt Sue enter his gym. His skin tingled, and he smelled that strange mixture of ginger and lily, sort of an Asian sweet-and-spicy smell. Turning around, he saw her looking aloof in another dark navy suit as she watched Mandy begin her warmup laps. She even wore her hair pulled up in a proper swirl that crested at the top of her head. But he remembered how she'd gone wild in his arms last night. Beneath Sue Ling's prim veneer pulsed the soul of a wildcat.

He closed his eyes and tried to focus. The volleyball season had just begun, and he already felt behind. Especially with half the team out with the flu, they were losing ground fast. Unfortunately, after a night spent fantasizing about what he'd started with Sue Ling in her parking lot, he wasn't thinking about volleyball. He was planning how he could catch some time with Mandy's very proper seductress of an aunt. And now she appeared in his gym, not just dropping her niece off, but finding a spot on the bleachers to watch while her sensuous lips dipped into the swirling depths of her morning coffee. God, how long could a man keep an erection before his brain completely dried up?

He needed to stay away from Sue. At least while he was coaching he had to keep her far from his thoughts. Yet seconds later he found himself settling onto the bleachers beside her.

"Good morning," he said, gratified that his voice wasn't completely thick with lust.

"Morning," she returned, her lips forming a rich red curve.

"Mandy looks a little tired this morning." He didn't know why he said that. His thoughts were someplace else entirely. On Sue's cleavage, to be specific. The top buttons of her blouse gaped open, and from his angle they allowed a silent peekaboo with her lacy bra.

"Girl talk with our friends Ben and Jerry." She paused as she pressed her lips to her coffee mug for a long sip.

He nodded, unable to resist touching her arm, slipping his thumb beneath the cuff of her blouse to stroke the satiny skin underneath. "Ice cream. The bonding tool of women." She shivered. He was sure of it. "You're distracting me," he said on a low growl.

He watched as a fire kindled in her dark almond eyes. "I'm just watching my niece play volleyball."

"You're making me think about stripping you naked beneath the bleachers. And that's the only part I can say aloud."

Her skin flushed a dusky rose. "Not one for subtlety, are you?"

"You're the hottest woman this side of a lava flow. No, Sue, I am not subtle. I'm going to take you into my bedroom, strip you naked, and eat you up one side and down the other." He leaned in, watching her eyes widen with excitement. "Then I'll really get started."

She swallowed convulsively, then suddenly straightened, her expression cooling to glacial in the blink of an eye. "You must have me mistaken for someone else," she said primly. "Have I mentioned that I'm an accountant? I wear conservative clothing and put my hair in a bun. A librarian in 1812 couldn't be more old-fashioned than I am. What makes you think I'll respond to talk like that?"

"Because yesterday, when I put my hands on your perfect breasts, you made a sound that makes men's teeth sweat."

Her breath caught, and she licked her lips before pressing them tightly together. "You're a social studies teacher," she said, her voice strained.

"And you're an accountant. Come over tonight."

She shook her head, flashes of panic lighting her eyes. "I can't. Mandy's staying with me, remember?" But she wanted to. He read hunger in the way she bit her lower lip, moistening it with her tongue.

"Find a baby-sitter," he urged. "Pick me tonight, not them."

She hesitated, her body echoing the same trembling desire he felt. Then suddenly she stood up, scrambling away from him. "No My family comes first." Then she sailed away, her heels making hard chips of sound on the floor before the fire doors clanged shut behind her.

Mitch didn't move. He sat on the bleachers, staring at the dark gray doors, knowing he'd just erred badly. He hadn't lied when he'd called her the hottest woman this side of a lava flow. Sexy, smart, and funny, she fascinated him. And worse yet, she came from a good, wholesome family. When she'd first approached him at the restaurant, he had thought her an exotic Chinese fantasy come to life. Last night she'd shown him so much more, and now he was more intrigued than ever.

Except he'd just led with his groin, pressing the sexuality button as if her body held the only attraction. She fascinated him on so many different levels, but he'd never get her to believe that now.

He needed to step back, get some perspective. Great men in history had either succeeded or failed based on their ability to clearly see themselves and how they fit into their situation. Now was his turn. Unfortunately, logical clarity had never been his strong suit. He tended to feel a situation and then proceed exactly as his gut dictated. But right now his gut told him to point grappling guns at Su Ling and reel her in.

But why? One week ago the thought of dating a traditional Chinese girl would have given him hysterics. He didn't go for silent, repressed types, and certainly not good girls who wanted permanence with a husband and a family. The thought of a mini-van and a lawn mower gave him the chills. His oldest possession was a hunk of moldy cheese in the back of his refrigerator.

Except that wasn't true anymore. His apartment was filled with stuff he'd had for a couple years now. He'd signed a two-year teaching contract. And last week his best friend's new baby had brought out unexpected fatherly urges in him. So much for the freewheeling, no-strings-attached lifestyle he'd originally planned. Now he was suddenly thinking about his own picket fence surrounding a huge backyard filled with dark-haired girls giggling over Barbie dolls and mischievous boys tossing a football around with him. And at the center of it all stood Su Ling, looking all proper while beneath her lurked a wanton.

Except he'd just come on as the type of sex-starved bad boy his father hated and her mother feared. When had that persona become a habit? Especially here, a long way away from his dour parents? Sure, he'd been primed at the restaurant, having just escaped their suffocating home at the holidays, but here, in his real life, he'd long since thrown adolescent rebellion away.

Or had he? He didn't know, but he sure as hell needed to find out. He didn't even know when it became so important to him, just that Su Ling seemed key in this vital search. As if she held a secret he needed to ferret out. And if that meant pursuing her slowly, quietly, but with the gentle persistence of a steady stream of water, then that was what he'd do.

Even if he had to be a gentleman to do it.

Chapter Three

*S*u Ling was being stalked. Not literally, but she definitely sensed a focused mind at work. The pattern began the very day she'd entered the Franklin gym, her body pinging and zinging like a live pinball machine. Mitch did that to her with his slumbery eyes and his cocky swagger that made her toes curl. He'd pressed her that day, obviously wanting to pursue these terrifying feelings, and she'd bolted. She'd acted like an uptight prude and made an exit that would do an Ice queen proud.

She'd blown it. But maybe that was for the best, she told herself. Mitch made her think and do things so unusual for her unobtrusive life. Motorcycles and wet T-shirt contests. When had she even thought these things, much less done them or said them to her mother? Never. And probably never again. Which meant that when she reverted to her more typical, dull identity, Mitch would dump her as boring. In short, they didn't have a future together, she told herself. Which meant she needed to stop obsessing about Mitch, stop replaying his every word, every nuance until she nearly jumped out of her skin.

But she kept running into him. He'd happened to be nearby when Su Ling picked up Mandy after school. His manner remained courteous and friendly without any sexual overtures, and this new conventional Mitch was so respectful, she didn't know how to stop their conversation. He politely inquired about her job. She responded equally politely before turning to leave. But then her matchmaker niece piped up with the truth.

"She hates it, but doesn't know what to do about it. Maybe you can help her, Mr. Kurtz."

And that spelled the end of her afternoon as the two ended up discussing her difficult, frustrating, and possibly deceitful boss for the next two hours. He picked up the same discussion the next day at the same time. Then Friday afternoon, they shared coffee for an hour while Mandy searched through the school library for a reference book. Now they met every day after school, talking about whatever came to mind.

Next came volleyball. Su Ling no longer went to Mandy's morning practice, but she did attend the last two matches. She couldn't seem to stop watching Mitch. He had such a focused intensity about him whenever he coached, giving the girls everything he could from the sidelines. He really cared about each member of his team, urging them to do their best. Then, when he paid for celebratory Happy Meals after the game with the fifty-dollar bill he'd lifted off of her that first night, she was hard-pressed to keep from melting right then and there.

So went the next ten days. They spoke every afternoon for as long as Mandy could find an excuse to stay in school. Then last Tuesday, Mitch appeared at Su Ling's favorite bookstore just when she and Mandy'd stopped in with Auntie Wen and Uncle Sammy to listen to a new jazz group in the café. They all sat together sharing cocoa while Mitch tossed irreverent comments into Auntie Wen's critique of popular music. Ten minutes later, matchmaker Mandy took her great-aunt and -uncle away to search for books, leaving Mitch and Su Ling alone to debate the pros and cons of large families. While he listened intently to her, rather than the soft music, she found herself confessing that her relatives often took advantage of her but she couldn't seem to say no to them. Her family supported her when life became uncertain, and she didn't want to upset the balance.

Then yesterday, while she sat with her father and Mandy at the movies, Su Ling could have sworn she heard Mitch's voice. Turning around, she discovered he'd slipped in beside her niece and was explaining the complex plot to the young girl. He'd even hung out after the showing, discussing the movie's trial scene with her father while Su Ling and a giggling Mandy tossed popcorn at the two men.

In short, Mitch had become a regular, if unpredictable, part of her day. She would have been thrilled by the situation except for one thing: All traces of sexual interest had completely disappeared. Throughout the week Mitch remained unfailingly genteel—almost formal—as they interacted. Even his laughter had been respectful, flowing about her like a warm pool of sound, soothing her fears without stirring up any red flags.

But she was stirred up. It was now Saturday evening, Mandy was spending the night at a friend's, and all Su Ling could do was pace her condo, worry more holes into her favorite sweats, and feel tormented by fantasies about a man who apparently no longer desired her.

Until the doorbell rang and she opened her front door to see Mitch standing there, a dozen roses in his hand and a come-hither look in his eyes. She just stood there and stared at him, gripped in a rush of electricity that short-circuited her brain whenever he looked at her. "Mandy's at a friend's tonight," she said stupidly.

He grinned. "I know. She's kept me quite up-to-date about her schedule lately." Then he offered her the roses. "Can I come in or should I just leave these leaning against the door?"

She let him in, of course. No matter how much she lectured herself that this could be a mistake, she couldn't bring herself to give up the tingling awareness he brought to her life. As if everything, including herself, sharpened into its individual, most distinct form.

"Thank you," she said formally as she accepted the roses and buried her nose in their bouquet. "They're beautiful." What was it about roses from a man in a leather jacket that turned her insides to jelly? "I'm not really dressed for company," she apologized.

"I'm not company," he quipped as he pushed his way into her living room. "I'm your niece's social studies teacher."

She laughed. "Since when do teachers make house calls?"

His back was to her, his leather jacket stretched taut against his broad shoulders, but then he turned, giving her a sideways smile that emphasized his chiseled face even as his earring flashed at her. "I'm just helping you rationalize my presence. If you like, I can ask about her research project. How's it going? Do you know?"

She shook her head, heading for her kitchen and a vase. "She's remarkably evasive whenever I ask about it."

He shrugged as he plopped down onto her cool blue sofa. Then he stretched out his arms and crossed one denim-clad leg over the other in the most blatantly male pose she'd ever seen. His jacket slipped open, revealing a soft burnt-orange sweater, while his gaze seared across her living room as if staking out his territory. On her couch. When her Mandy buffer was long gone.

And why did the sight make her want to leap on him, rip off his clothes, and nibble on every inch of his hard, powerful body?

"You've got the right idea," he said.

She blinked, startled. "What?"

"With Mandy. Let her handle this on her own. She can't learn responsibility unless she's given the opportunity to either screw up or come through."

"Oh." She felt her face heat with mortification. "I just hope my sister agrees when she discovers I've blown off the rules. Mandy and I've watched TV on school nights, even went to a movie. We've eaten ice cream and popcorn until I felt sick. I haven't even checked her homework, much less made her practice violin."

He grinned as he stretched his long legs out in front of him. "It's good for her. Haven't you seen how much happier she is? She's even laughing during practice."

Yes, Su Ling had noticed. If she hadn't seen the change, she would have long since succumbed to the Chinese guilt that constantly dragged on her conscience. "I just hope she keeps up with things. I'm not exactly fostering the study habits of a future doctor or lawyer."

"Doctors and lawyers are overrated."

"As opposed to the exciting life of a motorcycle sex god." She gasped. God, had she really just said that? His grin told her she had.

"That's what I like about you," he said as he slowly unfolded from the couch. "Just when you convince me you're completely prim, you say the most arousing things." He started moving toward her, a predatory gleam in his eyes, and she knew that long-limbed saunter would end up with her beneath him doing the most . . . *Oh, God.* She wasn't supposed to be thinking that way.

"Mitch—" she began.

"Call me Dragon. Your throat gets this sexy burr when you say it."

She swallowed. "Dragon . . ," Lord, he was right. She did put a throaty purr to the word. "Um, Mitch, you know that I'm not what you want, right? I'm not who you think I am."

"Exactly what do I want?" he asked, his hungry grin more than telling her the answer. He was still advancing upon her. She had placed the roses on her dining table, but was now backing up into the breakfast bar, leaving a rapidly narrowing two feet between them.

She tried to slide sideways, but he easily cut off her exit. "W-well," she stammered, "you think I'm this reckless biker groupie. The kind who picks up men in restaurants and makes out in parking lots. But that wasn't really me. I can't be that kind of woman even if I wanted to change for you. Which I don't. 'Cause I like me. I mean, I'm happy with who I am. And I don't do that," she finished lamely, belatedly realizing she was babbling.

He slowed, straightening as he seemed to study her. "So you don't pick up men."

"No."

He smiled at her adamant tone. "And you don't haunt me at night and interrupt my day, distracting me at times when I really should be doing something entirely different?" He sounded almost angry, and yet his words sent a tingly rush of flame through her body.

"I do?" she whispered.

He hitched his hip, leaning it against the table while she stood less than a foot away from him, poised to run. "You do," he affirmed. "I can't stop thinking about how you come alive in my arms," he continued, "shedding that prim exterior like so much excess clothing."

She swallowed and looked away. Her body felt alien to her, soft and womanly and prickly hot, too. He touched her chin, startling her with the heat in his fingertips — electricity that set her nerves dancing. "Okay!" she suddenly exploded, jerking away from him, "we've got chemistry. Woo-hoo!" she mocked, though her voice remained unsteady. "But I don't just hop into bed with the first guy who . . ." She stumbled to a stop. Who what? Turned her body into a punk-rock show of fantastic sensations? Who looked at her when she spoke? Who gave her that same absolute focus he showered on his students? The kind that made a woman feel like she was the center of his world?

"What's wrong with chemisty?" he challenged. He did that to her a lot, she realized, tempting her to do and think the most unorthodox things. "Have you ever felt this" — he gestured vaguely between the two of them — "this draw before? This absolute certainty that biologically, at least, we're a perfect match?"

She swallowed, his level gaze daring her to admit the truth. "No, I haven't. But I'm not just a creature of biology."

"I never said you were. I said . . ." He paused, then frowned slightly before allowing a slow smile to heat his expression. "I've said too much, haven't I?"

Then, before she could respond, he closed the distance between them, possessing her lips with a fierceness that sent rockets straight down to her core. She didn't put up even token resistance. He brought his mouth down to hers, and she devoured him. When his hands found her waist beneath her sweatshirt, she drew them higher, placing them on her naked breasts as she ground her pelvis into his.

"You know what you are?" he half groaned, half spoke against her cheek. "You're a bad girl in a good-girl dress. A rebel fighting for freedom."

She shook her head, trying to draw his lips back to hers. "No . . . no, I'm not."

She felt his smile against her mouth as his tongue darted out, teasing her lips. "Then push my hands off your breasts," he challenged. "Knee me in the groin." He took her hand and pressed it hard against his erection. Without conscious thought, she stroked his incredible length, marveling at the texture and the power of him even as his heat seared through his jeans.

"Oh, God," she moaned, not knowing if she were pleading for strength or simply awed by his power over her.

"I'm not stopping," he warned as he pressed more fully into her hand. "Not until I'm so deep inside you I can't find my way out."

Su Ling felt a shudder of hunger grip her body. She never thought she'd be turned on by dirty talk, but the more graphic he got, the more she wanted it. Part of her still fought. Logical Su Ling kept screaming that sex without substance only led to disaster. Sex-kitten Su Ling completely ignored her. At least until the phone rang.

The electronic trill seemed shrill and insistent. Especially as her reason latched onto it full force, slipping images of car wrecks, heart attacks, and plane crashes into her mind until she had to break away from Mitch. Until she pushed at him, gasping for breath as she tried to stumble toward the phone.

"Leave it," he begged, still holding her back, still manipulating her nipples in a way that made her body arch and her knees go weak.

"It might be Mandy," she whispered, already too far gone to care.

Fortunately he remained more responsible than she. Acknowledging the possibility, he slowly released her, dropping a gentle kiss along her forehead before reaching past her to pick up the phone. Then he silently passed it to her.

"Su Ling! Are you there?" her boss bellowed at her long before she pressed the receiver to her ear.

"Settle down, Frank. I'm here." There was nothing like her boss, Frank, for cooling off overheated blood. Meanwhile Mitch stood across from her, his eyes still dark with passion, his hands still touching her, stroking her arms, caressing her hands before wandering to more intimate places. She resisted. No way did she want to mix Frank with Mitch, even subconsciously.

"You've got to come in, Su Ling. I need you to go over the figures on the Collins-Hawking merger."

She grimaced, already knowing where this was headed. "It's Saturday night, Frank. If it's that urgent, I'll come in tomorrow."

"Can't. This deal is going to hell in a handbasket, and I need you to sort it out."

She ground her teeth, impatiently batting away Mitch's hands as she took out her frustration on the wrong target. Except Mitch was remarkably persistent as he slid behind her, wrapping his hands around her belly and whispering in her other ear.

"Say good-bye, Sue."

Su Ling jerked her head away. "Tomorrow, Frank."

"What's the problem?" he returned, his voice hard. "Got a hot date? Too bad. Need I remind you that all the partners in this firm are men? If you want to break through that glass ceiling, you gotta go the extra mile. And you're not going to do it without my help."

She closed her eyes. She'd heard this song before, and for the thousandth time she questioned its truth. Was this a promise she could count on? Or was he just using her? She didn't know, and that kept her firmly under his thumb.

"Look, it's late and I'm tired of arguing," Frank continued. "So get your tight little ass in here and go over these figures or don't bother coming in Monday."

"Yes, Frank," she said wearily as she hung up the phone.

"Tell me you're not running away again." Mitch sounded equal parts pleading and resigned.

"Sorry. My boss is having a crisis." She turned to face Mitch, but the sight of his ruffled hair nearly undid her. God, she so wanted to quit her job.

"First your family, now work. I'm beginning to see a pattern here."

She sighed. "It's a corporate merger. The biggest we've ever handled. Big crisis when it starts to sink." She moved down the hallway intending to change her clothes. The feel of her breasts against the inside of her sweatshirt reminded her much too clearly of what she was giving up. Of what she could be doing with Mitch rather than spending an eternity in hell with Frank.

Mitch walked with her, his long stride easily keeping pace. "So they call you on a Saturday night to rescue them. On the biggest deal the company's ever done. Except two days ago you said no one had talked seriously about giving you a partnership."

She nodded, suddenly excruciatingly aware of Mitch entering her bedroom. Her queen-size bed loomed large in her mind as she mentally painted them both there. What would they be doing? What wouldn't they do? The very thought made her mouth go dry, and she had to turn away. Unfortunately she caught Mitch's gaze in the mirror, and she knew he was thinking the same thing. Knew he wanted the same thing. On her bed. Right now. Without reservation.

"Quit." His one word came out hoarse, and she knew it must have cost him to say it because his hands were clenched, his entire body still taut and rigidly hard. "They're using you."

"I can't quit." She forced herself to look down, away from the palpable draw of his eyes. Blindly gathering blouse and pants, she rushed into her bathroom to dress. Then, just to increase the distance between them, she deliberately put the coarsest meaning possible on his actions, knowing it wasn't the whole truth but unable to face his full meaning. "I can't quit just because you're horny," she said through the door. She thought he would answer, but he remained silent until she emerged fully dressed, feeling once again encased in an armor he couldn't penetrate.

How wrong she was. Less than two seconds after opening the bathroom door, he was reaching for her, holding her arms, keeping her in front of him as he spoke. "Yeah, I'm horny," he admitted. "But I'm not ruled by my lower half."

She stiffened. "Unlike me?"

She felt his hands clench on her arms before he abruptly released her. "I didn't say that." Suddenly he spun away, running a hand through his hair. "Damn it, Sue, I have no problem understanding work emergencies. Hell, the after-school life of a teacher often feels busier than the in-class time." He turned back to her, frustration clear in his tight shoulders and clenched expression. "I'm trying to be understanding here, but it's hard when I've finally gotten you alone." He took a deep breath, then released it slowly. "You've talked about your job often enough. You suspect he's just stringing you along. So cut the cord, already. Or are you just using him as yet another excuse to get away from me?"

She lifted her hand and gently touched his broad chest, feeling the muscles ripple as she allowed her fingers to trail down his belly. "I'm not running from you," she finally admitted. "I ought to be. My mind tells me I should, but . . ."

He grabbed her hand, drawing it up to his lips, sensuously kissing her palm. "Then stay."

She shook her head, nearly killing herself as she firmly withdrew from his caress.

"This isn't just sex," he said. "You know that, don't you? I . . . It's more than that. You're funny and smart, and I think we'd be good together."

She stood there, a half step away from her car keys, her back to him while inside she felt completely raw. She didn't even have enough perspective to analyze the conflicting emotions roaring through her. All she could do was stand immobilized while she simply felt . . . everything . . . and yet nothing with any clarity.

He stepped around her, facing her directly as he made his case. "I know it's hard, but take a stand against this Frank. People will control you if they can."

She frowned slightly, hearing something deeper in his voice. Something key. And it was so much easier to focus on his inner life rather than her own. "I take it you've got personal experience with this," she said. When he hesitated, she knew she'd struck gold. So she folded her arms and gave him a level stare. "You're asking me to quit my job. I think you can give up one personal story here."

He reached for her, but she backed away, letting her posture communicate that she wouldn't be distracted. Eventually he relented. "My parents were incredibly controlling. They decided before I was born that I'd be a lawyer. Looking back now, their demands don't seem like a whole lot, but at the time I thought I'd explode."

She nodded sympathetically, remembering her own childhood. "Adolescence."

He quirked an eyebrow. "Maybe. Except I did something about it. One day I packed my things and rode away. I've never looked back."

She frowned. "You didn't even say good-bye?"

"I left a note." Then he grimaced. "Kinda childish, huh? But the point is, I hated the situation, so I changed it. And I survived. I found a job, put myself through college, and here I am." He reached out, and this time she let him capture her hands. "Don't stick out a lousy situation hoping it'll get better. Life doesn't work that way. You've got to change it yourself. Take charge."

"It's not that simple," she hedged.

"Of course it is."

She bit her lip, considering. "So you have a good relationship with your parents now? All's well that ends well?"

His hands slipped away from her. "I see them on holidays."

From his tone, she could just guess how much he dreaded the onset of Christmas. Then she flashed on the image of him when she first saw him—shaggy hair, huge obnoxious earring, a rebel don't-mess-with-me air right down to the dragon tattoo—and suddenly she understood. "That's why you looked that way at my father's party. You'd just come back from your parents', where you dressed and acted like a jerk, didn't you?"

He stepped backward. "The situation's complicated."

"Sure it is. What are they? Good, solid Midwestern stock? The thought of having a biker boy for a son just gives them spasms, doesn't it?"

"They kept pushing. Night and day." He shifted, obviously uncomfortable. "My father's an Illinois supreme court judge."

Oh, Lord, she could just picture it now. Mom and Dad Judge and their biker-boy son. "I bet that tattoo looks great in the holiday photos."

"I wanted to teach," he said defensively.

"Spare me the excuses, bad boy. Just because you glory in irresponsible rebellion doesn't mean the rest of us are that stupid." Then she stood at the door, her keys in hand as she waited for him to leave her condo.

He echoed her stance, hands clenched by his sides as he stared at her. Just looking at him like that made her want to throw it all away—her job, her family, everything—just to run into his arms and kiss away that lost look in his eyes. But she couldn't. They were talking about her job. Still, it took all her strength to stand there without compromising, waiting for him to precede her out the door.

"Do you even like accounting?" he challenged.

The question hit her squarely between the eyes. No one had ever thought to ask before. Not even her. But she didn't have the energy to face the problem right now. Frank was waiting, and Mitch was too distracting for her to reevaluate her life right then. So she just stared at him, her lips pressed together, her mind whirling in chaos.

"Fine," he finally spit out. "Fine with me." Then he stomped out, his body rigid with anger. She'd barely finished locking her door when she heard his motorcycle roar away.

"Yeah, fine," she muttered as she made it to her car.

Two hours later she was still muttering. Except now she sat at her desk, grinding her teeth and cursing her work, her boss, and life in general. As much as Su Ling fought the realization, Mitch's words were affecting her.

Did she hate accounting? She certainly hated Frank, her rude, domineering chauvinist of a boss. And she hated that she was sitting here, working on a Saturday night when she could still smell Mitch on her skin, still thought of him whenever her hair slipped out of its knot to slide across her neck, and still wanted to jump him in the worst possible way. Good God, she suddenly realized, if Frank sauntered in right then and offered her a partnership on a silver platter, all she'd want would be to go home and make love with her new boyfriend.

How could she make a serious life decision when she was this aroused?

At that moment Frank walked into her office with another stack of figures. Su Ling looked up from her computer and gave him a steely gaze. "I expect a partnership offer on Monday morning."

He blinked, obviously startled. Then suddenly he burst out laughing. "Good one, Su Ling. Here's the next set."

Su Ling swallowed. Normally she would cave at this point. She'd join him in the pretend joke, saving herself the embarrassment of asking for something he obviously wasn't going to give her. Not this time. "I'm serious, Frank. I've been going the extra mile for seven years now. I thought if I worked hard, the rewards would come naturally. But they haven't. So either I get a partnership offer Monday morning or I'm gone."

"Partnership politics are dicey," he hedged. "But I'm pulling for you, Susie. Really, I am. But it's just not possible right now."

Su Ling sighed, kicking herself for her own stupidity. Mitch was right. Frank had been using her just as she'd suspected for months but had been too afraid to face. Squaring her shoulders, she mentally pulled forward an image of Mitch. Then she went one step farther, actually adopting his personality just to get her through this moment. She was mentally wearing his motorcycle jacket when she closed her laptop.

"What are you doing?" Frank demanded, his voice suddenly shrill with panic.

She imagined slipping on Mitch's gold hoop earring as she reached for her purse.

"This is important!"

She not only mentally put on his tattoo but added another one all her own: a tiny, grinning dragon along her inner thigh. Then she felt strong enough to speak. "You're an asshole, Frank. I quit."

Chapter Four

*N*o one was worth this. Not even the sexiest, funniest, smartest, most intriguing woman he'd ever come across. No matter what mysterious hold she had over him, whatever secrets his soul seemed to want to ferret out of her, Sue was not worth it.

Mitch kept repeating that mantra as he streamed down the highway. Contentment required only the open road, a powerful engine, and much warmer gloves. Damn, it was cold. Even his throat felt raw from the icy wind. He'd even started coughing.

Odd how he never noticed those little discomforts before. Night or day, January or June, he'd go riding, wandering where the whim took him. But not tonight. Instead of merrily anticipating the possibilities ahead, he spent the ride obsessing about Sue. She'd called him irresponsible. Him! As if *he* were the one who kissed like hot licorice, getting them both all revved up—again—before bailing—again. And this time she bailed to go to her dead-end, frustrating job.

Just how many times would she pick her family, her job, or some other excuse over him? And how many times would he keep coming back, begging for more abuse?

No more. He was through with her. Time to get on his motorcycle and ride away just like he'd done as a kid.

He eased off the throttle and leaned into a Chicago suburb exit. He hadn't gone north on purpose. Simply hopped on his bike and rode. But lately whenever he hit the open road he'd head north, back to his old stomping grounds. Back home. Here to relive bad memories, he guessed. To remind himself of what he'd left behind: stifling demands, loud arguments, and parents who could see only what looked good on a résumé, not what their only son wanted.

Well, he sure showed them, Mitch thought to himself. He had his own life now. A career he loved, lived his way, and had created with his own sweat. Not a dime borrowed from the old man, despite his father's dire predictions.

Mitch felt his motorcycle slow to a stop. Again, apparently by habit, he had pulled into his favorite of the old stomping grounds — a risky, low-life bar. One with loud music, fast women, and just about any recreational drug a teen could try. Except looking at it now, he felt a chill of horror. Same name, same location, but now he saw a tacky bar where rich teens hung out to pretend at being bad. His years teaching teenagers, even in a sleepy college town like Champaign, had shown him true rebellion, real parental abuse. His childhood didn't come close.

Was it possible? Was Sue right? Had his glorious, in-your-face rebellion against Nazi-like parents actually been nothing more than normal adolescence? His father had been strict, yes, but abusive? Certainly not. And Dad's relentless demands, the endless life-is-hard lectures coupled with all those trips to Ivy League schools — had they truly been torture?

Mitch felt anxiety burn in his stomach as he got off his bike.

He winced at the teen mobiles parked in the lot. Everything from kiddy motorbikes to Daddy's cars clogged the blacktop. He even saw trigonometry homework crumpled on a dash.

Then he stepped into the bar and tasted his own doom. The entire memory of his teen years shattered as he crossed the threshold. Kids hung out here. Even the bar wasn't much of a bar. Beer on tap, of course, for the college set, but his "perilous biker bar" specialized in soda and nachos. The air wasn't even smoky as baby-faced boys talked dirty around pool tables.

He felt a shiver chill his spine as he walked slowly through the dark shack. From all around, spoiled rich kids pulled out their tough-boy acts while jealously admiring his leather jacket. And then, as if he weren't already miserable enough, the bartender hailed him.

"If you're looking for your kid," he said, "there's a back room down that corridor."

Mitch groaned. He couldn't help it. He remembered the back room. He'd strutted around for weeks once he'd been admitted into that "secret" hiding place for the truly tormented. He used to think even the cops didn't know about it. *Yeah right.*

"No, thanks," Mitch muttered past the cold burn in his throat. "The kid I'm looking for isn't here." The childhood he'd expected wasn't here. And if his entire youth had been a mirage, then what did that mean about the man he'd become?

He glanced at his reflection in the mirror behind the bar, startled to see that his image fit right in with the boys around the pool tables. His clothes might be more expensive, but the attitude and the look were all the same. Was it possible? Could Sue be right? Was he still stuck in his teenage rebellion?

He wandered back outside in a daze, pulling on his helmet and starting up his bike without conscious thought. But reality hit him even harder as he began to maneuver his cycle out of the lot. Again, out of habit, he turned toward his parents' home. The need to confront his parents pounded through his temples, giving him a first-class headache. But he couldn't do it yet. He didn't know what he'd say. Or what he'd see. How much of his childhood had been fabrication? Had he left home as a bold adventurer striking out on his own? Or in a childish fit of pique?

He looked down at his hands and realized he was shaking.

This was Sue's fault! Without her he never would have come here. Never would have seen the truth behind the memories. He didn't know if he hated or loved her for the revelation.

Opening up the throttle, he headed for the highway. Visiting the bar had been enough soul growth for one night. Now he needed his own bed so he could bury his head beneath the covers. Except half an hour later he admitted defeat. He'd long since lost feeling in his hands, and his sight was blurring, the lights of oncoming traffic smearing unrecognizably. Simple exhaustion sent him reeling to a seedy motel right off the freeway.

Twenty minutes later he dropped heavily, blissfully into sleep.

Nine hours later he was still in bed, shivering with fever, coughing his throat raw, and cursing his too-thin gloves along with the too-thin blanket and the too-lumpy bed. He'd caught the same flu that had taken out half his volleyball team.

Sunday came and went in a gray blur of misery.

All he remembered of Monday was calling in sick. Or dead. He wasn't sure which.

By Tuesday morning the lure of his own bed drew him back onto his bike. By nightfall he crossed his own doorstep. Somewhere, in the dim recesses of his bleary brain, he saw the blinking light on his answering machine. He even managed to hit the button just before falling onto his couch.

"You were right," came Sue's lyrical voice. "I quit. Call me. We can spend all of Sunday together."

He squinted awkwardly at his wall calendar. What day was it?

"My word, do you look pathetic or what?"

Mitch cracked an eye, only to shut it again. He'd had this dream a million times. Sue came in bearing cookies and ice cream and kissed away his pain. Except this time Sue was fully dressed and carried a bowl of yellow stuff, which she put in the microwave. Frankly, this fantasy didn't measure up.

"You know," continued his disgustingly nonsexual fantasy, "when you didn't call, I thought you were just being childish. Sulking or something. But when Mandy said you weren't in school, I began to wonder. Now I feel really bad about thinking all those mean things about you, because honestly, Mitch, you look half-dead."

"Yadda, yadda," he muttered. "Get to the good part."

His dream woman paused. "What?"

"The stripping-naked part." Then he cleared his throat and didn't pass out from the pain. He must be feeling better, he realized. Perhaps well enough to enjoy his fantasy for real. He opened his eyes, squinting against the light. Meanwhile, dream-Sue folded her arms and laughed. The musical sound rolled around his head, teasing away the pain.

"Well, I guess you aren't dead if you're still making passes."

He frowned. That didn't sound like any fantasy-Sue he'd create. Then his stomach rumbled—good and loud—as he smelled something strange and yet foodlike all the same.

"Feel up to some Chinese broth?" His stomach growled again, and she laughed. "I'll take that as a yes."

He didn't respond. Instead he began pushing himself upright as he fought to clear his fuddled mind. On the one hand, he didn't want to give up this Sue-fantasy, even if it ranked low on the spice meter. On the other hand, if she really stood next to him, then he definitely needed to wake up, because, sick or not, Sue and he were alone. He liked fantasies, but reality held a billion times more appeal. If only his head would stop spinning.

"Here you go." She gently settled down on the couch, her special ginger/floral scent focusing his thoughts as nothing else could.

"Sue?" he croaked. "For real?"

"For real, bad boy. Now take a bite." She lifted up a spoonful of . . . yellow pudding and green onions? "It's a Chinese thing. Chicken broth and steamed egg. Trust me. You'll like it."

He meant to turn away, planning on a big bowl of Wheaties, but his stomach wouldn't let him. It wanted food now. So he obediently opened his mouth. Moments later he lifted the bowl out of her hands and wolfed it down as if the yellow goo contained the elixir of life. And maybe it did. After all, God's handmaiden herself had served it to him.

"Sue?" he began again. He still couldn't quite believe she was here.

She arched an eyebrow at him. "You expecting somebody else?"

The food settled his stomach and soothed his throat, but his brain remained fuzzy. "Did I tell you to get naked?"

She grinned. "Yes, but I wouldn't want you to have a coronary just yet."

He set down his empty bowl, groaning as his head dropped into his hands. Sue was here. Alone in his apartment. And he hadn't the mental focus to seduce her.

"I've got a couple hours, Mitch, if you want me to stay."

His head jerked up painfully. "Stay," he croaked. Again she laughed, and he closed his eyes, enjoying the sound. It settled into his insides, putting everything in its proper place. God, he could sit and listen to her forever. It just felt *right*.

"Fine by me," she answered. "We can watch TV or you can sleep—"

"Talk. We'll talk." The last thing he wanted to do was sleep through their precious time together. If God truly smiled upon him, no mothers, nieces, sisters, fathers, or bosses would dare interrupt this time. He dropped his head back against the couch, letting his eyes rest on her face. "You talk. I'll enjoy."

He didn't quite believe her blush. She literally glowed with beauty. "Okay," she said. "What should I talk about?"

"About how I'm right, and you're wrong." She had said that, hadn't she? On his answering machine? "Oh, yeah," he quickly added. "And how quickly I can get you in bed."

She shook her head even as she dropped a kiss onto his cheek. "Sorry. I don't sleep with the dead."

"Just keep talking. You're making me stronger by the second."

Su Ling did not want to be in line. She did not want to wade through the endless piles of red tape required to register late at the University of Illinois. She certainly didn't want to be standing in line, her feet going numb, while she waited to file more paperwork.

She wanted to be with Mitch. They'd talked for hours yesterday, sharing the silly intimate details of their lives and thoughts and hopes and fears until exhaustion finally claimed him. Even then she hadn't left, but sat on the floor watching him breathe, wondering at the strangeness of life that she would think naughty thoughts about an unshaven, tattooed, rebel wanna-be. That had been his last confession: the wild youth he hadn't really had and the fear that his life was built on a lie.

She hadn't known how to respond except to help him look

at the truth. He loved teaching and was phenomenal at it. She, on the other hand, had no job, no career, and no idea what to do with her time. Meanwhile, her family had thrown a fit, and she'd had to endure endless lectures on reckless impulsiveness.

Mitch had laughed at that, obviously wanting to talk more, but losing the battle with exhaustion. His last suggestion had been to take a couple classes at the U of I while she figured a few things out. Then his eyelids had finally slipped down as he sank into much-needed sleep. In a supreme act of will, Su Ling had not joined him in his bed, curling up in his arms, but had gathered her things and left.

Now, a day later, he was at school while she stood in line at the registrar's office, counting the seconds until she finished with all this red tape. She'd already called in her mother to drive Mandy to volleyball. If this line took much longer, she wouldn't even get to see the match.

Then, praise God, it was her turn. Fifteen minutes later she slammed her briefcase shut and dashed to her car before careening down the road to Mandy's school.

She arrived in time to see a dismal score in the second game. Franklin was losing badly. Their serves went wild, their hits seemed erratic, and nowhere did she see Mandy. She did, however, see Mitch, looking like death warmed over as he croaked out encouragement from the coach's seat.

Where was Mandy? She wondered at first if her niece was hiding in the locker room. But as the match wore on to its depressing end, Su Ling realized Mandy wasn't even there. Seconds later she'd whipped out her cell phone, images of crumpled cars and mangled bodies flashing though her mind. It took her two tries to dial her home number, and when she finally pressed the phone to her ear she couldn't hear for all the noise in the gym. She thought her mother had answered, but when she spoke into the receiver, asking what had happened to

Mandy, all she heard was agitated Chinese, spilling out in a flurry of nonsense.

"Ma Ma!" Su Ling interrupted, rushing toward the fire door so she could hear more clearly. "Is Mandy okay? Is she there?"

"Here, yes!" came her mother's clipped tones. "Okay, no. She is spoiled. Spoiled rotten. You must come home!"

Su Ling heard only two out of every three words, but she caught the gist of it. "I'll be there right away."

She was just heading out when Mitch caught up to her. "Sue! What happened? Is Mandy all right?"

She nodded, unable to resist pressing her hand to his pale cheek. "I think so. Ma Ma kept her home. What about you?"

"I'm fine," he obviously lied. "Can you wait while I finish with the girls? Then we'll go together."

She nodded, unable to resist, especially when he flashed her a seductive grin. He might be sick, but he still could tempt her into doing just about anything.

They made it to her home in record time. Su Ling didn't even realize the problem until too late. Perhaps her lack of foresight showed how much Mitch had soaked into the fabric of her life. In two weeks he had somehow blended seamlessly into her days. Then she pushed open the door to see Ma Ma calmly serving *another* blind date green tea on her living room sofa.

She groaned, everything suddenly becoming clear. "Ma Ma." She sighed, already guessing that her mother had manufactured a tragedy to get Su Ling home to meet another dragon man. "Why didn't you take Mandy to the volleyball game?"

Ma Ma looked up, her face pinched into a sour expression. "She did not finish her homework. 'B's! And a 'C'. You haven't been checking her homework. Why is he here?"

Su Ling almost did it. She almost said, *Mitch is here because I love him.* She hadn't even fully realized her feelings until the words nearly slipped past her teeth. Thank God she'd long since mastered choking back hasty words. Ma Ma would flip if she knew, not to mention sending Mitch—a.k.a. Mr. Independence—screaming for the door. So she sidestepped the issue. "Ma Ma, you remember Mitch Kurtz. He's Mandy's teacher and coach."

"Of course." Ma Ma was all smiles. "Mandy will not play volleyball anymore, Mr. Kurtz. Her grades are too poor. Thank you for coming." Then she turned her back on him as she smiled at the plastically perfect man sitting on the couch. "Su Ling, this is Mr. Tseng, a technician at the hospital. He is studying to be a doctor."

Su Ling gritted her teeth, steeling herself against the rebellion surging within her. Right now she had to get through this as quickly as possible. She had to get her mother and this new dragon out of her home so she could take a few minutes to examine her feelings. Hopefully with Mitch. Unfortunately that meant politely playing Ma Ma's matchmaking game.

Stepping forward, she extended her hand. "Hello, Mr. Tseng, I'm afraid—"

"I'm not just Mandy's teacher," Mitch interrupted, his voice hoarse. "I'm also Sue's boyfriend."

Su Ling spun around, a thrill zinging down her spine. Though he'd progressed to boyfriend status in her own mind, she'd never expected Mitch to say it out loud. That he did had her grinning from ear to ear. Unfortunately Ma Ma wasn't nearly as excited.

"Of course you're not," she snapped. "You're a waiter."

Su Ling released a groan, recognizing one of her mother's favorite tactics. She knew good and well that Mitch was a teacher, but she pretended to forget when she wanted to insult him. That way she wasn't insulting him. She'd just forgotten. Except Mitch had every right to feel offended, especially when Ma Ma tried to slam the door in his face.

Mitch stopped the door with a single press of his hand. Moments ago his pale face had looked sallow; now Su Ling saw the dark flush of heat suffuse his skin. Then, before she could say anything, a tearful Mandy slammed out of the guest room, running not to her aunt, but to Mitch.

"Mr. Kurtz! I tried to go, but she wouldn't let me. Did we win? Are we still going to play in the tournament? Is everyone mad because I didn't show?"

"Calm down, Mandy." That came from Mitch, his expression softening as he smiled at the girl. Unfortunately he didn't get any farther before Ma Ma stepped in again.

"No, no! Your homework. Violin. Piano. Those come first. No sports!"

"But—" her granddaughter cried.

"And you, waiter-coach, leave now!"

"Ma Ma," Su Ling began, trying to soothe her agitated mother.

"And you"—Ma Ma pointed a long, dark red fingernail at Su Ling—"you have a guest. How can you be so rude?" She made shooing noises at Mandy before becoming all smiles for the tall, awkward-looking Chinese man still sitting on the sofa. "Please excuse the chaos. My granddaughter, so impulsive."

"That's not fair!" screamed Mandy. "Ma Ma said I could play! Mr. Kurtz, don't kick me off the team. Not until—"

"Mandy!" That came from Su Ling, startling herself and everyone. Who knew she had the lungs to silence everyone? "Go do your homework," she snapped. "And Ma Ma—"

"Yes," interrupted Ma Ma. "You have much homework. Everything behind!"

"But—" the girl whined.

"If you'd done your work in the first place," cut in Mitch, his voice the most level of all of them, "you wouldn't be having this problem, would you? You've let everything go since your Mom left, haven't you?"

Mandy couldn't argue that one, so with a petulant frown she turned and stomped away. Then Su Ling turned toward the soon-to-be doctor, but once again she was forestalled as the man stood, his hand extended. "I'm so sorry. I don't know why I let my mother talk me into these things."

"Because we're cursed by them as babies, conditioned to follow their every psychotic whim," she quipped, earning a handsome smile from the gentleman but an angry gasp from Ma Ma. Then, before Su Ling could take back her hasty words, her mother nodded, angry tears shimmering in the older woman's eyes.

"Yes, yes. You should go," she said as Mr. Tseng moved toward the door. "My daughter is not worthy of you. Go. Find a good girl. One who honors her mother. Who knows the sacrifice . . ."

Ma Ma continued while her doctor dragon left, but Su Ling had already focused elsewhere. She turned to Mitch, seeing him wobble slightly with illness despite the flush that still heated his expression. "Why don't you sit down," she coaxed, "before you pass out."

Ma Ma roughly pushed between the two of them. "No, no! He cannot stay." Then she turned to Su Ling, true distress in her eyes. "What has he done to you? This busboy has sold you drugs. You are on drugs!"

"No, Ma Ma—"

But her mother wasn't listening. She had turned around to poke her sharp nail into Mitch's chest. "I could get you fired. I will tell the school board. Getting my daughter hooked on drugs."

"Ma Ma!" Su Ling exclaimed, but Mitch had already grabbed hold of her mother's thin hand, firmly setting it away from him.

"I am not involved in any type of drugs, Mrs. Chen—"

"You lie!" she screamed, pushing him away, turning desperate eyes back to Su Ling. "This is what happens with drugs. Your niece . . . failing! Your job . . . gone! Your mother . . . a curse! Look at him, Su Ling! Look! This is the life you are buying with your drugs. Tattoos. Motorcycles."

"Don't be ridiculous—" Su Ling began,

"Amanda!" Ma Ma screeched. "Pack your things! You will stay with me."

From down the hall Mandy poked her head out, confusion and defiance already forming in her expression.

"Stop it," Su Ling snapped, her temper getting the better of her. "Mandy is perfectly safe."

Her mother shook her head. "You brought him here. To your home." Then suddenly, the color drained out of her mother's face. "You are sleeping with him. You will get AIDS! Amanda, quickly! We must go!"

"Mrs. Chen, please," interrupted Mitch, his voice low and soothing. "I don't have AIDS."

Su Ling closed her eyes at Mitch's gaffe. He couldn't know it, but Ma Ma hadn't truly thought they were sleeping together or that Su Ling would get AIDS. But Mitch's four words seemed to confirm her mother's real fear: that Su Ling was sleeping with Mitch. Which naturally then rolled into all the other fears.

Ma Ma gaped at him, her mouth opening and closing in horrified shock. Meanwhile, Su Ling took the opportunity to try to mollify the situation. "I'm not sleeping with him, Ma Ma. It was a joke." Once again Su Ling knew it was the wrong thing to say. Yes, it might calm her mother, but she could see Mitch stiffen at the insult. Meanwhile Ma Ma continued her tirade.

"Some joke! Amanda! Hurry!"

"Ma Ma, Mandy is fine here. And she wants to stay with me."

"She doesn't know," she shot back. "Nobody knew about your drug-dealing dishwasher."

"For the last time, Mrs. Chen," Mitch said through gritted teeth, "I'm a teacher. Your granddaughter's social studies teacher."

Ma Ma practically hissed at him. "I will tell the school board, and you will be fired. You stay away from my daughter!"

It wasn't a true threat, though once again Mitch couldn't know that. Ma Ma often said all sorts of wild things she had no intention of following through on, but the steel in her mother's tone sent chills down Su Ling's spine. Ma Ma was truly terrified for Su Ling. Unfortunately, one look at Mitch's face and Su Ling knew he was barely holding on to his temper. She couldn't blame him. In less than five minutes, Ma Ma had dismissed his life's work, called him a diseased drug dealer, and threatened his job.

Su Ling looked up at Mitch, praying he understood. "Perhaps you should go."

"What?" He gaped at her, obviously *not* understanding.

"Just until I get things settled down."

Then, to make matters worse, Ma Ma actually taunted him. "You are not wanted here."

Mitch kept his eyes on Su Ling, his pain obvious though his back remained straight and proud. "Is that true? Am I not wanted?" He swallowed. "Are you choosing your family over me again?"

"Yes!" answered Ma Ma.

"No!" put in Su Ling firmly. Then she sighed. "Ma Ma, you should go home," she said in as soothing a tone as she could muster. "I know how upsetting this is. Give me time to sort things out."

Her mother hesitated, eyeing both Su Ling and Mitch with a suspicious expression. "He must go first."

"He will," Su Ling lied. "But I need to talk to him. Explain things."

Ma Ma folded her arms and glared. "Then I will wait."

"Don't bother," he said coldly. "I've seen this pattern before." He turned to Mandy, where she peered out of her doorway. "I'm glad you're okay, Mandy." Then he turned and headed for the door.

"Mitch, hold on—" Su Ling began, but once again her words were drowned out by someone else. This time it was her niece as Mandy came bolting down the hall.

"Mr. Kurtz! Wait!"

Mitch stopped, turning even as Ma Ma tried to grab her granddaughter. "Go back to your room!"

Su Ling gave up. She couldn't control this mayhem. She shouldn't have even tried. Then as she collapsed down onto her sofa, Mandy turned her large, adoring eyes on her grandmother. "Please let Mr. Kurtz talk to Auntie. He's really nice. I think they'd be great together!"

"Don't be ridiculous," snapped Ma Ma.

"Take her out to dinner!" Su Ling ordered, as stunned as everyone else by her bellow. And in the startled silence that followed, Su Ling marshaled enough brainpower to press her advantage. "I intend to speak with Mr. Kurtz right now, Ma Ma. Why don't you take Mandy to dinner? You can lecture her about the evils of drug use. And in the meantime I will set things straight with Mitch."

She didn't think it would work. Su Ling had never spoken so forcefully to her mother before. But to her amazement, Ma Ma reluctantly nodded. "Very well," she said as she canted an evil look at Mitch. "We will be back immediately. Be gone by then."

Neither Mitch nor Su Ling responded as Mandy caught

her grandmother's hand and gently tugged her out the door. In fact, neither of them moved until the ding of the elevator penetrated the heavy silence within the condo. Even then Su Ling waited until she heard the rumble of the elevator doors shutting before releasing a heavy sigh and letting her head drop back onto the couch. Only then did she dare look at Mitch.

He hadn't relaxed one iota. If anything he held himself more rigid, haughtier. "What did you want to talk to me about?" he asked stiffly.

She sighed. "Try to understand. My mother's afraid. She doesn't know who I am when I'm with you. Hell, sometimes I don't even recognize myself."

"Do you know what an accusation of drug dealing will do to my career?" he snapped. He turned toward her, the movement stiff with suppressed anger.

Su Ling straightened, trying to explain. "She's just afraid. She won't go to the school board. She didn't mean it."

"Yes, she did. She'd eat glass to protect you." He sounded envious.

"She won't do it. I swear. I'll make sure." Then she waited in silence, studying his expression as he at last softened, the anger slowly draining from his body.

Eventually he shifted, wearily settling onto the couch beside her. "She's trying to control you."

Su Ling shrugged. "She's my mother."

"That makes it okay?" He didn't even try to hide the disgust in his voice.

"Of course it's not okay. But that's the way she is."

"Only because you allow it." He twisted to look at her. "Stand up to her. Tell her to mind her own business."

Su Ling shook her head, horrified by the family breech that would occur if she took the direct approach. "I still do what I want. It just takes more effort. More finesse."

Mitch exhaled a long, loud sigh that seemed to sink him down into her couch. "So you manipulate her while she manipulates you. Can't you see how much energy you waste on that nonsense? Just take control. Like you did with your job."

She squirmed nervously on the couch. "This is my family. I can't just quit them."

"Why not?" Then before she could argue he straightened up, pressing his point further. "Don't you ever do what you want, what feels right, and damn the consequences?"

"Mitch—"

"Listen to your gut," he interrupted. "What do you feel right now?"

She hesitated, only now understanding what she wanted, what she felt.

"You're thinking too much," he pressed. "Just say it. I won't be shock—"

He didn't get any farther. Su Ling took over his mouth mid-word, kissing him with a ferocity that shocked her. And for the first time in her life her actions felt absolutely, totally, and perfectly right.

Chapter Five

*M*itch felt completely lost in a maelstrom of emotions, feelings, and thoughts, none of which made any sense, but all of which felt absolutely wonderful. As he kissed Sue's mouth, held her perfect breasts, even stroked the satiny flesh of her perfect thighs, he knew he had finally found *it*. He'd spent years searching for it, aching for this kaleidoscope of experience—wonder and hunger and even that razor-thin edge of fear all wrapped up in one amazing moment.

But this engulfed him in more than a moment. Minutes, hours, aeons of sensations spun through him, taking him well beyond what he'd ever been, and centering him in the most unlikely place—in a woman. In Sue.

Never had he wanted to pleasure a woman more. Never had he felt more fear that she wouldn't like his body or his touch or him. And yet she left no time for fear. Her first kiss robbed him of breath, and from that moment on they seemed to adore each other—together.

He wanted to touch, taste, and exalt every part of her. He left her mouth to pull open her blouse, kissing down her neck as he found her incredible breasts. Impatiently pushing away her bra, he stroked and squeezed them, thrilling at her gasps as he took her coral nipple into his mouth, teasing it with his tongue.

She began tugging at his shirt, stripping it away from him, but he barely noticed until he felt the satin slide of her skin against his. And as their naked flesh touched, his body became attuned to hers. He felt her quiver against him, communicating the same trembling awe and fear. But when he looked into her eyes, silently sharing his own anxiety, she began to smile, a soft curling of her lips even as she let her legs relax open.

"Sue," he whispered, amazed that he could speak at all. "I've been with . . . I've done . . ." He swallowed, searching for the words. "This is different. I know what you're feeling with just a touch." Then, as if to prove the point to himself, he lightly stroked his hand across her breast, luxuriating in the curve and the point on a purely sensual level, but stunned by the emotional ripples within him. He knew she loved his touch, wanted more of it. More of him. "It's never been like this before," he repeated. "God, Sue, I want you, but . . ."

"Afraid?" she whispered.

"Awed."

She reached forward, stroking her hands across his chest, and he felt tiny explosions reverberate through him as she released a soft laugh. "Someone suggested I stop thinking. Just feel. But you know what?" she asked as she leaned forward to kiss his chest. "I think I've never been so sure about anything in my life."

He closed his eyes, glorying in the sensations, but then she pulled away.

"Look at me," she whispered. And he did. His eyes flew open to watch her rise up off the couch. He watched, his mouth going dry as she shrugged out of her open blouse, her glorious breasts bobbing just in front of him. Then he heard the slow *rrrrrrrr* of her skirt zipper slipping lower and lower, and his blood and eyes followed the movement south. With a playful wiggle she slipped the skirt free, exposing—*oh, God*—thigh-high hose and the sexiest, tiniest scrap of thong lace already darkened with her moisture.

"Mitch . . ." Her voice was a throaty purr, but she had to stroke his chin to get him to look up. "I love you," she said.

There it was. His answer. Love made this different. This wasn't about bodies. It was about souls. He didn't know how to answer, so he did the only thing he could. He worshiped her. He glorified her every cell, every curve and ripple and moan and gasp.

He went to his knees before her, kissing her belly, stroking his tongue around and beneath her thong. And when her knees began to buckle, he caught her, easing her down as he used his teeth to pull the fabric away. He kissed her everywhere, spreading her open to revere her private places. He felt her tension build and decided her pleasure was just beginning. Indeed, he wanted to spend his life giving her joy in any way he could.

"Mitch." She moaned as he pushed his thumb into her.

"Mitch!" She gasped as he tasted her. *"Mitch!"* she cried as she arched beneath him, bucking as she grabbed hold of him, dragging him upward across her body. "All of you," she demanded. "Now!"

He wanted to give her everything. Everything he was, everything he had, everything he ever would be. He wanted to place them before her as tokens of his reverence. Instead she tugged his pants away, freeing him to do what she demanded. So with one deep, full stroke he entered her, touching her as deeply as he knew how, wishing he could give her more, while all the time his body shook with need.

She cried out in ecstasy, and he repeated the thrust, wanting to prolong her joy even while the fire entered his mind, overwhelming his restraint. In. Again. And again. Until he burst open, pouring himself into her as she shook with the power of her own fulfillment.

His last thought before collapsing beside her was that he had given her everything he had and more, and yet he'd never, ever felt more complete.

He floated in a pool of absolute contentment. No thoughts clouded his feelings. If anything, flashes of memory only enhanced his mood. He recalled Sue's body shuddering around him. Her giggle as he stumbled when he scooped her up and carried her to the bedroom. Her body flowing around him as she settled her head onto his shoulder, her breath a sweet caress. And best of all, a total suffusion of joy when she'd whispered, "I love you."

God, he felt blessed.

Then a ripple of unhappiness swirled through his pool. Sue was leaving his side. Dimly he recognized sounds in the distance. Noises from the front hallway. The whisper of clothing against skin, probably as Sue dressed, then the muted plop of fabric hitting the floor. He struggled up to consciousness, coming awake as the bedroom door shut and voices filtered in through the doorway.

"Su Ling! You look so relaxed. Isn't it good to be finally rid of that man?"

Sue's mother. Coming back with Mandy. Mitch's eyes flew open as he scrambled out of bed, scanning the room for his clothing, spotting them in a heap on the floor.

"Ma Ma, you have to stop. Mitch isn't a drug dealer or anything bad."

He listened to his love's voice as she chastised her mother, smiling as he anticipated her proud declaration. She loved him. They were in love. Meanwhile, he hastily pulled on his pants, wishing he had nicer clothes to wear before his woman's mother.

"In fact," continued Sue, "I . . . Well, he's . . . Ma Ma, he's a very nice man."

Mitch paused, his hands clutching his shirt. *Nice?* He sounded like a pet.

"Well, of course. Waiters are paid to be nice—"

"Teacher, Ma Ma." At least Sue sounded annoyed.

"Them, too. But he is not for you. You know this, yes?"

He waited for her swift denial, but as the silence stretched Mitch felt his soul grow cold. Was it possible? After everything they'd just shared, after everything they'd just done, would she still choose her mother over him? Was her good-girl persona so ingrained that even love couldn't crack it?

An old anger began to burn in him, feeding on the tangible presence of parental disapproval. He'd left his home because of this. Unreasonable condemnation had fueled his teenage rebellion and still made him torture his family with shaggy hair, outrageous earrings, and a really bad attitude over holidays. Put simply, his parents hated his choices—to play hockey, to buy a motorcycle, to teach middle school—and all too soon their contempt became as natural as his rebellion. So once again he faced parental scorn, and once again it pushed him into mutiny as he sauntered out of Sue's bedroom with only his low-slung jeans on.

"Yes, Sue," he called, "tell her how I'm not for you."

Mrs. Chen whipped around at his sudden entrance while Sue's sigh echoed in the taut silence. But the person Mitch spotted first was Mandy, her eyes widening with shock and teen speculation. Seeing her made him instinctively want to cover himself, but it was too late. Teen presence or not, he had to brazen it through.

Mrs. Chen reacted first. She began spouting a flurry of Chinese, adding wide gestures and dramatic expressions, but Sue didn't appear to listen any more than he did. Instead she turned to him, her eyes wide and tragic. "You couldn't just let me handle it, could you? Geez, Mitch, they're my family. Let me deal with them my way."

He took a step forward, hating to see the pain in her eyes, but still driven to defend himself. "Your way leaves me hidden in the back room like some shameful secret. Just tell her you love me, and she has to accept it!"

Mrs. Chen abruptly switched into English, physically stepping between her daughter and Mitch. "You told me he had gone. You told me he wasn't for you."

Sue shook her head, tears shimmering in her eyes. "You said that, Ma Ma. Not me."

The pain in her voice spurred Mitch to act, determined now to end this scene as quickly and painlessly as possible. And that meant showing the truth to Sue's mother. So he gently but firmly took hold of Mrs. Chen's arm, pulling her back far enough to allow him to slip an arm around Sue's waist. "No, I haven't gone. And I'm not going."

In less than a second Mitch realized he'd erred. Mrs. Chen's expression shifted into pure hatred. This woman would bury a cleaver in his chest if it meant protecting her daughter. And right now she obviously thought him the devil incarnate.

Mrs. Chen pulled herself upright, and Mitch instinctively tensed, sliding in front of Sue in case her mother became violent, but neither of them had the chance. Sue roughly pushed them both apart. "Stop it! Both of you!" she shouted.

Mitch straightened, intending to say something—what, he had no clue—but something perfect. Something that would show both mother and daughter that he and Sue belonged together. But as he desperately searched for the right words, Mrs. Chen pulled herself together, speaking in Chinese with great dignity while her daughter pulled her arms against her chest in a defensive posture.

He didn't know what her mother said, but Sue's response was very clear. "Of course I love you, Ma Ma. And my family. But I'm an adult. You must allow me to make my own mistakes."

"Aha!" cried her mother in English. "You admit it." She pointed her dark red fingernail at Mitch. "He is a mistake."

For his part, Mitch felt his heart shrivel with cold. Why couldn't she just say the truth? That she loved him and damn the consequences? "Maybe you're right," he said. "Maybe this whole thing is a mistake."

She shook her head, a single tear slipping free. "I didn't say that."

Her mother began speaking, but Sue held up her hand, shooting her mother a stern look before turning back to him. "I'm asking you." She took a deep breath. "I'm begging you, Mitch, don't make me choose between you and my family."

"God, Sue, can't you see how much pain they're causing you?"

"My name is *Su Ling*!" she exploded. And when he just stared stupidly at her, she shook her head, her tone and her shoulders dropping in weariness. "Mitch, I'm Chinese. I can't just throw my family away because they're inconvenient."

He took a step forward. "Stop thinking so much. Go with your gut. It feels right between us, doesn't it? It has to. You said you love me." He watched as she closed her eyes, drawing herself together. Even her posture became firmer.

Then she opened her eyes, shifting to look at her mother. Inside Mitch began to glow with joy. She was going to tell her mother to butt out. This was her life. And, miracle of miracles, her next words confirmed it.

"Ma Ma, I do love him." Then she turned to him, and he felt his happiness start to sink. "But I love my family, too. They're a part of me. The man for me will recognize that."

He shifted his gaze to her mother, seeing the triumphant gleam in her eyes. "And what if your family doesn't accept him?" he challenged. Because from her mother's expression, hell would serve frozen margaritas before that woman accepted him.

Sue hesitated, shifting her gaze to her mother. "They love me, too. We have to find a way to work it out."

"Work it out with your family?" he drawled, thinking of his own family—the bitter arguments, the ugly words. Some things, he knew, never ran smoothly.

"I will not choose between a man and my family." Sue stepped toward him, her heart in her eyes. "If you love me, you'll help me find a way."

He tasted bitterness as he spoke. "If you loved me, you wouldn't need my help. You'd know that my love . . ." He took a deep breath. "That our love comes first." He crossed to the door then, intending to leave. That was how he'd ended his last bitter argument with his father—by just walking out. But before he could close the door on the one woman he'd ever truly loved, he had to try one last time. "I make you happy. You know I do."

She shook her head, the tears flowing freely down her cheeks. "Not if it means I have to break with my parents. Are you truly happy—truly whole—without your family?"

He didn't answer, knowing he'd been defeated. She would always be tied to her mother's strings, always bound by their choices, not her own. Swallowing his anger along with his regrets, he grabbed his shirt and jacket and walked out.

Chapter Six

*O*ne week later Mitch knew he'd made a mistake. All his life he'd trusted his gut. If he felt pain, then something had to change. So years ago he'd walked out on his parents, and now he had a good job, a good home, a good life. All in all, a good decision.

Except he didn't feel so good right now. He couldn't shake the thought that Su Ling's refusal to break with her family, to stick by them through the good and bad, gave her something he'd lost in his adolescence. Misguided or not, her family would go through hell, even brave a potential drug-dealing psychotic to protect one another. Wasn't that worth preserving?

He'd told himself that no woman, not even Su Ling, was worth this agony. He'd repeated it a million times as he tried to focus on the wonderful life he had without her. But every time he told himself, the words sounded hollow. As if a part of him were missing. As if *she* brought him something he hadn't had in a long time.

But what?

He mulled over their times together—the best and the

worst—and he nearly laughed out loud at his stupidity. What was missing from his life? Why did he feel so alone? Because he was alone. He began teaching children because he loved children. His first mind-blowing attraction to Su Ling came when she'd offered him not only a dinner with her gorgeous self, but all her relatives as well. Then came the time spent discussing, arguing, and laughing . . . over what? Mandy. And Su Ling's family. Sure, she'd used them as an excuse to run from him. But that had only increased his soul-deep need to pursue her.

Could it be that easy? He knew he loved her—loved her wit, her strength, her prim exterior, and her wild-woman interior. But when he pictured their future together, he saw a family. One with children *and* grandparents.

God almighty, she was right. Her family was a part of her. And part of what he loved about her. He didn't want her to break with her parents. He wanted her parents to accept him. But when Ma Ma had proved difficult, he'd simply walked out, just as he'd done to his own parents. Instead of sticking it out, instead of finding a way through the problem, he'd just walked.

What an idiot!

But how could he fix it? How could he show Su Ling he valued her family? And in a way that would convince Mrs. Chen, too? Obviously words wouldn't be enough. He had to show them that family mattered to him, and that he honored family ties.

He looked at his closet. Buried in the back, in a box that had followed him from move to move, lay a picture album. A pathetic album, actually, one that contained three pictures. Christmas candids, to be exact, of his parents, his sister, and him happily tearing apart presents. The rest of the pages remained blank, empty except for his intention to fill them one day with pictures of new memories, new family. Except now he knew he'd never be able to fill the latter pages until he reconciled with the earlier ones.

In short, he had to talk to his parents again. He had to honor his own family ties before he could accept someone else's.

He took a deep breath and picked up the phone, dialing quickly before he changed his mind. His father answered, and over the heavy beating of his heart, Mitch spoke, saying the words he should have said years ago. "I'm sorry, Dad. Not for the way my life's turned out, but for everything else. Can we try again? And this time I won't be such a jerk."

Victories come in small pieces, Su Ling reflected with a sigh. After Mitch left, Su Ling finally had it out with her mother. Ma Ma had to respect Su Ling's choices, she'd said. Family needed to support, not dictate. If Su Ling quit her job, her mother needed to have faith that Su Ling would find another. If Su Ling picked a man, then her mother had damn well give him a chance. After all, Su Ling had respected her mother enough to give all those dragon men a chance. Didn't Su Ling deserve that same respect?

Of course, Ma Ma had readily agreed. She'd already gotten what she wanted: Mitch, irretrievably gone. Ma Ma had left, firmly putting "that horrible dishwasher man" out of her thoughts, but Su Ling remained miserable, mourning what she might have had with Mitch. If only she'd been a little stronger, thought a little faster, had it out with her mother a day, an hour, a minute earlier. Maybe things would be different. But it was too late. Mitch's face when he'd walked out told her she'd chosen her family over him one time too many.

At least it'd worked out for Mandy. The family had been so upset by Su Ling's rebellion that they quickly folded when Mandy followed her aunt's example. The girl flatly told her mother and grandparents that she'd given violin and piano a chance. She hated them. Now they needed to let her try something she liked: volleyball. In fact, the Chens caved so quickly that now everyone—grandparents, grandaunt, and granduncle—all dutifully filed in to watch the first of Mandy's tournament matches. Score one victory for self-determination.

The cost, of course, had been Mitch. Now more than ever Su Ling knew that she loved him. She loved how she grew stronger around him, finding value in herself. He helped her stand firm against an abusive boss and a frightened, domineering mother. What would happen to that strength without him beside her? In keeping the structure she'd always relied upon, had she thrown away the one person who forced her to grow, to become better?

She wanted a second chance with him, but she doubted Mitch would risk his heart again. He'd come in second—to her family and her job—too many times for him to believe she'd put him first from now on. So she decided to act—publicly and in full view of her family—hoping to show him once and for all that part of her would always be his. Forever. If only she could stop shaking long enough to do it.

She arrived late, of course. Her first day of classes had been a lot harder than she'd expected. But she would adjust. Thanks to Mitch, she had enough determination to keep at it despite the temptation to grab the first accounting job that came along. She would *not* run to the easy, familiar road again.

She hurried into the gym, immediately spotting Mandy in play, her rosy-cheeked happiness clear. Her family, Mandy's mom included, occupied the center black hole of Chinese stoicism in the middle of the bleachers. But as Mandy executed a beautiful spike, Su Ling caught Ma Ma's sudden beaming smile amid the Chens' polite clapping.

Su Ling absorbed these details in a flash as she paid for her ticket. But the center of her attention focused on Mitch as he called to his team from the sidelines. He looked different, she realized with a touch of sadness. None of the haggard exhaustion seemed to dog him as it had her. Instead he seemed relaxed, almost happy in a crisp new suit with a stylish tie. He'd even cut his hair, though the cubic zirconium still flashed from his earlobe.

He looked up and saw her. Something unreadable flashed across his expression, and Su Ling felt momentarily paralyzed, wondering if he could see the apology in her eyes and the love in her heart. But before she could guess at his thoughts, a stylish brunette touched his arm, physically drawing his gaze away from Su Ling.

Su Ling bit her lip, looking down at her feet as she made her way to the bleachers. Just over a week, and already Mitch had found another woman. She'd missed her chance. Looking up, Su Ling couldn't stop herself from studying the brunette. She sat in the bleachers behind Mitch, occasionally turning to talk to a handsome elderly gentleman and his wife. Her parents, no doubt.

Su Ling almost laughed. Not only had Mitch picked up another woman, but one who came with her own family encumbrances. Obviously Mitch could tolerate family interference with the right woman.

Meanwhile the match continued as the Franklin team struggled. All through it, Su Ling fought her tears. Just because things didn't work out with Mitch didn't mean she regretted the experience. She was a stronger woman because of Mitch. Or so she told herself, even as her mother reached out and patted her shoulder in sympathy. That was the thing about Ma Ma. The woman could be totally clueless, but she was always there and she always cared.

The volleyball match finally concluded with a Franklin rally ending in victory. Parents and friends stood in the bleachers, all cheering and chatting and generally getting on with their lives. All except Su Ling, who felt completely numb. Then the principal grabbed a mike and asked for everyone's attention.

"Mr. Kurtz has made an unusual request, but since he is one of our best teachers, I've decided to indulge him," the principal said as she offered the mike to Mitch. But he simply gestured sideways to the brunette's father, who took center stage as if he were born to it.

With a formal air, the older man bowed first to the principal, thanking her and calling her Madam Principal; then he walked across the gym floor, approaching the Chen family in an equally dignified manner before bowing deeply to Su Ling's father.

"Mr. Chen," he intoned. "I am James Kurtz, an Illinois supreme court justice and father to Mitchell Kurtz, teacher and coach to your granddaughter."

Su Ling's gaze flew to Mitch, who was watching her with the type of vulnerable intensity she'd seen from him only when they were in bed. And as she colored at the memory, her sluggish brain finally assembled the pieces. The elderly couple were Mitch's parents. Which meant the brunette was his sister.

Mitch had made up with his family! The very thought stunned her. And its ramifications . . . She hadn't a clue. And all the while Mitch's father continued to address her father, elaborating on his son's accomplishments and stellar qualities. In fact, Su Ling had to stifle a laugh when his father extolled Mitch's strong "independent streak."

But then Justice Kurtz bowed again deeply. "I am not completely familiar with Chinese customs regarding a courtship request, but please understand that I and my family, and most especially my son, would very much like to learn. He respects your family and your culture, and we all hope you will accept this token from us to you." Then he presented a small black jeweler's box to Su Ling's father. "It has been in the Kurtz family for six generations, and now we present it to you."

A hush fell over the gym, but it was nothing compared to the sudden stillness in Su Ling's heart. Everyone craned their necks, trying to see into the box her father opened. Then Su Ling saw Ma Ma raise her eyebrows, obviously impressed. "Dragons have good jewels," Ma Ma whispered.

Then the box snapped closed as her father gained his feet, also bowing deeply to Justice Kurtz. Next came the long, formal recitation of the Chen family's lineage and accomplishments before her father accepted the gift on his daughter's behalf. And then her father turned slightly, his smile showing his approval even as he looked to Su Ling's reaction.

She had none. She sat completely frozen by the conflicting emotions at war within her. Five minutes ago she had resolved to try to live without Mitch. But now? She didn't want to guess.

"I think," continued her father, "that this is America. Perhaps we should allow your son to begin his courtship in person." Then he passed the jeweler's box back to Justice Kurtz, who gave it to his son.

As if by magic, or perhaps it was because of Mandy's sudden whispers, the bleachers in front of Su Ling magically cleared as Mitch, black box in hand, approached her. She watched as he swallowed nervously before dropping down on one knee before her.

"Su Ling," he began, his voice starting out soft, but gaining in strength as he spoke. "My father, who turns out to be a much smarter man than I ever gave him credit for, suggested I start out with the basic facts." He took a deep breath. "Fact one: I'm an idiot. Fact two: I love you. I love you because you're gorgeous and sexy and funny and really, really smart. So smart, in fact—number three—that you were right. Your family is part of your strength, and I wouldn't want you to give them up. I wanted you to make all the changes, when in truth I was too cowardly to learn from you." He twisted slightly, indicating his parents and sister, both standing nearby watching him. "I need family. Yours and mine." He looked back at her, holding out a huge diamond-and-ruby ring. "Will you marry me and join our two meddlesome, overbearing, wonderful families together?"

Su Ling reached out, touching not the ring, but Mitch's face. "No," she whispered. And at his stricken look, she rushed to explain. "No, Mitch, you were right. I was hiding behind my family, always running to them for support instead of standing on my own two feet. You taught me that." Then she paused, still trying to believe it was possible. "Did you make up with your family for me?"

He shook his head. "I did it for me. But I never would have realized how much I missed them if it weren't for you. And your clan," he added with a wry sideways glance at the Chens. Then he pulled the ring out of the jeweler's box. "All mature, responsible, unimpulsive people need family around. It grounds them to the past and helps keep them strong for the future. Did I mention that I love you?"

She grinned, for the first time knowing that both her heart and her mind agreed. "I love you, too. But don't quite lose that bad-boy look," she said as she leaned forward to whisper into his ear. "I like my wild dragon—and have a new tattoo to prove it. A tiny one—all dark and mysterious—on the inside of my thigh. Perhaps I'll let you find it on our wedding night."

His eyes glittered. "Have I mentioned that I really, really love you a lot?"

"Have I mentioned that I'll definitely marry you?"

He slipped the ring onto her finger while around them the stands erupted into cheers. And in the background Su Ling could hear her mother repeating to everyone who listened, "I picked him. Dragon for dinner. Good family. Good husband. I picked him. Now maybe she will listen to her mother. Chinese superstition not so stupid anymore."

The Spice Bazaar

BY
SABEEHA JOHNSON

Chapter One

"*I*'ve found the perfect "husband for you, Nalini. He's successful, handsome, quiet, thoughtful." Showla Aunty's matchmaking words lifted Nalini's spirits as she sat in her cubicle, working on a marketing plan for a new kitchen appliance. Waiting to meet the perfect husband was like waiting to exhale. And she'd been waiting for three long years. Each call from a matchmaker took her on a wild roller-coaster ride of hope, then plunged her into the deep, dark well of disappointment, then lifted her back up to heights of burning expectation, such as she now felt. In two hours she'd have her answer—the perfect husband or another unacceptable match.

In the last year, the push to arrange a suitable marriage for her gained velocity around the United States, from one Indian community to another, linked by zealot matchmakers, mostly self-appointed, like Showla Aunty. Nalini thought fondly of how these well-meaning ladies e-mailed, faxed, phoned, and met each other, over numerous cups of hot chai. They sat studying names and data on eligible young men and women, whose names they recorded in huge old-fashioned ledgers as though to pay homage to the ancient custom. They upheld the rules and formalities that had been observed by her parents, grandparents, and ancestors going back centuries in India. Because she was born in America, Nalini had modified the old rules by asking her parents if she could first meet a prospect and decide if they'd get along. Since others her age were also asking for such an opportunity, they had agreed.

As Nalini looked over product research on her computer, she sighed. Tonight's meeting had to work, because in two weeks, when she turned twenty-five, all those efforts would dry up like a pot of soup forgotten on a stove top. She checked her reflection in the small mirror on her cubicle wall. Her large almond-shaped eyes, smooth complexion, black shoulder-length hair, slender curves, and sprightly spirit made her feel young and vivacious. But by Indian standards she was poised on the brink of spinsterhood, a pebble about to be washed away in a stream full of driftwood.

If she married outside her religion sometime in the future, her entire family and community would condemn and shun her. Still, she'd explored that possibility by dating three Americans, of European background, briefly. Not one seemed interested in anything more than a good time, and she hadn't had a good time with any of them. But those experiences crystallized her vision of her future. She wanted a husband who shared her values, her culture and heritage, someone her whole family could relate to, someone she could raise children with in the comfortable setting of a home unsplintered by cultural differences.

Her grandfather's wish to see a great-grandchild before he died pressed on her. At eighty-two, he was the only one of five siblings without a great-grandchild, and getting cranky over all the jabs relatives leveled at him for sending his only daughter to live in America, where family values didn't include respect for elderly relatives' wishes.

At last six o'clock lazed by and Nalini hurriedly began to neaten up her desk when the phone rang. Her mother's voice, swelling with excitement, said, "Nalini, keep an open mind.

You need someone dependable, quiet, practical, and patient. You're far too independent and talkative. Too impatient. Your life must be balanced with the appropriate partner. Showla Aunty says Dilip has these qualities, which have made him so successful. His accounting firm's spun off three branches. He's quite a catch."

Nalini secretly hoped this prospect was also romantic, somebody she'd find attractive on all levels.

"It's your decision not to have us there," her mother said reproachfully.

The last three meetings with marriage prospects had been disastrous. The pressure of two sets of parents watching had made it impossible to act normally, so Nalini had begged them to allow her to do this alone. "It's okay, Mummy. You won't have to fly from Chicago for this meeting. If things don't go well, no time's lost."

Her mother sucked in her breath. "Nalini, don't take out a black tongue. How many times have I told you not to think negatively before meeting a prospect? That just makes such thoughts come true. Center yourself and go forward, dear, with an open mind. Remember the name of the restaurant you're going to is Spice Bazaar. There wasn't time to get his photograph, but he'll find you."

"Yes, Mummy. I've already looked it up in the phone book. I'll call you afterward and give you all the details. I have a good feeling about this."

Nalini dashed home to change into a forest-green shalwar outfit, loosely draping its matching chiffon scarf around her shoulders. Since three years ago, after the first prospect, a wiry engineer, had turned touchy-feely, Nalini now made a point of transporting herself and meeting in a public place. She rushed to her car and drove madly through the traffic-clogged streets of Vienna, Virginia, impatiently taking shortcuts through leafy side streets, past a mishmash of homes on tiny lawns. Blooming azalea bushes, climbing roses, and banks of impatiens added the exuberant touches of early summer. Someday soon, she'd have a garden. . . .

Her heart beat wildly in ancipation. What would he look like? Would they like each other? Would he find her attractive?

The sign SPICE BAZAAR, with its red lettering bouncing playfully on white, rose to the right, and Nalini pulled into the small parking spot next to it. With one last look in the mirror to fluff up her hair, she walked into the restaurant, quickly surveying the area.

The grocery store, with its crowded, spicy-smelling aisles, was full of middle-aged ladies picking over fresh bitter melons, fenugreek, green mangoes, and yard-long beans. Some of them were lugging huge bags of basmati rice and lentils to the cash register.

The back of the store opened onto a neat restaurant, with a hand-carved wooden screen and white walls hung with paintings of palm tree–lined beaches and the Himalayas. She walked past chattering groups of American diners and nervously seated herself at one of the tables glistening with crisp blue linens. Nearby, a husband and wife were trying to finish their meal and quieten three screaming children at the same time. In the far corner, a gray-haired, bespectacled man sat reading the *India Weekly* newspaper. Nalini stared at the paintings, thinking that at this very minute she'd rather be on top of the jagged, snow-covered peak of the Himalayas instead of on display for someone who could easily turn out to be another wrong guy.

The waiter, a scrawny fellow, approached her with a big smile and handed her a menu. "Today's specialty is fish in a spicy sauce cooked in banana leaves," he said.

She opened the menu but her eyes kept returning to the café entrance and her watch. Having arrived a fashionable fifteen minutes late, she was alarmed that she'd been sitting alone for five minutes more. What if he didn't show up? What if he'd been here and left?

"I'm waiting for someone," she said quietly to the waiter, "a Dilip Joshi. Has he been here? Maybe he's in the store."

"I will check for you, madam."

The waiter left and she focused on the menu, ignoring the curious eyes boring into her. The menu featured vegetarian and nonvegetarian dishes. The half page devoted to flat breads pleased her. Chapathis, paratas, naan with onions, with sesame seeds, with fenugreek leaves, stuffed with ground beef, with cauliflower and peas, with different lentils. Some were layered and fried. Others were tandoori-oven baked. Breads took so much time and technique to make, and the frozen ones she bought from the Indian grocery stores never tasted as good as the freshly made ones. She busied herself studying the menu while impatiently waiting for the prospect to show up.

"Hello, Nalini?"

She glanced up into deep chocolate–brown smiling eyes. Her heart skipped a beat as their gazes held, mingling in a startling warm caress. Showla Aunty had outdone herself This was the handsomest man Nalini had ever seen. He looked to be in his mid-twenties. His hair, parted on the left side, glistened as beautifully black as a quiet night. She took in his high cheekbones, long, straight nose, and chin with the most beautiful dimple, and sighed. She had always wished she had a dimple. It made a face so distinguished.

"Are you Nalini?" he asked.

She jumped. "Yes, I'm Nalini, and I was told—"

"Yes, yes, Showla Aunty called. We were expecting you."

"Are your parents joining us?" She didn't mean to sound so alarmed and silly, but that was a question she'd failed to ask Showla Aunty.

"No, no. My parents are back in Bombay. They might come for a visit soon, but they don't like to leave their old friends and relatives. Their comfort is all wrapped up in going to the same jeweler and the same sari shops and the same shoe shops. They came here once, two years ago, over the Christmas holidays. They liked the Christmas lights but hated the heavy winter coats and the pressures of life in the States." He sat down across from her and continued, "They felt it was too formal a lifestyle here. People didn't know their neighbors. They couldn't understand why Americans are so abrupt and busy all the time. You know, I tried to explain how much there is to do here in one day. But they think people should learn to relax and not take all the little stuff so seriously."

Nalini couldn't take her eyes off of him. He spoke with warm affection for his parents. There was none of the embarrassment or apology others used in describing similar scenarios of parents visiting from other countries. Unlike other men, Dilip talked so easily and openly on their very first meeting, she felt she'd always known him.

"I love my new country. Americans are wonderful people." His eyes filled with amusement. "I've been here only eight years, so I'm still an FOB."

"Fresh off the Boat? No, you're too Americanized to be an FOB."

"According to Showla Aunty, Nalini, your parents live here in the States. . . ."

"Yes. They live in Oak Park, a suburb of Chicago. That's where I was born."

"So they're well used to heavy winter coats by now." He chuckled. "And you're a bona-fide American."

"Are you going to think me an ABCD?" she teased.

"I considered it," he teased back. "But you don't look like an American-Born Confused Desi. Are you? I mean confused?"

"Of course." She laughed. "Which one of us isn't? It's impossible to explain you're born here but look foreign." As understanding softened his eyes and he nodded, she continued, "At one job interview I was asked where I was from. And when I said Illinois, the man repeated very slowly, like this"— she imitated him, opening her mouth to form each word distinctly separate from the last— " 'But *where* are you *originally* from?' "

He threw back his head and laughed so loudly the children at the next table quit crying to watch him. "So did you call yourself an American Indian? Or did you say you were an Indian-American?"

"I was confused." She laughed. "I tried to stick to the facts . . . born in Oakbrook, Illinois. I think I lost that job because the man had never interviewed an Indian or anyone who looked Asian before."

"Their loss. Definitely their loss."

She sighed. "That job paid much more than I make now, and the offices were plush. They had upholstered chairs, matching curtains at the windows. Every employee got fresh flowers on Mondays. And every three months they got to select a new painting from an art gallery for their office walls. I was depressed for weeks about not getting that job." She fell silent, realizing she had never admitted her feelings about losing the better job to anyone before.

"Gold cages do not make happy birds. Old Sanskrit saying," he said, and winked.

She smiled appreciatively. He didn't look down his nose at her, as so many competitive peers would have if she confessed she didn't get the first job she applied for. Indians were extremely competitive that way, but he made her feel better, reinventing an old Sanskrit saying.

And she never imagined Showla Aunty's phone call would produce a man so handsome, so easy to talk to, so open and friendly, and so Americanized even though he'd come to the United States only eight years ago. She could imagine spending her days and nights with him, laughing and talking and teasing.

The waiter arrived with a tray bearing a plate of samosas and two glasses of soft drinks that he set carefully in front of them. He bowed and scraped and asked in a most deferential tone, "What else may I bring you, sir?"

"Nothing for now," Dilip said without taking his eyes off Nalini's face. As soon as the waiter was out of earshot, he leaned forward. "Where have you been hiding all this time? Why haven't I seen you before?" he asked, deliciously tangling the deep browns of their eyes.

Her face and heart filled with warmth. Her hand shook as she tried to lift the glass, and she quickly set it back down. "What do you mean?" she said as evenly as she could. "I just told you I grew up outside of Chicago. I went to Northwestern University and moved here two years ago when I took the second-best job."

"I mean why haven't we run into each other in these twenty-four months since you moved here? Seven hundred and thirty days?"

"Because you've been hiding," she giggled. "Showla Aunty said you don't go to Indian community events, and I've only gone to one Diwali celebration and one wedding. I didn't know anybody except friends of my parents, the Raos. They took me under their wing and tried to introduce me to people. Maybe you were there."

His eyes swept across her with the rapt absorption a jeweler devoted to a rare diamond. "If I'd seen you, trust me, I would remember."

Her cheeks flushed, and her heart fluttered. She looked deeper into his eyes, searching for signals of false flattery, but could find only deep sincerity, a wistfulness and regret over the lost twenty-four months that she'd been in the area. Slowly she returned the compliment: "I guess if I'd seen you, I would have remembered. . . ."

"What's this 'I guess' business?" He laughed. "You're not sure at all, are you?"

"No, no, I would remember you. That dimple . . ." She quickly bit back further descriptions that would be considered too forward in an Indian girl meeting a marriage prospect for the first time. She had been coached to act shy and hard to get. But so far all that had gone out the window, and she was talking to him as though she'd known him all her life, and now she couldn't stop. "I'd have remembered your face. You're handsome," she said.

"So you noticed? Now which angle do you think is best?" He presented one profile, then the other, with an exaggerated tilt of his head. Then he gave her a dancing smile.

She couldn't stop laughing. "Stop it. You're too vain," she said. "You must have been a spoiled baby."

He shook his head mischievously. Then he continued with aplomb, "As the only son, I was the rajah of the house, maharajah of the neighborhood. The *hijras* were constantly coming to the house to dance. And the women of the house were rubbing black coal on my forehead and paying the *hijras* to take their evil eye somewhere else."

Nalini laughed at the vision of the ladies rubbing coal on his baby face to drive off the *hijras,* men dressed as women, who claimed they'd cast spells on babies if they didn't get money. Her mother had told her what a nuisance those *hijras* were in Bombay.

"I'm glad you were saved from the *hijrahs,*" Nalini said, wanting to add, *and saved from other brides*. They sat, their glances wrapping them both in magic. She lowered her lashes shyly and gazed up again to find him studying her with a tenderness that spoke of the many things he liked about her.

He rose slowly from his chair, never taking his eyes off her face, and smiled down at her. "I have to do something. I'll be right back. It'll only take a minute," he said, and went back into the store.

She watched him walk toward the front of the store, a muscular man with the easy gait of an athlete. When he disappeared out of sight, she took a forkful of the samosa. The buttery pastry melted in her mouth around a spicy potato-and-pea filling almost as good as her mother's. She knew her mother and father would like him, although on second thought, they might say he wasn't serious enough. But on formal occasions Dilip would be serious. Of course he would. As Showla Aunty and her parents had said, she needed somebody serious to balance her own freewheeling, impulsive personality. A thousand questions about him were crowding her mind. Did he read books? What kind? Did he have other hobbies? Could he cook? What expectations did he have of a wife? What did he think of her working with men? Going to business lunches and dinner with men?

These last questions had been issues with other prospects, who wanted her to continue working to add her salary to the household bank account. But they were threatened by the one-on-one interactions with other men her job required. After the first prospect had told her she'd have to quit, Nalini had made a point of bringing up her job description, using it as a barometer of a prospect's mind-set.

Even the ABCD men were uptight about their wives' professional relationships with other men. One had actually asked her if she would quit and work in a nursery school. "If you work with children, no one will start any scandals about seeing you in restaurants with different men," he'd said. Nalini had fled, drawing the wrath of the matchmaker and her parents, who had told her she should have just nodded along and refused him later through the proper channels. If she continued to act the way she had, word would spread through Indian communities that Nalini was a loose woman. She should always wait. . . .

Suddenly alarmed, she craned her neck, looking for Prince Charming. He couldn't have fled because of anything she said, could he? Had he been testing her and she'd failed? Why had she flirted? Why had she ignored the rules of the first meeting? The man reading *India Weekly* was watching her carefully, as though trying to understand how an Indian girl could have been so bold, joking and laughing. Oh, why had she acted without thinking? Self-consciously, she composed herself, lowered her head, and sat pondering the sudden departure of the most fabulous man she'd met.

Then she tried to flag down the waiter and question him, but he left with some new arrivals' orders without even looking in her direction. Nalini played through her meeting word for word, gaze for gaze. No, she reassured herself, he would be back. He definitely appeared to be interested in her.

Lokesh Mehta walked into his tiny office at the far end of the Spice Bazaar, torn between doing the right thing for his friend Dilip and his own urgent desire to explore the intriguing possibilities in Nalini Gupta. Yesterday, when Dilip called him to "check out the chick Showla Aunty dug up from somewhere" he had reluctantly agreed. Lokesh hadn't meant to impersonate his friend. He was only going to chat with Nalini, then call Dilip. If his report proved good, Dilip would drive over and finish the interview with Nalini.

So Lokesh had walked into the restaurant, expecting another haughty, calculating, and reserved female like so many others Dilip and he had been lined up with. But Nalini was a breath of fresh air, open, friendly, easy to talk to, and a pleasure to look at. He sat at his desk still relishing the spark in her dark brown eyes full of mischief and laughter. They had hit it off right away. They enjoyed the same sense of humor.

Nalini didn't play the usual female games of self-importance, and she certainly didn't look down on him for being an FOB. So many times the ABCDs he'd met let him know immediately that he was a second-class citizen and that he couldn't possibly relate to them, even though they shared the same cultural background.

He picked up the phone to dial Dilip, then set it down. If he told him Nalini was a gem, Dilip would be racing over in his Ferrari to claim her. Lokesh wasn't sure Dilip was worthy of Nalini. Although they had been friends for years, Lokesh was not blind to Dilip's faults. Money was very important to Dilip, sometimes too much so, and his sense of humor could be as nonexistent as real red hair among Indians. But he had promised his friend he would look Nalini over, and Lokesh couldn't lie to Dilip now. He knew that the matchmaker, Showla Aunty, praised Nalini, but Dilip had not believed her. And now Lokesh was hoping Dilip wouldn't believe him either.

As Lokesh reached again for the phone it rang so loudly he grabbed it. "This is *Mataji*," his mother's voice crackled from Bombay. *"Acchi khabbar hai."*

The good news she announced was that a matchmaker had found the "perfect match" for him in Bombay. The prospect was a woman doctor. Not only would she draw a big salary, but her parents were offering a huge dowry in cash, plus twelve gold and diamond jewelry sets and two around-the-world first-class tickets with stays in five-star hotels. "You won't have to worry about keeping your business afloat," his mother enthused. "We've met them and like the doctor and her family. She's pretty and was raised just like you. She'll keep our culture ever present with you. It'll comfort us to know we haven't lost you to America. Your father and I want you to come here as soon as possible for the wedding. I'll tell the matchmaker we have informed you and we accept the offer."

She hung up before he could say anything. *Mataji* had be-

come clever that way. She knew even though he would probably agree to please his parents, he might ask for time to think
it over and change his mind a dozen times, as his cousin had.
Or refuse, as some of his friends had.

Lokesh set the phone down. His mind refused to dwell on
his future bride, lingering instead on Nalini's big, almond-
shaped eyes. He walked in a daze to the restaurant through his
shop, nodding to customers he knew.

A big smile lit up Nalini's face when she saw him, and it
gladdened his heart even as he realized he hadn't called Dilip.
And Nalini still thought he was the match who had been
arranged for her. About to blurt out the truth, he saw her exu-
berance at seeing him again and changed his mind. He wanted
to spend a few more minutes in her warm and sunny company,
letting her laughter sweep away all his nervousness. He would
tell her his real identity soon.

"My apologies. I had to make a phone call. Now where
were we?" Dilip sat back, broad shoulders relaxed, the glass
raised to his perfect mouth.

Relieved that her basic instinct about him had held true,
Nalini studied his lips, then the intricate way his long fingers
circled the glass, before she remembered his question and
blushed. She couldn't say, "You were enchanting me." She
took a sip of water. "What do you do when you're not working? Do you read books?" she finally asked.

His eyes lit up. He grinned. "Yes. I really enjoy books and
movies about the West, with those cowboys rounding up cat-
tle, talking in grunts. I've never been on a horse, but if I had
to cross a mountain, and riding across it was the only way, I
bet I could do it."

As he went on, Nalini was surprised at the intensity with
which he spoke about the Wild West. She had expected him to
be interested in business manuals strategizing on mergers and

acquisitions. Showla Aunty had described him as a serious accountant who spent long hours at work. But obviously, when he left the office, he left his work behind and lost himself in adventure, definitely a plus in her mind.

He ordered dinner for both of them. She watched the way he moved his glass with his strong, long fingers and licked a crumb of samosa off his lip with the tip of his tongue. When the waiter tried to tell him about something happening in the store, he lifted his dark, thick eyebrows and the waiter bowed and fled. The man had style and authority but Nalini wondered why the waiter was trying to get his attention. Well, Dilip was easy to talk to and the waiter clearly found him approachable.

"And what kind of books do you like, Nalini?"

The softness with which he rolled out the three syllables of her name melted her. She sat basking in these new and exciting feelings. Not one prospect, whether found by a matchmaker or by herself, had ever made her feel this way.

She told him about the adventure stories she enjoyed: Patrick O'Brian's high-seas sagas, Dick Francis stories about the world of horse racing. Dilip, too, had read a couple of those novels and they talked animatedly.

When the two waiters brought the food, they had to join up another table to set it all up. The spicy fragrance of cumin and coriander, the rosy color of tandoori chicken, the saffron tint of the vegetable pullau with green peas were pleasing enough. But he had also ordered malai kofta, which were vegetable balls cooked in a creamy curry, the spinach saag panir, potato patties stuffed with peas, a mung dal, two kinds of raitas, pakoras, plain white rice, and six different kinds of parathas.

Watching them set up the feast, Nalini chuckled. "There's enough here to feed at least six more people," she pointed out.

"Or at least three fat ones." He laughed. "I want to make our first meal together as memorable as possible."

Since her move to Virginia, Nalini had missed her mother's

big dinners. Nalini cooked twice a week and ate leftovers in between. But although she wanted to dive right into the feast, another rule of the matchmaking interviews was that the woman should play with her food, acting as though she had sampled far better cooking, even if she had to eat again later. Nalini followed that advice for a few slow forkfuls, but she couldn't continue the charade. Besides, Dilip helped himself to everything with such boyish enthusiasm that she reasoned pretense would make him self-conscious. "I've never eaten here before. The food is excellent," she said.

"I'm glad you like it, because it's one of the best restaurants in town," he said proudly. "Only the finest and freshest ingredients are used in this food."

From his familiarity with the place, wandering into the store and back, nodding at various people, the waiter bringing problems to him, she figured he was a regular here.

When four different types of desserts arrived, they both leaned back in their chairs, letting the rest of the meal settle in. She liked Dilip. Showla Aunty had done well. Her watch reiterated that—they had been together almost three and a half hours without her even thinking once of getting away. But now she had to scrape herself off the chair and leave. The rules required her to thank him graciously and drive away. If he wanted to see her again, he'd have to go through the matchmaker.

"Thank you for the dinner and conversation," she said, carefully avoiding any adjectives, just as she was supposed to do. She reached for her purse.

"Wait," he said. "Will you write down your phone number for me?"

Nalini paused, perplexed at his request. The matchmaker surely had provided him with the basic contact information.

He touched her hand, sending heat roaring through her. "I

want to see your handwriting," he teased, handing her a page from a tiny notebook he pulled from his pocket.

She dug out a pen from her voluminous purse, acutely aware of his gaze upon her. Her hand trembled as she wrote down her name and phone number, printing each letter carefully. Still, her nervousness created an extra "L" in Nalini. She sheepishly struck it out and handed him the paper. This had never happened in her life. It was almost as though she already wanted to display a fuller version of herself to him, tossing in an extra saucy "L." She blushed.

He slid it in his black leather wallet and returned it to his hip pocket. "We'll meet again soon," he said, rising to pull her chair back for her and grazing her shoulders with his fingers.

Forcing herself to move away from his warm and sexy presence, she flung the strap of her purse over her shoulder and looked up at him. From her height of five feet, three inches in heels, he appeared to tower over her — an Indian almost as tall as a Sikh. But thank goodness he didn't cover up that dimple with a beard.

When she got in her car, instead of driving away she circled the Spice Bazaar, waiting to catch a glimpse of him leaving. But a car honked her back into reality, and traffic kept her in her lane all the way home.

That night her starry-eyed, breathless phone reports to her mother, then to Showla Aunty, created celebrations all around. They were thrilled that at last, as they said, she had met her soul mate.

Her mother put her father on the phone and he said, "Nalini, this is very very good news. Dilip's family is highly respected. His father is a heart surgeon and his mother is an anesthesiologist so they have a high standing in any Indian community. They're extremely well off and it'll be such a pleasure to form an alliance with their good family." She listened with greater interest now than she had ever paid to their social commentary on the self-appointed prestige and position doctors occupy in the Indian community. Most of the doctors they knew in Chicago were ridiculously arrogant, braggy and one-dimensional, but Nalini couldn't imagine Dilip's parents being that way. There wasn't one ounce of pretense or arrogance in Dilip.

"Showla Aunty, we know, will be burning the phone lines, firming up the match," her mother said. "You spent three and a half hours with him without any disagreement. You have no complaints. I'm sure he didn't either, so we'll hear from them by tomorrow." Her mother was already setting the wedding date and worrying about how she could have everything in place in two weeks. They wanted close relatives and friends to fly in from Bombay, London, Paris, Singapore, and all over the U.S. "We're inviting at least 500 people," her mother chattered excitedly. "I'll start calling hotels. They're open all night."

Nalini, bursting with happiness, didn't even know how her employers would react to her request for two weeks off in the middle of their busy season but at this point, she didn't care. She had found the perfect man.

Chapter Two

Lokesh still hadn't called Dilip, but decided he would do that from the privacy of his home. As usual, he locked up the shop and drove to his nearby apartment. He quickly tossed out the ads that filled his mailbox, said hello to the old lady who lived on his floor, walked into the dark interior of his apartment, and turned on the lights. It seemed emptier than usual. An image of Nalini waiting for him here after work popped into his head, but he ruthlessly suppressed it. He went to his den, lined with books and framed prints of snowcapped Rockies and palm tree–laden island beaches, and studied the message light flickering red on his answering machine, dreading the news that awaited him.

Finally he punched in and listened. Three messages from his mother, each one more frantic than the last, urged him to buy his airline ticket to Bombay as soon as possible, telling him the matchmaker had reported back that the parents of the doctor, named Jamuna, were thrilled he'd accepted.

"Jamuna had applied for a U.S. visa and it arrived today. That's such an auspicious sign of the joining of our two families. And Lokesh, let me mention to you again how fortunate we are to find Jamuna. She's a respected doctor, and she's so very, very fair-skinned. Just like your father's sister, Reema."

Lokesh threw himself into the closest chair and groaned. His Reema Aunty was almost an albino and highly regarded throughout Bombay for her light skin; her coloring had garnered her a marriage to a wealthy but dark-skinned industrialist. But his Reena Aunty's vanity and meanness to people of darker skin and lesser station in life bothered Lokesh. He thought of Nalini and her chai-with-cream complexion that he wanted to touch with his fingertips and lips. Her black hair with its brown highlights, as though the sun had kissed it, hung like a curtain in his mind to screen his thought from the stranger his mother was so anxious for him to marry. Nalini with the dancing dark, big eyes had chased away all his troubles.

The name, Nalini, kept blowing through his mind like a soft, cool, welcome breeze on a hot day. For the first time in months and months, he had laughed and joked and enjoyed himself with natural ease. Nalini was the first woman who'd asked him if he read books rather than performing the usual dance to figure out his salary, the size of his home, et cetera. He, too, wanted to discover everything about her as a person.

And for the first time in his life, he wanted to share all his hopes and dreams and fears.

But he hadn't shared the truth with her. This fact was out of character for him and made him terribly uneasy. "Let me think in an orderly manner." He began analyzing his new feelings. "It's natural for a man to get nervous before his wedding. So of course he goes out of his way to be charming to a young woman he likes and feels sorry for. That's all it is, that's all I'm doing," he told the palm tree in the painting on his wall.

He had left his aging parents in Bombay and moved to the United States to pursue opportunities in the high-tech field, made quite a bit of money, added to it by investing in a friend's software company, then bought this grocery store because he wanted to do something new and adventurous in a people-oriented business. But he should have researched the market more thoroughly instead of following tips from acquaintances, because within six months two other Indian grocery stores had sprung up in the area. To compete better, he had added the little restaurant that became an instant hit. But overall the store was losing money. He hated to sell Spice Bazaar, because he enjoyed the variety of customers. If he expanded the restaurant he'd do really well, but he didn't want to overextend himself.

Lokesh had been honest about the state of affairs with his parents, which led to their seeking out a bride with a large dowry. His dad had used his mother's dowry to set up an electronics business; his sister's husband had used her dowry to open up a manufacturing plant. Lokesh agreed to the plan because he knew that once the expanded restaurant began making money, he'd be able to return the dowry to his wife. A matchmaker was called upon to arrange a suitable marriage, one that balanced the needs of two honorable families. Love would come later. As would romance. He knew all that.

But now Nalini was filling him with different ideas. Why else would he try to impress her with a feast at the restaurant?

Why else would he take down her phone number? And above all, why would he lie to her, concealing his true identity?

Lokesh tried to get hold of himself. In India people met and fell in love only in the movies. A happy ending never came of such nonsense in real life. His cousin, Govind, had been swept away by romance and married a Parsi woman. But they weren't accepted by the Parsis or the Hindus and had to make a home in New Delhi, where no one knew them. Even when couples married within their subsects of Hinduism, these love marriages did not work out. Lokesh knew there was only one responsible choice to make.

He went to the phone with a measure of regret for what might have been. He would call Dilip and tell him Nalini would make a perfect wife. Lokesh slowly dialed the number and listened to it ring endlessly. He was about to hang up when Dilip picked up the phone, practically panting.

"Lokesh, I only picked up because I saw your phone number on my caller ID. Showla Aunty's been dialing every few minutes. I'm about to unplug the phone for the night."

"Listen, Dilip, I met Nalini. She's a bright, friendly, modern girl. She's nice and attractive." Lokesh deliberately kept his review bland without sacrificing the truth.

"*Aray Yar,* hold on." Dilip switched to Hindi. "Well, if there's nothing objectionable about this girl, I guess it's time to do my duty to my parents and culture. I just don't know how to break the news to my girlfriend."

"Ah," Lokesh said. "That will be messy."

"Yes. Marina will have a difficult time understanding an Indian arranged marriage. Especially since she imagines herself in love with me. Well, we're about to go on vacation to the Florida Keys for three days. Perhaps that will be a good, relaxed setting to tell her."

"Wait, Dilip, don't you want to meet Nalini before you decide?"

"I will after I return from Florida. There's just no time before. Besides, your recommendation is good enough for me. After all, it doesn't really matter *who* I'm marrying, as long as I am getting *married.* Good night, Lokesh, I'll talk to you when I am back."

Lokesh hung up, disquieted by Dilip's attitude. Despite his acceptance of the system, Lokesh also recognized that in arranged marriages, husband and wife often operated as separate entities, coming together as a unit for the children and for their families. Dilip's indifference to his future bride seemed to portend an indifferent marriage. Nalini didn't deserve to be treated that way. Entering an arrangement with Dilip, only to be treated as his formal companion at family and community events, would squeeze the laughter out of her.

The next evening after work, Nalini opened the door to her apartment and ran to pick up the ringing phone. A rich male voice said, "Hello, we met yesterday."

She felt a flush of happiness. "Showla Aunty said you were out of town on business for three days." That news had rankled her and her parents. Although he had accepted the match, his unavailability was inscrutable. Was he playing hard to get, or was he really gone? As her father had said, they had telephones in other cities. He must have a cell phone. "Where are you now?" she asked.

"Can you have dinner with me? I'll explain everything. And oh, I'd rather that your family and the matchmaker not know about it."

"Yes." She glowed, flattered that he wanted some private time with her free from everyone else's scrutiny. This was a real date. She had fantasized about a courtship before marriage, a time to get to know her future husband, a time to relish each delicious moment together, charting a life together.

"Meet me at Peking Duck at Nineteenth and M," he said. "How about an hour from now?"

She agreed. Humming softly, she went to change. After rejecting at least a dozen outfits, she decided on a powder-blue shalwar set. The pink paisley border of the chiffon scarf made a nice edging below her dark hair. She applied a small, round pink bindhi on her forehead, matching lip gloss, and a couple of squirts of jasmine perfume. With her heart beating wildly, she drove to the Chinese restaurant twenty minutes away, in Washington, D.C.

He was waiting for her, a dark, handsome dream with the dimple she longed to touch. His stark white shirt set off his wheat-colored complexion and his eyes glowed with warmth and pleasure. He stood up to pull out the chair for her, and his hand lingered on her shoulder, pressing the chiffon so softly against her neck she trembled and lowered her lashes.

"You look beautiful," he said. "Just as I remembered."

Showla Aunty's advice—*Don't act forward. Act shy,*—stopped Nalini from complimenting him back. She leaned back in her chair and tried to appear calm while her heart fluttered.

"I brought you something," he said, reaching for a package on the floor. "Don't laugh when you see it."

The small package was wrapped in a forest-green foil, the same color as the outfit she had worn yesterday. His detailed observation of her attire thrilled her, and she carefully ripped the paper along the taped edge and opened the box. The sight of a pink lotus bloom surprised her, and when she touched it she burst out laughing. He had brought her a plastic lotus, slightly lopsided, overly stiff in form, overly bright in color.

"Didn't I say don't laugh?" he asked in a mock huff. "I couldn't get the real flower, even though I called at least a dozen florists."

She could barely speak, she was so touched. "You called a

dozen florists to find me a lotus? That is so sweet of you. How did you happen to think of a lotus? Oh, of course . . . but no one's ever given me a lotus before."

"I was hoping they hadn't. Although your name—the beautiful flower of India—seems to call for it. This one is plastic, but there's nothing plastic about you."

"This will keep forever," she said, touching its ugly pink petals that appeared more beautiful to her than the lotuses she'd seen in Florida's Cypress Gardens. So much thought and effort lay wrapped in the bloom, it brought a new glow to her face. "Tell me, what does Dilip mean?" she asked.

She thought he looked uneasy as he began to reply; but then the waiter arrived with enormous red menus stamped in gold Chinese lettering, propped them on their white plates, and began reciting the day's specials. After he left, Lokesh started going through the different items on the menu, recommending more dishes then she could possibly eat.

"You're not trying to fatten me up, are you?" she teased, thinking how lucky she was to have inherited her mother's fast metabolism.

"Of course not. You're pleasantly slim," he said. "Do you cook?"

"Oh, yes. All different kinds of food: Indian, Thai, Italian, French, Vietnamese, Korean, Spanish."

"Stop." He laughed. "I haven't tried to cook anything but vegetarian hamburgers and a few different kinds of dals. You sound like a gourmet. Where did you develop such an interest in international cuisine?"

She was relieved that he cooked. Some of the men she'd met made it clear that they expected her to do all the household chores. "I always thought sampling the food was almost like traveling through countries."

"Right now we're in Peking. Tomorrow we'll go to the

Great Wall of China . . ." he said in the exaggerated tone of shared mock adventure.

"Oh, I've always wanted to do that," Nalini said softly, imagining them traveling together around the world, sharing their thoughts and impressions. "I'm also eager to visit the Taj Mahal."

"It's beautiful in the moonlight. When I was there, I was alone. It's such a spectacular tribute to love that it must be shared. I wish I could've taken you." He got very quiet and took a sip of water.

She watched a mix of emotions cast clouds across his face. Remembering how he'd asked her so wistfully where she'd been hiding all these years, Nalini's heart melted further. She almost dared to say they could go after they were married, but then he spoke.

"We don't have to go overseas. The United States has fabulous places to visit," he said.

"Yes, it does. Like the Grand Canyon, the Rockies, Montana's big sky. Out west's where you want to go, right?" she asked.

"Yes, I haven't had time to travel there yet. But we can go . . ." He glanced away, gulped, and continued, "Well, there's also New Orleans, with jazz and dancing in the streets. I'd like to see the Alamo, Vermont, Capistrano. And from now on I'm going to make time and go, even if it's for a weekend."

She smiled. He wanted to share the world with her, and she wanted to give him a world of happiness.

They ordered egg rolls, shrimp with broccoli, and Szechwan chicken, and continued talking animatedly about places they'd been and places they'd like to see.

Her excitement grew as she imagined traveling with him, combining adventure with the intimacy she longed to have with him, from sharing the same tube of toothpaste to the same pillows. She loved his new pledge to go places, to adopt a new lifestyle full of impromptu weekends, falling asleep in each other's arms in new and exotic places, watching the sun set over different mountains and oceans and prairies.

They ate in dreamy silence, their gazes mingling more heat than the Szechwan chicken.

"I'm so glad I met you," Nalini said, forgetting all the rules in her burst of joy.

He smiled and let his exquisite chocolate-brown gaze linger on her lips, leading her to wild, tumbling thoughts of the passion and tenderness that awaited her on their wedding night. He reached across the table and patted her hand.

"I'm glad I met you, too, Nalini," he said so softly, with such feeling, that even the waiter, who'd arrived with the check, hesitated to interrupt.

At his discreet cough, Nalini said, "I guess it's time to leave."

He paid. "Let's go to the Mall," he said.

"Oh, you like shopping? That's wonderful," she exclaimed.

"Actually I meant the National Mall. Let's just drive around and see the beautiful monuments in the moonlight. Since we can't get to the Taj Mahal tonight." He laughed.

"Where's your flying carpet?" she joked.

"It flew away. I must have used the wrong password," he joked back. "This way to my new mode of transportation. Follow me."

He drove an old white van, which surprised her. With his success she was sure he would be driving a Ferrari or at least a BMW. But of course, the man had too much class to show off. The more she thought about it the more it impressed her. He helped her climb into the van, touching her elbow and spreading heat down to her toes.

The Nation's Capitol was fairly quiet at eleven o'clock. A few limousines sidled along K Street. Without the vendors the sidewalks looked wider, cleaner. Big planters full of blue petunias splashed color under the streetlights. Dilip swung a left on Fifteenth Street and circled around the White House, which was lit up like a beautiful white cake.

They said nothing to each other, but the silence wrapped them as comfortably as a cherished old quilt. The faint smell of Dilip's musky aftershave pleased Nalini's senses as she admired his sculpted profile in the dim light of the van. They passed the tall Washington Monument on the right, rising as a beacon of hope to people from around the world, with the round-domed Jefferson Memorial beyond it and the Lincoln Memorial on the left.

He parked and led her up the marble steps of the Lincoln Memorial, with its strong white marble columns supporting a giant rectangular roof. "Lincoln is my hero; he freed the slaves," he said as they walked around the enormous statue, tracing the cold marble lines of Lincoln's sleeves with their fingers and reading the plaques telling the president's story. They studied the excerpts from the famous Gettysburg address that Lincoln had jotted down on the back of an envelope. "Lincoln's on our five-dollar bill," he said.

She nodded. He hadn't even gone to school here, as she had, but they shared an interest in American history and an admiration for these awesome leaders who made this nation so great. They connected on so many levels that a quiet pleasure lightened Nalini's heart. They stood on the top step, soaking in their grand setting, reveling in having found each other, letting their feelings speak to their hearts.

"Let's sit on the steps for a while," he said.

The marble step felt cool, and a small breeze ruffled her hair. He sat down beside her, their sleeves rustling electricity between them. The fragrance of summer flowers filled the air. But only his musky aftershave sweetened her senses.

He leaned closer, their arms brushing to their elbows, and

they sat that way for a long time. "What do you miss about your old life?" she asked.

"The ocean. In Bombay we walked along the beach and ate bhel puri and drank coconut milk. Juhu Beach, where young people go to try to meet their soul mates. Girls and boys walk in separate groups, pretending not to notice the person they are crazy about. Here, the Reflecting Pool is our ocean. And I'm sitting with you," he said; then he put his arm around her.

She welcomed the sizzle of his skin through the cotton and chiffon. She could feel the strength of his muscles and nervously allowed herself to lean on his shoulder. He drew in his breath, and his arm tightened around her. They sat looking at the stars and the dark water lit up with ripples of light from a distant moon.

His words, their roundabout message about soul mates, gave her the courage to lean toward him, letting her hair graze his face, making her keenly aware of his rustling breath. People walking around them became distant, watery images brushed on a forgotten canvas. For this moment in time, other tourists, work, the rest of the world receded in outgoing waves on a Neptune tide, leaving them alone in a blaze of unspoken desires.

They must have sat that way, bonded, listening to each other's heartbeats, for a gloriously long time before he said, "If we were in an Indian movie, you would now be dancing down these steps and I would burst into song. Then the chorus would appear from somewhere, beating on drums and swinging their plaits."

Nalini laughed. "We'd dance up and down these steps for a few hours. Then you'd mysteriously appear in some other clothes, like a nehru jacket or a khaki safari suit. Big, exotic flowers would start blooming all around." She patted her purse, where she had carefully placed the plastic lotus, her first gift from him that she would always cherish. Remembering the matchmaker's rule to be the first to leave, reluctantly she said, "I have to go to work tomorrow."

He stood up and held out his hand for her, clasping her fingers tenderly in his. They walked hand in hand down the steps and to his van. She lingered for another look at her magical surroundings, wanting to hang on to their night under the stars forever. From now on, no matter how many people walked through it, the Lincoln Memorial would belong only to them.

He was quiet on the ride back to the Chinese restaurant, but she talked about her family, filling him in on how her dad had been recruited by an engineering firm to move to the U.S., and how her mother still talked about the culture shock.

"They sound like nice people," he said.

"I wish you could meet them immediately. Maybe we can fly to Chicago this weekend," Nalini said, seized with the impulse of sharing him with the other two people she loved the most in the world.

"Weekends are crazy at the Spice Bazaar," he said.

"The Spice Bazaar?" She was confused as to why that would affect his schedule.

"Hmmm, yes," he said, clearing his throat. "The owner is a friend, and he asked me to look in on it this weekend while he visits his brother in, umm, California."

"Well, okay. You'll meet my family soon enough," she said. "You'll all get along."

He walked her to her Mercedes in the empty parking lot. "Be careful driving home," he said, and for a minute, as he leaned across to open the door, she thought he would kiss her. In anticipation she lowered her eyes and waited, but he only sighed and touched her cheek with one finger, making unspoken lingering promises, heating desires.

"Can we go out to dinner tomorrow night? We haven't tried Mexican food," he said after a small pause.

She got into her car and rolled the window down. Looking

up at him, his eyes shining in the moonlight like dark pools of chocolate, she sighed. She suddenly realized that he had never explained about the business trip Showla Aunty had mentioned, but Nalini supposed the matchmaker had been wrong. He clearly wanted to pursue the match. "Yes," she agreed to the date. Then, much to her own surprise, she lifted a finger and touched his dimple, one grazing, caressing touch that clamored for further attention, but she pulled back, delighting in the surprised affection flooding his eyes. Then she drove away, relishing the feel of his skin still imprinted on her finger.

In her rearview mirror, she saw him standing beneath the neon sign of the restaurant, touching his chin at the exact spot where her finger had lingered, and her pulse raced wildly.

Chapter Three

*H*e didn't mean to continue the deception. In fact, Lokesh had fully intended to disclose his real identity, but . . . Nalini was a gem. Sitting with her under the stars, feeling the silky strands of her hair brush across his face, hearing her sweet sigh as he leaned closer, he couldn't bear to let her go. Confessing would have ended the evening abruptly, and he had wanted to draw out their time together as long as possible. He despised himself for continuing the pretense, but his desire to be with her was stronger. But he'd have to confess soon.

He picked up the phone and then set it down, chuckling over the remembrance of her shocked expression when she had opened the plastic lotus. He knew, from the way her long-lashed eyes rested on the package, that Nalini had noticed he'd matched the wrapping paper to her outfit from their first meeting. No words were necessary. When their gazes locked, her large, honest brown eyes expressed all he needed to know. And, repeatedly, he saw tenderness for him, and it gladdened his heart.

Lokesh shuffled the papers on his desk, approving spice orders, stopping himself from signing, *Dilip*. He knew the perfect opportunity to spill the truth would have been when Nalini asked the meaning of Dilip. But he had conveniently used the waiter's interruption to change the subject, and such subterfuge bothered him. Not once before in his life had he deceived anyone; doing so now, to someone he truly liked, someone so innocent and open and trusting, really upset him. He picked up the phone, thinking he'd just blurt it out, and if she hung up, he deserved it.

He was interrupted, though, by his capable assistant. "A man is here from a restaurant."

"Send him in." Lokesh dropped the phone back into its cradle and pushed the packages of saffron into a neat pile on his desk. The shipment had just come in, and at the price saffron commanded, he wanted to check each package to make sure it was the real thing.

A tall Sikh entered. "I'm Jagdish Singh," he said, sinking down into the only guest chair. "I own three restaurants, two in Maryland, and the Curry Commotion in Washington, which President Clinton and his staff liked so much. I have yet to find a reliable supplier of the extremely high-quality ingredients we use. I need the freshest possible coriander, chilis, curry leaf, and all the other Asian vegetables, but end up with greens that vary in grade like bird feathers."

"We can guarantee consistent high quality. Have you looked in the store?"

"Yes. This is not my first visit. I've been checking your store against the one we now use. You have better things at better prices. And if you agree to work with us, it'll save us many headaches." He detailed the finances.

Lokesh steepled his hands in silent prayer to Lakshmi, the goddess of wealth. If the Sikh meant what Lokesh thought he meant, business was about to pick up.

"I can personally help you select whatever you need. This saffron just came in." He handed over a bag with the orange strands. "We can go into the store and you can pick out the best of everything."

Jagdish Singh held the saffron package up to the light, squinted at it, then ripped it open to smell it. Lokesh poured water into a small glass and set it on his desk. The restaurateur dropped a few strands in it and stroked his beard while the water turned the rich, dark color of tangerine peel dipped in henna. "Yes, this is real," he acknowledged with a smile. "I'm tired of receiving the dyed blades of grass and other junk passed off as the real thing and at really big prices."

Lokesh nodded. "But that's been going on for centuries all over the world," he said.

"This is how I want things done. I'll sign a yearlong contract I'll bring later. For now, I'll take this entire lot of saffron. My chief cook is already collecting what he needs from your shop. Here's my card. If you receive any new shipments of fresh vegetables or fruits from the tropics that're not on the list, please telephone me."

After the Sikh left, Lokesh allowed himself a victorious pump of his arm. Landing a restaurant account was a huge step in stabilizing the store's revenue. He could count on getting paid on a specific date instead of worrying how many customers were going to walk into his store in a given month.

Still beaming with success, Lokesh took stock of what the chief cook had purchased, and realized they had emptied the whole aisle of lentils. Grinning, he hurried to the phone to put in a rush replacement order. By the time he completed other business the day was over. He glanced at his watch and called out to his assistant, "I'll let you lock up tonight. I'm late for a meeting." Ignoring the curious glances of his employees, he got in his van and drove to Casa Mexico, wishing he had time to change out of his work clothes before meeting Nalini. He had selected Casa Mexico for the same reason he'd picked the Chinese restaurant: Both were in Washington, D.C., where he hoped they wouldn't run into any other Indians. The desi network was as fluid as a river, carrying gossip on its strong currents of exaggeration and speculation. And Nalini needed to be protected from gossip.

"My name is Lokesh," he kept practicing aloud, debating when in the evening to announce it. Saying it immediately upon arrival carried merit at first. As soon as it was in the open he could be relieved and spend the rest of the dinner begging for her mercy. Then the fear that she might simply walk out forever overcame him. The best time to tell her, he decided, was as soon as they finished their meal, so at least she wouldn't leave without a good dinner. But he had to tell her.

Inside the dimly lit restaurant he stood next to a wall covered with large sombreros and red-striped serapes, observing Nalini. She was a vision of beauty in a plum outfit of silk and softness, sitting at a table in the next room, carefully reading the menu. Her dark hair gracefully draped her sweetly shaped face, and her long lashes covered big, brown, almond-shaped eyes he adored. She looked so vulnerable, a girl alone, waiting on destiny. Deep in his heart he knew he was the right man for her, but a glance out the window at her Mercedes brought on doubts.

Ever since he had met her, his heart had been filled with so much tenderness and caring he hadn't stopped for one minute to assess himself properly. He didn't have Dilip's money and probably never would. In the eyes of the world, and certainly those of her family, he was only a shopkeeper. Even with the new account with Jagdish Singh, the Spice Bazaar was still small potatoes. Nobody cared that he had a master's degree in business and had left a good job in high tech. Dilip had position in the Indian community. Lokesh had so much less to offer—was he being fair to Nalini? It was impossible, in any case; they were both promised to others.

She looked up, and when her eyes met his, a smile of genuine pleasure lit her face. He, too, smiled and rushed forward, quickly smoothing down his freshly combed hair for the umpteenth time.

"I apologize for arriving late," he said, sliding into his chair.

"I just got here myself. Things were crazy at work today. Too many things going wrong. Too many meetings. So I'm very glad we're having dinner together this evening." As soon as she said that she looked away, as though she didn't want to appear too eager.

He reached out and held her hand in his, stroking her long pink fingernails, circling the simple but elegant ruby ring on her finger. She blushed, and his heart pounded at the reaction their touch had created. Her fingers grew warm in his, and he longed to hold her in his arms. Their eyes met again, and hers told him so many warm and tender things that no words could convey. He eagerly soaked in those special messages, feeling the intensity escalate in their touch till she withdrew her hand shyly, circling the water glass tightly, but not before he'd seen it tremble.

"I put the lotus in water," she said coyly, knowing he would get the joke.

He did. He laughed. "It'll grow and you'll have many lotuses, just like the one I gave you. They'll all grow and bloom," he said. And they both groaned. They ordered Mexican combination plates and began to talk about India, how Nalini had never been there but wanted to tour Bombay, where her parents grew up. Relaxed, he began talking about how the monsoons drenched rich and poor alike, the traffic, the human commotion, the palm trees on the beach, Bollywood movies, how the Portuguese name, Bombay, given by the Portuguese rulers, was changed by zealot patriots to the city's original ancient name, Mumbai. Nalini asked questions and listened intently to every word he said.

Under her sunny gaze he fingered the dimple on his chin, enjoying the way her eyes followed his every move. He longed to lead her out of the loud and crowded restaurant to a patch of privacy beneath the stars and moon and caress her face, stroke her silky hair, and press his lips on hers.

She looked equally dazed. They barely touched their food. "Showla Aunty sent your resume and it has your address. But I couldn't tell if you live in a house or an apartment. What is it like?"

From the manner in which she asked—slanting her head, throwing in a sigh—he could feel the urgency behind her question. She wanted to be alone with him as much as he wanted to be alone with her. He gave her a deep, deep look that said, *Yes, I, too, want you in my arms;* then he summoned the waiter. After he paid, they walked out to her car.

"I don't want to appear too forward, Dilip, but can we go somewhere to talk? Maybe a quiet coffee shop?" Nalini asked.

He longed to say yes, but her calling him Dilip had pulled him back into the cesspool of his dilemma.

"I, too, would like to talk. There's something important I must tell you. Dilip . . ."

When he paused, Nalini said, "Oh, I looked it up on the Internet. It means 'king.' "

And just like that, the opportunity to confess was gone. Nalini looked so trusting and innocent, Lokesh could not bear to disillusion her. She placed her delicate hand on his arm, and he nearly jumped from the contact. He craved to take her to his small apartment and adore her with more than his eyes. But the more honorable side of him protested such behavior. She thought he was Dilip. And Lokesh . . . well, he, too, had an expectant bride waiting for him.

"Nalini, my dear, it's getting late. Why don't I meet you for lunch tomorrow at noon at Thai Emporium? There's a serious subject we have to discuss."

She smiled and played with her hair and looked at her left hand, as though imagining it with a ring. When she drove away he felt abandoned in a world totally empty of laughter and happiness. And despite himself he began dreaming of buying her a ring, a gold band designed with a lotus set in diamonds.

Visions of Dilip formally proposing to her at lunch had Nalini on cloud nine the next day. Even her coworkers commented on her glow.

As Dilip had requested, Nalini had kept their dinner dates a secret from her parents, making excuses about working late, shopping, seeing friends. And she was relieved not to be hounded with questions about those meetings. Already her mother had called several times about wedding details, the Mandap, or canopy, she'd rented for the ceremony, the garland of red roses that were ordered. Showla Aunty was calling Dilip's parents on a daily basis for their input. They had discussed the dowry. It surprised her that Dilip wanted a dowry, but she decided the parents were asking for it, not Dilip. Her parents had set aside a fund for it practically since the minute of her birth, so that request could be met easily.

"I leave it all to you, Mummy," she had said compliantly, knowing her mother's organizational and party-giving talents, and to offset the little bit of guilt at keeping the exact nature of Dilip's courtship from her parents. She loved that Dilip was courting her personally, and the way he couldn't wait to see her, even inviting her to lunch. She didn't doubt for one minute the fact that he wanted to propose to her in person, even though their match had been made in the conventional way. Dilip was so romantic and so much fun. She could hardly wait to see him. In fact, she had left work at eleven o'clock to get her nails done. Her hands should be polished and elegant to complement the ring Dilip would give her. In the Indian culture the jewelry was selected by the groom's family. But Dilip was taking charge, and Nalini didn't doubt for one minute that he, not his parents, was selecting the ring. It would reflect his taste and symbolize the time he spent to please her, and she was delighted by that idea.

When he walked into the restaurant he smiled, but in a vague manner. He looked tired, with big circles under his eyes and hair standing up over his ears, and overall his spirit appeared as rumpled as grass trodden by horses. He patted her hand in a distracted manner; then he held it tight, as though he never wanted to let go, and her heart hammered with the same sentiment. He leaned forward, lifted her hand to his lips, and kissed it, sending electric shocks of excitement through her. Then he withdrew his hand and asked her solemnly about work. They ordered their meal and talked about Thailand. Each of them wanted to travel there, and to Japan and Hong Kong. She teased, "You want to go to Japan so you can be with the geisha girls."

He laughed. Then he got extremely quiet, his mood shifting like a sunny sky turning dark and cloudy, casting his face in mysterious shadows.

"What is it?" she asked, suddenly agitated.

"I like you very very much," he said sincerely. "You make me happy. You're bright, funny, and sincere." He looked sad. "We've had a good time, don't you think? What do you think about me?"

His expression surprised her. Not one negative thing bristled between them. They got along in so many ways. Their relationship had blossomed from the first meeting. So why the uncertainty? Maybe he thought she didn't like him as much as he liked her. But she loved him. Knowing it was too soon to declare herself in such a forward manner, she said, "I like you very, very much." She reached across the table to place her hand over his, feeling the warmth gathering below her palm. "I've enjoyed every minute with you. . . ." She squeezed his hand. "I think you're wonderful."

He sighed.

She loved the way he didn't mind being reassured. He was so genuine. So unlike those Indian men who never let anyone see their real selves, always in charge, always arrogantly confident of their charms. "You're very thoughtful and considerate. You like adventure, the West, exploring different cultures through their food. I can hardly wait to go to Bombay. You can help me discover my heritage. I feel strongly that children should know and understand the backgrounds of their families."

He dropped his fork. She set hers down and took a sip of water. An unusual awkwardness descended, causing her to squirm. The word *children* must have taken him aback. Her mother always said men were intimidated by the responsibilities entailed in raising a family. "Your own father got so nervous," she'd say, "he spilled his tea when I told him I was pregnant." Why had that slipped out about children?

"Okay, we don't have to rush off to India. I only get two weeks' vacation, and that will be . . . Oh, I've already asked my boss. He was reluctant—said it was a busy time now—but when he heard the reason . . . Oh, they're so happy I'm getting married."

He didn't appear to be listening to her. Head lowered, he sat a dreadfully unknown thousand miles away. Last evening he had said he liked her, but now his forehead was creased, his eyes veiled. She began to panic that he had changed his mind.

"Showla Aunty is talking to your parents. You know that. We don't have to worry about any details. My mother is very organized. You will get along very well with her. She worked as a bookkeeper once and thinks very highly of accountants. Dilip, they can't wait to meet you next week. She loves the name Dilip. So do I."

"How about Lokesh?"

His barely audible voice startled her. "Pardon?" she said. "What did you say?"

"Lokesh," he said loudly. "Lokesh," he repeated even more loudly. "How do you like the name Lokesh?"

"It's not so bad." Bemused by this change in subject and wondering if that was the name he had always thought of bestowing on his son, she quickly added, "It has a nice ring to it."

He reached for his pocket and her heart missed a beat in anticipated relief. She spread her hand out on the white tablecloth beside her white plate, letting her freshly done nails shine a feminine, pink invitation.

He pulled out a tissue and dabbed his forehead with it, and she noticed the perspiration beading back up again. She withdrew her hands back into her lap to twist the napkin. Embarrassed by her eagerness Nalini asked, "Why do you like the name Lokesh?"

"Because it's mine." His chin shot up.

She laughed. "You obviously don't like Dilip."

"At this very moment I don't."

Confused but determined to salvage the situation, she plunged forward with conversation. "Oh, everybody has ideas about their names. I went through a phase where I didn't like mine. I must have been about ten, and the other kids in my class were mispronouncing it all the time. It made me feel so different from all the blond kids. I wished my name had been something that crosses cultures, like Shielah, or Gita. But my parents said they wanted to preserve my Hindu heritage with a name that couldn't be mistaken for anything else but Indian. Now I'm proud of my name, and since you gave me the lotus it's taken on new importance, a romantic nuance in those three syllables. So one day you'll like your name, Dilip." She pronounced it in the dreamy manner she reserved for her private nightly fantasies about him.

But his eyes didn't sparkle with her sexy rendition of his name. He dabbed at his forehead with more tissues. Then he blurted out something she couldn't understand.

"Slow down; what is it, Dilip?"

"Lokesh," he repeated. "My name is Lokesh Mehta. I am not who you think I am. My apologies. I'm very sorry I didn't tell you right away. My reasons are too difficult to explain. I was selfish. I wanted to be with you and hear your laughter and see your beautiful face and be with you. I couldn't help it. I haven't slept well since we met because my heart is with you and my duty is elsewhere."

She strained to understand his words. This handsome man, the one she thought was her soul mate, was not Dilip? Was that what he was saying? Confusion and alarm twisted her stomach. "I don't understand," she stammered. "Showla Aunty arranged my meeting with you . . . maybe she got your name wrong . . . maybe she wrote it down wrong . . . maybe my mother and I misunderstood. . . ."

"Unfortunately no error of that nature was made."

"Then how is it that you and I are —"

"You must forgive me for this deception. There's no one responsible for this except myself. Dilip is a good friend of mine. He asked me to . . . well, to meet you on his behalf, and I did. But before I could introduce myself properly you assumed I was him. And I found you so beautiful and so intriguing I forgot . . . No, that is a lie. I wanted to keep talking to you. I kept thinking of you and postponed the honorable thing. I'm deeply apologetic."

Nothing made sense. Waves of anger rocked her even as she tried to think through this mess. If this wasn't Dilip, why had he agreed to marry her? Showla Aunty had spoken to him and his parents. Wasn't that what she'd said? Or was she also playing some stupid game? Matchmakers were known to stop at nothing to achieve success. As one of her bitterly divorced cousins said, they were always in search of victims to bring into the system of arranged marriages. She had even heard of marriages where the bride discovered the groom was incapable of pleasing a woman, so a friend or a brother was recruited to consummate the marriage. Outraged at such a plot, Nalini shuddered.

She didn't want an arrangement of that sort. She wanted love, laughter, romance, and all those lovemaking rituals learned together with a husband who adored her. But Dilip hadn't even shown up. "Is Dilip gay?" she asked bluntly. "Tell me." Her voice quavered.

Shock widened Lokesh's eyes. He coughed.

"Tell me, please," she begged. "Is it the story of a man who cannot please a woman, who recruits a friend?"

He began laughing, a surprised little burst, then with genuine merriment. "No, he's not a homosexual."

"Then why did he ask you to meet me first?" she demanded.

"He was tired of matchmakers introducing him to unsuitable girls. He had meetings to attend, a million-dollar business to run. Dilip is a very busy man."

"Too busy for a meeting with a future wife," she said bitterly, twisting the napkin.

"Oh, he'll meet with you. There's plenty of time for that." Lokesh's voice sank.

"Of course I'll meet Dilip. And you . . . you go around

doing this for all your friends? Looking over prospective matches for them? Is this some kind of service you run, or do you just enjoy making women miserable?" Her sharp tone barely conveyed the outrage she felt toward the man sitting across from her. "How dare you do this to me?"

His hand flew out to cover hers and she untangled it. Flinging her hands under the table, out of reach, she said, "I'm stunned. As for there being plenty of time, there isn't. Our marriage plans are going forward. My mother is looking into hotels; she's probably booked one today, put down a large deposit. My parents have talked to Dilip's parents in detail. Oh, how could I have overlooked the fact that you said your parents lived in Bombay? Showla Aunty had said they lived in L.A. My marriage to Dilip is public knowledge now. People all over the world are hearing the news from both families and buying airline tickets. I feel ill."

"Please accept my apology."

"You deceived me. For such a straightforward-acting and -talking man you led me to believe you and I, well, that you and I . . ." Her own foolishness and this man's sordid deception were choking back whatever words she could find to convey her anger.

"I didn't deceive you about my feelings for you. You and I have a bond. We're made for each other, Nalini. And that's the only excuse I have for carrying on this imposture for as long as I have."

Her laughter was low and bitter. "Oh, you know how to say all the right things to please a woman without ever revealing who you are. Do you work with Dilip?"

"No, I own the Spice Bazaar. Dilip and I became friends when I was new in this country."

"And all those silly film stories from Bollywood are still so fresh in your mind you're actually acting one out. Next thing you know you'll kidnap Dilip and ask for a ransom in kisses."

He laughed then. For the first time since he'd sat down opposite her, he laughed and couldn't stop. She supposed it was ridiculous, the whole situation a farce that wouldn't be believable on film. Yet she couldn't find it in her to see the humor.

Her eyes grew moist. "I misplaced my trust in you. You shouldn't have misled me," she said, picking up her purse.

"Wait. Let's start all over again. Please forgive me."

Forgive him for making her believe she'd finally met her soul mate? Forgive him for making her believe the matchmaker had at last succeeded? She stood up so suddenly the small table rattled. Holding her head up high against the threatening tears, she fled.

Chapter Four

As the restaurant door closed behind Nalini, Lokesh dropped his head into his hands. He knew his confession would upset her, but he had underestimated his own agony over her stunned reaction. Watching her sweet face crumble, her eyes moisten, her chin go up, drove home the cruel truth that he had lost Nalini's affection, if he had ever had it in the first place. He went over everything she'd said, word for word, torturing himself. *Of course I'll meet the real Dilip,* she'd said. And Dilip, Lokesh knew, could turn on the charm, bestow upon her solid-gold trinkets that would make his plastic lotus seem cheap and graceless. Why had he acted so impulsively? Why did he see her again after the first meeting? Why had he meddled in the arrangement of her marriage?

Totally distraught, Lokesh sat listless at the restaurant until the waiter finally suggested in a mild way that they needed the table for someone else. Tipping him extra, Lokesh left wishing he could chase after Nalini. But the memory of her angry eyes and her justifiably haughty departure cautioned him against intruding in her life more than he already had. He wanted desperately to protect her from a cold marriage with Dilip, but no solution presented itself.

At home the message light blinked red, and he punched it. His mother's voice, filled with excitement, told him, "Lokesh, Jamuna's family wants to know where you want to go on your honeymoon. They've heard of Niagara Falls and are eager to supply all tickets and accommodations. They want to know if they should make the arrangements. Call me at once."

Lokesh could barely focus. A good woman waited somewhere in Bombay to marry him, and she was the last thing on his mind. How had he sunk to this depth? Was his treatment of Jamuna any better than Dilip's of Nalini?

On his kitchen counter lay a stack of papers covered with small drawings of the lotus ring he had fantasized about presenting to Nalini. Insanity could be the only reason for such childish behavior. As a grown Indian man he had to do the right thing and fulfill his obligations to his family. He crumpled up the papers and tossed them into the garbage. Never again in his life could he look at a lotus anywhere—in a painting, on fabric, in a pond—without remembering Nalini's lovely face. He wished he could erase the past few days, but Nalini's countenance, voice, and laughter teased his body and mind unmercifully.

For the next two days Nalini moved in a cloud of misery, impatiently waiting to meet the real Dilip and fuming over the impostor. She desperately wanted to tell her parents what had happened, but afraid of their reaction were she to halt the wedding preparations. The only thing she could do now was to meet Dilip as soon as possible and hope he was an acceptable groom. As for Lokesh . . . well, she refused to waste another thought on him.

But her mother could still sense that something was wrong. "Are you okay, Nalini? You sound so quiet," she said during one of their many phone conversations.

She clutched back her tears and said, "I'm just nervous, Mummy."

"It's only natural. Dilip will be back from his trip tomorrow and he'll call the minute he gets in. He's such a busy boy, working so hard to ensure a good life for you two. So really, there is nothing to fret about." Then her mother switched to the next wedding detail.

Nalini went to bed early, trying to banish images of Lokesh's dazzling smile; they kept popping up even as she hated him for leading her on. When the phone rang, she didn't want to pick up, but changed her mind at the sound of the real Dilip's voice on her answering machine. "Hello, I'm here," she said quietly.

"I'm so sorry I had to go to Boston on business before getting a chance to meet you. And then I had one appointment after another. I couldn't even call. But I was thinking about you every minute. I'm most eager to finally meet you. How about dinner tomorrow night?"

She let his apologies soothe her anger. As a businesswoman she understood the pressures. "Where would you like to meet?" she asked formally.

"How about the Peacock Restaurant? At seven? We can get to know each other at last. Again, sorry about this delay. I've been on pins and needles to see how we will suit."

She hung up slowly, unsure of what to expect. Dilip sounded polite and charming enough, but then, so had Lokesh.

When Dilip hung up, he sighed with relief. Nalini sounded sweet and uncomplicated, exactly what he wanted in a wife.

He was looking for a pliable helpmate, one who would not make life unpleasant for him were she to find out the truth— that he had a girlfriend. For it had become very clear to Dilip in Florida that he was not ready to give up Marina. His American girlfriend was sensual and free in a way that no Indian could ever be. So while he resigned himself to marrying an Indian girl, he refused to deny himself the excitement he shared with Marina.

Of course, the situation was delicate. He had tried to bring up the subject of his familial obligations, and Marina had crinkled up her nose in incomprehension. "But, Dilip," she had said, "you're an American now. Surely you can choose your own wife." And from her coquettish tone of voice, he knew she expected to be that choice.

Well, if he handled the situation properly, Dilip would have both the bride his parents wanted, and the woman he desired in his bed. He dialed Lokesh. "*Yar,* I'm following your recommendation. Nalini and I will meet tomorrow. And Marina . . . well . . ."

"What of Marina? Was she upset about the marriage? Will she cause trouble for Nalini?" Lokesh's questions came like bullets.

"No, no. Nothing to worry about, my friend. I have . . ." Dilip sighed. "I have not told her yet about Nalini. Marina . . . she is a treasure. She's wonderful, the woman of any man's dreams. We had a wonderful three days in the Florida Keys, and I do not plan to let her go."

Dilip thought he heard a swear word. Then the phone went dead. He redialed. "Lokesh, we got cut off. I want you to plan on attending my wedding."

"I don't have time to talk now," Lokesh said, and hung up.

Dilip stood in his spacious apartment overlooking Rock Creek Park in Northwest Washington and puzzled over his friend's lack of interest. But then he suspected that Lokesh was worried about his business. He could help Lokesh by extending him a personal loan or sending him customers, but wondered if his friend's pride would force him to refuse the help. Well, he would wait until Lokesh asked directly for help, rather than offend him with an unsolicited offer. Meanwhile, he had a neglected betrothed to charm.

He called the Peacock Restaurant and reserved the best booth. An extra seventy dollars ensured that an additional special request would be executed exactly to Dilip's specifications.

Then Dilip returned to the bedroom, where Marina lay in a black teddy, her blond hair spread out like a golden fan on the pillow. The peach satin sheets and her black teddy highlighted her beautiful creamy white skin, and he went to her with the fervor of a man finding an oasis in a desert.

Nalini, wrapped in a purple sari with a pink border and a matching purple blouse, arrived at the Peacock Restaurant the next evening, nervous about meeting the man whose proposal she had been tricked into accepting. Remembering her dates with Lokesh, she sighed, still trying to erase him from her memory. Inside the restaurant the maître d' stepped forward, and as soon as Nalini gave him her name he bowed. "*Sahib* is waiting, madam; follow me please," he said. The restaurant's pale blue walls were decorated with large murals of peacocks dancing in gardens bursting with red roses. Crisp white linens covered the tables, with centerpieces of vases of fresh red roses and ferns. Melodious Indian music played softly in the background.

They walked past several tables with chattering American diners. From a distant corner, a young but gray-haired, hawk-nosed man watched her curiously, and her heart sank. But the maître d' didn't stop at that table, and she thankfully followed him into the back room. With a flourish he lifted a curtain of long strands of hanging blue beads. "*Sahib,* your lady is here," he said with a bow.

With her heart beating wildly she stepped into the private alcove. Dilip, in an exquisitely cut blue suit, stood up to greet her. He was good-looking in a different way from Lokesh. Dilip wasn't quite as tall or muscular, and his hair was a lighter shade of brown. His longer face and slim eyebrows over wire-rimmed glasses exuded a sophistication and intelligence that impressed her. After all, he was very successful, and his appearance showed every bit of it.

"Nalini, I've thought about nothing but you for three days and nights," he said. "You're even more beautiful than I imagined."

She sat down, a little surprised by his obvious interest. Wasn't this the same man who had sent his friend to scout her out in advance for him?

"How was your trip to Boston?" she asked, not wanting to start off the evening with an immediate confrontation.

His eyes grew distant, as though his trip to Boston didn't exist in his memory at all. "What?" he asked.

"Boston, your business trip?"

"Fine. Just fine."

"Were you trapped in meetings the whole time, or were you able to go out and walk around Beacon Hill and sightsee?"

This time he focused, as though remembering that grueling trip. "I was trapped. Meetings went from breakfast through late dinner. I only saw the inside of the hotel. I could have been anywhere from Boston to Wisconsin or home here in Washington."

She wondered where he'd gotten his fresh tan being indoors all day, then decided he probably went to a tanning booth to get that even, reddish complexion.

"Now, Nalini, tell me about *your* job."

Pleased at his interest, she began telling him about her marketing plan for a new skillet that worked like a wok. He listened quietly. When she finished he said nothing. He didn't even make a joke, as Lokesh might have. . . . But why was she even thinking of that impostor? Everyone agreed she needed somebody serious to balance her levity, and Dilip had that quality in spades. She continued, "I'm really happy with my job. When I first came here I wasn't certain about the decision, but the company where I really wanted to work turned me down."

She proceeded to tell him the story she'd told Lokesh about the interviewer. Dilip nodded. She thought of joking about being an ABCD but didn't. After all, he was one, too. She waited for him to comment, to make up a Sanskrit saying as Lokesh had, anything to make her feel better, but Dilip said nothing. She wondered if he felt as awkward as she did.

The waiter arrived with a variety of spicy starters—vegetable pakoras, papadums, samosas—and they ate quietly for a few minutes. The red-and-white floral centerpiece at their table caught her attention. "Such beautiful roses and baby's breath," she said.

"Yes. When we marry, we'll have a big garden, and you can tell the gardener to grow all the flowers you like," he promised.

She smiled, thinking how much she would enjoy looking out at the colorful flower beds from the windows. She started to feel better about the match. Dilip was attractive, and she appreciated his direct discussion of their future. "Do you have a house?" she asked.

"No, I'm in a large apartment over in Rock Creek. But I would like us to live in a house, which you can choose for us. I'll have a realtor take you around. Just make sure it's in a desirable neighborhood, and that it's big, with large downstairs rooms for entertaining and at least six bedrooms."

At least he wasn't controlling, like other Indian men who

would insist on selecting the house. "We don't need six bedrooms. It's too much to take care of," she said. "Three will be fine."

"Oh, Nalini, you won't have to lift a finger. We'll hire a maid and a cook or a combination housekeeper and cook. We need six bedrooms so when our parents visit they have their own wing. And then, of course, when we start having children . . ."

Yes, her grandfather needed great-grandchildren! She wondered how many children Dilip wanted to have, but didn't feel it was the right time to ask. Now, if she were talking to Lokesh, she could make a joke by saying, *If we have two sets of twins we can fill the house fast,* and then Lokesh would joke back that quadruplets were the best way to go.

"I think we'll have beautiful children if they look like you," Dilip said, interrupting Nalini's thoughts and making her blush. "I just remembered a business call I must make, so please excuse me."

"Sorry I'm late calling," he said into his cell phone.

Then he listened for the longest time, causing Nalini to wonder if somebody was filling him in on a problem. His dark brown eyes shone as if he thrived on the challenge of smoothing over a crisis. As a career woman, she understood the drive and energy required in doing a job well, and admired Dilip for it.

When he hung up after setting up a meeting time with his associate, his face lit with an anticipatory smile. It faded as Dilip returned his attention to Nalini. "Sorry. One of my accountants is a little long-winded. She explains everything methodically, from A to Z." He paused for a sip of water. "When you and I are married, you're going to find I'm gone many evenings and sometimes on weekends, too. Running the three companies takes a lot of time and energy. As a marketing executive, you're used to that, aren't you?"

She nodded, pleased that he treated her as a peer. "Yes, when we're on a special project sometimes I have to work late. Sometimes we have to meet clients for lunch or dinner," she said, waiting for his reaction. If he wanted her to quit or flinched at her entertaining for business, she couldn't agree to marry him.

The waiter brought several dishes and set up a feast, reminding Nalini of her dinners with Lokesh. Certainly he and his buddy, Dilip, were the same in this, at least. Neither asked her what she wanted to order, but that didn't faze her. She didn't mind the man taking charge here, as long as he allowed her freedom elsewhere.

When the waiters left, Dilip said, "Nalini, you were talking about your job. I understand a lot of business is conducted over meals. I wouldn't want you to lose a client or be left out of the loop with your boss because you refuse to have lunch with them. Nor do I object to your working late to get your job done. Now, would you like some tandoori chicken?"

With tremendous relief she took a helping and reached for a paratha. Dilip was really a good match. He didn't expect her to waste her education by giving up her career. And he hadn't even asked how well she cooked, just simply informed her that a hired cook and maid would do the work. He knew how to respect and take care of his wife. Then why didn't she feel more excited?

"I can't believe Showla Aunty did so well," he said, smiling at her fondly. "And Lokesh was totally correct in his report about you. He called you smart, charming, pretty. And he's right."

She slowly ripped a piece of the paratha and chewed it, thinking of Lokesh and how he'd fooled her. Trying not to sound as angry as she felt, she asked, "Tell me, why did you send Lokesh in your place?"

He chuckled. "I met so many inappropriate women through

matchmakers, and my schedule is so hectic. Since Lokesh had to be at the Spice Bazaar anyway, I thought it would be an easy enough thing for him to first make sure you were suitable wife material." He polished off the last forkful of tandoori chicken on his plate, helped himself to some rice that he set on one side of his plate, and put the curries on the other; then he mixed the two carefully.

Nalini was bothered by this attitude, although she supposed it did make good sense for him to try to cut the fat out of his schedule. But still . . . She opened her mouth to ask how many meetings it was to have taken Lokesh to form an opinion on her, then quickly took another morsel, changing her mind. Obviously he had decided on his own to keep seeing her, just as he said. Dilip hadn't asked him to. Her heart beat wildly. Despite her anger, she couldn't contain her curiosity about Lokesh. "Well, since you trusted him to meet me first, tell me about this guy," she said in a casual conversational tone.

"He's a decent, hardworking guy . . . a little staid. But he's a good friend. His shop isn't doing as well as he thought, because he won't do what other merchants do."

Staid? Words in defense of Lokesh rose up like soldiers prepared to fight. But Nalini took a deep breath and reached for the bread basket. She could eat these fresh breads forever, just as she could talk to Lokesh forever, without ever getting bored. "What do other merchants do?" she asked, helping herself to a naan.

"Well, you know they can play with quality—take saffron, for example—and pass off inferior goods for more money. Or they confuse the shopper by posting sale signs on rice bags, saying three for so many dollars, but essentially they're charging more. It's standard practice but Lokesh won't do it." Dilip dipped a piece of tandoori chicken in yogurt raita and ate it. Then he sampled other curries on his plate. "You must try this saag panir," he urged her.

She took a spoonful of the spinach-and-cheese curry from the serving dish. Dilip's description of Lokesh surprised her. After his masquerade she'd decided Lokesh was a flimflam man, but now she was hearing about his honesty, though Dilip, the astute businessman, obviously considered it stupidity. Again she wanted to defend Lokesh, but calmed herself down. A good man didn't deceive customers, but good men didn't always finish first. Suddenly concerned about Lokesh, she asked, "If his shop fails, what will Lokesh do?"

"If he had accounting skills, I'd hire him. But he can always go back to working for a tech company as a software expert. It was silly of him to give up that great career and buy that shop," Dilip said, looking at her a little curiously. "I imagine you're asking about him because I sent him to meet you first?"

"Of course. And also because he's the only person we have in common," she said easily. But a perplexing tenderness settled in her heart even as she still hated Lokesh for leading her on. "This food is wonderful. Thank you, but now I have to get home," she said.

"Wait, our dessert hasn't arrived." Dilip stood up and rattled the beaded curtain in precise, tight movements, so it made a distinctive *rap, rap, rap* sound.

Nalini laughed, watching Dilip wave to the waiter in an authoritative way that was almost comical in its exaggeration. Not one but *two* waiters and the maître d' came running, "Sir, how can we please you, sir?" He didn't blink an eye at their deferential treatment. A man in command, he simply returned to his seat and swept a hand over the table. The two waiters began clearing the table immediately, almost falling over each other. She chuckled again. Next he waggled his eyebrows at the maître d', who turned and fled. Nalini thought back to Lokesh's quiet authority as he waved off the waiter at their first dinner. But now that she knew he owned the Spice Bazaar, she refused to let it impress her as much as it had then.

"Who owns this restaurant?" she asked Dilip, half expecting him to announce ownership.

"I don't know. An idiot, probably. The service was slow," he said.

She didn't think so. The waiters were respectful of the privacy of the beaded booth. But Dilip was looking at his watch again. She lowered her head. Perhaps he found her company tedious. After all, they hadn't laughed or joked as she and Lokesh did. Despite all of that she was willing to accept the match. Dilip would make a fine husband. And love would come after the marriage. Dilip was a man she could love in time — unlike that impostor, Lokesh.

The tinkle of music interrupted her thoughts. The beads rattled as the curtain parted, and the maître d' stood with head bowed, arms outstretched, hands holding a large filigree silver-covered dish. A musician played the harmonica while another accompanied on the flute. "Allow me, sir," the maître d' said, placing the dish on the table.

"Dismissed," Dilip sang out, and they edged away backward, getting enmeshed in the beads swinging from their touch before finally jerkily disentangling themselves.

Nalini couldn't quite stifle her laughter.

"They're acting like monkeys," Dilip harrumphed.

"I'm too full for dessert. I have to get home. Thanks for dinner," she told him.

"Wait, you've got to have some. I insist. I ordered it specially for you." He whisked off the cover of the dish to reveal dozens of traditional sweets such as her mother made, round, diamond shaped, oval, with different flavors of creamy almond, pistachio, cashew, and cardamom. They were arranged in a circle around a single red rose.

"Beautiful." She sighed, touching the soft petals of the rose.

"It's in full bloom, as our marriage will be, Nalini."

She smiled wistfully at his romantic analogy. Yes, she

would like that. Together they would make their marriage
bloom. They shared the same ideas about work, success, and
raising a family in a house full of love and a garden full of
flowers. "I'll taste one dessert and then I really must head
home," she told him, picking up a pistachio sweet and biting
into its soft green sweetness.

"Wait, Nalini. Let's eat the sweets carefully. It's important
to notice the shape and consistency. That's how I like to eat
dessert, savoring every bite. Don't rush. Don't bite hard."

He picked one up. She followed suit. They ate several. She
enjoyed the ritual, pleased to be connecting with her future
husband.

And then she picked one up that seemed heavier than the
others. She rolled it around in her fingers and looked at it carefully. Its shape was rougher. It bulged. Afraid the almond in it
hadn't been shelled, she broke it apart. And there, gleaming
brilliantly, lay a large diamond ring. It fell from her fingers to
the plate with a sharp clunk.

"You can wear it now. I'd like to see how it looks on your
finger," he said proudly. "Go on, put it on."

Surprised beyond belief, she wiped it with her napkin, then
slipped it on, letting the sparks from it bounce off the crystal
glasses.

"You and I are now engaged," he said matter-of-factly. "We
can inform our parents and Showla Aunty that I've given you
the ring."

She didn't know how to respond. It was a far grander diamond than she had ever expected to receive, yet she didn't feel
the joy she'd always thought she would at wearing an engagement ring. And now she didn't know if she should leave as
she'd announced or wait. The rules didn't cover this. She finally said, "It's a beautiful ring. I'll enjoy showing it off."

He chuckled approvingly.

After an awkward silence, she said, "Well, it's getting late. . . ."

"I'll escort you to your car."

Nalini waited for him to suggest another date, but when he didn't she asked, "When will we meet again?"

He looked blank for a second, then said, "Oh, I'd like nothing better than to have dinner with you again tomorrow. It's hectic at work, but we'll just have to make time for each other. Are you free to meet me here? Same time?"

Wanting to please, she acquiesced easily. "I'd love to have dinner with you tomorrow, Dilip."

"There's my Ferrari over there; I'm assuming this is your Mercedes." He walked her to the only other expensive car within sight and looked carefully at it. "Hmm . . . this is five years old. I'll get you the latest model after we're married. Nalini, the thought of meeting you for dinner tomorrow night will keep me in a good mood all day. I'll try to wrap everything up as close to six as possible. Here's what we'll do . . . I'll call you sixish at your apartment just to make sure nothing's come up. Okay?"

"That's fine," she said, opening her car door, wondering if he was going to hug her or kiss her. After all, they *were* engaged now. She waited for a couple of moments, then got in the car, rolled down the window, and looked up at him. Suddenly she noticed the chin she was staring at didn't have a dimple. The face looking at her showed impatience instead of the dreamy desire that Lokesh always projected. *Oh, Lokesh, Lokesh,* her heart pounded.

"I can hardly wait to see you tomorrow. Drive carefully," he said, turning away toward his car. "Be sure and let everyone know we're now engaged."

Driving home, Nalini kept glancing at her ring, delighting in its spark but still oddly unsatisfied. She shook off the feeling. A major decision had been made. She sighed with relief.

She no longer needed to face the apprehension and humiliation of meeting new prospects. Dilip was so decisive. He didn't waste a minute. He found her attractive and thought she was the perfect wife for him. As she got home and unlocked her door, a strange sense of deficiency nagged at her. Dilip had made no attempt to hold her hand or to touch her. In fact, he hadn't even slipped the ring on her finger. Nalini's mind filled with Lokesh and his warm, tender eyes and how he found so many ways of brushing her arm, patting her hand, how he'd sensuously fingered his dimple after she touched it, how they could talk forever, how they shared so many interests. She fought the improper desire to call him and tell him about her engagement.

To banish him from her thoughts, she deliberately went to the phone to tell her parents the good news. As her mother raved, Nalini's spirits lifted. Her father got on the phone, and the happiness in his voice pleased her. They were ecstatic about Dilip's plans for buying a big house, hiring help, planting the garden, buying the new car. They wanted all that for her and she did, too.

"Showla Aunty is the best matchmaker. I'll call her immediately to tell her that Dilip gave you a mega diamond ring," her mother said.

Too restless to sleep, Nalini then called her best friend, Meena, in Chicago, and a few other friends, who were all thrilled for her. Some of them envied the fact that she got to meet her future husband before the wedding and that he planned to court her and get to know her.

Ready for bed, she gathered up the pile of junk mail cluttering the kitchen counter. About to toss it in the trash, she noticed the plastic lotus Lokesh had presented to her. After he confessed his deception, she'd come home furious and seized the bloom to rip it apart, but the tough plastic made that impossible. Now there it lay in the wastepaper basket, ugly and beautiful all at once, reminding her of the time Lokesh had spent looking up the meaning of her name and trying to find a real lotus. Moved in an inexplicable tenderness, she picked up the flower and set it gently on her bedside table.

Chapter Five

At the office, Nalini shyly flashed her ring and reveled in the raves over the size of the diamond and its beautiful setting. Her friend Chelsea said, "I won't miss your wedding. A bunch of us will drive to Chicago for it." Nalini hadn't known her colleagues very long, but they were planning to make the twelve-hour drive for her wedding, and it heightened her sense of belonging.

Her boss came in to tell her how much he liked the marketing plan for the wok-skillet. "I heard your good news. We're happy you're getting married, but we don't want to lose you . . ." he began.

"Oh, I wouldn't think of leaving this job. I love it here," she said. "My fiancé agrees." Just voicing that word, *fiancé,* thrilled her. After three years of waiting and wondering about the man she'd marry, at last she had found a good man who wanted to give her the best in life. She suppressed any misgivings about the occasional doubts that had arisen the previous night. They had another date, and she was sure it would be more comfortable that evening.

But that date never happened. Dilip called her at her apartment, as promised, and said he was still in a meeting and would call back in half an hour. She waited and waited, checking her watch every few minutes, brushing her hair, primping, but an hour went by before he finally called again. "Look, I'm still trapped in this meeting. We're working on a big merger and this could run very late. I wouldn't think of keeping you up; you've got to get to work early. How about dinner tomorrow night? I can't wait to see you. I've been thinking about you every minute."

Nalini hung up, disappointed. Oh, well, she'd see him tomorrow. She changed out of her fancy teal-colored sari, washed and creamed her face, and tied her hair back in a ponytail. Fixing a bowl of cereal for herself, she sat down at the dining table doodling with some watercolors. Soon a landscape of a beach with palm trees emerged, reminding her of Lokesh and how he missed Juhu Beach in Bombay. Was he home this minute or still at his store? What did he do when he got home? Nalini closed her eyes in exasperation, wondering why she was thinking about Lokesh and not her handsome fiancé.

She leapt, startled, when the phone rang. If Dilip was now free, she could dab her makeup back on and get re-dressed to meet him. But it was her mother on the line. "Mummy, Dilip had to work late, so our dinner got canceled," she said, unable to hold back her disappointment.

"That's how it is with successful men, Nalini. If Dilip didn't take his work seriously he wouldn't be able to provide you with all the things he promised. So don't worry. You've already met with him and talked with him. That's more than you would have with a true arranged marriage. And there'll be years and years for you and Dilip to have dinners together," her mother told her.

And she remembered every single word for the next two nights when Dilip canceled with similar reasons. Work was hectic. The meeting ran late and another one was starting. He couldn't wait to see her. Tomorrow, same time, same place. *Let's meet for dinner.* Well, tonight, for the fourth time in a row, when she heard those same words from Dilip, she hung up more frustrated than ever. After saying, *Let's make time for each other,* he couldn't. Was she so wrong in expecting him to make her his top priority? She was his fiancée now. She went into the bedroom, grumbling, to change out of the blue sari with a red border, when her eye fell on the lotus. At least Lokesh showed up when and where he said he would. He took time off from running his shop to sit in the moonlight with her. He made time to have dinner with her. And Lokesh put his feelings on the line, asking her if she liked him.

Seized by a sudden impulse to see Lokesh, she grabbed her purse and ran to her car. Before she could calmly evaluate her actions she'd driven to the Spice Bazaar, parked, and entered. Once inside she moved purposefully toward the farthest aisle, which was stacked high with sacks of basmati rice, while quickly scanning the entire area for Lokesh. Not finding him, she went to the restaurant, surveying its blue-and-white interior for the man she desperately wanted to see. The waiter from the other night steepled his hands together in the Hindu greeting. "*Namaste,*" he said. "Would you like a table?"

Her stomach growled on cue. "Yes," she said.

He led her to their old table. Several patrons looked up from their meals to observe her. An Indian woman seen dining alone was of interest to all the busybodies in the community, and Nalini was glad that not too many knew her by name or sight. She sat down and focused on the menu, remembering the feast Lokesh had ordered. The waiter, instead of pressing forward with a pitcher of water or a menu, disappeared. She imagined he'd gone to bring out someone's order.

When she next looked up, her heart stopped. Lokesh stood dazzling a smile at her, debonair in a red-and-white-striped shirt. They looked at each other for the longest time. Nalini relished the sparks in his dark eyes, reflecting his joy in seeing her again. Finally, when she tore her gaze away and glanced down, he pulled out the chair opposite her and seated himself.

"So you like our food?" He smiled.

"The bread here is quite good."

"Anything else?" he asked, looking so deeply into her eyes she blushed. "Nalini, I see you're wearing Dilip's ring. . . ." He trailed off, lowering his head as though to avoid the diamond on her finger.

She slipped her hand under the table, out of sight, reminded of her new status as a fiancée. What was she doing here anyway? Suddenly embarrassed, she said, "I have to leave."

He reached out then and held her right hand securely in his, sending electricity coursing to her toes. The touch seemed so natural, establishing a searing connection with a tender request for her to stay. Nalini thought of Dilip, how he had presented her the engagement ring without attempting any sort of physical contact.

She pulled her hand away, looking nervously around at the other patrons. They appeared wrapped up in their own conversations. She sighed with relief. "I shouldn't be here," she said, but she remained glued to her chair.

"Of course you should be here," Lokesh said vehemently. "Why shouldn't you be? We have good food. You can go to any restaurant you like, even this one. You can look for groceries in this store, rent a movie, get carryout. There are many, many reasons for you to come here anytime you need to. I'm always here."

He said the last softly, with so much caring in his voice she glanced away, fighting a tear. Why couldn't she and Dilip talk this way? This conversation was much more personal than discussing the size of a house or a new car. But she couldn't dwell on that. Just as her mother said, Dilip worked hard so he could give her all those things, and success meant long hours and dedication.

The waiter hovered. Nalini took a deep breath, then gave in. "Okay, I'll have chicken vindaloo, naan, partha, chapathi. . . ."

Lokesh laughed. "Bring the basket of bread. Start with vegetable pakoras and bring some samosas. Make it enough for both of us." When the waiter left, Lokesh said, "You look wonderful tonight. Your sari reminds me of a sunrise over the Indian ocean . . . the border is the exact red that appears first every morning over the blue water."

"Oh, I so want to see—" She bit off her sentence. She'd have to tell Dilip that she wanted to travel to India. They hadn't talked about doing anything fun like that. "Did Dilip tell you . . . well . . . that he'd proposed?"

"He just said you were getting married soon." His eyebrows pulled together as his face turned to stone.

Nalini nodded. Lokesh was clearly uncomfortable talking about Dilip, and for good reason. She had come with a vague notion of getting reassurance from Lokesh that Dilip wasn't always such a workaholic, but realized how silly that was. Lokesh could not be trusted where Dilip was concerned. And yet, sitting here with him, she found it hard to believe him dishonorable.

The appetizers arrived, and she turned to the food in relief, helping herself to a spinach pakora, so crisp and spicy. He watched her eat, and she looked at the dimple on his chin and glanced away, remembering how firm his skin felt and how he'd stood in the light tracing her touch with his finger.

As he felt her eyes roam his face, he again touched the dimple ever so slightly. She felt almost compelled to reach across the table and trace its small, shallow dip but diverted her hand to another pakora.

"How's work?" he asked with genuine interest while helping himself to a samosa.

She watched his long fingers around the fork as he dipped the morsel in red tamarind chutney. Absently she replied,

"Fine. My boss liked my marketing plan for this new wok-skillet."

"That's great. Really great. How is it better than a regular skillet?"

"It has a small, shallow bottom with higher sides so it works like a wok. But it's nonstick, and with a special kind of heavy bottom it works well for heavy frying." She was getting warmed up to the topic and was surprised at his continued attention. "It goes in the oven. You can steam in it, and it's fancy enough to be used as a serving dish."

"Have you tried it? How did it work? What did you cook? Chinese combined with Indian?" The questions tumbled out.

"Yes, of course I tried it. Cooked prawns in an onion-and-coriander sauce with coconut milk. It was delicious. You'd have liked it." Nalini cringed. What *if* he would have liked it? She wouldn't ever be cooking for him. Just Dilip, her future husband—Dilip, who had been so silent when she told him about the campaign, who didn't go below the surface, didn't ask questions, didn't comment or joke or even continue a conversation.

"I wish I had some of those prawns. You should have called me. Next time don't hesitate. I'll come running. I'll even try to catch the prawns, at least shrimp, in some river and rush them to your brand-new wok-skillet."

He said it with such pronounced sincerity she laughed. "Don't be silly. A cowboy wouldn't know how to fish."

"Not true. As a vegetarian, I'll have to learn to catch shrimp and fish to survive. All those big cowboys eat are beefsteaks and venison."

They finished their meal. His good-natured company put Nalini in a good mood. She forced all her doubts about Lokesh and Dilip away, wanting to savor each minute of her time with Lokesh.

"Now, would you like to meet Jefferson?" he said.

"Who is Jefferson?"

"He's in his own monument next to the Lincoln Memorial on the Mall."

Her heartbeat quickened. She sighed, remembering that starry night when they had sat on the steps of the Lincoln Memorial. How could she do something so simple and beautiful like that anymore? The engagement ring weighed heavily on her finger. But when their eyes locked she knew she would follow him.

Lokesh rose from his chair, nodded toward the waiter, and, ignoring the questioning look from his assistant, walked out of the store. When he got to his van he leaned against it and waited with excitement. He shouldn't be taking his friend's fiancée anywhere. He shouldn't be continuing to court her. Soon she would belong to Dilip. Soon Lokesh would be left with only the memory of her smile, her humor, her beauty. And soon innocent Nalini would be engulfed by a marriage that would stifle her vitality. Lokesh himself would have a Bombay bride expecting to win his heart. He and Nalini would follow the ancient customs and duties of arranged marriages as so many before them had. But this moment belonged to them. And he intended to make the most of it.

He watched Nalini leave the restaurant and walk directly toward his van with an undulating grace like the most beautiful starlet in Bollywood. No words were spoken till Lokesh got on the Beltway. "Nalini, do you like to dance?"

"As in Kathakali? Or Bharat Natyam? I took a few lessons in Chicago, but I'm not cut out for those classical dances."

"I'm not talking about Indian dances. I thought we could go to a nightclub. I have a jacket in the backseat, and you look ravishing." He glanced over at her. Even in the dim light of the van's interior, her classical profile, her slender neck, and the poised set of her shoulders delighted him.

"What about Jefferson?" she asked with exaggerated interest, teasing him. "We can't keep him waiting."

"He's been waiting for two hundred years; he can be patient a little while longer," he said, enjoying how well they connected. He drove down Canal Road, with its long tree-lined border of the famous C&O Canal below them. A few joggers and bicyclists were still out. He pointed to one of the narrow houses clinging to the top of a steep hill on the left. "That's where the movie *The Exorcist* was filmed," he said.

"I saw that one! It was so spooky. Those stairs are very steep, and there must be a hundred of them." She shuddered.

He continued past Key Bridge into Georgetown, where the sidewalks bustled with tourists window-shopping the boutiques. The idea of going to a nightclub and taking Nalini publicly in his arms on the dance floor thrilled him, even though he wasn't an experienced dancer. In fact, he'd tried it only a few times at community-center functions—with older ladies, since young men and women didn't dance together unless they were married. But now he wanted to experience dancing with someone he truly desired in his arms.

Despite the heavy traffic and the lack of parking spots, soon they were pulling in near Hot Gossip, with its flashing chili-pepper lights. He put on his navy-blue blazer, opened Nalini's door, and escorted her out on the street. As they walked, squeezing past other pedestrians, he protectively placed his hand on her back.

The heat of Lokesh's palm through the back of her silk blouse radiated through Nalini. She wanted to lean back into his palm and feel his breath on her neck, but kept walking forward slowly. Inside the doors of Hot Gossip music throbbed from the floor to the ceiling, with rainbow lights swinging in a splashy rhythm. Nalini blinked, adjusting to the lights, the black walls, the laughter, and the crowd of fashionable people. Several people turned, filled with curiosity about her sari.

A tall man with a blond beard and blond hair styled back fashionably approached. "May I have the pleasure of this dance? I was a Peace Corps worker in India—"

Lokesh stepped forward. "I'm with her," he said firmly.

"Oh, sorry, I didn't see you. Hope you and your girlfriend have a wonderful evening," the man said, slowly walking away, glancing back at Nalini.

The word *girlfriend* sent an exquisite tremor through Nalini. She'd never been anybody's girlfriend. The three men she'd gone out with had logged negligible time with her. Nobody had taken her dancing. And like other Indians, her parents hadn't allowed her to date or to go to school proms or dances. Now she wondered how she'd do with Lokesh. As long as she didn't step on his toes she figured he wouldn't complain too much.

"Lokesh, are there any desis in this place?" The flashing lights made it difficult to see into all the alcoves in this room, and Nalini had a sudden flash of fear about being seen by somebody from the community. "Should we really be here?" she asked.

"I don't see any, but if it makes you uncomfortable we don't have to stay. But Nalini, why don't we dance once and then you can decide?" He took her hand in his and led her to the crowded dance floor just as the music changed to the popular Frank Sinatra tune "Strangers in the Night."

Even at arm's length she could feel the heat between them, palm to palm. His left hand glided down her back to settle on the bare skin where her blouse ended and her sari's petticoat began. His first touch tingled her spine. He spread his palm wider to encompass more skin and more warmth. His other hand pressed hers tighter as he pulled her closer. Their intoxicating intimacy, the music, the romance around them prompted her to lean her head against his shoulder. He stroked her back, running his fingers in a maddeningly sexy drift, and she closed her eyes, absorbing the moment, letting her breasts crush against his hard chest.

She had never felt this thrill before. Her arms wound around his neck, and her palm rubbed against his hair, relishing its rough texture. Then the song ended and they returned to a newly vacated booth. Nalini wanted to leave now, to go home to her pillow and guilt. But he ordered them drinks, and she knew they couldn't just walk into a club, dance, and leave. So she sat quietly, unable to look at Lokesh for fear all her emotions would show as plain as letters printed on a page. These new feelings needed to be sorted out before she revealed them to anyone, even to the source of their creation, who sat across from her. When their eyes met he took her hand in his, and they sat observing others dancing, freely embracing, kissing. But those people were Americans, from a free society that she and Lokesh lived in but weren't really a part of.

The music flowed beautifully around them. Their drinks arrived and they sipped quietly. Then Lokesh said, "Nalini, I have something to tell you. . . ."

She said, "What is it?" But when the music swallowed her words, she moved closer.

He leaned closer also and spoke loudly and clearly. "My parents have found a match for me in Bombay and are proceeding with the arrangement."

Nalini gasped in shock and hurt. "Do you know her? Have you met her?" Her alarm bounced over the music, and she realized how jealous she sounded. She lowered her eyes.

"I won't see her before the wedding. She's a doctor. Jamuna's her name," he said. "Like you, I have little choice in the matter. I promised my parents they could find me a bride."

The ring on her finger emphasized his words. She had no choice in the matter; she couldn't let her parents down any more than he could. The system, full of family expectations and plans, would squeeze out their individual wishes and keep them apart. And as much as she had no right to expect it, she had a wild wish that Lokesh would refuse the match to pine for her. She felt ridiculous going to his store, flinging herself at him on the dance floor. Oh why, oh, why, had she done this? She knew no good could come of it. Anger at herself, at him, at the situation, sickened her.

"I'm grateful for this chance to enjoy each other's company," Lokesh said. "I will always treasure it. But after you and I are married to others . . . I know we'll still see each other. Dilip and I are friends. But for the sake of our spouses we can't be this close again," he said in a gruff, firm tone.

A heavy cold gripped her heart. So this was what breaking up was about? Chelsea and her other American friends had shared their heartaches with her. But their breakups came after many dates and many months. Lokesh and she hadn't even had a relationship in conventional American terms. So why did it upset her so much? Tears lapped against her eyelids. "Can we leave now?" she asked.

"Of course," he said, summoning the waiter.

When he tried to take her hand to escort her through the crowd, she held back. In the car they remained silent, each trapped in a separate misery, unable to voice their morass of feelings, powerless to fight tradition.

"Thank you for dinner," she said formally, as he pulled up next to her car by his store.

He walked her to her car. "Nalini, I really had a great time. I enjoy your company . . . you know that. But I wanted to be up-front with you, to not deceive you about anything else. I didn't want you to hear about my arrangement from Dilip. The last person in the whole world that I want to upset is you. But I can't stop you from marrying Dilip. He can give you the best money can buy. And I'm always here if you need anything else."

She got in quietly. "Okay, good-bye," she said, averting her eyes from the dimple that winked on his chin. Soon another woman would be claiming it. *So let her.* Anger flared up again. How dare Lokesh give that little speech at the club about maintaining proper distance? As though she'd implied that she would flirt with him after she was married, that she'd consider him anything more than her husband's friend, as though she cared if she ever saw him again. Why had she ever gone to his store? Why had she ever lowered herself that way? Humiliated, she let the tears flow as she drove home.

Glad no one else was on the elevator to see her tearstained face, she took the elevator up to her fifth-floor apartment and, head still bowed, walked down the hallway. She fished out the key from her purse and almost stumbled on a three-foot-tall package wrapped in gold-and-red paper. The card on top of it carried her name. She opened her door, dragged the package in, and ripped open the card.

A dozen roses for every day we've been apart. Dilip. The red and white long-stemmed roses were set in a tall porcelain vase with blue hearts on it. Nalini wept out of relief. At least this part of her life was on track. At least Dilip cared about her. He worked hard, as her mother said, to give her the best in life. Once they got married, Dilip would make time for her. She shouldn't have questioned his devotion to her. He must have felt terrible canceling all those dinners with her, to send such an extravagant bouquet. She bent down and inhaled their sweet fragrance. Then she lifted the heavy vase and set it on her living room coffee table. She traced a blue heart with her finger, positive that there would be many more romantic gestures in her future with Dilip.

In the bedroom she changed into a blue nightie, washed and creamed her face, and tied back her hair. Then her eye fell on the plastic lotus sitting on her nightstand. Determined to wrench all traces of Lokesh from her heart, Nalini tossed it into the wastebasket, washed her hands, and went to bed dreaming of a big house with a lovely garden filled with sweet-smelling red and white roses, lacy ferns, and big white dahlias.

Nalini filled Lokesh's every waking moment. He could smell her perfume, like sweet jasmine on a summer night. For the rest of his life it would haunt him. As long as he lived he would feel the softness of her skin and the whisper of her breath in his ear as they danced. Nalini had brought him more joy than he had thought possible. On the dance floor his thoughts had roved wildly, filling him with wishes far beyond his control. He had barely prevented himself from begging her to marry him, but the ring on her finger — a heavy warning for all men to keep away, had snapped that impulse out of him. Still, the temptation to cast aside tradition, parental wishes, and a whole way of life was so strong he knew that if he didn't distance himself he might actually ruin her reputation and disgrace their families.

Already his affection for Nalini blazed as obviously as the tropical sun in the summer. Even the waiter knew, running into his office the previous evening and telling him, "*Memsahib* is here" without any prompting or instructions to notify him. Lokesh had rushed through the store, wondering if she was with Dilip. When he saw her alone his heart had thrummed wildly. His restaurant lit up with her beauty. He wanted to take her in his arms and tell her how much he missed her, how he dreamed about her, how he worried about her future. But he couldn't behave so inappropriately. He choked back the words, looking at the ring on her finger, remembering Dilip's totally dispassionate announcement that he was going to marry Nalini. How could he have even befriended such a blind fool like Dilip? And how was he going to caution Nalini about her future husband?

"*Sahib,* the restaurant owner wants to talk to you," his assistant told him from the doorway of his office.

"Send him in," Lokesh said. As the Sikh came in he stood up and steepled his hands. "*Namaste ji,*" he greeted him. "Please sit down."

Jagdish Singh slid into the chair. "My cooks at all three restaurants are most anxious to make you our supplier of bulk goods. We're very pleased with the quality of everything we've used from your store. And I've brought a three-year contract."

"*Shookriya,*" Lokesh thanked him, taking the papers he extended. "May I look these over?" he asked, and began reading the contract. It was a standard form of agreement, specifying quantities of staples — masala, herbs, vegetables, and fruit — dates of delivery, et cetera. Lokesh picked up a pen and signed all three copies.

They shook hands and the man said, "My brother is setting up a catering service and we'd like you to become a supplier for that venture as well. I'll bring a contract to you next month."

Lokesh couldn't stop smiling. These agreements ensured steady income so he could expand the restaurant without dipping into reserve funds. He called out to his assistant to bring in a plate of sweets for the new and honored customer, who happily helped himself to several almond confections before leaving.

The phone rang and a man said, "I understand from Jagdish Singh that you're a reliable supplier. I'd like to meet with you about the possibility of supplying my restaurant, the Brave Tiger, and my brother's, the Green Mango Bistro."

Now Lokesh couldn't believe his good luck as the man discussed his specific needs and the revenues the account could generate. When he hung up, his business worries, which had been sitting on his shoulders like oxen-pulled carts, lifted, and he relaxed, again thanking Lakshmi, the goddess of wealth, from the bottom of his heart.

The phone rang once more and his mother greeted him, bursting with happiness. "The wedding plans are now in place. Jamuna is such a wonderful, sweet girl. She was first in her class in medical school but is so modest and kind and beautiful. I'm calling to ask you when you're coming to Bombay. Your father and I want you to get here at least one week before the wedding. Now tell me, son, when are you coming?"

The smile faded from Lokesh's face. This was the tenth call from his mother, and her excitement was as high as the Himalayas, but he couldn't share her enthusiasm—or summon up any anticipation to meet such a wonderful, intelligent wife. "I'll check with the airlines and call you next week, Mother." Hanging up, he wallowed in misery. His business was finally soaring, but his personal life was sinking deeper than ever. He needed a wife, he needed children . . . he needed Nalini. But he couldn't have her. Wishing he could go to her, he sat with his head in his hands.

Chapter Six

Dilip's red and white roses brightened up Nalini's cubicle at work. Coworkers and boss came in to admire the display of three dozen blooms she'd brought in, along with his card. "He sounds so romantic," they exclaimed. And when she described the vase with the blue hearts on it, the women practically swooned and wished their boyfriends or husbands were as sentimental.

After work that evening, Nalini changed out of her business suit into a crimson silk sari with hand-painted white rosebuds on it. But she couldn't quite quell the worry that Dilip would cancel again. To divert herself, she sat painting another watercolor of the garden she'd have, full of flowers and butterflies and singing birds.

Finally the phone rang, and with trepidation she picked it up. "Nalini, meet me at the Peacock Restaurant as soon as you can get there," Dilip said. "I can hardly wait."

It took forever to get to the restaurant, frustrating Nalini, who was just as eager as Dilip to move forward with their wedding plans. She would not allow herself to be distracted by a laughing, handsome, dimpled deceiver anymore!

Inside the Peacock, the familiar birds danced on the murals. A musician sat in the corner, legs crossed, playing the sitar. She scanned the interior full of patrons but couldn't find Dilip, and her stomach knotted. "This way, madam," the maître d' said, leading her to the beaded booth in the back. Somehow Dilip had managed to appropriate the same private booth again.

When she parted the hanging beads, they clattered. Dilip stood up with a big smile. In his navy-blue suit he looked sophisticated and powerful. "Hello," she said shyly, waiting to see if he would hug her.

"Hello, beautiful. Sit down, sit down; let me feast my eyes on you. I haven't seen you in so long . . . I remember every feature so vividly. Your beauty leaves an impression on a man's senses."

Overcome by his flattery, she sat down across from him and set her purse beside her. "I'm glad you could get away today," she said without rancor. After all, his roses had so prettily apologized for the previous evenings.

"I wanted to make time for you. I thought of you every minute. But the meetings went late into the night. Did you get the roses?"

"Yes. That was really sweet of you. They're beautiful. I took them to work with me, and everybody came by to say how beautiful they looked. And I loved the vase. The pattern is so sentimental."

He looked blank for a second, then quickly said, "I'm so glad you liked the roses. I told the florist to make the best possible arrangement. When you have your garden you can have as many rosebushes as you want."

"I'm thinking twenty-five," she said saucily, waiting for him to groan or make a joke or increase the number.

"Whatever you want." He bent over the menu. "I'm on break between meetings, so let's order."

She flipped open the huge blue cover of the menu but could hardly focus. His abruptness startled her. If only he'd said that twenty-five was too many or too few. If only he'd asked what color roses she would plant. Lokesh's smiling face crowded the print off the menu. The nagging realization that the florist had selected the vase with the blue hearts and the color of the roses distressed her. Dilip's serious nature didn't leave room for sentimentality, and, like an idiot, she had believed he'd taken the time to personalize the flowers. Oh, why couldn't Dilip be as playful as Lokesh?

The waiter arrived, and without even looking at the menu she ordered tandoori chicken, parathas, and daal with loki. Dilip ordered several other dishes in a purposeful manner. This wasn't going to be a leisurely "let's get to know each other" meal full of laughter and fun, as they had been with Lokesh. No dancing would follow.

Not about to give up on trying to connect, she set her hand deliberately within reach of his. "Everybody exclaims over the ring," she said, hoping he'd at least touch it, as even strangers did to acknowledge its existence.

"That's a four-carat diamond. It *should* impress." He smiled but made no attempt to pat her hand.

"Yes, it's so big and heavy. I'm trying to get used to it," she rattled on.

His cell phone beeped and he pulled it out of his pocket. "Eight o'clock meeting," he said, then held the phone to his ear for the longest time.

Nalini tried to stay patient, tried to hold on to her mother's words—that only a hardworking man could be successful enough to give her all the things she deserved. They would have a lifetime to get to know each other better. Yet she couldn't stop the irritation at this monopolizing assistant calling and interrupting her date.

"Sorry," Dilip said, finally putting his phone away.

"Have you ever been to India, Dilip?" Nalini asked, determined to make the most of the short time she had with Dilip. "I'd love to go to Bombay, maybe even for our honeymoon, and walk on Juhu Beach, eat some bhel puri, sink our toes in the sand."

Shock widened his eyes. "Why would you want to go to India? It couldn't possibly compare to Hawaii. That's where we're going for our honeymoon."

"You have no desire to go see the land of our ancestors?" she asked.

"No, I don't. But if you want to go to India for a few months after we return from our honeymoon, there's no reason you can't. I'll make arrangements for you to stay in first-class hotels and hire a car with a chaffeur. My parents' friends will be happy to show you around."

Heatedly, she said, "There's a good reason I can't go to India for a few months. I can't just take off from work. And going by myself wouldn't be any fun. I'd want to travel together with my husband."

"I can't take off that much time. It's decided that you'll take your vacation and go to India alone," he said, glancing at his watch.

The food arrived as her stomach churned. Had he even heard her objections? Nalini took a deep breath, battling her disappointment and anger. She reminded herself that neither Dilip nor she was used to talking like husband and wife. Dilip was the boss of his own company, so surely he wasn't used to consulting someone else before making a decision. She would just have to make a point of disagreeing forcefully enough so that he didn't say peremptory things like "It's decided."

He ate rapidly, mixing curries and rice in methodical circles, then asked, "So have you been to Hawaii? It's a tropical paradise. After my last visit there I decided it was where I'd bring my bride. You don't have any objections, do you?"

At last he asked her opinion and showed interest in a place other than his office. She was willing to meet him halfway and let go of her anger. "I'd love to see Hawaii."

His wide grin and newly relaxed manner reassured her. His earlier abruptness was probably due to hunger. Endless meetings could tire anybody out. Lokesh would have made some joke about going to Hawaii to bake themselves on the beach, but laughing wasn't as important in a marriage as trust and companionship. "How many days' honeymoon?" she asked, picking up her fork again. The daal with chunks of loki, the long baseball bat–size squash tasted wonderful with parathas.

"Two weeks. You should make arrangements with your firm. If they refuse to give you the days, just take unpaid leave. This is an important time for us, and I want to have you with me every minute of the honeymoon. We'll stay in the best hotels and dine at the finest restaurants. We'll stroll on the beach."

"Yes, this is an important time for us," she agreed enthusiastically. "We'll get to know each other intimately, our likes and dislikes, our feelings, the way a real married couple should. We're really busy at the office right now, but of course they'll give me the time off. Some of my friends from work are coming to the wedding. Have you invited anyone from your business?"

"No. I try to keep my office life separate from my personal life. But a lot of other friends are coming. It's a long list I e-mailed to my mother. She's looking forward to having you join our family. I know you'll like my parents. They're serious like me."

She laughed then. At least he knew himself well. "Yes, you are serious. What do you do for fun?"

A strange expression crossed his face. He hooded his eyes, shifted in his seat, then said, "Work. Work is fun for me. You told me you enjoy your job, so you understand?"

"Yes." She nodded, pleased he remembered her comment from their last dinner. "But is there something you like to do outdoors? Play golf? Sit under the stars?"

He laughed and his whole face took on an appealing charm. If she could only make him laugh more. Well, on their honeymoon she'd work on that. Sometimes it took a while for people to enjoy each other's sense of humor.

"I'm serious. Wouldn't you enjoy sitting on the marble steps of a monument, weaving a dream future in the moonlight?"

He laughed even harder now. "That's the silliest thing I ever heard, sitting on the steps of a monument at night. Only people without anything better to do can waste time like that."

Thinking of how much she had enjoyed sitting under the stars with Lokesh, Nalini felt her heart sink. Well, she'd teach Dilip the magic of a night full of stars, small breezes, rippling water, and sleeve-rustling passion. On their honeymoon she'd have Dilip all to herself. He'd be more relaxed.

"Tell me, did your boss like your marketing plan?" he asked.

Trying to banish Lokesh from her thoughts, she said, "Yes, he was gung-ho about it. He even put a memo in my personal file praising it."

"That's excellent." Dilip grinned. "You're smart and ambitious. You'll go far; I'm sure of that. I don't understand women who refuse to work."

She swelled with pride. At their last dinner he'd made it clear that he appreciated career women, but it pleased her to hear it again.

"Oh, I don't ever want to just stay home. I like working," she said.

"You don't have to stay home. I already told you we'll have a staff, and that includes a live-in nanny. My wife will get the best in life. And you're going to be my wife. Oh, you're beautiful. I'm very pleased. Showla Aunty did well." He popped the last bit of food on his plate into his mouth, wiped his fingers on his napkin, and then summoned the waiter hovering just beyond the beads. "As I told you when you got here, I have to leave. But we'll meet again tomorrow for dinner. Same time. Same place."

Dilip paid the waiter and they walked out together. A strong, cool breeze ruffled her hair across her face and fluffed the sari's end off her shoulder. It bared her tightfitting blouse and her midriff, but Dilip didn't seem to notice. He sprang out of range of the wind-whipped silk and kept walking forward.

Nalini grabbed the errant end of her sari, wrapped it around her shoulder, and held on to it with one hand. "There's my car," she pointed out.

When she opened the door, Dilip said, "You didn't lock it?

You should always lock your car. I worry about your safety. Promise me you'll always lock your car?"

Pleased by his concern, Nalini said, "I promise."

"I'll see you tomorrow. I can hardly wait. I'll bring some brochures of Hawaii and we can decide on a hotel. I'd better rush now." With that he strode off, the navy-blue suit disappearing in her rearview mirror.

At home she kicked off her shoes and called her mother to tell her they would be honeymooning in Hawaii. Mummy loved details and information she could then dole out, crumb by crumb, to others in the community. Her mother's proud intake of breath erased the last bit of doubt Nalini had about the choice. "Dilip's invited me to dinner again tomorrow. He's going to bring brochures so we can select a hotel." Nalini particularly liked this invitation to make a joint decision, and her voice hummed.

"The other details of the wedding are coming together nicely," her mother said, pleased.

Listening to her mother's report on caterers, the hotel, and the florist, Nalini sighed with contentment. Her grandfather's airline ticket had been purchased. One of her uncles planned to accompany him and arrange for a wheelchair at the airports.

"What else did Dilip say?" her mother asked, ready to absorb anything else her daughter could provide on her new son-in-law.

"Well, Dilip got quite upset that I hadn't locked my car. He made me promise I'll always lock it."

"That's exactly the kind of husband you need. Someone to look after you." Her mother clucked.

"The best thing, Mummy, is that he respects me as a career woman. Dilip says I don't have to quit my job even after we have children. A live-in nanny will take care of them."

Her mother cheered. "What a sensible boy. Marriage is all about adjustments, Nalini. If you're patient with him he'll do everything in his power to give you things you want. Remember that always."

In bed, she let her mother's words tuck her in, wrapping her in reassurance.

Lokesh didn't even have to look up Nalini's number. It had been stuck indelibly in his memory since his first glance at it. He picked up the phone and set it down several times. He longed to see her one more time while they were both free, and have a softer farewell that would not linger with such a sour taste. With her in his arms on the dance floor, he'd soared to heaven, her hand clutching his with a feminine need, her breasts crushed softly against his chest, her thigh quivering against his. Words weren't needed to tell him she felt the same strong bond that drew him to her, kept him awake at night, worried him about letting her go to the passionless marriage Dilip planned with her.

But if he called her now, what would have changed? Duty had an iron grip on his future. Jamuna waited in Bombay to marry him. And he couldn't hurt Jamuna, an innocent woman, either.

He sat agitating for a long time, letting the apartment darken around him. Still restless, he grabbed his car keys to drive around, hoping the activity would shake off his desolation.

But after driving aimlessly about, he found himself across the street from her address. The brick building looked posh, neatly landscaped with flowering shrubs and stone paths edged with patches of lawn. He sat in his van, picturing Nalini relaxing in that garden, imagining her rushing for work, bright-eyed, in the morning, sitting on her balcony reading the adventure novels she loved so much. All the apartments were lit up. An old man walked by holding his gray-haired wife's hand, making Lokesh long for a life like theirs with Nalini, sharing memories day by day into old age. He couldn't stand staying away from Nalini any longer. He dialed her number on his cell phone and waited nervously, listening to it ring and ring and cursing Dilip for taking her out to dinner.

He disconnected the ringing phone and was about to drive away when he decided to give it one more try. He pulled back into his parking spot and pressed the redial button.

"Hello?" Nalini's light, sweet voice filled his ear. "Hello?" she repeated.

"Nalini, this is Lokesh. . . ." He trailed off, uncertain of her reaction, unsure of what he'd say if Dilip was with her.

"Lokesh," she said under her breath.

Did he imagine a note of joy in her voice? "Can I see you? Are you with . . . ?"

"I thought we agreed not to do this. You have somebody waiting for you in Bombay."

Her voice sank, confirming his feelings that she cared as deeply for him as he cared for her. And he had no ready answers. "Last time we met I wanted to let you know my situation. But . . . I do not want that evening to be our last memory."

A long silence later, she said, "Lokesh, you want me to meet Jefferson?"

He laughed in relief, feeling like a condemned man who had just been granted a stay of execution. "Yes, Jefferson's waiting in his round memorial. And I . . . I am waiting in the street below your building."

"You're here? Why don't you . . . I'll be down in a few minutes."

The evening turned beautiful. He knew she wanted to invite him up to her apartment but changed her mind for the same reason he wouldn't go up there.

Nalini quickly brushed her hair, and rifled through the closet for a suitable outfit. The green suit she'd worn the first time she met Lokesh hung lopsided from a hanger, and she pulled it out. It reminded her again of the plastic lotus, which she'd rescued from the trash after realizing she just wasn't ready to part with it yet. Lokesh's thoughtfulness contrasted with Dilip's rush-rush attitude, his honoring of appointments so different from Dilip's constant cancellations.

As Nalini applied fresh makeup, she thought how glad she was that Dilip had canceled yet again tonight.

She knew she shouldn't be so thrilled to see Lokesh again. What was the point? A woman named Jamuna would claim Lokesh soon, and she herself would become Dilip's wife. "I need a friend," she said aloud, thinking how badly she needed to laugh away her troubles and relax with someone who understood her.

He stepped out of the van, a tall, strong anchor in her sea of woes. Dressed in a cream-colored shirt and jeans, he looked comfortable and comforting — and handsome. A brilliant smile lit up his face as he stretched out his arms, but she quickly shook her head and climbed into the passenger seat of the van.

He climbed into the driver's seat and buckled up. "How're you?" he asked.

The tenderness in his voice brought a tear rolling down her cheek.

"What happened?" he asked, starting the engine and driving away.

"Dilip canceled again," she wailed. She hadn't intended to share this with anyone, certainly not Lokesh. Such admission of Dilip's poor treatment of her made her feel foolish and spoiled, but she couldn't hold it in any longer. She hadn't even called her mother, because she knew the lecture — about adjustments and the hard work necessary for success — by heart. Those were valid points but didn't help erase her growing trepidation that she rated low on Dilip's priority list.

"He keeps canceling. Meeting after meeting, so late into the night? Every night? How can that be?" she asked.

His face hardened but he said nothing for the longest time. Then he said, "Nalini, don't cry. I'm sure he's trying to finish taking care of business before he and you . . ."

Lokesh gripped the steering wheel and continued driving. Nalini tried to take comfort in his words. A businessman would do exactly what Lokesh said, wrap up all his projects before a long vacation. Dilip just wanted to be able to devote his total attention to his bride. She wiped away her tears. Dilip was meticulously planning their honeymoon; he *was* showing her that she mattered to him.

"Nalini, if you don't like Dilip's canceling dates, you should tell him how you feel."

That made sense. She should be herself. How would Dilip ever know his behavior upset her if she didn't tell him? Somebody had to break down those formal barriers between them. Her spirits lifted.

"At least you've met Dilip. I haven't even seen Jamuna," Lokesh said.

Jealousy filled her. She didn't want to hear that name. She didn't want to think of Lokesh married to the other woman — or to anybody else.

"Where would you like to have dinner?"

Nalini appreciated being consulted. Remembering Dilip's "same time, same place," she shuddered. "How about Italian?" she suggested. "There's a new place called La Dolce Vita that got good reviews in the *Washington Post*, and it's in Georgetown, right on the Potomac."

"Yes, I read that as well," he said, passing the White Hurst Freeway and Key Bridge and continuing on M Street.

Georgetown swarmed as usual with tourists and suburbanites. Lokesh took a side street and found a parking space. They walked to the restaurant down the block and into its pleasantly dim interior, where grapevines climbed white pillars to sprawl from the blue ceiling, displaying huge bunches of purple grapes between large clusters of leaves.

"Would you like a grape?" he joked.

"I'd better say no before you give me plastic grapes," she said coyly.

"Did you throw away the plastic lotus?" He laughed.

"No," she admitted shyly. "It reminds me of you."

"I'm not plastic; see . . ." He extended his arm for her to feel.

She placed two fingers on his hard biceps and withdrew them with exaggerated alarm. "Oh, no, it's all plastic." She laughed.

The maître d' smiled. "Ah, *amore*." He sighed, leading them to a corner table. Nalini blushed with guilt before following.

Lokesh sat opposite her. "I remember this beautiful forest-green shalwar suit. You wore it the first time I met you."

"And you matched the wrapping paper to it."

He smiled. "It wasn't easy."

She couldn't help thinking sadly of Dilip's red and white roses and the vase with blue hearts that he obviously didn't know anything about. Dilip always said the right words, but his gestures lacked any personalization. She'd have to get used to that. To prevent herself from bursting into tears, she asked Lokesh, "How's business?"

"Surprisingly good. It seems that I'm a restaurant supplier now."

Nalini was gladdened by Lokesh's elation as he elaborated. Lokesh's sticking to high principles had paid off. "Will this give you more free time?" As soon as she asked, she realized how he'd be using that free time—to go to India to marry Jamuna.

"Yes, this comes at a practical time," he said.

Nalini was leaving in two days for her own wedding and had to take care of last-minute details, shopping and cleaning her apartment and finishing up the project at work. "I'm leaving on Wednesday for Chicago," she finally said.

"Are your parents still in Oak Brook?"

"Yes. The house is filled already with relatives. And we're expecting five hundred guests. It's going to be crazy. The wedding's at the Marriott. Did you get an invitation?"

"Yes, I did," he finally said. "I have to send you a gift."

"Make sure it's something plastic," she joked gamely, but her heart ached.

As the waiter brought them menus a bell started ringing loudly somewhere. People began jumping up from their tables and running toward the door.

"Come on." Lokesh pulled her by her hand. "It's the fire alarm. Come on."

She grabbed her purse, but the crowd made it impossible to move forward. Smoke came curling thick from the kitchen. A woman screamed as other patrons began to swear and jostle each other. "Don't anybody move; sit down," somebody shouted.

Lokesh grabbed napkins off their table. "Here, cover your mouth so you don't inhale the smoke," he said. They stood together, helplessly watching the crowd of hysterical diners trying to stampede to the front door.

"Sit down. Exit in an orderly fashion," the maître d' yelled.

"Like hell we will," a thin man cried out.

"He's right," Lokesh said. He grabbed Nalini's hand and raced her away from the crowd toward the kitchen.

Before she could protest that they were heading into the fire, he kicked open a wide door and pushed her out. Then he turned and yelled, "Come this way. This door's open."

They emerged coughing and thankful onto a narrow alley stacked with enormous brown trash bins. The smoke hurt her eyes and she rubbed them, noticing Lokesh help an elderly man whose walking cane was stuck between the bins. All the evacuees clumped together, shaken by the fire, which now shot small flames through a back window. They pushed forward from the alley to the street, pleased to see the other diners pouring out of the front door, unhurt. The fire engines roared in, screeching traffic to a halt. "Move back," the firefighters yelled.

"Let's get out of here. We're just in their way," Lokesh said, handing their napkins to one of the waiters looking anxiously at all the customers leaving without paying their bills.

They began walking away from the crowd toward the car. Relieved that nobody was hurt, she asked, "How did you know where to find that door, Lokesh?"

"Because of the Spice Bazaar. I've had firefighters come in and discuss evacuation procedures, so I'm habitually checking for emergency exits," he said. "Are you okay? Wait." He gently brushed off her hair. Then he hugged her.

People streamed by, but Lokesh and Nalini didn't notice, too focused on reassuring each other they were both alive and unharmed. Finally she forced herself away from him and said, "Somebody might see us. The Indian community network is incredible, you know." It sounded weak even as she was saying it.

"Yes, it is," he said. "So are you still hungry?"

"How about takeout? Then we can picnic. I'm not sure I'm ready to be near another kitchen so soon," she quipped.

"A great idea." He swung around on his feet, surveying the restaurant signs nearby. "A new Indian carryout restaurant called Samosa Palace opened on K Street. We'll drive there, get a bagful, and go visit Jefferson," he said.

In the van they talked about the shock of the fire, its possible causes, and the swiftness of the fire department's response. As they crossed the Potomac, he fantasized aloud. "One day we'll go on a cruise on the river, one of the dinner cruises. Won't that be fun?"

"That'll be wonderful. I've only been on a boat once before, when we went on Lake Michigan. On my dad's boss's boat," she said, ignoring reality rising up in thorny reminders. They weren't going anywhere after tonight except into the arms of strangers. But who needed to think of that now? She looked at his profile so long, he turned to her.

"What're you thinking of?" he asked.

"Why some people have dimples and others don't," she said flirtatiously.

He laughed. "When I was a little boy, this bully in our neighborhood called me the boy with the flowerpot. I was only six and I looked all around me for a flower pot. Then he pointed to my chin. I burst into tears and ran to my mother. She and my aunties immediately rubbed black coal on my face to drive away evil spirits, like that boy."

"That jealous little thing," Nalini said, thinking how much she liked Lokesh's stories about his childhood. She knew nothing about Dilip. He volunteered so little.

"That jealous little thing is now a big-shot newspaper editor. We're now friends. Every time I call him he says, 'Hey flowerpot,' and we laugh. You'll meet him. . . ." He fell silent.

She knew reality had prickled him, too. They would never meet each other's friends. Their lives were about to speed off in opposite directions. He took a right on Eighteenth and a left on K and double-parked in front of Samosa Palace. The shiny-fronted new carryout was crowded, but she spotted Lokesh in line and her eyes wouldn't leave his compelling figure. When he emerged, she chuckled at the huge bag in his arms.

"I got a large sampling of all the snacks they had, and mango and guava juice," he said. "Let's go see Jefferson."

They drove past the White House, looking grand with its

big lawn and magnolia trees, past the imposing gray government buildings to the National Mall.

"One day, when you're not in a sari, we'll have to climb to the top of the George Washington Monument. It's got eight hundred and ninety-seven steps," he said.

"Better not wait till we're too old," she joked.

"Yes, next week will be too late," he joked back, but his laughter died. They both knew next week would be too late for anything they'd ever do together.

She stared straight ahead, wishing for a solution, wishing this night would never end.

"I'm not sure you can actually take food up into the monument," he said, pulling into a parking spot. "So let's picnic on the grass here." He took his jacket from the back of the car and laid it on the grass for her to sit on.

Nalini spread it out so he could join her. They sat eating samosas, looking up at the obelisk of the Washington Monument with its ever-present stream of gawking tourists. The gingery fragrance of the food, the warm breeze rustling the leaves of the big oak trees, and the stars reflected in the Reflecting Pool made her sigh. No matter where she was with Lokesh—in the van, in a restaurant, on the street—she found the setting beautiful.

"How do you like these samosas?" he asked.

"Not as good as the ones at the Spice Bazaar."

"You said the right thing. You're clever," he said, pulling her closer to him and impulsively kissing her on the cheek.

She pulled away before her emotions could spin out of control. "Let's go meet Jefferson," she said.

They drove the short distance, parked, and walked up the steps, admiring the pillared front. Inside his 129-foot-high marble dome, Jefferson's bronze statue stood surveying the Tidal Basin lined with the famous cherry trees that drew tourists from all over the world in April, and the Potomac

River beyond. They read the inscriptions, then sat on the steps side by side, letting their sleeves touch, feeling their hearts beat.

"This is our last night together," he said, taking her hand in his. "Are you nervous about your wedding?"

"Yes. Are you about yours?"

"Yes," he said, clutching her hand. "I haven't met Jamuna. I haven't even talked to her on the phone. I don't know what to expect."

"Didn't you get a picture?" she asked, curious despite her unwillingness to imagine him with someone else.

"No. I didn't ask."

His worried voice and face made her want to take him in her arms and comfort him. Instead she offered a fair solution. "You could call her up, Lokesh. Just as you told me to let Dilip know my feelings, you can talk to her and see if she has any questions. Or ask her some questions about her likes and dislikes."

Lokesh's face reddened. "This is so awkward. Here we are sitting at the foot of Jefferson, the man who wrote the Declaration of Independence, but we're unable to declare ourselves independent of our culture," he said.

She understood his torture. Her heart also ached. Even if Lokesh asked her to marry him, she couldn't bring shame on her family when they had given their word to Dilip's parents and the wedding plans were in full swing. She leaned her head on his shoulder. His arm tightened around her. They wanted so much more. The stars twinkled. The Tidal Basin reflected the streetlights in shimmering ribbons on dark water. They sat knowing this was the last time they would meet this way, without others, freely experiencing the joy of their closeness.

Finally, after an eternity of peace and joy, Nalini reluctantly said, "Lokesh, I have to leave." What was the point of compounding all that she was going to miss? Why add to her own torture? If she didn't leave now she might be reduced to tears and reveal her total vulnerability.

He rose and held out his hand for hers. She stood up and they walked down the steps to the van. He helped her in, then got into the driver's seat, and they began heading back to their individual futures. Nalini knew from Lokesh's face and the firm pressure of his hand over hers that he wanted her to be with him forever, and she sighed over the futility of it all.

"Do you have a ride to the airport?" he asked.

"Yes, Dilip's sending a company car to take me. He's coming two days later. Too much work." Hours earlier that had hurt, but now it was nothing compared to parting with Lokesh forever. "And you?"

"Someone from the Spice Bazaar will give me a ride."

They talked about the logistics of their life-changing journeys as though transportation were the most pressing problem to be resolved. They compared notes on their last flights, the delays, the bad food. They clung to trivia.

When they got to her apartment building, she dredged up the energy to say brightly, "Good luck. Thanks," and turned for the door.

But before she could reach it, he pulled her into his arms and stroked her hair. His lips grazed her cheek and she sighed, nuzzling against him, listening to his heart pound. He lifted her chin with his fingers. She closed her eyes, recalling her fantasies. It was now or never. She reached for his chin and kissed his dimple. He trembled against her, then placed his lips on hers, lightly kissing them while caressing her back. She pressed closer, deepening the kiss and her desires.

He pulled away. "Nalini, Nalini, much as I crave you, I can't take advantage of you. You'll hate me forever if we did what we both long to do." With that he climbed down from the van, came to her door, and helped her out. "I'll wait to make sure you get into your building safely," he said.

She walked away feeling as if another planet, a somber place with a cold and proper future, awaited her with a man who couldn't be anything but proper.

Chapter Seven

*H*er mother and father, wreathed in smiles, met Nalini at O'Hare Airport in Chicago. Behind them stood a throng of relatives and friends chattering in excitement, craning their necks, and waving hello. The eldest of them stepped forward and threw a garland of marigolds around Nalini's neck as flashbulbs popped and cameras clicked. "Show us your ring," they called out.

She held it up, and their oohs and aahs made her smile for the first time in days. "You'll make a beautiful bride, you lucky girl, marrying such a handsome and successful boy," her mother exclaimed.

Her relatives' warm, generous celebration of her upcoming wedding brought tears to Nalini's eyes. An arranged marriage involved the entire community. Every one of these women had experienced the nervousness, uncertainty, fear, and excitement of marrying a stranger. At least she'd met Dilip, though she couldn't say she knew him as well as she knew Lokesh. *Ah, Lokesh.* She didn't realize she'd said Lokesh's name aloud till she felt the silence around her and saw her mother's face twist with curiosity, then suspicion. "Lokesh?" she asked Nalini.

A young acquaintance stepped forward. "No, I didn't bring the baby. Lokesh doesn't do well in crowds. Nalini, it's so sweet of you to remember my baby's name. You told me how much you liked the name when he was born." All the ladies, including her mother, beamed approvingly, and Nalini quickly thanked her lucky stars at the coincidence, vowing never to think again of the man on his way to India to claim Jamuna.

"Don't look sad," the young woman said. "You'll have babies of your own soon. And Dilip's going to hire a live-in nanny for you."

Mummy had spread the word. Nalini busied herself rummaging through her purse for luggage tags to hide the alarm she felt at having her own babies—Dilip's babies—while he talked endlessly on his cell phone to business contacts. For the first time in her life she wasn't sure she wanted children. But her duty to produce the first great-grandchild calmed down her rising rebellion.

They all piled into different cars and headed for her parents' house. "Your mother's invited everybody to the house for dinner tonight. For the next three days our home will be lit up with honored guests for your wedding," her father said, patting her hand.

"When is Grandfather coming?"

"Tomorrow morning. He hasn't been feeling well, and your uncle changed his tickets from last week so he could fight off the cold bothering him," her mother said.

"I hope he feels better," Nalini said sincerely. She worried about her grandfather's health. He used to visit every couple of years, and she truly loved seeing him. But he had canceled his last two visits, saying the journey halfway around the world was exhausting, unless, of course, it ended with Nalini's wedding.

"Our out-of-town guests are all arriving at different times for the next three days. And they're staying with friends or in hotels. Showla Aunty is coming the morning of the wedding. She's walking on clouds at her successful match. Dilip's parents will come tomorrow for the Mehendi, the henna ceremony, and dinner."

In three days Lokesh would be arriving in Bombay. "What is the Bombay airport like?" Nalini asked.

Her parents exchanged curious looks. "What does the Bombay airport have to do with Dilip and his parents?" her mother asked sharply.

"I was thinking of Grandfather . . . how he'd get around," Nalini lied.

"The airport is always a mess in Bombay, but your uncle will take care of your grandfather. Don't worry, child."

They were pulling up at the house, a spacious four-bedroom brick colonial painted white with green shutters and large front door. On either side of the house evergreens screened off the huge backyard and garden full of childhood memories of picking flowers and chasing butterflies.

"I'll cook pullau and make saag panir," Nalini said.

Her father laughed. "You've always had a helpful nature, Nalini. Even as a little girl you were dragging clothes to the washer. Clean clothes." He chuckled fondly. "But this is your wedding. We're having all the lunches and dinners catered from tonight on. The Mehendi-night buffet will be served in the tent."

"Come look at the tent," her mother said.

They walked through the house to the backyard.

It looked festive, full of round tables under red floor-length tablecloths. The folding chairs were covered in white with big bows pleating the fabric in back. The buffet table stretched at the far end of the tent. "I ordered huge bouquets of white and red roses, like the ones your Dilip sent you, for all the tables. We couldn't find vases with blue hearts. . . ."

The excitement in her parents' and guests' voices lifted Nalini's spirits. So what if Dilip hadn't personally selected the vase and flowers? He'd thought of ordering them for her. And it had cheered her up when Lokesh had announced his marriage to Jamuna. Her heart ached.

"If we were in India, we would put lotuses on the tables to match your name," her dad said. "We looked everywhere but couldn't find a single lotus. Not even a plastic one."

Nalini nodded, trying not to think of how Lokesh had managed to find one, and how much she treasured that gift. She'd even brought it with her as a good-luck charm. But why look back at a useless situation? The bustle around her told her she'd made the right choice. Everything was proceeding as it should.

"I'm here, I'm here. Nalini, this is so exciting." Her best friend, Meena, arrived, hair done up in a stylish chignon and wearing a pale pink sari.

Nalini brightened with genuine delight. "Let's go and unpack," Nalini suggested; she wanted some private time with her friend.

The two went up to Nalini's old room, where her two suitcases had already been delivered. Meena chattered about her own wedding last year. "It's a good thing they'll make a video, because it's hard to remember everything and everybody. This is so exciting. At least you've met Dilip. Tell me about him."

"He's wonderful," Nalini said, and burst into tears.

Meena rushed to close the bedroom door. "What is it? What happened?" she asked.

Nalini couldn't find words to describe the grueling sense of defeat at losing Lokesh. Till she boarded the plane that morning, her heart had pounded wildly with ideas of him appearing to beg her not to marry Dilip. At Dulles Airport in Virginia, she made a point of boarding the plane last, dragging her feet, scanning the area for signs of Lokesh. But he never came. She'd sat through the flight, lecturing herself for her foolishness. He hadn't even called to say good-bye.

"What is it?" Meena asked again. "Is there someone else you want to marry?"

The blunt question sliced through Nalini. "Of course not. I'm just nervous," she said vehemently. "Why would you even ask something like that?"

Meena's face squared in determination. "Nalini, you're like my own sister. I know your heart is aching. I've never seen you this upset before. And I don't want you to make the same mistake I did. Instead of telling my parents I wanted to marry Govind and not Prakash, I went ahead—"

"Govind? You never told me this, Meena! I remember Govind from high school, but I didn't know you and he were seeing each other. Why didn't you tell me?"

"For the same reason you're not telling me about your real love. We've been best friends since kindergarten, but we were all raised never to share our most important feelings with anyone. We have to guard our family reputation against gossip. No one, not even your best friend, is to be trusted. So I didn't tell a soul that Govind and I were sneaking around and meeting at the movies. I was so frightened of getting caught I kept all this secret, even from you, and guess what? I'm now married to a couch potato who grunts a response when asked something, claps his hands if he wants another beer, and watches every dime I spend. There's no fun or laughter. . . ." Meena burst into tears. "Don't let this happen to you. Speak up now," she urged her friend.

Nalini had had no idea of Meena's unhappiness. "Why don't you tell your parents to talk to your husband?"

"I did. Several times. But you know, once you're married you keep your mouth shut. You go around pretending or your husband and in-laws make things worse for you. It brings shame on your whole family."

"But you can't keep living this way."

"I'm getting used to it now. It's okay. Don't worry about me. I just don't want you to make the same mistake. I didn't even tell Govind I was getting married. I saw him at a party and his accusing eyes told me I should have. We could be together now. But it's too late for me. You're not married yet, so tell me, who is he? Why're you crying?"

"Nothing can be done, Meena."

"Don't be so sure. I can step in and help. I'm a married woman now, with more freedom to speak on your behalf."

"Nothing can be done," Nalini repeated, but then the words, bottled up in her heart, began pouring out. She told her friend about Lokesh Mehta, how he had only been looking her over for his friend in the store he owned, called Spice Bazaar. She told Meena about Dilip—all the broken dates, the distance he kept, his glib lines, his late meetings, his total indifference to anything romantic.

"Nalini, why didn't you tell Lokesh you wanted to marry him?"

"Don't shock me, Meena. I'm not that bold. I made it as clear as possible, but he's going to his arranged marriage in Bombay."

"Give me his number. I'll call him and tell him he's making a mistake."

"No! Please don't call. Nothing can be done now. I thought he might come to the airport but he never did. He doesn't want to marry me. I can't put a blot on my family name. The scandal would kill my mother."

Her protests fell on deaf ears. Meena picked up the phone, dialed information, got the number and called Spice Bazaar. "Is Lokesh there?" she asked with the authority of a relative. "Oh, okay. Will he be back tomorrow? No, there's no message."

She hung up slowly and said, "The man said Lokesh left town. He's on his way to his wedding."

Nalini calmed herself down and wiped her tears. "I'm going to push him out of my mind. Everything's going to be fine with Dilip and me. There'll be the phase of adjustment. And really, there's nothing wrong with Dilip. I can't complain."

The door burst open. Her mother walked in and said, "Of course there's nothing wrong with Dilip. What makes you even talk that way?"

"Mummy, you didn't hear the first part of it. I was just telling Meena how much I like Dilip. How wonderful he's been." Nalini practiced what she'd just vowed she would do. By centering all her thoughts on Dilip she could keep Lokesh from entering her mind.

Her mother beamed. "Here are some Mehendi patterns for tomorrow. Select one. The woman will be here later this afternoon to apply the henna to your hands; then all the other ladies will choose their own patterns. Meena, you can see what you like also."

Nalini selected a simple pattern of small flowers, and Meena liked the stars. Then her mother said, "Let's go over these clothes for tomorrow's ceremony."

She opened up the closet door. "Oh, Mummy, you've bought so many saris and shalwar outfits," Nalini cried out, fingering a beautiful forest-green silk sari.

"I did. You know about some of them, but I had your aunties in Bombay shop for us, and all these arrived a week ago. I think they did really well with the fabric and colors. All these'll be taken to the hotel and displayed as your trousseau. They will set up tables, and I've asked a woman in the community to work as a guard, because we'll be displaying all your jewelry and household goods, like the new toaster, et cetera."

"Mummy, I don't need a new toaster."

"Yes, you do. It's all part of the trousseau. People need to see our daughter going into marriage with her own proper possessions. Come, those are downstairs."

That began the first of several meetings about the trousseau

in which the rest of the guests participated, offering their two
cents on how best to display all the goods, dishes in front,
with silver trays behind those, et cetera. As the center of attention, Nalini rushed around automatically, then sat through
the dinner that went late into the night, and filled the next day
with more preparations and last-minute shopping. She welcomed the activity, throwing herself completely into helping
her mother, nervous after a phone call from Bombay telling
them Nalini's grandfather's ticket had been changed again.
He didn't feel well but would be arriving the next day.

Throughout all this, Lokesh kept popping up in her mind,
whether she thought of him or not. Imagining him going to
meet Jamuna in Bombay stabbed daggers into her already
wounded soul. If only he'd asked her to marry him, she
might have said yes. She might have called her parents and
begged them. But he didn't. She sighed. As the last gesture
of an independent woman before her marriage, she took a
five-dollar bill, kissed the picture of Lincoln on it, folded it
carefully, and thrust it under the strap of her bra, close to her
heart.

When the henna artist arrived and applied the leaf paste to
her hands in the flowery design she'd selected, and worked
on Meena's, the two friends sat holding their hands up in the
air, trying to keep the paste from smudging the design before
it dried. Women from their community played the sitar and
the tabla and sang traditional songs that teased the bride,
whose feet were now being decorated with the same henna
pattern.

"How do you feel?" Meena whispered, using the music to
give them privacy.

"Fine," Nalini replied. "I've moved on from my silly ex-
pectations. It's all behind me." The lack of contact with
Lokesh helped her focus on her own future. She attributed
Meena's unhappiness with her husband to the adjustment all

women faced. Meena had been married only a year, so things would straighten out soon. Already not a trace of yesterday's sorrow clouded her friend's face. She talked animatedly to her husband on the phone. Nalini applied her observations about Meena to herself. A moment's sadness, a few complaints, or a few disappointments did not affect marriage.

After two hours they washed their hands and feet, oohing and aahing over the beautiful red decorations imprinted temporarily on their skin, adding to the festive feeling of the occasion.

"Dilip's parents are here," her father called out.

"Come, my daughter, meet your future family," her mother said.

Nervously casting one last look in the mirror, Nalini followed her mother upstairs into the living room. Dilip's parents were friendly and good-looking, tastefully dressed, displaying the same prosperity and sophistication as their son. They embraced her and made much over her, setting her mind at ease about her reception in their family.

A small, round-faced woman with hair dyed red from henna arrived and drew Nalini into her arms. "Without even meeting you, I knew from our phone conversations how to match you up with the perfect husband," she bragged. "Dilip is a most eligible bachelor. You and he will lead a long and blissful life together. I am so good at this."

"Showla Aunty," Nalini exclaimed, pleased to meet the woman she'd talked to so many times on the phone.

As the music got louder and more and more guests arrived, Nalini was swept away by the celebrations for her wedding. Late that night, when the guests were gone and her parents and she had hashed over the evening, she reached into her cosmetic bag for some night cream and found the plastic lotus. She touched the garish petals tenderly before letting the flower float into the wastepaper basket. "Good-bye, Lokesh," she said, falling into an exhausted sleep.

But he appeared in her dreams to tease her.

When Lokesh got back from shopping and walked into his store, his assistant updated him on the afternoon's activities, then casually added, "A lady called you. I told her you left the country and were on your way to your wedding."

"Why did you say such a thing?" Lokesh tried to curb his anger.

"Sir, because you said you were leaving and you had a suitcase in your hand."

"But I was only returning the suitcase to get a bigger one. Why would you think I'd leave without a proper announcement? Did the lady leave a name and number?"

"No, she sounded very disappointed. Then she hung up."

Lokesh could think of only one lady who would call him— Nalini—and his heart ached for her. He wished he had her phone number in Chicago, but even if he had it he couldn't call there, because a young woman about to become a bride didn't receive phone calls from other men. He couldn't tarnish Nalini's reputation.

He couldn't sleep that night. When his mother called to discuss his arrival time in Bombay, he asked her several questions about Jamuna. "Does she laugh a lot? Does she have a sense of humor? Does she like her work?"

Finally, his mother said, "You'll know the answers very soon. Her education and other information are listed on the résumé we faxed you."

Nalini had filled Lokesh's thoughts so completely, he'd simply tucked that résumé into a drawer in his desk. Now he pored through it, dismayed at how impersonal it was. He couldn't quite imagine what this Jamuna was like. If he were in Bombay he could have gone by the hospital where she

worked and tried to see what she looked like, how she treated
patients and coworkers. Was she a nice person or was she arrogant? In trying to do the culturally right thing he had given
up Nalini, and that thought splintered his very soul. He paced
his apartment like a madman. How could he have let Nalini go
when he didn't even know if Jamuna truly wanted to marry
him and move to the United States? He had given up somebody he loved for a total stranger.

Nalini's dazzling smile, her teasing laughter, her eagerness
to explore different cuisines, her spontaneity and her love of
travel made her unique. As he folded back Jamuna's résumé,
Nalini's voice whispered again, *Just as you told me to let Dilip
know my feelings, you can talk to her and see if she has any
questions. Or ask her some questions about her likes and
dislikes.*

Lokesh unfolded Jamuna's résumé, tapped her office number on top, and looked at his watch. In India they were nine
hours ahead of the United States, so Jamuna would have just
arrived at work.

He dialed.

The wedding day dawned to an excited chatter floating
from room to room, jolting people out of bed. Not that Nalini
had slept well. First she woke up at midnight, thinking Lokesh
had just said, *Gold cages do not make happy birds.* She'd cried
out his name. But of course he wasn't there. After getting a
drink of water, she sat up in bed in the dark, imagining stars on
the ceiling and Lokesh beside her. When she fell asleep at last,
she dreamt fitfully of Jefferson reading the Declaration of
Independence.

Then she thought she heard Lokesh call out her name, separating the three syllables in his inimitable, masculine, sexy
way. They were side by side in a van. He turned his face toward her. She reached over and kissed his dimple. "Do you

like to dance, Nalini?" he whispered in her ear and she cried out his name and reached for him. But only heartless darkness enveloped her.

Exhausted and still haunted by her dreams, Nalini could barely eat the bowl of cereal her mother set before her as she chattered about the arrival of Grandfather that evening about two hours before the wedding.

"We'll pick him up, bring him back here first. Then we'll change. It'll give your grandfather a chance to rest up a little. Then he can go with us in the bridal procession," her father said.

Along with family friends, they loaded up three cars with the trousseau clothes, dishes, and appliances and ferried them to the hotel, where friends waited to set up the display. The phone kept ringing off the hook. Dilip's parents called to say that a few more guests had been added to their list. Her office friends called to say they had arrived and to ask if she preferred that they bring the gifts to the house or leave them at the hotel. With the caterers setting up lunch, Nalini told them to come on over.

While guests sat drinking hot chai and coffee and looking through her childhood pictures, Nalini and her mother drove to get their hair and nails done. They rushed back home to make sure all the guests were well fed and to check messages and tie up loose ends. On this roller coaster, Nalini moved about in a dizzy state of excitement, greeting new arrivals and meeting relatives from overseas she'd never seen before.

She drove with her mother to the airport. Her father drove separately so that there'd be enough room for all the luggage and the people.

"In three hours, my darling, when the wedding ceremony is over, you will belong to another family," her mother said, with tears in her eyes.

"I'll always belong to you and Dad," Nalini said fiercely.

"Hush, don't talk that way. We know that's a fact, but officially you'll conduct yourself as Dilip's wife . . . and you like his parents, right?"

"Yes, I do. They're warm and friendly. They made me feel right at home," Nalini said.

They pulled up behind her dad at the crowded curb marked ARRIVALS. SHORT-TERM PARKING. He went in while they waited with the cars.

Nalini casually looked out at the terminal and her heart stopped. The world buckled and shifted beneath her as she tried to comprehend what she saw. "Mummy, did you say Dilip is already here?"

"His mother said he came in yesterday. He's doing the proper thing, keeping his distance from his bride. You'll see him in two hours."

"I'm seeing him now," she said woodenly.

"What do you mean, you're seeing him now?"

"There, Mummy." Nalini pointed toward Dilip. He was embracing a blond woman in a short red dress.

"Oh, he's handsome. Just like you said," her mother exulted, setting eyes for the first time on her future son-in-law. "But . . . who's the woman? I don't know of any blondes who married into his family. A close family friend, maybe?" A hint of nervousness quivered her voice.

Her mother's attempts at explaining the scene on the curb frustrated Nalini even more. Dilip and the woman were obviously not related or being friendly. The tight clinch and the locked lips churned Nalini's stomach. Her immediate reaction was to hide her outrage and pretend nothing unseemly was going on, that she had only mistaken the man for Dilip. Or to swim away on her mother's conclusion that the woman was married into Dilip's family or a harmless old friend. But then Lokesh's voice came roaring through her mind, telling her, *You should tell Dilip how you feel.* Lokesh's words renewed her confidence. She had to face this. "Come, Mummy, let me introduce you."

Her mother quickly turned off the engine and followed, clutching the car keys in her hand. They stood close together, waiting to get Dilip's attention. But oblivious to their presence, he continued stroking the blonde's hair, kissing her with a passion far beyond anything a family friend would merit.

Enraged, Nalini stepped forward and tapped him on the shoulder. "Hello, Dilip," she said. "Who is this?"

Dilip swung away from the woman, but the blonde clung to him. "I'm his girlfriend," she announced.

Nalini fought back her tears and asked the sheepish Dilip, "Girlfriend?"

He shrugged guiltily, then flinched as Nalini's eyes widened in disbelief.

"I'm Nalini's mother. Stop this bad behavior at once. Dilip, you're demonstrating poor, poor, poor character," her mother cried out. She grasped Nalini's hand and yanked her back to the car.

Nalini wept angry tears. "Why did he agree to marry me when he's involved with somebody else? Mummy, I can't marry someone who deceives me. He never even put the ring on my finger. He's been distant and aloof, and here he is . . ." She couldn't say *French-kissing the woman* out loud. They'd both seen what he was doing.

Dilip tapped on the window. "I'll see you at the wedding ceremony," he said hopefully, before dashing off.

"What a jerk." Nalini fumed. "He acts like I'm a piece of furniture. Mummy, I can't marry him."

"If we weren't here to receive my father, I would race after him and plunge my spare car keys into his dirty mouth," her mother said, wiping a tear from her face. "But we must gather our strength and, for now, pretend nothing has happened. Our relatives have traveled a long way."

They saw her father waving to them and jumped out to greet her grandfather, frail and tired, in crisp white clothes, slumped in his wheelchair.

"Don't weep, my child. Your joyous tears upon seeing me again make me feel glad I made this arduous journey," her grandfather said.

After they put the luggage in her dad's car and helped her grandfather get in the front seat with him, her uncle got in the car with Nalini and her mother. Worry scrunched her mother's face, but they couldn't talk about the mess they'd discovered without alarming the relative who'd traveled so far. So they listened to her uncle's report of their trip.

As soon as they got home, Nalini fled upstairs to her room, closed the door, and wept. She was such low priority with Dilip that two hours before the wedding he was smooching with his girlfriend, who had obviously flown into town. Was she going on their honeymoon, too? No wonder Dilip wanted her to go to India for several months alone. All the canceled dates, his rush to get away, now made bitter sense as did the phone calls that interrupted the dates that they did have. The marriage she'd agreed to enter was the gold cage Lokesh had warned her about, even last night, in her dreams.

Her father and mother came in and sat on the bed with her. "Your mother told me what happened. We cannot tolerate such disgusting behavior. Our daughter will not marry someone with such poor character," her father raged. "We'll return his false symbol of commitment through the matchmaker." He picked up the diamond ring she'd flung on top of the nightstand.

"Thank you." Nalini wept. "Please send everybody away. I can't face them."

"We'll hold our heads up high. You haven't done anything bad. Listen, my daughter, it's too late now to notify all the guests. Many have already gone to the hotel. So we'll go also.

And I'll have to make an announcement—let everybody
know what happened so Dilip doesn't snag some other innocent girl into this kind of marriage. Come, daughter; get
dressed for a public farewell to a rotten man and a celebration
of your being saved from him."

Instead of the elaborate red-and-gold wedding outfit, Nalini
dressed in the new forest-green silk sari, remembering how
Lokesh had liked her in that color. She rescued the poor lotus,
stroked it, and put it back in her underwear drawer. Despite the
bad start, Lokesh had ultimately proven himself the better
man. She would keep the memento of their special time together, and wished him better happiness with his doctor than
she had had with Dilip.

When they arrived in the wedding procession at the hotel,
Nalini was at once mortified and relieved. With her parents'
backing she didn't have to marry the deceptive Dilip. They
walked solemnly to the head table, which was decorated with
the white and red roses that she now despised. When all the
guests were seated, instead of escorting the bride to the Man-
daap, her father whispered to Nalini and her mother, "The bas-
tard's actually here, pretending nothing happened." They
turned their faces away from the groom's side of the room and
sat solemnly, heads bowed. Then her father stood up and began
in a hollow voice that was barely audible on the mike, "Thank
you all for coming today for my daughter's wedding. Due to
some new developments I stand humbly before you—"

"To introduce the groom," a familiar voice said loudly.

Nalini's heart began to pound as she saw Lokesh, dressed in
a dark suit, standing tall and handsome and reliable beside her
father. He covered the mike with one hand and whispered
something to her father. They both turned toward her. "Please
excuse me for a moment. Enjoy your drinks," her father said

into the mike, signaling to the waiters to serve the guests, who were craning their necks curiously.

Nalini's eyes locked with Lokesh's, and electricity shot through her as his message of unconditional love echoed her own. She left the table and stood to the side. He rushed up. "Marry me, Nalini," he said. "I can't live without you. You're my only love."

"What about the doctor in India?" she asked.

"I called her, just as you suggested. She doesn't want to marry me. She doesn't want to leave Bombay. She loves someone else; he's from a different caste, so her parents were trying to break it up by marrying her to me and sending her away to America."

With five hundred people watching, she couldn't throw herself into his arms. Her heart pounded. Her eyes filled with love for him. "I'll marry you," she said. "Mummy, Daddy, I want you to meet Lokesh Mehta, the finest man I know. Daddy?"

Lokesh stepped forward and said, "Sir, I know you don't know me very well yet, but I promise you I'll move heaven and earth to make your daughter happy the rest of her life. I'm well able to take care of her. I own a restaurant and store called the Spice Bazaar. Nalini means more to me than life itself. May I have your blessings to marry your beautiful daughter?"

"Do you want to marry this man, Nalini?" her father asked, eyes sparkling.

"Yes!"

"Look at our daughter's face light up. Look at the happiness he's already brought Nalini. Come here, my son," her mother said, hugging Lokesh. "She called out your name when she got to Chicago without even knowing it. I wondered then."

"You appear to be a decent fellow, a business owner, and well mannered enough to properly seek our blessings. I'm most happy to meet you and look forward to getting to know you," her father said. "Do you have any family with you?"

When Lokesh shook his head, her dad said, "You have all of us. Come with me. We'll proceed with the religious ceremony now and hold a civil ceremony after we get the papers."

He walked to the podium. "Ladies and gentlemen, it is my pleasure to introduce to you the groom, Lokesh Mehta. Goodbye, Dilip."

Shocked whispers buzzed through the crowd. As Dilip's mother peppered her erstwhile son with urgent whispers, Nalini's father called Dilip's parents over and told them what had happened. As they left, he led a round of applause. "Let the ceremony begin," he said joyously.

The Hindu priest stepped to the center of the canopy, decorated with cascades of roses.

A distraught Showla Aunty appeared by her father's side. "What's going on?" she demanded. "What are you doing to my perfect match?"

Nalini patted her on her back. "It's okay, Showla Aunty. Without even knowing it, you had an integral role in my meeting Lokesh. Thank you. I'll explain everything later."

Three elderly ladies from the community stepped forward and tied the end of Nalini's sari to Lokesh's wrist, and the oldest of them said, "The bride and groom will now walk around the fire to begin their wedding ceremony."

Lokesh dazzled a smile to Nalini, and the two lost themselves in their tangle of loving gazes as they floated forward to the canopy.

Love.com

BY
KAREN HARBAUGH

Prologue

*M*rs. Miyazaki adjusted her bifocals and peered at the sleeve she was hemming. It was sheer white transparent georgette, 100 percent silk, part of a kimono-sleeved floor-length duster that she had designed to go on top of a slim, strapless wedding dress. The dress was made of white double-weave matelasse silk, and the dress's hem had the same pearls embedded in the occasional patterned curl of the fabric. But the duster's silk was so light it had been difficult spreading it on her cutting table. She had had to turn off the fan in her shop and Scotch-tape the georgette to the brown paper on the table so that it wouldn't move. She had become too warm without the fan, and she didn't like too much heat. But it was worth it.

She could imagine the effect: Her customer, Joyce Vanderhoof, would float down the church aisle, the duster delicately fluttering around her shoulders and drifting behind her as if she were walking through a mist. Joyce would wear a small silk hat with a pointed brim, tipped just at the middle of her forehead, and no veil; the duster would act as the veil instead. Very sophisticated, Mrs. Miyazaki thought, even though it was unusual to wear such a thing over a wedding dress, but her designs were always unique. She was very proud of that.

She sighed. If only it were one of her daughters instead of

Joyce! Not that she wanted Joyce not to marry — she had been
the one to find her customer the perfect man, so she could not
regret that! Besides, it was one more jewel to put in her crown
as the Blind Date Empress of the neighborhood.

Mrs. Miyazaki allowed herself a small self-satisfied smile
as she set another tiny stitch in the rolled hem. Yes, they said
it behind her back, but she knew what her neighbors and her
regular customers called her. It was well earned, and she was
proud of it. There could be nothing better than tailoring and
sewing the best kind of clothes and making sure her customers
were happy. And they were always happy when she made a
good match for them, whether it was in clothes or a marriage
partner. What could be better than that?

Mrs. Miyazaki's smile turned into a fierce frown. What
could be better would be if her children were not so stubborn
and became married themselves. It did not sit well with her. It
was like using cheap rayon lining under high-quality gabardine
wool for a business suit. Very bad. How could she truly claim
the title of the Blind Date Empress when her own children
failed not only to marry, but even to go on the dates she
arranged for them? It was a shameful thing. If she had less self-
discipline, it would be difficult to hold her head up in public.

So she tried not to think about it . . . but it was difficult not
to think about it when the orders for wedding dresses — her
favorite thing to design and sew — came in, and none of them
were to be her daughters'. No blind dates, no engagement; no
engagement, no wedding dress; no dress, no marriage . . . and
no marriage meant no grandchildren. It was embarrassing, especially when all of her friends had at least *one* child who had
married, and all of them had grandchildren, yes, even her own
sister, who was one year younger than she was! But none of
her children would listen to her about marriage and grandchildren. She had felt like giving up on them so many times.

Mrs. Miyazaki peered at the hem of the silk duster again,

and her lips twisted in frustration. She had made a crooked stitch. See what thinking of no grandchildren had done? It had made her sew inaccurately. Very bad. She liked the clothes she made to be perfect, from creating the pattern to the very last stitch. Carefully she unthreaded the needle and pulled out the stitch, then threaded the needle again.

Her lips pulled in firmly in a determined line. The sooner she married off her children, the better for her peace of mind and the quality of her work.

Amy. Mrs. Miyazaki sighed. Amy was her oldest daughter, twenty-nine years old. Twenty-nine! She would start with Amy, because she was the oldest. But . . . it would be difficult.

All women had a measuring tape in their heads when it came to men. It had nothing to do with their private parts, but much to do with how well a man could fit into their lives. Some measuring tapes were as short as a ruler; some were too long; and some women measured men with barely any seam to let out when they grew, which was why, Mrs. Miyazaki thought, women chose men who did not fit well into their lives.

Amy had a very tall measuring tape for men. She had been engaged, and her fiancé had died. It was difficult enough for a woman to remarry when divorced or widowed. But Amy had always been a cautious girl, and since Jeffrey had died, her measuring tape would always be too big for whatever man she met, which was why her dates always came up short. She had become too . . . controlled. Yes, that was it. Too controlled, someone who did not enjoy life.

Mrs. Miyazaki understood, of course. She herself had loved her husband at first sight, and they had been married for forty years before he died. He had loved and cared for her in return, and never criticized when her first few pregnancies ended in miscarriages. Then in the next few years they had four healthy children! Oh, how he had celebrated each one, and held them as if they had been golden treasures. Yes, she could understand her daughter—she herself could not marry again after such a good husband.

But Amy was not her mother, and she had not spent any time in a marriage at all, nor had she had any children. It was not the same, and Amy was young enough to find another good man, and a full life—with children. Besides, Amy was too young not to enjoy life. Didn't she, Yoshino Miyazaki, enjoy life very much? And she was over sixty already. There was no excuse for a young woman like her daughter not to enjoy life.

Mrs. Miyazaki pressed her lips together in determination. Yes, she would start with Amy. She would do everything in her power to make sure Amy became married, and she would plan it carefully. Was she not a samurai's daughter? The ancient blood of warriors flowed through her heart. Therefore she would plan her daughter's future with all the strategy of a warrior before battle.

Mrs. Miyazaki gazed at the hem of the duster and nodded, satisfied. It looked quite good, if she said so herself. Joyce would look beautiful, and she was marrying a very nice man, especially picked by Mrs. Miyazaki herself. She carefully put the duster on a hanger and put a protective plastic bag over it before she hung it up next to the finished wedding dress. Then she went to her sewing notions drawer and put away the thread.

Her gaze fell on the middle drawer and her hand hesitated over it. Strategy was one thing, but luck was another. You could set up a situation, but if the timing was not right, or the blind date incompatible, or the stars and moon not in their right positions, all could go wrong.

She pulled open the middle drawer and searched—yes, there it was. She smiled. Yes, this would work. She would give it to Amy as a present . . . and the next wedding dress would be for her own daughter; she would make sure of it.

Chapter One

*A*my Miyazaki moved her pressure-sensitive mouse pen over the tablet and watched the cursor move it back by 75 percent. There. Perfectly pixeled. She gazed over the Web page with satisfaction. Not bad. Not bad at all.

Buzzz!

The sound of the doorbell startled her and made her hand jerk over the tablet. Probably a solicitor; she'd ignore it. She glanced at her computer monitor and grimaced. The table she had made on the Web page was now too large. She hated for her work to be out of order. She liked order. Lots and lots of order. It made life smooth, serene, and uncomplicated. A small niggling voice in her mind protested, but she squashed it. She was a competent businesswoman, a Web guru, a woman of sense and insight. Smoothness, serenity, and a calm, Zen-like life was what she aspired to. She breathed in, breathed out. Calm . . . calm . . .

Buzz! Buzz!

Amy sighed. It was not a solicitor. The persistency of the sound had to mean it was family, probably her mother. She went to the door and punched the intercom. *Beep!*

"Hello! Amy-*chan*, are you there? I need to talk to you. Huh. Maybe on a date? What is he like?"

Amy groaned. It was her mother—the farthest thing from Zen-like calm. In fact, if there was anything Zen-like about her mother, it was those incomprehensible Zen koans, or those stories she'd heard about Buddhist monks who had a habit of popping up at odd moments and whapping acolytes upside the head in an attempt to shock them into enlightenment. Problem was, her mother created more whapping and shocking than enlightenment.

No doubt she was visiting to convince Amy to go on yet another blind date. It was inevitable—her mother was the Blind Date Empress of her neighborhood, after all. Everyone knew it, and once her mother got word of the unofficial title, she took pride in it, and tried to get everyone who entered into her shop fixed up with whoever she thought was most suitable. So far Amy had been able to resist her matchmaking attempts. She preferred to make her own choices and her own destiny, thank you very much.

Amy wondered if it would be better to pretend that she was in the middle of a meeting. She glanced at the clock at the right bottom corner of her monitor. Six-thirty—not likely. Mom knew she never had meetings past six, and even if she did, the problem was that her mother was fully capable of giving her the third degree later on.

She sighed. "Hi, Mom. Come on in." She pushed the door-release button. It would take three minutes for her mother to come upstairs. She'd have to think of a reason why she couldn't go on a date in the next few weeks, so that her life could continue in its nice, neat way.

Her gaze caught the stack of unopened mail on her desk. If she was very, very lucky, she'd have a request for her services among them . . . no hope in e-mail—she had looked over that already. Amy picked up the first envelope and looked at it. CDI Corporation. Maybe someone referred a client to her? She opened it. *Mega-Vites! Sure to enhance your love-life!* She shuddered and hastily shoved the glossy pamphlet into the shredder. *Great.* First her mother, and now the junk mail was ragging on her about her love life.

She frantically sifted through the mail and turned over a mustard-yellow envelope—Nakagawa Enterprises—from a

town in Washington state. She frowned. Junk mail or a potential customer? *Please God, let it be a customer, one that I can
leave town for, please, please, please.*

> Dear Ms. Miyazaki.
> We have heard of your award-winning business de-
> sign services and would like to talk to you about helping
> us create a logo design and stationery for our upcoming
> new business and its Web site . . .

Yes! Amy barely kept herself from yelling the word aloud.
She hastily scanned the rest of the letter and grinned. *Thank
you, God.* The senior owner of the company in Seattle was
old-fashioned and wanted to see her work in person, not via
e-mail. *Not a problem.* It was always best to meet the customer
in person anyway. She heard her mother's firm footsteps approaching the door, and her grin grew wider. *Very much not a
problem.*

Amy opened the door at her mother's second knock, and
enveloped her in a hug. "Hi, Mom! Come on in." Amy bit back
a wince; she hoped her glee at having found a way out of her
mother's near-term matrimonial machinations wasn't too obvious. Her mother gave her a suspicious look and wheeled in
a small cooler—a cooler no doubt filled with obento boxes
full of food. Amy's heart sank. Her mother was bringing out
the big guns. "Tea?" she asked.

Her mother looked thoughtful. "What kind?"

"*Genmai-cha,* premium green, or buckwheat."

"Premium."

"Of course," Amy replied, and smiled heartily. "Nothing
but the best for my mom."

Her mother's suspicious look grew. "You do something I
don't know about?"

She *had* overdone it. "No, nothing. I'm just happy to see

you. It's been a while, hasn't it?" Amy gave an apologetic grimace. "I've been working a lot lately."

Mrs. Miyazaki's expression softened. Hard work she could understand—Amy knew that her mother had had to work hard all her young life until she met Amy's father, and by then the habit had been so very ingrained that she kept working, developing her tailoring shop until it was one of the most exclusive places to have clothes made. Amy remembered that when she was a child, she'd watch wide-eyed as her mother would take the measurements of starlets for the Academy Awards in her cluttered workshop. She'd spend days looking for the right fabric and the right color. She worked hard at pleasing her customers. Amy smiled slightly. Or rather, bossing her customers around until they conformed to her notions of correct fashion. But her customers never minded it, and in fact seemed to seek her opinion more than ever.

Her mother patted her arm. "You work too hard, Amy. It is not good for someone your age to work so hard, not to enjoy life."

Amy's smile turned dismissive. "Oh, Mom, I'm twenty-nine, for heaven's sake. I'm fine. Besides, you worked twice as hard when you were my age."

Her mother frowned. "Yes, but I was married and had children, so I had an excuse. You do not."

Amy groaned. "Oh, not again!"

Her mother looked at her sternly. "Huh. Fine. You are not fine. You are not happy and you are too skinny. Look at that. Your bones are sticking out." She poked a finger at Amy's shoulder bone for emphasis, then turned to the cooler she had brought with her. "You eat yet? Six-thirty already. I brought some makisushi, how about that? Homemade. And chicken yakisoba—your favorite, all nice and warm in this box." A warm, spicy aroma permeated the air as Mrs. Miyazaki opened the cooler.

Amy's mouth began to water. She had forgotten to eat lunch and had just worked through it, wanting to get the Cyber-aquarium Company's Web site updated before she quit today. She'd also just barely nibbled on the pizza she had ordered at three o'clock—delivery pizza, the kind that became limp and moist once it cooled. *Chicken yakisoba . . .*

She gazed at her mother and a brief smile flickered over her mother's face. Amy's suspicion grew. On the other hand, if she said yes to the food, her mother would expect her to listen to whatever proposal she might have and carry it out. Homemade food usually had strings attached, and the strings were usually tied to a blind date with someone she would much rather avoid. Strings attached to anything her mother did usually meant that life would become much more complicated than Amy wanted. *Zen-like calm. Calm,* she reminded herself.

She tried not to look at the food her mother began to lay out on the table next to her desk. "No, no, Mom, I'm fine. I've had a slice of pizza, really." Pizza she barely touched, instead of yakisoba noodles sautéed in sesame oil, soy sauce, and a dash of red pepper flakes, lightly tossed with seared pan-fried slices of chicken.

"Pizza. Huh. What kind of dinner is that? No vegetables. Greasy. All that fat. Better you eat yakisoba and sushi, and look, I have miso mackerel and pickle radish."

Dread made Amy's appetite recede slightly—her mother must have one huge agenda on her mind, bringing this kind of meal. She believed that a traditional Japanese meal was the best in the world, which meant that if she presented it, she also had a major agenda to serve with it. If Amy refused, she might just offend her mother to the point where she would not speak to her for at least three weeks. Her heart sank.

On the other hand, if her mother was intent on arranging yet another blind date, it might be a good thing if she *was* offended for that long.

"No, I'm fine." Amy tried harder not to look at the steaming obento box of yakisoba. "The pizza was good enough."

"Pizza is not good enough. Too much fat. You should eat better—you're too skinny; you look like you have tuberculosis," Mrs. Miyazaki said, oblivious to contradiction.

"Mom, I don't have tuberculosis. I just wasn't that hungry."

"First sign of tuberculosis," her mother said firmly. "No appetite."

Amy began wishing she hadn't answered the door. "No, seriously, I don't have tuberculosis. I just went to my physical two weeks ago. Doctor says I'm fine. Perfect health. See?" She pinched her own cheek. "No blusher, nothing to worry about."

Mrs. Miyazaki ignored her, continuing to lay out the food on the table next to Amy's desk. She picked up the yakisoba bowl and stuck chopsticks in it, then brought it to Amy. "Eat," she commanded.

"Mom, I don't take bribes." Sometimes the direct approach worked—sometimes.

Mrs. Miyazaki raised her eyebrows. "What bribe? I just brought supper for my favorite daughter." She waved the bowl, Svengali-like, under Amy's nose. "Mmmm. Gooooood. If you won't eat, then smellllll . . . so gooood for you . . . tastes soooo good." She deftly picked up a bit of chicken and popped it into her own mouth. "Mmm. Delicious. Too bad you ate the pizza. This is the best yakisoba I have ever made. Yum, yum, yum." She raised her eyebrows, gazing at Amy with a hopeful expression. "Too bad you are not hungry. I made this especially for you, and now you don't want." She let out a long, sad sigh. "I worked hard to make this, after all day I sewed and sewed."

Amy groaned. If she didn't know any better, she would

think that her mother was a mischievous *oni,* a Japanese
demon tempting her into doing something very, very disrup-
tive. She crossed her arms. No, she wouldn't feel guilty. Her
mother did work hard, but it wasn't as if she didn't have an
army of seamstresses at her beck and call either, not to mention her youngest daughter, Naomi, doing much of the cutting
and seamwork.

Amy's gaze fell on the envelope from Nakagawa Enterprises she had set down next to her computer monitor. She
looked again at the yakisoba bowl her mother hopefully held
up to her. However, she could use that bit of business to get out
of whatever her mother had planned for her and still have the
yakisoba. If she did that, she could at once avoid any blind
dates and at the same time avoid any accusation that she had
caused her mother to lose face by refusing the blind date, as
well as not offending her by refusing the supper.

She sighed and smiled. "Oh, all right," she said, and held
out her hand for the bowl.

Mrs. Miyazaki beamed. "See, I knew you were hungry,"
she said as Amy wolfed down the yakisoba noodles.

Her mother settled down in the chair next to her and put
some noodles in another bowl. She took another experimental
taste and nodded her head. "Yes, this is the best I have made.
Very perfect."

Amy scooped some makisushi into her mouth with her
chopsticks, closing her eyes again as the sweet-sour taste
flowed over her tongue. God, this was good. It was the best;
her mother was not only one of the finest tailors around, but
she was an incredibly good cook, too.

She heard a satisfied sigh and glanced at her mother, who
was wearing a speculative look. Amy braced herself. *Great.
Here it comes.*

"Amy . . . I want to talk to you about something."

"Oh?" she replied, trying to sound nonchalant. *Right.* Like she didn't know what was coming. She always hoped, though, that the conversation wouldn't come around to going on a date.

"It's about Mrs. Tanaka." Mrs. Miyazaki gave her a hopeful look. "About her store. They not do so good." There was a certain satisfaction in her voice. It wasn't malice, though; her mother had a heart as soft as premium silken tofu underneath her tough samurai exterior, but she did take an inordinate amount of satisfaction when her business sense—which was very canny—came through. "I tell them, 'Go to my Amy; she will make a better stationery, and the Internet store on the computer,' and they will have more customers. But do they listen? No! Now they have less business." Her mother nodded in satisfaction. "This is what happens when they do not listen to me—do I have good business? Yes. Do I go to my daughter to make the stationery and the advertising on the computer? Yes. My business is even better now. But they did not listen to me . . . until they see Jackson Edsel come to my shop."

Amy put down her chopsticks. "Jackson Edsel came to your shop? For what?" Jackson Edsel was the latest daytime-TV heartthrob in *As Life Turns,* and both her mother and Mrs. Tanaka were avid viewers. She herself didn't watch it, but her mother usually gave her a scene-by-scene synopsis whenever she visited.

Mrs. Miyazaki's smile grew even more satisfied. "He wanted a chartreuse casual suit jacket made of boiled wool, but I told him this was a very bad color for him and the boiled wool would make him look fat. Also, I told him he would look much better in a cool gray-colored suit jacket made of cashmere." She frowned. "He is a good actor, and very handsome, but he does not know anything about clothes."

Amy winced. "You told him all of this?"

Her mother raised her brows haughtily. "Of course. He is a

Winter, not an Autumn. So he said I was right, and he ordered more clothes. I will be very busy for the next month now. What's the matter? He is very nice man, and he promised he would come for more clothes. Also, he gave me an auto-graphed picture."

Amy's wince turned into a wry smile. Of course he'd come back. Her customers always did, despite —or maybe because of—her sartorial bullying.

"So I said to Miyoko, 'See, Jackson Edsel come to my shop because of my Amy's stationery and the computer thing. Amy make you the store on the computer, Jackson Edsel come to your store, too.' So now she wants you to make the computer store and the stationery."

For a fleeting moment Amy allowed herself the fantasy that the Tanakas wanted her to create a Web site and redo their store logo. They owned a very stylish jewelry store just on the edge of town. She'd been hinting around that they might want to update their logo and advertise their one-of-a-kind jewelry with their own Web site, but they'd been hesitant because they weren't computer-savvy. In fact, they still used their second cash register they'd bought in 1972. Still, their jewelry designs were exquisite. . . . She looked up from her empty bowl of yakisoba and caught another speculative look on her mother's face. *Yeah, right.*

"So I said, maybe James can have lunch with my Amy, because he knows the computer things, and they talk a little bit—"

"James!" Amy shrieked. "What are you thinking? James is a slimeball!" There it was, the blind date setup. She knew it was coming . . . but James Tanaka! "Mom, you know he's a butthead. I'm willing to bet he's what's made their business decline, if the Tanakas took it into their heads to bring him back into the business again."

Her mother folded her hands calmly on her lap. "Maybe

they think about it, maybe they not. Maybe if you talk to James and make their computer store, they find someone else to do the computer stuff, but you do the stationery."

Amy groaned. "Mom, look, I know you came here to set me up with a blind date. But James? Come on! *You* don't even like him. I'm about as likely to date him as . . . as Jackson Edsel would be likely to date me."

Her mother brightened. "You want to date Jackson Edsel? Hah, I will set it up; you will see—"

"No!" Amy jumped up from her chair and began to pace. "I do not want to date Jackson Edsel. I do not even know Jackson Edsel. I haven't even seen him on TV."

"You should watch," her mother said encouragingly. "Very educational."

"Educational?" Amy stared at her mother.

Mrs. Miyazaki nodded wisely and tapped her head. "All about the psychology. All about life and true love." She sighed sentimentally. "Okay, so maybe not James Tanaka. Maybe Jackson Edsel—"

"No, Mom, seriously, I'm not interested," Amy said desperately.

Mrs. Miyazaki nodded. "Yes, I think Jackson Edsel would be better for you," she said.

"No, Jackson Edsel would *not* be better for me," Amy said firmly. "Besides . . ." She picked up the letter from Nakagawa Enterprises and waved it in front of her mother. "Besides, I have to go out of town on business. *Important* business."

"Where?" Mrs. Miyazaki raised her brows suspiciously. "Who?"

Amy sat down again at her desk and let out a breath, relieved that she remembered before she became too agitated. "Kent, Washington, up north. Nakagawa Enterprises."

Her mother frowned. "Huh. Nakagawa. Sounds like a merchant's name. They probably not samurai, or even scholars."

"Mom, it doesn't matter in America—you know that from your citizenship test. Besides, if they do have merchant ancestry, then their business will be a good one and they'll pay me lots and lots of money for my work, right?"

"Hmm." Her mother continued to look doubtful. "Maybe they from *yakuza* family."

Amy rolled her eyes. "Oh, right. The Japanese Mafia grows cabbages in Washington state. I don't think so." The unruly part of herself perked up its ears at the idea of dating a *yakuza,* but she squashed it.

"Maybe they grow something else?"

Amy picked up the letter and looked it over. "Produce and a dot-com. The father's the farmer; the son's the head of a startup dot-com business, and they want to have an on-line order system for their grocery home-delivery business."

"Not good," Mrs. Miyazaki pronounced in dire tones. "Dot-com is like junk bond. Not stable. Bad investment, just like I told Mrs. Tanaka. But she did not listen. Better long-term, blue chip investment." She sighed and shook her head. Mrs. Miyazaki, Mrs. Tanaka, and a handful of other neighborhood women commonly met every Wednesday for tea, sushi, and the trading of stocks and investment information. Amy had attended one of their meetings once; the get-togethers reminded her of a Tupperware party of elderly female Wall Street sharks. They even played short trivia games about stock market history.

"I'm not investing in them, Mom, just doing a job."

"Huh. What if they not pay you?"

"I'll hound them until they do." Amy shrugged. "Look, it's not a big deal. I'll be up there for a month or so; then I'll be back. I'll even talk to the Tanakas, but *not* to James."

Mrs. Miyazaki frowned, then pointed to Amy's computer. "Who is going to take care of your computer when you are gone?"

"Cousin Nicky."

Mrs. Miyazaki pursed her lips. "He is only sixteen!"

"Yes, but he's a computer genius and knows these computers backward and forward and is better at fixing them than I am."

"He does not care about money," her mother said, obviously putting up a fight.

"He does care about skateboarding, and I have two tickets to a Tony Hawk skate demo at the skate park." Amy grinned. "You seriously think he's going to say no?" Thank God she had those tickets. She had thought of keeping them for Nicky's birthday, but this was an emergency.

"Hmph," Mrs. Miyazaki said, and Amy knew it was going to be the closest her mother would get to an admission of defeat. "Maybe the owner is a nice man . . ." her mother said hopefully.

Amy closed her eyes, searching for that elusive calm and failing. "Don't go there, Mom," she said at last. "It's business. That's all." She opened her eyes and thought for a moment that a satisfied look crossed her mother's face, but Mrs. Miyazaki turned and busied herself with putting the empty obento boxes into the cooler.

For a moment Amy wondered if her mother knew the Nakagawas . . . but no. So far as she knew, her mother had never gone up to Washington state, and didn't know anyone there.

She began to help her mother put away the empty obento boxes, but Mrs. Miyazaki stopped her.

"No, no, I do it. Wait. . . ." She dug into her purse. "I have to give you something."

Amy grinned. "It's not my birthday, and you won't get me to go out on a date with James Tanaka, gift or no gift."

Mrs. Miyazaki shook her head and smiled. "Forget about James; he's no good anyway." She pulled her closed hand from the purse.

"Mom!" Amy protested. "If he's no good, why were you trying—"

"Desperate." Mrs. Miyazaki waved one hand at her in dismissal. "Desperate for a marriage and grandchildren. It make me crazy sometime—my own younger sister have grandchildren, but not me. Sometimes I cannot even look at her from shame." She sighed. "Never mind; this is more important." She opened her hand. "See? This is for you—good luck and happiness and having fun, because you work too hard."

Amy drew in a soft breath. "Ohhhh. It's lovely." She picked up the tiny jade sculpture and turned it in her hand.

Two entwined dolphins danced on green jade waves, each minute detail lovingly carved. The dolphins' beaks curled up in mischievous smiles, and their eyes seemed to gleam as Amy turned them over in her hand. On the topmost dolphin's dorsal fin was a small hole—she could put it on a necklace. A gold chain fell into her hand, and she looked up.

"This for you, too," her mother said, and looked at her gravely. "It's magic."

Was there worry in her eyes? Amy's heart softened. "Don't worry about me, Mom. I'm okay." She kept a skeptical expression from her face—she didn't believe in magic, but her mother did, and it would hurt her to say otherwise when she was giving her this gift.

Mrs. Miyazaki patted her hand. "Don't tell me not to worry. Of course I worry. I am a mother. Mothers always worry." She hesitated. "See these dolphins? They are happy. They have fun. You should have fun, too."

Amy sat down abruptly in sudden worry. This wasn't like her mother. Her mother was a taskmaster, Mrs. Nose-to-the-grindstone. Maybe she had some kind of serious disease, and this was her way of telling her family. She swallowed down her fear and looked keenly at her mother. "Mom," Amy said tentatively. "Mom, are you all right?"

Mrs. Miyazaki looked at her for a moment, puzzled, then burst out laughing. "No, no. Me, I'm tough. Funny I talk about working too hard, huh?"

"Yeah." Amy grinned, relieved.

Her mother's expression sobered. "So when I say you work too hard, have no fun, it means something, *anno ne?*" She nodded toward the letter from Nakagawa Enterprises. "You go to the Nakagawa company, you work for them, then stay extra week, two weeks after. Have some fun. Maybe date—"

Amy gave her a warning look.

"Okay, maybe not date." She took Amy's hand and curled it around the dolphins. "But have fun, like the dolphins." She nodded firmly. "I will tell Nicky I buy him two skateboards if he work for you extra week, two weeks, and a year pass to inside skate park."

Amy's heart melted and she kissed her mother's cheek. "No, no, you don't have to do that. I'll pay."

Mrs. Miyazaki shook her head. "No, he not care about money, only computers and skateboard." She smiled suddenly. "But Nicky is a good boy. He get straight 'A,' you know that? I give him present for that, present from me, his favorite aunt Yoshino."

Amy looked into her mother's eyes, seeing the concern. She turned and gazed around her office, at how everything was neat and in its place, controlled and precise. Suddenly she didn't want to be controlled or precise; she wanted to be . . . messy. She drew in a deep breath. She hadn't been messy for a long time. Messy and wild and . . . and all that kind of thing, the way she was before Jeffrey, her fiancé, had died. She looked at her mother, whose expression had grown hopeful.

Amy shook off the feeling. *No.* It was much better to be serene and have everything in order. She was a responsible adult, and had her own business to run. But she looked at her mother's expression, which had turned from hopeful to mournful. Her heart twisted painfully.

"All right, I'll have some fun while I'm away," Amy said reluctantly. "A few days of vacation after I'm done with the Nakagawa job." That should do it. It wasn't necessary to disrupt her life for longer than that.

Her mother's lips closed stubbornly for a moment; then she shook her head. "Two weeks. Or else I will tell James Tanaka to ask you for a date when you come home."

"All right, all right! Two weeks."

Her mother beamed, and foreboding crept into Amy's stomach, right on top of the yakisoba she had eaten. She was going on a vacation. Her life was going to be messy for two weeks as a result, because it was on short notice and she hadn't anything planned. She glanced at her laptop. Nothing said she couldn't take her laptop and do some business while she was on her "vacation." The foreboding receded.

She managed to smile at her mother. "Two weeks. I can handle two weeks."

Mrs. Miyazaki nodded wisely, and smiled a small, secretive smile. "It will be good for you, Amy. You will see. Now, put on the necklace; let me see what it looks like on you." Amy sighed and put the dolphin pendant around her neck. She met her mother's eyes, and Mrs. Miyazaki smiled at her again, this time all innocence. Amy gazed at her for a moment and pursed her lips. Was her mother up to something?

Mrs. Miyazaki raised her brows. "What?" she asked.

"I know you, Mom," Amy said. "Every time you get that innocent look, I know you're thinking of some way to arrange a blind date."

Her mother threw up her hands in exasperation. "I already try with James Tanaka. You don't want him. Okay. I try with

Jackson Edsel. A TV star! You still don't want. For now, I give up."

Amy looked at her mother, whose expression had grown hopeful.

"All right, I'll have some fun while I'm away."

Her mother smiled and patted her hand. "You good girl, Amy. I just wish happiness for you, you know?"

Amy's heart warmed, and she pressed her mother's hand in return. "Thanks, Mom. You know I love you, right?" She enveloped her mother in a hug.

And her eye fell on her laptop computer, all nice and orderly and neat in its case. It called to her, *Take me! Take me now! You need me! Think of all the work you could do—on the plane, on the train, in the cab!*

She could do that. She'd take the laptop on the shuttle plane, get a good hour's or more worth of work done in flight, not to mention during the hours of wait time before the flight. Not that she needed it for the Nakagawa site—she always did the mock-up site beforehand on her own server before she transferred it to her customer's, so the Nakagawas could see the site and thumbnails from their own computers. It would be handy for the Nakagawa job and she could also work on the Alexander Web site later, and get it done way before deadline, and then she'd have time to stuff in another project during her two-week vacation . . . . A feeling of relief came to her. Her life would be even more orderly and safe if she took her laptop along.

She released her mom and smiled widely. "Thanks for the suggestion, Mom. I'll do that; I'll see about having some fun." It wasn't a lie. She did have fun making up Web sites and logos, while she wasn't sure what kind of fun anyone could have in Washington state.

Her mother looked at her gravely. "You promise?"

Amy smiled and nodded. "I promise," she said, and crossed her fingers behind her back just in case.

*   *   *

Two weeks later Amy sat in the airport terminal and opened her laptop. She had an hour and a half before she'd board the plane—plenty of time to get started on the Alexander Web site. She pushed the on button and waited for the computer to boot up.

Nirvana's "Smells Like Teen Spirit" suddenly burst from the laptop's speakers, and she barely caught the computer before it fell to the floor. "What the hell . . . ?" She straightened the screen and stared at it.

An animated picture of her cousin Nicky grinned from the monitor.

"Amy, dude!" said the virtual Nicky. "Sorry about the hack, but highest bidder wins. Your mom offered me two tickets to a Rodney Mullen skate demo, plus a backstage interview for my e-zine, and Rodney trumps Tony Hawk every time, 'cause the Rod-man almost never demos, plus he skates street, not vert, and I am totally into street." The animated Nicky scooted back and forth across her screen, doing a couple of 360 flips from time to time.

Amy closed her eyes. *Great.* She should have known her mother was up to something, but she didn't figure that she'd try to interfere with her laptop. She opened her eyes as the volume of the Nirvana song got louder. She almost switched off the sound when the virtual Nicky stopped his skateboarding and spoke again.

"Ah, ah! Don't touch that switch! You want to get past this hack, you have to listen. I've written a little timed code for you, but you've gotta guess what the password is. Yes, timed, Amy, dudette. The password won't work until a month and a half is up, which means Nicky the Virtual Computer Dude is your friend until you're done with your job up north, and take your vacation.

"Don't worry; I'll take care of your computers at home—

no hacking there, I promise. Sorry about this, but dude, it's Rodney Mullen. I mean, *dude!* Anyway, the password's hella simple; it's just one of the tricks that the Rod-man created."

Amy groaned. She had learned enough about skateboarding from Nicky's conversations to know that his hero had invented at least 95 percent of the hundreds of skateboard tricks in existence.

"Sorry about this, but, like, Aunt Yoshino talked to some skate dudes, and it's not like she could take back the tickets."

Of course. Her mother had an extensive web of contacts that made the CIA look like a second-rate detective agency. Still, maybe she could get into the computer and—

"Oh, and dude, don't bother to unhack it, 'cause I put in this program that'll blow away your registry and config files. I call it 'da bomb'—get it? But I did load some hella cool games like 'Awesome Skater Tricks' that'll work if you get bored. Just press the F5 key if you want to get to the games."

She was going to kill Cousin Nicky when she came back home. Then she was going to have a little talk with her mother. . . . Amy sighed and shut down her laptop. She didn't dare try out her Web program to see if it worked. Who knew what Nicky had done to it, and the way it sounded, she'd be reloading and reconfiguring her computer if she did it before her "vacation" was over. She closed the laptop with a decided snap.

She wouldn't think about that now. She at least had her personal digital assistant and could do a little work on that—notetaking, basic design ideas, some little sketches on the mini graphics program she had loaded on it a month ago. Thank goodness she had that, anyway, little enough though it was.

Her flight number suddenly blared from the loudspeakers and she tucked the laptop into its case, picked up her carry-on bag, and headed toward the boarding dock. She sighed again. The bad thing about not having her laptop in working order was that she'd pretty much be left to her own thoughts, and frankly she'd rather not. She knew what would happen: She'd start thinking of Jeffrey again and get all depressed, and her concentration would be off. Bad for work, and work had been her salvation.

Her mother didn't understand. Sure, she understood that losing Jeffrey was a great loss. Who wouldn't? But Amy hadn't ever felt anything for anyone except Jeffrey, and that had taken a long time to develop. He'd been her friend, and then her lover, and then he'd asked her to marry him. She had grown to love him in a calm, comfortable way. That was the way love was supposed to be, never mind her mother's romantic sighs over true love and love at first sight. Love simply didn't happen at first sight.

The thing was, Jeffrey had died, and her love life wasn't comfortable anymore. There were all these dates her mother had tried to arrange for her, and she had felt nothing but . . . well, nothing. Not even a warm comfortable feeling. It was more like yucky awkwardness, which she had never felt with Jeffrey. It felt more like her life had whirled out of control—or worse, was in her mother's control, if her mother's chaotic activities could be called control. Amy smiled absently at the cheerful flight attendant as she boarded, then found her seat, luckily by the window. At least she could distract herself by looking at the scenery.

No such luck. A few minutes into the flight showed nothing but clouds below. The flight was on the empty side, and she didn't have anyone sitting next to her. Half an hour passed, and she had gone through all her notes on her PDA, with nothing more to do.

So, thoughts. No—no thoughts. She thought of the computer games Nicky had loaded on her laptop. No, she wasn't that desperate. She picked up the in-flight magazine instead and opened it at random.

"*Now's the time for a romantic getaway to . . . Hawaii!*"

Amy slapped the magazine closed before she could read any more romantic getaway ads. She looked at her laptop again.

Skateboard video games. *Uh-huh.* She sighed, booted up her computer, and hit the F5 button.

Chapter Two

T   *he great samurai warrior Miyamoto Musashi smoothly cleans his sword of blood and sheathes it. He surveys the damage he has done and smiles in grim satisfaction. He has battled long and hard against the army of oni and sorcerers. . . .*

But wait! A mist arises from one of the sinister, dark portals he had thought he had sealed. He puts his hand on the hilt of his sword, ready for any threat, any evil. He pulls out his sword swiftly, a lightning flash in the dark—

The monitor blipped.

He pulls out his sword swiftly, a lightning flash in the dark—

Blip.

"Great." Kyle Nakagawa stared at the monitor and frowned, watching the virtual samurai repeatedly pull out his sword swiftly, a lightning flash in the dark. Another glitch in the game. He rubbed his eyes wearily. He'd been at this a bit too long. It was fun creating video games, and even more fun testing them, but a man's creativity had its limits. He rose and stretched, his joints cracking.

"What a slacker!"

Kyle turned and grinned at his cousin Dave, who tapped his wristwatch. "Yeah, yeah, I know, it's only—" He glanced at his own watch and swore. "Six-thirty. I'm supposed to pick up Ms. Miyazaki at the airport in half an hour." He quickly exited the glitching program and pulled on his jacket. Maybe he'd get back to it tonight.

"So you did decide to go with Miyazaki Web Design." Dave smiled an *I told you so* smile.

"Okay, Dave, you're right." Kyle held up his hands in surrender. "She's good." Very good. Each one of the Web sites she'd built reflected not her style, but her clients'. He'd seen a lot of Internet storefronts that looked pretty much the same from one to another, and it was easy to tell they'd been designed by someone who cared more about their own style than their clients' needs. But Ms. Miyazaki seemed to have a real feel for what her clients' businesses were all about, and— Kyle clicked his mouse on "reveal source," listed on his Web browser's menu—her code was very clean as well, technically very proficient.

His cousin grinned. "See, told you. Cami told me about her—she's on the Webgrrls list." Kyle suppressed a smile. Dave somehow always managed to slip Cami's name into a conversation one way or another—he was crazy about his new fiancée. They'd met on a blind date in San Francisco a few years ago and fallen in love on the spot.

Kyle allowed himself a wry smile at the thought. Blind dates. He was glad he'd escaped them after the first one; he'd choose his own date, thanks. The first one had been a disaster—thank God—because the woman had turned out to be nothing but a gold digger. She had heard he was the owner of a rising dot-com, and was sure she'd hitch up with a millionaire. Well, he wasn't the get-rich-quick type, but liked to build slowly over time . . . and it was a good thing, considering how the market had dropped out from under the overinflated high-tech companies in the late nineties. Nakagawa Enterprises was one of the few tech businesses that had survived and made a profit.

But Sandra, his blind date, had left as fast as the investors had, and for the same reason—no confidence in the market.

He caught Dave grinning at him. "What?" he said.

"I said, is she good-looking?"

"Who?"

"The girl you were thinking about."

Kyle's smile twisted. "Yeah. Sandra." He held up his hand again. "And no blind dates, man. They don't work for me. You lucked out, that's all, so don't try anything." He nodded at the e-mail from Ms. Miyazaki on the screen. "You aren't trying to hook her up with me, are you?"

Dave widened his eyes innocently. "Who, me? No way. I got the message the last time I tried to hook you up with someone. Kyle Nakagawa: Blind dates need not apply."

Kyle gazed at him suspiciously for a moment, then nodded. Despite his put-on innocent look, Dave's voice sounded sincere.

"Besides," Dave continued, "Uncle Toshi cleared her before she came here."

"True," Kyle replied, and relaxed. His father was picky about anything to do with his produce company, and had the last say, which was fine with him. Kyle had a lot on his hands anyway.

He looked at his watch. "Speaking of which . . . think you can pick her up?"

"No way," Dave said firmly. "Have to see about the repairs to two of the trucks at the Auburn farm, and then I'm out of town tomorrow. You go."

Kyle glanced at his computer. He'd like to figure out that bug before he quit for the day. Maybe he'd be able to get it worked out later if he took a break from it.

He nodded. "Not a problem." His stomach growled. It wouldn't hurt to get some food, either, and if Ms. Miyazaki was open to it, they could talk business over dinner. He glanced at his cousin again, whose face grew suddenly still. Dave was very, very bad at hiding his thoughts. Something was up, he was sure, but he didn't have time to investigate it now. He looked at his computer and smiled, thinking of the challenge of figuring out the glitch. Business first, then the pleasure.

By the time Amy got off the plane, she was in a foul mood. It had been a long time since she had been on a plane, and she had forgotten how much she didn't like them. They were noisy and boring, especially without a working laptop, skateboard video games notwithstanding. A drunken man had decided he'd talk to her, and it had taken a few minutes before she could get the flight assistant to haul him away from her. She had had snack food only, and it had made her think of her mother's chicken yakisoba.

And thinking of yakisoba wasn't good, because now that she thought about it, if it hadn't been for her mother's yakisoba, she wouldn't be here now. She usually did her business via e-mail and the Web — she could have convinced the senior Mr. Nakagawa that she could have worked that way.

But no. She'd had to give in to the chicken yakisoba, and because she gave in to that, she had to find a face-saving way to get out of her mother's attempt at matching her up with James Tanaka. And that meant finding a way out of town, because there was no way her mother was going to let her alone unless she left for a while.

Amy sighed. Kent, Washington, which was probably in the middle of Podunk-land. Amy took a quick glance out the airport windows at the gray skies that looked about as grouchy as she felt, and grimaced. She was no doubt going to have to wait outside on the passenger curb for Mr. Nakagawa, out in the wet, and she was probably going to freeze to the bone before he picked her up.

Her stomach growled, and she thought briefly about getting a quick snack at one of the airport cafés, but decided against it. The junior Mr. Nakagawa had e-mailed her and said she'd be picked up precisely at six o'clock, and if he was going to pick her up at the passenger curb, then she'd best be there at the designated time, or else he'd have to drive past the passenger-pickup station more than a few times before he'd see her. Best not to make extra trouble for her customer—bad business, that.

The baggage claim was crowded, as she had expected; the bags from two flights had been combined into one carousel. Amy worried her lower lip. She hoped it wouldn't take too long to get her luggage. With her luck it'd be the senior Nakagawa picking her up at the airport, and if he was as picky as he had sounded from his son's description, he'd be irritated at her lack of punctuality.

She knew these elderly Japanese gentlemen—enough of them had passed through her mother's shop for her to be very familiar with them. The older they were, the more demanding they were of their women, worse if they were well-off. The younger generation was better, and she had been lucky enough to have found that Jeffrey didn't care about social status, and neither did his parents. But the rest of them . . . woe be to you if your mother was a war bride. Didn't matter the background—you could be related to the emperor, but if your mother had been a war bride, particularly if she married a non-Japanese, you were beyond the pale.

Amy never could figure out what the issue was about that—maybe they thought the war bride was "no better than she should be" or some rot like that. She was pretty sure her mother had been snubbed socially, even though she had never shown she was even conscious of the snubs. Her mother had a lot of pride; she saw no reason why she should be ashamed of marrying her soldier husband—he was of good family, after all, and hers was even better.

But it was probably why Amy's mother had worked so hard at making her tailoring shop one of the most sought-after in the city . . . and taken such perverse glee at her reputation as the Blind Date Empress of her neighborhood. It scandalized the elders of the well-to-do Japanese-American social circles and made her the envy of them, as well. But, as her mother had said, she was the daughter of samurai, and normal social conventions didn't apply to her. A smile came to Amy's lips. For all her mother's buttinsky ways, she admired her for her boldness, for not being typical of the stereotype of the traditional meek Japanese woman. But then, samurai women—women of the warrior caste—had never been typical.

The thought made Amy smile more widely. She always felt better thinking of her samurai heritage, for all that she would tell her mother such things didn't matter in American society. She felt tough thinking of it, capable of handling anything. Samurai women had been entitled to carry—and use——a sword. She closed her eyes and imagined herself in full samurai garb, pulling out her sword and slashing at whatever obstacles were in her way.

She opened her eyes and looked at the crowd that was nearly obscuring the baggage-claim carousel. She looked up and saw her flower-print canvas bag coming down the ramp. Not a problem. She imagined herself cutting through each space that existed between the passengers' bodies, and slipped neatly to the edge of the carousel just as her bag came around the corner. She snatched it up and pulled it off in one smooth sweep of her arm.

"Nice move! You travel often?"

Amy jumped and turned around to find herself looking

straight up at Clark Kent. Except she was no Lois Lane and could see past the black-framed glasses to the Superman under them. Long, tied-back, blue-black hair, large brown eyes, high cheekbones that slanted down to sensually, smiling lips above a cleft and stubborn chin. She looked away, flustered; then her gaze caught the worn jeans taut around well-muscled thighs. She swallowed and raised her eyes to his chest—that was better. The sweatshirt he wore covered up what she was sure was a firm torso.

"Ms. Miyazaki?"

She lifted her eyes to his face again, surprised. "Yes, how did you know?"

His grin grew wider and he held out his hand. "Kyle Naka-gawa. You were the only Asian woman wearing casual clothes and carrying a laptop." He nodded at her pink Henley shirt and blue corduroy slacks covered by a long blue duster. "Typical West Coast wear for female techies. If you had been from Japan, you would have worn something far more conservative."

She wasn't used to men commenting on her clothes, and she felt a little defensive. She retied the belt on her duster more firmly, hoping it made her look neater, then realized that she hadn't looked in a mirror for the last hour or two, and her hair was probably a mess. "Not professional enough?" she asked, and couldn't help the defiant note in her voice.

He looked her up and down slowly and consideringly, and his grin grew even wider. "Not at all." He spread his arms out slightly. "See? Typical Northwest wear for male techies, com-plete with nerdy glasses. Except, damn, I forgot my Mariners hat."

A laugh suddenly bubbled out of her, her bad mood dis-sipating, and she clasped his hand. "Nice to meet you, Mr. Nakagawa."

His hand came over hers, strong and warm, and as she

looked into his eyes his expression softened and even became a little shy. "Kyle," he said. "Call me Kyle."

Amy looked at the strong hand covering her own. Her heart did a little flip, her stomach fluttered, and she mentally cataloged all the clichéd things a woman's body was supposed to do when in the presence of a highly attractive man. She swallowed again. This was, of course, just a physical attraction. Nothing more than that. Never mind that she hadn't had anything more than a mild aesthetic interest in whatever good-looking men she had encountered in the past few years. This was business, and it was best she kept it that way. She didn't really know if he thought he was in any way attracted to her. Besides, she didn't believe in love at first sight, and even thinking of such a thing right now was pretty damn silly.

She looked down at his hand holding hers again. He suddenly released her. "Sorry." He smiled again, this time with a tinge of embarrassment. "I'll get your luggage."

"Oh, that's okay, I'll—" She bent toward her suitcase.

"No, I'll—"

Whap!

They both rose, rubbing their heads. Kyle winced. "Sorry. My bad. I'll make up for it." He lifted her suitcase as if it weighed almost nothing. "I parked over at the parking garage, not far from here." He jerked his chin away from the baggage carousel. "You hungry?"

"Yes!" she said. "I'm starving. They didn't serve much on the plane, I'm afraid, just snacks."

He grinned. "Great! We can go to a restaurant, or . . ." He gazed at her speculatively. "We can go to my place and I'll cook you up some chicken yakisoba."

"No!" Amy said, and realized suddenly that her voice had risen. "That is, er, I'd like to go to a restaurant, please." Chicken yakisoba. She looked at him, and a sudden suspicion entered her mind. She wondered if her mother had some-how . . .

No. No, she wouldn't. Business matters were off-limits. Amy had made this very clear to her mother the last time she had tried to set up a blind date with what Amy had thought was a potential customer. The man had made some moves on her while she was trying to find out what it was that he wanted on his Web site, and she had been so surprised when he grabbed her for a kiss that she had instinctively used her aikido and flipped him to the ground. It had been a complete disaster of what she had thought was a business lunch, and she was half-angry, half-relieved when she had found out that he hadn't had any work for her at all . . . unless it was the kind of work she might do flat on her back. She had been furious when she found out that her mother had set it up, telling her that it was business, not pleasure.

Kyle held up a hand. "Not a problem—restaurant it is." He looked a little disappointed, and Amy's suspicions grew.

"This *is* a business meeting, right?" she asked. "So that we can go over your requirements for your Web site?"

They passed into the parking garage and he turned to look at her, clearly puzzled. "Sure. Why else would I—" He stopped suddenly, a horrified look coming over his face. "Oh, man, you thought I asked you over to my place because— No, hey, I wouldn't do that. . . . I mean, you're very attractive, and sure, I'd . . . What I mean is, this is business—"

She smiled, relieved, and put her hand on his arm. "That's okay, and I'm sorry I thought you were . . ." She made a face. "Well, you know, sometimes it happens."

He nodded, then looked embarrassed. "I wasn't thinking, obviously. Thing is, I have this great recipe for yakisoba I wanted to try out, and since I have people over all the time for dinner, I just assumed . . ." He shrugged and grinned, then moved around a bank of elevators to the line of cars on the other side. "But you're not from around here."

She looked a question at him as he stopped by a Ford Explorer and unlocked the doors. He grinned again and bowed to her after he hefted her suitcase into the backseat. "Kyle Nakagawa, at your service: video-game developer, produce manager of Nakagawa Enterprises, and host of *Cooking with Kyle*."

"You have a cooking show?" Amy asked as she climbed into the SUV. "How did that happen?"

"Came by it naturally." The Ford Explorer roared to life and he carefully backed it out of the stall. She watched as he skillfully maneuvered it out and around the obstacle course of construction and oncoming traffic. "My dad has a farm, and he had a lot of family recipes, some of which came from a greatuncle who used to be a noodle cook and then a sushi chef. I seem to have inherited the skill. Good thing, too, because I can't resist good food." He patted his nonexistent stomach. "But it's a side hobby. My main business is my video-game development, which is going pretty well right now, despite the downturn in the tech sector."

Amy gave him a sidelong look. "I'm surprised that you didn't decide to do your father's logo and Web site yourself."

He glanced at her ruefully. "I don't have the artistic talent. You *did* look at our envelope and logo, right?"

She remembered the dull mustard-yellow envelope with the sheaf-of-corn logo and nodded.

"It was done up by my great-aunt Fumiko, who had all the artistic talent of a rock. A nice lady, and I liked her, but nothing would convince her that she couldn't design her way out of a paper bag, and she did the logo as a favor for Dad. There was no way he could get out of it without offending her, so we went with it."

Amy nodded, totally understanding. That was the way it was with family businesses. Sometimes you had to let the elders have their way, unless you could get around them somehow. She looked around at the decked-out dashboard of his car. It hadn't hurt their business, so far as she could see. "She doesn't mind the change now?"

Kyle looked embarrassed. "Well . . . she's dead."

"I'm so sorry. . . ."

He shrugged. "We miss her, but she's been gone for over seven years."

"Seven years!" If they were going to change the logo, she would have thought they'd have changed it sooner than that.

"Yeah, you'd think we would have changed it sooner than that," he replied, echoing her thought. "But I left it up to Dad— he was closer to my great-aunt than I was—and he never brought it up until three weeks ago."

Three weeks ago. That was the very day her mother had come over offering yakisoba. Amy looked at Kyle in suspicion.

He caught her glance and his eyebrows rose. "What?" he asked.

"Do you by chance know my mother?" she asked, and watched him carefully.

"What's her name?" He kept his eyes on the road, but there was nothing but friendliness in his voice.

"Yoshino Miyazaki," she said.

"Nope. Why?" The Explorer slowed down a windy hill, and rain began to splash against the windshield.

Relief settled through Amy's chest and she sighed, but shook her head. It was complicated, she was tired, and she didn't feel like explaining at the moment. "Oh . . . she has a great chicken yakisoba recipe," was all she could say. "I was wondering where you got your recipe." *Right.* That was like asking whether someone from New York knew your uncle Joe.

He looked at her, then shrugged. "My cousin Dave gave it to me," he said. "He's as good a cook as I am, except he never took it to a professional level."

Coincidence then. Amy felt a little embarrassed at suspecting that he might have had some connection with her mother. He seemed to be an up-front kind of guy, and genuinely puzzled about why she'd ask that question.

"We're here," Kyle said.

The car turned into a driveway, and Amy gazed up at a narrow house set up against a hill. She breathed in the smell of the salt water as she opened the door of the Explorer and turned around to look out of the garage door. "We're by the sea," she said.

Kyle nodded. "Puget Sound—we're in Redondo, but the office in Kent is just ten minutes away." He jerked his head up toward the house as he took out her luggage. "I keep this place for my software team if we get to crunch time, or if we're brainstorming another game. It's fully networked and has a kitchen, bedrooms, all that, if they need it. We're just starting on another project, so it's all yours." He trudged up the stairs, and Amy followed. He flicked on the light. "Here we are."

She drew in a breath and let it out in a long sigh. It was gorgeous. Big picture windows to the west showed an expanse of sea and shore beneath stormy gray clouds. The wind had whipped up peaks of water into a white froth, and the setting sun was a thin brilliant line of white and red light between the clouds above and the dark line of mountains below. There were a few computer desks and computers toward the back of the room away from the window, with short partitions separating them; no doubt the sun sometimes caused a glare on the monitors. Still, she couldn't wish for a better place to work. She'd always dreamed of a home or workplace by the sea, but that was way over her budget.

"It's beautiful," she said, turning to Kyle. "Are you sure you wouldn't rather have me over at your office? I mean, what if I just drift off looking at the sunset and don't get any work done?"

He grinned, and she briefly closed her eyes. He had dimples—they showed up clearly in the light of this room. She loved men with dimples. Amy tried not to think about it, but focused her attention on his words instead.

"You'd think that," he said. "But there's something about this place . . . well, let's just say none of us at Nakagawa Enterprises has had a problem getting our creative juices going when we work here." His grin turned into a grimace. "I normally would have you over in our Kent office, but we're expanding and the mess and noise from remodeling near the cubicle where I'd normally put you is annoying. In fact, it's so bad I've let some of my employees telecommute from home. I think you'd be more comfortable here." He glanced at the dimming sunset and then at his watch. "You still want to get some dinner?"

Her stomach growled, and she put her hand over it. "Yeah, I guess so," she said. "Give me time to freshen up?"

"Not a problem. Here, I'll take your stuff to the bedroom."

She followed him to another room just off the living room. It was large, and though in good taste, sparsely decorated. Kyle placed the luggage near the bed. "I'll take just fifteen minutes," she promised.

He nodded. "I'll get one of the computers booted up, and make sure you're up and running." He left and closed the door.

Amy leaned against it and let out a deep breath. She was half-glad she was going to be here by herself. It was much safer that way. Being around him was nerve-racking. Truth to tell, every time she looked at him she wanted to take off those glasses to see if he really did look like Superman underneath. In fact, she wanted to see if he looked like Superman all over. He had hefted her suitcase as if it'd been nothing, and though she kept herself fit, the idea of getting one of those wheeled suitcases had been pretty appealing after lugging it to the baggage check-in at San Francisco. She was not used to this. She was used to lean techie types, not someone with long, sleek black hair who looked like he could bench-press a truck. She looked out of the bedroom's seascape window. It was a good thing she was going to work here instead of at Nakagawa Enterprises' offices. The view from the window wouldn't be as distracting as the view Kyle Nakagawa offered.

Her stomach growled again, and she straightened herself, then walked to the bathroom. This was business, not *The Love Boat*. She'd better get a handle on her hormones or else she'd be mooning about Mr. Nakagawa, not focusing on getting the job done. She turned on the faucet. She'd wash up, put on something less rumpled, then go out to dinner—

With the most delicious-looking man she'd seen in a long, long time.

Amy let out a groan and gave her wayward thought processes a mental slap. *Enough of that!* She fiercely twisted the faucet to freezing cold and plunged her face into a handful of water. *There!* That should keep her mind disciplined. Her mother used to say that there was nothing like freezing water to keep your mind on your priorities.

Amy washed, dressed, and touched up her makeup. She glanced in the mirror, satisfied that she looked professional enough. She took in a deep breath, opened the door, and met Kyle Nakagawa's shyly smiling face. Amy closed her eyes and barely bit back a groan.

Unfortunately, her mother was wrong.

Kyle Nakagawa had watched Amy Miyazaki close the door behind her, then repeatedly whacked his fist against his forehead. *Damn.* He was sure he had made a complete fool of himself. First he ruffled her feathers at the airport, then he clumsily whacked his head against hers when he tried to pick up her luggage, and then he almost blurted out what he wanted to do with her as soon as he looked at her: get her into bed and have wild, impossible sex with her.

Stupid, stupid, stupid. He could whip up a video-game scheme in no time flat, he could toss out quips on his cooking show, but put a gorgeous woman in front of him and he gained all the mental capacity of a small soap dish. Her eyes dominated her small, elfin face, and she would have looked ethereal if she hadn't pulled in her belt and suddenly revealed very womanly curves. It drove him wild.

And not just gorgeous. It just took one look from her large, vulnerable eyes, and he wanted to protect her from whatever hurt she might have suffered . . . and he was sure she must have. There'd been a wariness in her eyes, the kind that he'd seen too many times in the stray dogs and cats he kept on adopting. He knew that look: *Are you going to hurt me, too?* And it was always his downfall.

The problem was, this was business. He didn't hit on his employees, and though she wasn't his employee but an independent contractor, the two kinds of workers were too close in his mind for comfort. Still . . . nothing said that he couldn't try again after the job was done.

The thought cheered him. It'd be strictly business until she was finished, and then who knew? Kyle looked around the room and nodded. It was a good idea to bring her here. He wouldn't be distracted by her presence at the office, and at the same time, maybe she'd think he was an okay kind of guy if he catered to her every working need.

The thought of catering to her needs brought a warm heat over him, and he shifted uncomfortably. *Don't go there, man,* he told himself. *Working relationship only—for now.*

The door opened, and he wanted to kick himself. First, because she'd changed her clothes, and her jeans stretched themselves around her derriere like a lover's hand, while her lacy sweater gently hugged her full breasts. Second, because he had just told himself he'd be hands-off for the duration of her contract time. Third, because she looked at him with those *help me* eyes, briefly closed them, and let out a breathy sigh between those kissable lips of hers, and for one moment she looked as he imagined she might look after some long, satisfying sex.

And fourth, because he knew he probably wore an inane, lust-filled grin that would have fooled nobody about what he was thinking. He looked away, hoping she hadn't noticed. "Uh, ready for dinner?" he asked, then mentally cringed. *Idiot.* Of course she was ready, she was standing there, wasn't she?

She smiled at him, the wariness disappearing. "Sure," she said. "Where?"

Damn. He hadn't even thought of where they might go. He'd been too preoccupied by his thoughts of sad eyes, tight jeans, and sex. He hastily went through the list of restaurants in the area that had good food and didn't demand evening wear. He stalled. "What's your preference?"

She was silent a moment; then a wry smile formed on her lips. "Not Japanese. What's typical in this area?"

This he could answer without looking like a fool. "It's a mix. Seafood, mostly, with fresh produce. Salmon's a specialty," he said, relieved. "Rick's Café Americana in Kent is one of my favorites, and it's not that far away."

"Sounds good to me."

Kyle nodded and led the way back to the Explorer again. As he opened the door for her, his ears caught the wind picking up speed and whistling around the corners of the house. He moved toward the garage entrance and let the wind gust over his face. It had a humid feel, and not just from their being near Puget Sound. He shook his head. The weather was changing — as usual. He hoped that whatever storm he felt was coming in wouldn't be too bad. The house was a solid one, but depended on outside wiring for its electricity, instead of underground cable. It wasn't unusual for a fierce storm to take down a few electrical lines and render the desktop computers useless. He had had generators installed a while ago, but she'd have to know how to turn them on. Well, he'd deal with it tomorrow, and get her a laptop and network it to their system. That would solve any potential lack of electricity.

The drive to Rick's was, luckily, not long. He kept the conversation on work, and she seemed to be comfortable with that, he noted ruefully. In fact, she seemed more willing to talk about work than she was to talk about herself or anything else. He began to wonder if that initial spark of interest he thought he saw in her eyes when they had met at the airport was purely imaginary. He sighed. *Probably.*

Rick's was an old turn-of-the-century house, on Central Avenue in Kent. Kyle watched as Amy looked around the restaurant entrance, her eyes alight with curiosity and her lips turning up as she sniffed the air. She closed her eyes again and let out a breathy sigh in that just-after-great-sex way, and what was worse, the sigh sounded very much like a sensual groan. His groin tightened, and thoughts of bed and sex flitted through his mind again. He fixed his eyes on the framed antique newspaper pictures of downtown Kent mounted on the walls and made himself read the captions that he had memorized already for years now.

It was worse when they began to eat dinner. He watched with fascination as Amy took each bite into her mouth, at how her tongue slipped out between her lips to lick off the alfredo sauce, and how it made her lips look slick and sensuous. Occasionally she would close her eyes as she savored the taste, and let out that breathy little sigh, which made him wish there weren't a tableful of food between them so that he could take her right there, never mind spectators.

"You like that, don't you?" he blurted. *That.* He didn't blame her for raising her brows at him. "Food, I mean." *Dumb.* Of course she liked food. Who didn't?

She smiled. "Yeah. Too much. The tastes and textures are seductive, you know?"

He watched her lips turn up at the corners as she took another bite of shrimp. Seductive. Yeah, he knew.

"If I didn't practice my aikido regularly, I'd look like a blimp," she continued.

"Aikido?" His interest perked up. "So that's why you can move so . . . uh, smoothly through a crowd." He caught himself in time—*sensually* was the word he was going to use. It was the other thing that had caught his attention, the way she moved, smoothly, with an easy flexibility. Flexibility. *Don't think about that, man.* "I'm into karate, myself."

Her eyes shifted and dropped to his chest, and she let out that breathy sigh again before she gazed into his eyes. Hope rose. Maybe she *was* interested.

Wait. This was business. He was going to wait until after she was through with the job. She'd take maybe a month to finish, she had said. A month. Then there was her vulnerable *help me* look. You didn't go charging in and have rambunctious sex with someone who had that kind of look. Sex didn't heal wounds, and sometimes it made the wounds worse.

She bit into a shrimp again, then licked her lips.

On the other hand, sex could be a comfort. He could be very good at comforting. He was a comforting kind of guy—everyone said so. He even cooked comfort food—chicken soup, miso soup, beef Wellington, you name it. Kyle imagined cooking up her favorite comfort food and watching her eat it, slowly, bit by bit, hearing her soft, sensual, groaning sigh. Then he would peel off every bit of clothing she had on, slowly, and hear her make the same kind of sigh as he made love to her, slowly, and then faster—

"What?"

He blinked. She was looking at him, her head cocked to one side, as if she was puzzling something out. "Excuse me?" he said.

"You were staring at me, not saying anything. Do I have

food on my face or something?" She brushed her fingers over her chin.

"Uh, no. You look fine." *Fine. Right.* She looked like a starving man's feast, and he felt like he'd been on a fast for forty days and forty nights.

"How long have you studied karate?" she asked.

"Most of my life," he said, relieved to be taken away from his thoughts. "My dad was big on self-defense."

She looked a question at him, and he thought he saw some sympathy there. He smiled wryly, remembering his childhood. "Nothing bad, no more teasing than any other kid might get. But my dad remembers . . ." He paused, thinking about the land his father farmed. "My dad remembers the internment-camp days in Puyallup. He was very patriotic, and his oldest brother was a hero to him—my uncle was in the Four-forty-second Regimental Combat Team. So he practiced karate, thinking that when he was old enough, he'd go in the Four-forty-second, too."

Amy laid a hand on his arm, a comforting gesture. "I'm sorry."

Kyle shrugged. "Old history, and my family was lucky. We had good neighbors, mostly Italian. They kept and worked the land for us until the war was over, and gave it all back, every bit. My dad said the farm looked as if his family had never left. He doesn't dwell on it—no need to. We've done well."

She nodded her approval, then gave him an impish grin. "Black belt?"

"Yeah, how did you guess?"

Her grin grew wider. "Every guy I've met says he has a black belt in karate."

He laughed. "And they didn't?"

"No." Her impish smile increased, making her look even more elfin than before.

"How did you find out?" he asked, intrigued.

"I eventually sparred with each guy and kicked his ass."

"Tough gal," Kyle said, smiling, and relief settled in his stomach. Not so vulnerable, then. She could hold her own. He liked that, and it meant his protective instincts were all wrong . . . like the rest of his instincts about her. Still, he wondered how she sparred, and what kind of aikido she used.

"Samurai," she said, lifting her chin in mock hauteur. "I can't help it."

"I'm scared now," he said, pushing his empty plate away from himself. "You'll want to spar with me, a poor farm boy, and you'll break me in pieces if I do." He caught the attention of the waiter and asked for the check.

She looked him up and down with an assessing eye. "Okay, I've upgraded you to a brown belt."

He laughed. "Thanks. But how do you know I'm not just a weakling white belt?"

There was no way he was a white belt, Amy thought. She watched the way he reclined in his chair, and remembered the way he had walked and moved—with an easy grace that belied the strength he'd shown. You didn't get that way without extensive training. "You didn't break a sweat when I said I kicked ass," she said instead.

He grinned, and the dimple appeared again in his cheek. "I could pick you up with one hand," he said. "I'm not going to whimper just because you *say* you kick ass." He nodded to the waiter after signing the credit-card slip, then rose from the chair.

The dimple and the thought of him picking her up with one hand almost made *her* whimper. It occurred to her that she'd like to see if he'd try, and then she'd get into a real sparring match with him, and she'd toss him to the ground, and maybe he'd try to trip her up and wrestle her down right there beside him on the floor. They'd continue to wrestle a whole lot until they got all hot and sweaty, sort of the way they could get if they had sex.

Amy slid her gaze away from him and was glad the light in the restaurant was dim, because she was sure she was blushing.

Oookay. Enough of that kind of thinking. "Since I'm here to work, and we can hardly fight here in the restaurant, it's a moot point." She rose from her chair, picked up her sweater, and pulled it on.

He chuckled as he opened the door to the cold night air. The wind blew her hair into disarray, and she pushed it away from her face so that she could see him more clearly. He gave her an assessing glance, and his grin grew wider.

"Oh, I don't know about that," he said. "Tomorrow's Saturday. I figured you needed the weekend to settle in. You want to spar, we can do it tomorrow. There's an exercise room at the house you're in . . . unless you're afraid." There was definite challenge in his voice and a twinkle in his eye as he opened the door to the Explorer.

Amy wasn't sure if he believed her, and his challenge provoked her. It'd be pretty amusing to see that grin wiped from his face when she tossed him to the floor. She could do it; she had dropped larger men.

"You're on," she said, and closed the door of the car.

Chapter Three

*S*he must be crazy.

Amy stretched out her muscles, then jogged in place for a couple of minutes to warm herself up. She flexed her hands and shook them out. Kyle would be here in about fifteen minutes, and she was going to kick his ass. Just thinking of it had kept her up half the night, and images of him under her—and over her—on the floor haunted her dreams.

But she was a professional . . . professional Web designer and graphic artist. Professionals didn't kick their clients' asses.

They came in, assessed their clients' requirements, and created Web sites and office forms that would help their clients run their companies efficiently. They didn't go out to dinner on their clients' tabs, and then proceed to challenge them to a duel.

Well, okay, she hadn't done the challenging, but if she were truly the self-controlled, self-disciplined person she had been for so long, she wouldn't have agreed to this. She would have smiled politely and not even mentioned the word *ass*, let alone the kicking of one.

But there had been that challenge in Kyle's voice, as if he didn't believe her, and she had a hard time backing down from a challenge. She supposed it was because there was samurai blood in her, as her mother said. She couldn't imagine a warrior woman backing down. And yet . . . she'd been able to ignore other challenges to her competency before. She didn't care for the most part what anyone thought of her. Nothing said she had to take up this challenge.

Amy jogged in place again, and something bumped up against her collarbone. She lifted her hand and touched the pendant her mother had given her, then stood still, bringing the carved dolphins into view.

A small, superstitious shiver went through her. Her mother had said it was magic. Nonsense, of course. But her mother had given it to her after telling her she wanted her to have fun, to enjoy life, after trying to arrange a blind date with James Tanaka. Well, here she was, not working, but about to toss a great-looking guy to the floor. She supposed it was a form of fun.

Supposed. Right. Truth was, most women would think it was enormous fun to wrestle a guy like Kyle Nakagawa to the floor and have their way with him.

She didn't believe in magic, but thinking about her mother's efforts at matchmaking did make her think about seeing Kyle again and wonder if, after her contract work was done, maybe she could take a bit of vacation and see him on a noncontract basis. A date, in fact. It wouldn't even be a blind date; this would be all on her own. She liked the thought of that. Blind dates made her feel . . . well, as if she didn't have any control over her destiny. As if she were very bad at picking men. Well, she wasn't. She had picked Jeffrey, after all, and he had been perfect for her.

Sadness threatened to overcome her, but she pushed it away. He was gone, and nothing would bring him back. Maybe she should look forward to the future. She never would forget him, but maybe her friends—all right, even her mother—were right. Maybe there were other good guys out there, good guys who wouldn't leave, wouldn't die on you, and who weren't jerks. Maybe Kyle wouldn't object to a date after this.

Amy rolled her eyes. *Uh-huh.* As if he'd want to date her after she kicked his ass. It had been a good way of getting rid of the blind dates her mother had arranged for her in the past. She hadn't wanted to date after Jeffrey died, and yet her mother kept on pushing men on her. When she mentioned aikido as one of her activities, they'd boasted that they had a black belt in this, that, or the other martial art. Well, she'd proved them wrong.

Kyle . . . Well, maybe he was a brown belt, and she didn't doubt he lifted weights. But she wouldn't go easy on him. When someone challenged you, you were honor-bound to do your best. She'd been taught that all her life.

The doorbell rang, and she heard the door open.

"Hey!" It was Kyle's voice.

Amy drew in a deep breath and calmed herself. "Hey, yourself!" she called.

She heard footsteps near the door and looked up. She drew in another breath, then gave up any pretense at slowing down her pulse rate, because if she drew in as many breaths as she needed to center herself, she'd end up hyperventilating.

She knew this sparring match was going to be difficult. He wasn't wearing his Clark Kent glasses—he must be wearing contacts—and yes, he looked like Superman, the Dean Cain version, complete with washboard stomach. He wore a tank top and sweatpants, instead of the loose karate shirt and pants her past opponents had worn. There wouldn't be much to grab on him so that she could throw him. There was just the skintight tank top and . . . skin. Lots of bare, sun-bronzed skin that shifted over muscles like rippling water over granite. His sweatpants were the loosest thing on him, but the thought of grabbing a handful of that made her feel a little dizzy when she imagined where her hand might land. He smiled at her. And then there was that damned dimple.

Amy swallowed and wet her lips. *Discipline, girl! Keep your mind on the job.* He was just another guy, just another opponent. She'd toss him, she'd hold him down, and he'd cry uncle. End of story, and she'd get back to being the professional graphic artist and Web designer she was. He'd keep his distance once she beat him. Date? Forget it.

The thought of being a professional and not dating him threatened to depress her, but she dismissed it. It wasn't anything new and she hadn't felt depressed about it before. No need to feel it now. She watched him stretch and warm up, then pulled her gaze away. Best she pay attention to her own warm-up.

Amy jogged in place again, then stretched one more time. She looked up at him. "Ready?" she said.

"Yeah," he said, and an intent look came into his eyes. They bowed to each other and took up their stances.

Kyle moved first, circling around her, his movements pantherlike. She watched him, concentrating on his eyes for any hint of his intentions. A flicker, and he made his move.

She leaped and whirled away, and his outstretched leg missed her feet. She grinned fiercely. So he knew some karate, but that move was an easy one to avoid. Was he being easy on her? If so, he'd learn different. She feinted toward him, inviting a strike, and he did just what she intended and struck out with the side of his hand. It took only a gentle grasp of his hand to lead his *ki*—his energy—past her and, with an extra push of her foot for emphasis, make him land hard on the ground.

"Brown belt," she said, leaning over him. "Just as I thought."

He twisted his body, and her breath left her as she landed with a hard thump beside him. He rolled over on top of her. "Wrong," he said, grinning. "Black belt. I was *sensei* and taught a karate class for a while some years ago."

She found her breath at last, but as she gazed into his eyes she lost it again. His grin faded. She could feel his heartbeat against hers and was suddenly conscious of her hand on his chest. His skin was smooth, and the muscles beneath were as hard as she had thought they might be. He bent his head closer to her and she slid her hand upward, behind his neck, and let loose the elastic that held his hair in place. It flowed over on either side of them, a dark, sleek river, and she pulled him down and kissed him.

Kyle groaned and moved his hands from her shoulders to her waist, then gathered her hips hard against him. It made her kiss him more deeply, wildly, and she didn't care whether she had control over herself or not; he felt too good to let go.

She slid her hands up beneath his shirt, wanting to feel more of him, and then it was gone, a soft *whushing* sound telling her that his shirt had landed not far from where they lay on the mat. Her own tank top slid up, his hands following the shirt's path and moving gently over her breasts. His lips found hers again, and then descended to her neck, and then her col-

larbone, disturbing the chain that held the dolphin pendant and
following the line of it down between her breasts. The waist-
band of her sweatpants rolled down, and his hands followed
them down, moving them off her hips and off her legs.

His kisses disturbed the pendant, and it reminded her of
blind dates, and how she wasn't going to date Kyle because
she would throw him to the floor and make him cry uncle. It
reminded her that she had to be disciplined. "We shouldn't,"
she whispered.

"I'll stop if you tell me to," Kyle said, and kissed the tip of
her breast. She moaned and pushed at the edge of his pants.
She didn't want to tell him anything but *Hurry, now, please.*

"Please," she said, and tugged at the tied cord at his waist.
For a moment his weight left her, and then flesh met flesh. He
moved on her, slowly, his skin liquid against hers, slick and intense all at once.

"God, Amy," he whispered. "This is too good. Too good.
We shouldn't—" She kissed him again, and a groan came deep
from his throat. He pulled away. "Wait. Not here." He rose,
then scooped her up in his arms easily, as if she weighed nothing. He took her into the bedroom and laid her gently on the
bed. She closed her eyes, not thinking, just wanting him on her
again, hard and hot. There was the sound of ripping foil, and
the bed dipped, and then he was on her, his fingers moving
over her breasts and her hips and then between them. She
opened her eyes widely then, and stared at him.

Kyle looked at her and kissed her gently, brushing the hair
from her face. He couldn't resist her, not the way she looked
at him in that vulnerable way of hers, not the way she felt beneath him, strong and lithe, or the way she licked her lips and
breathed in just the way he thought she might when he'd imagined her hot and ready beneath him. He touched her, and she
closed her eyes, moaning, and then what resistance he had left
disappeared, and he entered her.

She cried out, and her hands seized his shoulders and then his hips, urging him on, pleading with him. It made him wild with wanting her, and he thrust hard. She arched her neck, and a sobbing cry came from her as she shuddered beneath him, and he burned with need until he burst with it, deep inside of her.

He sank down on her, then moved them onto their sides. He gathered her close and stroked her hair. It felt soft, as soft as her cheek. He lifted her chin and gazed at her as she stared at him, her eyes soft with spent passion and confusion. Something twisted inside of his chest, and he knew that he didn't want her to go away after a month. "I'm glad we decided to spar," he said.

A hesitant smile formed on her lips. "Should we have?"

"Yes," he said, and kissed her. Her response made him want her again, and this time he set her on top of him and watched her close her eyes and moan as she moved on him to their completion.

"We've known each other for only a day," Amy said at last, when her breath slowed and she slid back to her side of the bed. She moved her hand over his chest, loving the feel of it.

Kyle lifted himself up on one elbow and gazed down at her. A faint smile turned up the corners of his lips. "Do you believe in love at first sight?" he asked.

Her breath caught in her throat as she gazed at him. "I . . . I don't know."

His voice was serious, even though he smiled. "I didn't at first," he said. "But I think I do now." He pulled her to him, nuzzling her neck, then pulled the bedcovers over them. Amy put her head on his chest and closed her eyes.

She didn't know if there was such a thing as love at first sight. But if this comfort and the almost painful opening of her heart meant anything, perhaps . . . perhaps it might exist after all.

*   *   *

The next three weeks were unreal. By day Amy worked on
the logo and the Web site. Kyle introduced her to his father,
Mr. Nakagawa, and he was surprisingly easy to please. The
older man had only a few comments to make on her design before agreeing to it, and he smiled and patted her hand in a fatherly way that made her miss her own father.

By night . . . Amy drew in a long breath and shivered, almost enlarging the mountain-and-river logo one size too big
on her computer monitor, then wondered if the logo she'd created had been inspired by Kyle's —

She gave herself a mental slap and looked at the design
with an objective eye. It was a line drawing of Mount Rainier
with the Green River curling around it and forward into the
foreground, done in a distinctly Japanese woodcut style. It rep-
resented the Nakagawas' land and heritage, and Mr. Nakagawa
had nodded approvingly when he saw it. It was just what he
had wanted, he said, when she showed him how the Web site's
ordering system and database worked. The grocery-delivery
service would start small, just within a ten-mile radius. If it
succeeded they'd expand, but slowly. Nakagawa Produce and
Grocery was not going to follow in the footsteps of the failed
dot-coms of the late nineties.

After that it was easy. The Web site design fell together
well; despite the gorgeous view from her office window, the
work went quickly, as did the month she said she'd take to do
the job. She thought of her mother's urging that she take an additional two weeks off for vacation, and she glanced at the useless laptop she had brought along with her. It would be another
three weeks before it was up and working properly.

Meanwhile there was Kyle. If he wasn't working on his
cooking show, and if he wasn't working on his latest video-
game project, he'd come over for dinner, cook her a gourmet
meal, and then make love to her afterward, playfully or with

slow, deliberate seriousness, as if every part of her body deserved reverent contemplation. His eyes would gaze into hers as if he couldn't stop looking at her, and she began to believe, just a little, that he was serious when he said he'd fallen in love with her at first sight.

She was afraid of believing it, afraid of believing that she, too, was falling in love with him. It was less than a month! Nobody fell in love like that, so quickly. Or did they? Her mother believed it. Maybe . . . maybe her mother was right.

Amy smiled. Well, she wasn't right about one thing: Amy didn't need her mother's matchmaking to find a man who cared about her. She had done it just fine by herself. She'd been in control of the whole process.

She grimaced. Well, as in control as you could be when falling in love. Kind of falling in love. Well, mostly falling in love, she conceded.

The doorbell rang, and Amy hurriedly saved the Web page and closed the program. She turned in time to see Kyle smile at her, then pull her up into a deep kiss. He moved his mouth over hers slowly, sensuously, and touched her cheek with gentle fingers.

All the way falling in love, Amy thought, as she took his hand and pulled him into the bedroom. All the way.

Chapter Four

Kyle gazed at the small female figure on the computer screen, complete with battle gear and samurai sword. He put the character through her paces and watched as she sprang into a pitched battle with the figure of Miyamoto

Musashi. It made him think of Amy, and how she looked when he saw her stripped for sparring. Her tank top had hugged her body so that he didn't need to guess at the shape of her breasts, and her loose sweatpants had only made him want to strip them off so that he could see whether she was as lithe and strong as she looked on top.

Well, he had stripped them off later, but she had looked better than he thought, and he had felt about to burst thinking that she was letting him do this, letting him touch her and enter her until they both exploded with pleasure.

Okay, he was besotted. He admitted it. He'd told Amy he'd fallen in love with her at first sight, and maybe he had fudged a bit, because it was most definitely lust at first sight. But then she had looked at him with that fierce grin of hers as she circled around him in the exercise room, and he had wanted her body and soul right there. And now he had put her into his video game. Yeah, he was obsessed.

She hadn't come out and said she loved him in return, but he didn't expect it. It had been only three weeks, after all, and not everyone believed in love at first sight, much less actually did it. It would take time. But meanwhile she gave every sign she wanted to hold on to him as much as he wanted to hold on to her.

He whistled as he edited the program, then looked up as he heard a "Hey!" just outside his office. He turned and smiled. "Dave," he said.

His cousin lifted an eyebrow. "Happy, are we?"

Kyle shrugged one shoulder. "Could be." He turned back to the monitor, not wanting to give Dave the satisfaction of seeing the contented smile he was sure was on his face.

"So is Amy Miyazaki keeping you busy?"

Kyle turned back to him. "Amy Miyazaki. She's at the Redondo house, doing her work as usual, and doesn't bother me unless she has a question about the work."

Dave lifted an eyebrow, and his eyes glinted with laughter. "Uh huh. So she works in the evening, not during the day?"

Kyle could feel his face become warm. "Look, everyone needs supervision from time to time."

His cousin pulled up a chair and sat, shaking his head. "I thought you said she was competent. And yet, in the three days I've been back from San Francisco, you've had to 'supervise' her every evening, and gee, I don't recall seeing your car arrive from Kent in the morning. Your Kent home is *that* way, remember?" Dave pointed eastward. "She looks like one fine woman, too."

Kyle let out an exasperated breath. "Whatever. Just go away. I have work to do."

Dave's grin only grew wider. "I'll have to tell Cami it's a success." He rose and turned toward the door.

Kyle stared at him. "Excuse me?"

Dave looked back at him. "A success. Mr. 'I'm not into blind dates' Nakagawa is caught at last."

He swallowed. "Blind date. This whole thing about the logo and Web site was an orchestrated blind date?"

Something in his expression must have alerted his cousin to his state of mind, because Dave's face looked suddenly nervous and he shuffled his feet. "Er, not exactly, man. It wasn't my idea, seriously. It was your dad's. The logo and Web site needed to be done, and at the same time, it's been, what, three years since Sandra dumped you? You haven't gone out on a date since then. You're almost thirty. Uncle told me that at this rate, he wouldn't be alive to see any grandchildren. So I thought, Hey, Cami and I got hooked up via Mrs. Miyazaki down in San Francisco, and so why not you? I told Uncle about her and he told me to go for it."

Mrs. Miyazaki. Amy Miyazaki. Kyle looked at the small female figure on the monitor on his desk. It blurred in the angry red haze that seemed to have formed in front of him. A blind date. He remembered that Amy had asked if he knew her mother.

Really stupid of him. He should have known. You didn't meet someone who fit your specs by accident. It had been planned. What he didn't understand was why Amy didn't tell him that she'd come up here looking for a husband. He had thought she was more honest than that.

It didn't fit. She didn't seem to be the kind who went coldly husband hunting. On the other hand, he'd known her for less than a month. He didn't know anything about her, it seemed. He turned to Dave. "Does she know? Did she come up here looking to hook up with me?"

His cousin gazed at him warily and moved back a pace. "I guess so. She's Mrs. Miyazaki's daughter. She must have known and agreed to the whole thing."

Kyle stood up abruptly, almost upsetting his chair. "I have to talk to her."

"Look, I could be wrong. . . ."

Kyle glared at him. "Just shut up." He grabbed his coat and left his office, slamming the door shut.

Dave gazed at the shut door and grimaced. "Damn," he whispered. "I need to talk to Uncle."

Amy sat back and gazed at the computer monitor and then at the completed stationery that had just been sent to her. She was pleased with it. The Japanese woodcut design of mountain and river shimmered with the colors of blue, white, and green, and matched—as much as hard-copy colors could match monitor colors—perfectly. The Web site worked without a glitch—Kyle's testers had pushed the site to the max and hadn't been able to bring it down or break through the database. Combined with Nakagawa Enterprises' strong firewalls, it was about as secure as anything could be on the Web.

And it had to be the most incredibly fast job she had ever

done. It usually took her a month to do a Web site like this, but she seemed to have been working on overdrive this past three weeks. She was sure both Kyle and his father would be pleased.

She was done with her job here. She looked around at the room she'd worked in for the last three weeks, and sadness came over her, but she dismissed it immediately. What did she have to feel sad about? The job was done, but she was sure she and Kyle weren't. She'd take two more weeks and make it a vacation—she had been going to do that anyway. And then she could see about finding a place to stay around here, and still work with her clients long-distance. Most of her clients *were* long-distance, anyway.

She'd have to let her mother know. A part of her was reluctant to say anything about it, which was silly of her, because what did it matter that she was doing what her mother wanted? She wanted this, too, and it wasn't as if her mother had arranged it. Amy had fallen in love all on her own, all within three weeks.

Oh, it was crazy; she knew it. Just three weeks! But she seriously didn't know what more she could want in a man. Kyle was sweet, intelligent, great to look at, and great in bed. And dear God, the meals he cooked. His chicken yakisoba was even better than her mother's. She had to say that dinner was her downfall. She couldn't resist yakisoba, and the way he had looked at her as she had savored it made her think he had wanted to savor *her* just as slowly and intensely. In fact, he had waited only five minutes after she had put down her chopsticks before he picked her up and set her on the counter-top, pulled off her panties and had his way with her.

Amy shivered at the memory. Sex and food. Kyle and yakisoba. There couldn't be a better combination. And she had found him herself. It was fate; it was destiny; and even better, it had nothing to do with her mother's matrimonial machina-

tions. She grinned and picked up the telephone. If she crowed
a little, so what?

"*Hai!*" Her mother sounded cheerful when she answered.
No doubt she had had a good day at her shop, and perhaps had
matched up someone in a blind date. *Good for her!* Amy
thought. She felt expansive today, willing to let her mother
have her fun. It couldn't be at Amy's expense, after all.

"Hi, Mom!"

"Amy-*chan!* You happy? You work hard? You take vacation
now?"

Amy grinned. "Yes, yes, and yes."

Her mother chuckled. "Good, good! I am happy for you.
Always happy when my children are happy. I tell Nicky to
give you password. I bet you don't want to use laptop computer now anyway."

A niggling unease wiggled its way into Amy's stomach.
"No, I don't. I'm going on vacation, after all."

"Uh-huh. With that nice young man, Kyle Nakagawa, yes?"

The unease flowered into dread. Amy hadn't talked about
Kyle with her mother. She'd been too busy working on the
Web site and seeing Kyle at night to call her mother or mention anything about him. So how did she know his first name?
She had taken all the correspondence with her, and her mother
wasn't computer-savvy enough to know how to get into her
e-mail at home. If Nicky had let her look at her e-mail, she'd
skin him alive. . . .

"Did Nicky tell you about Kyle?"

"Huh." Her mother's voice sounded slightly offended. "I
don't need Nicky to tell me about Kyle Nakagawa."

Amy thought of her conversation with her mother not long
before she had left San Francisco, when she had failed to set
Amy up in a date with James Tanaka. She had thought her
mother had given up pretty quickly at the time, faster than she
had before. She swallowed, and thought about how Kyle had

seduced her with chicken yakisoba. He couldn't be party to—
No. He had said he had fallen in love with her at first sight. He
hadn't made that up, had he? She began to feel trapped, as if a
web were closing in around her.

"Mom, did you arrange this whole thing with Kyle?" She
had to know. She didn't think Kyle would be so ultratradi-
tional that he'd want to have someone matchmake for him.
Okay, so maybe it wasn't all that traditional, seeing as how a
lot of people did it these days. But why didn't he tell her that
he had wanted to meet with her as a potential mate? She
glanced at the Web site she had just finished and at the stationery on her desk. Did he really think she was any good at
this, or was he just playing along, the way he and his dad had
played along with his aunt Fumiko and her mustard-colored
corn logo?

She waited for her mother's reply, a bit long in coming.
Dread grew the longer her mother was silent.

"Well . . ." Mrs. Miyazaki said at last. "Maybe I help a little." Amy could hear just a bit of smugness in her mother's
voice.

"You *arranged* this whole thing? This whole project was
just an elaborate blind date?" She couldn't keep the anger from
her voice. All her work . . .

"Amy, don't get mad," her mother said calmly. "Why get
mad? He is a nice man. He cooks good and he is on TV with
his own show, just like Jackson Edsel, except not in a soap
opera. He makes lots of money, even if he has a dot-com business, and his father is also a nice man, make a good father-in-
law."

Her mother knew all about Kyle. All about him. She had
arranged this project, except it wasn't a real project but a front
for her mother's ambitions and matchmaking machinations.
Amy closed her eyes and groaned with mixed anger and embarrassment. She wondered if Kyle and his father even meant

to use her designs. Dammit, her Web designs were award-winners. She was a professional, and she worked hard on her projects. She really, really did not like anyone jerking her around like this. Not her mother, not Kyle, not anyone.

"Amy? You there?" Her mother's voice was worried at last. "I do this for your own good; you know that. You cry over Jeffrey too long; you need a better life, new love."

Jeffrey. She hadn't even thought about him. Guilt threaded through her anger and embarrassment, escalating both. There hadn't been anything she could do about his death, but she could control her life. Her life was her own. She wouldn't be manipulated or pushed around to other people's bidding. She thought of how she had let herself fall in love with Kyle, and how he had meant her to do it all along, seduced her with his food and the way he looked at her, and wrestled her to the ground. Her mother had arranged all of that. Her mother.

"Thanks, Mom," she said. She kept her voice calm, and she was glad of her control. "Thanks a lot. I'm finished with the project now. I'm coming home. Tell Nicky thanks for taking care of my servers, and if he doesn't give me the password to restore my laptop computer as soon as I arrive, I'll not only skin him alive but he won't get the Tony Hawk skate-demo tickets I've been saving for him." She hung up before her mother could reply, and didn't care that she would be offended with Amy for over a week for doing so.

She sat, shaking, staring at the Web site she had just finished. This whole thing had been a sham. Almost a month of work she could have done for someone else. Didn't her mother understand? She had her own business. Time was money. What if someone had come into her shop and asked her to make a dress, and then it turned out the dress wasn't wanted after all? She knew her mother would be furious if it had happened to her. Didn't she see the same thing applied to her?

And Kyle. How could he? He had even less excuse than her

mother. He was a businessman; he owned at least part of Nak-agawa Enterprises. Surely he could see that asking her to do all this work just to get her into his bed was a waste of time.

She thought of the time she had spent with him in bed, and a small part of her protested that it wasn't a complete waste of time, but she squashed it. He could have been up-front with her. He could have told her that he was looking for a date and a bedmate, not a Web designer.

She closed the program and powered down the computer. Her hands shook even more, and she closed them into fists. *Forget him. Forget the project; forget Kyle Nakagawa.* She was going home.

Furiously she ran to the bedroom and hauled out her suit-cases, then began stuffing her clothes into them without even bothering to fold them neatly, as she always had. A tear fell on the lacy sweater she had worn when she had first gone out with Kyle, and she rubbed at it, then gave up, because the tears were falling faster now, and she wiped them away from her eyes with the back of her hand.

Finally all her clothes were packed, and she closed the suit-case zipper with a fierce pull. She put on a sweater and called a cab. She had to go now. She'd e-mail Kyle later and let him know everything was done. She had uploaded the Web site and the logo to the public server already. It'd give him less of an excuse to hire a Web designer the next time he wanted to se-duce someone, she thought savagely.

The sound of a car came to her—it must be the cab. Amy hauled down the suitcases and pulled them out the door, stum-bling slightly and catching herself as she went down the stairs. Rain fell on her face, and she was glad. Nobody could tell she was crying if her face was wet with raindrops.

She brought suitcases down to the waiting car—no, it was a Ford Explorer, and Kyle was getting out of it. She pushed her wet hair out of her face. Fine. She could just tell him right here and now what she thought of him.

"Where the hell do you think you're going?" he said, his voice low and harsh. His eyes seemed to blaze in the darkness, and the light from the house outlined the muscles in his jaw.

"Home," Amy said. "The Web site is done and loaded. The logos and stationery are done. You don't need me anymore, and I don't need you." The words tumbled from her lips fast and furious, totally uncontrolled. She didn't care. She had had enough of control—God knew it didn't do her any good. Not when Jeffrey died, not now, when she looked in Kyle's eyes and knew he must have connived with her mother all along. "Thanks for the dates—but I don't need anyone to arrange blind dates for me. Not you, not my mother, nobody."

His face seemed to grow pale. "So you knew about it."

Her heart sank. He admitted it. "I figured it out," she said. "I'm not stupid. If my mom could see what a catch you are, of course I could. Of course she'd try to set something up. And you went along with it. I can't believe it." She put scorn in her voice, wanting to push him away, because being so close hurt her down to her heart. She looked up and saw her cab arriving. "Excuse me; my cab is waiting. I'm going home." She pushed past him, lugging her suitcases along with her, thinking once again that the next time she was going to get one of those damned wheeled suitcases, because making an exit with bags hitting her legs made for less of a graceful show than she wanted. If she left anybody, she wanted to make him regret it, dammit.

Amy took a last glance back at him, at the rain soaking his hair and his face. He stared at her, his hands in fists. He was saying something—she couldn't hear; the rain was falling faster now and was loud in her ears—but she didn't care. She hoisted her bags into the trunk of the cab, hastily climbed into the backseat, and told the cabdriver to get to the airport pronto.

She was glad she was sitting in the backseat. It wouldn't be so obvious that she was crying, and she could wipe away the tears in peace. She fished around in her purse for some tissues. *Great.* Nothing.

She looked up to find a box of tissues being handed over the back of the front seat, and saw the driver's sympathetic eyes. She took one, then wiped her face and blew her nose.

"Bad fight, eh?" he said with a lilt in his voice. He was from India, if she gauged the accent right, and, probably working his way through college. "I tell you, it's a bad thing to leave the man before he talks to you."

Great. Now she was even getting advice for the lovelorn from the cabdriver.

He gestured with one hand. "We have a better way in India—arranged marriages. But even so, there are little problems. I did not see my wife until three days before I married her. But it was good, because we came to love each other. Love comes slow, even in America. You can't speed it up. But you marry, you work it out, do you see?"

She thought of Kyle saying that he had fallen in love with her at first sight. Lust maybe. Not love. The cabdriver was right. She nodded.

Encouraged, the cabdriver smiled and gave forth more advice, most of which Amy didn't hear, because she drifted in and out of her own thoughts, remembering Kyle and what he said, what he looked like, and how she wished he hadn't agreed to this whole stupid charade. She wished they had come together without her mother's matchmaking, so that she could believe it was real, not forced, not put on.

She didn't want it forced or put on. She wanted it to be real. Because . . . because she was very much afraid—very *much* afraid—that she was still horribly, terribly in love with Kyle and there was nothing she could do about it. The realization brought fresh tears to her eyes, and the cabdriver gave her the whole box this time. She sniffled her thank-you into the tissues, and managed, by the time they reached the airport, to look as if she had not had any sleep instead of crying her eyes out.

Amy sighed. By the time she reached San Francisco she was going to be completely calm and controlled. She was going to put all of this behind her and concentrate on her business. It was what she had done after Jeffrey had died, and it had given her some order in her life, had put her back on her feet. She could do it again.

The cabdriver gave her a gentle pat on her hand as she paid him, and he set her suitcases on the passenger curb. "You work it out with your sweetheart, okay?" he said, and his look was so kind that it almost made her cry again. She nodded and smiled, not promising anything, and he looked satisfied. "Go in peace," he said.

The man's words gave her a measure of comfort, and she turned away toward the ticket counter. She was going home. Whatever additional comfort she would find, she'd find there. She was going to hole up in her condominium and not come out for a week. That would be her comfort. She liked to be alone, after all.

Somehow, as Amy boarded the plane and gave her ticket to the flight attendant, being alone didn't sound all that comforting.

Chapter Five

Kyle stood in the rain, watching Amy leave in the cab. She *hadn't* known about the blind date arrangement— he knew there had to be some other explanation than the one he had first hit on. Amy had been crying. He was sure of it. If she had been as gold digging as Sandra had been, she wouldn't have been in tears; she would have smiled, shrugged, and left, and he would have heard not one word more from her.

It had killed him to see Amy like that, dripping wet like a lost kitten, the *help me* expression back in her eyes. But he'd just stood there staring at her, anger and bewilderment making it impossible for him to speak. And when he did manage to open his mouth, all he could say was "Come back"—but she must not have heard because she had shut the door to the cab.

He shivered and looked at the house. He might be a stupid geekoid computer nerd, but at least he knew enough to get out of the rain. He looked around the house once he entered and saw the supply of the stationery Amy had ordered with the new logo on the top left corner. He had reviewed the Web site she had created for her father's grocery-delivery service, and saw the beta test reports—solid functionality. She did great work. Of course she would. She was a professional, and she worked hard. If she was looking for a husband, well fine. But all the evidence showed that despite their times together, her main focus was on the work.

He drummed his fingers on the desk and thought over her words. He had thought at first that she could have been part of this whole elaborate blind date scheme, but it was clear she hadn't known about it. Okay, so her mother—and his cousin Dave and his father—had colluded to bring them together. But Amy said she had *figured* out that her mother was behind this. It didn't mean she had known about it all along.

If she hadn't known . . . Kyle looked at the stationery again. She would have been furious at finding out that she had been led to believe she was contracted to do a job and that it was only a ruse to get her to meet him. He'd be furious, too, in her place. It was unprofessional as hell.

A niggling thought that his whole involvement with her had

been unprofessional entered his mind, and he winced. Well, okay. He should have kept his distance. But the fact was, she had wanted him as badly as he had wanted her. But he had told himself that they'd been on an equal professional footing, and that it wasn't a matter of her being his employee. She wasn't his employee—she was an independent contractor who owned her own business. Still, it wasn't like him to get involved with women like this. He liked to keep it clean.

Right. Kyle sighed. This was probably the messiest relationship he had ever been in. Amy was furious with him, he was sure, and rightfully so if she thought he had agreed to this whole crazy scheme his father and cousin had concocted.

He was going to get her back. One way or another, he was going to get her back. She was probably too angry with him to talk, or even want to look at his e-mails. But he was patient—patient enough not to go headlong into the dot-com craze, and so patient enough to wait for her, even though he had fallen headlong in love with Amy. He'd get the full skinny from his dad and Dave and then he'd figure out how to approach Amy, once enough time had passed for her to calm down. A week, max. She was a fiercely passionate woman, and he loved her for that, but she also had iron control over herself most of the time. A week was all he needed. He'd have to work hard, but he could do it.

Kyle rose from the desk and headed down to his Explorer. He was going have a talk with his dad and with Cousin Dave, and he suspected Dave knew it. No doubt they'd be waiting for him when he arrived. *Good.* His smile was grim. They were going to know how very, very displeased he was.

Amy had pushed her plush armchair up to the computer monitor and sat in the chair, a blanket pulled around her shoulders. Once again she found she had not done a thing on the

Alexander Web site, but had gone drifting off into her thoughts, which inevitably turned to Kyle.

She had no discipline where Kyle was concerned. She'd left him a week and a half ago, and all she could do was think of him, his shy smile, his gentle hands on her body, the feel of his sleek long hair. There had been a couple of e-mails from him, but she hadn't looked at them so far. They could wait. She knew if she read them she'd start crying again, and she hated to cry.

The computer monitor glared at her, and she pushed the mouse around, feeling guilty that she hadn't done any work for the last hour. She pushed the mouse away from her. She should take a break, look over her mail. Then she'd get back to work. The mail sat in a pile in her in-box; she hadn't looked at it for a few days. Mostly junk mail, she was sure.

Junk, junk, junk, junk. Amy tossed most of it into her shredder. A flat, hard cardboard envelope took her attention.

Nakagawa Enterprises. Amy swallowed. Probably from Kyle. She almost put it aside, then gave herself a mental slap. *C'mon, you idiot; get over it. You can't keep mooning about him for the rest of your life.* She opened the envelope and pulled out the compact disc.

Five Rings was printed on the front of the jewel case. One of Kyle's video games, it seemed, probably the one with Miyamoto Musashi that she had seen him working on. A sticky note was on the front of the case. *Give this a try—please. Love, Kyle.*

Love, Kyle. Her heart lifted. Did he love her still? Maybe it was just the way he closed all his letters. She smiled slightly. *Yeah, right.* She imagined him writing to his distributors with *Love, Kyle* at the end of his letters. She pushed the CD-ROM bay button, slipped the compact disc into the bay, and closed it.

The CD-ROM bay hummed and the program began. It was

a video game, and there was Miyamoto Musashi, but there was another character there with him, a female. Amy looked closer and shook her head, a reluctant smile coming to her lips. Miyamoto Musashi looked very much like Kyle, and the female warrior looked very much like her. She watched as the two clashed their swords, fighting their virtual battle. It reminded her of the time she had sparred with him in the exercise room, and how it had ended—in hot, sweaty, totally satisfying sex. She watched the small warriors fighting, and wondered how it would end.

The two clashed their swords one last time, and lightning struck both their swords, breaking them in half. The two figures dropped their weapons and the Kyle warrior swept the Amy warrior into his arms.

The program stopped, and words in an Asian-type font appeared on the screen: *To find out the exciting end of the adventure of Five Rings, click here.* An arrow flashed, pointing to a heart-shaped image with the words *love.com* in the middle of it. She hesitated.

The words disappeared, and one word replaced it. *Please.* She smiled reluctantly, and clicked the heart image.

Her Web browser fired up, and she was glad she had a high-speed DSL connection, because the love.com Web site she came to probably had the largest collection of heart, flower, and wedding-ring images she'd ever seen on the World Wide Web, and it would have loaded with snail-like speed if she had had a regular modem. Each one had a message in it when she rolled her cursor onto it. *I love you,* said one. *Come back,* said another. *It's not my fault!* She moved her cursor over a ring. The words *Marry me* popped up.

She moved her cursor away from the ring image and wet her lips. He wanted her to marry him. She shook her head. She had to think about it. They hadn't known each other that long, not long at all. But her hand moved the cursor over yet another ring.

Marry me popped up again. She moved the cursor to another. *Marry me.* Another. *Marry me.* Another one—nope. Amy giggled and then began to cry. *Marry me and I'll feed you chicken yakisoba for the rest of your life,* the last ring said. Chicken yakisoba. The man was ridiculous.

All right. One of the heart images had said it wasn't his fault. Maybe he had been as clueless about her mother's matchmaking scheme as she had been. She'd been so miserable, so angry, that she hadn't given him any time to explain. *My bad,* she thought. At least she could give him a call.

Amy reached for the phone, then noticed that she had a call waiting. Maybe it was Kyle. She dialed her voice mail and listened.

It was her mother.

"Amy-*chan,* you don't answer the phone! You don't answer the door! I know your heart is broken, and this makes me very sad. It is my fault you are sad." Her mother's voice sounded low, depressed. "I mess up this blind date. Now you are angry at Kyle Nakagawa, this nice man who would make a perfect husband for you, and makes better chicken yakisoba than I do, with his own TV show. It is not his fault! It is my fault, his father's fault, also his cousin's fault. We only wanted the best for both of you! You forgive me? I tell you what. I will go to Kyle Nakagawa on the airplane today, and fix it all up." *Click.*

Amy groaned and banged her forehead on her desk. *No. No, no, no, no, no. Not again.* She couldn't have her mother interfering again, not now just when Kyle had proposed, regardless of whether she intended to accept his proposal or not. But her mother's English had been very mangled, and it was clear to Amy that she was terribly upset. She was sure her mother was on her way to Kent, Washington, right now, if she hadn't already arrived.

Amy ran to her bedroom and grabbed a duffel bag—no time to pack anything other than the essentials, because she wasn't going to stay long. Only long enough to keep her mother from messing up any future relationship with Kyle. And if her mother dared think she was going to set up another date . . . Amy shuddered.

She drove her own car to the airport this time, recklessly parking it in the most expensive parking space at the airport. She thrust her credit card at the ticket counter agent, muttering, "Hurry, hurry," and hoping she could get a flight in the next hour that would have enough room for one more passenger. Her credit-card bill was piling up these days, but she didn't care. Anything was better than her mother interfering in her love life once again. She gave a small sigh of relief when the ticket agent found an exorbitantly expensive last-minute seat for her. *Whatever.* Whatever it took to get to her mother before her mother got to Kyle.

The wait was torture. Amy tried to occupy her thoughts with what she would say to Kyle, what she would say to her mother, and how not to embarrass herself when she got there. If she were honest, she had to say she hadn't been fair to Kyle. She should have stayed long enough to hear him out. But she had felt betrayed and trapped, and way, way out of control of the situation.

Well, she had had enough time to cool down and think, thank God. She had thought of the cabdriver's words, that love took some time to work. She knew she was in love with Kyle, but it was a very new kind of love, wild and crazy and not what she was used to, nothing like the calm, loving friendship sort that she had had with Jeffrey. Maybe it would last; maybe it wouldn't. But she was sensible enough to know that it would take time, and it would take some work. Everything took work, didn't it?

And Kyle was worth it. Beyond his looks, he was a kind-hearted guy, the sort who couldn't stop rescuing lost dogs and cats, and who could resist a guy like that? He cooked delicious meals, and he loved to watch her eat. He was smart, he was innovative, and he had drive and worked hard. If he hadn't been a conscious part of her mother's schemes, then he was probably as ticked off as she had been. But he'd responded with one of the most creative proposals she'd ever seen, and if he could reason things out, if he thought she was worth it, then she had to give him a chance.

Besides, if neither he nor she knew about her mother's machinations, then did it really matter? They had for all intents and purposes fallen in love with each other all by themselves. Nobody made them do it; they just did it. Amy shook her head at herself. She'd been stupid. Well, she wouldn't be stupid any longer.

The plane landed at last, and Amy rushed out to the cab station, grabbed the door of a cab, and jumped in. She gave the address of Nakagawa Enterprises in Kent, and waited.

And waited. It was rush hour on Interstate 5, one of the most notoriously congested highways in the nation. Amy groaned. *Hurry, hurry,* she thought. At least Kyle tended to stay late at work. She might catch him before he left. Five-thirty. The offices officially closed at six. *Please, please don't let me be late. Please don't let Mom get there before I do.*

The cab stopped at the office entrance and Amy hastily shoved two twenties at him and ran to the office door. She smiled at the receptionist and said, "Amy Miyazaki, and I'm here to meet Kyle Nakagawa—he's expecting me; I'll go in now," in the most cheerful way she could. The receptionist opened her mouth to protest, but Amy sped by her. She sprinted up the stairs and rounded the corner to Kyle's office.

He wasn't there. Amy groaned. *Great.* What if he had left for the day? She looked around frantically and caught sight of Dave, his cousin.

"Dave!"

"Amy—say, what's up? Why are you—"

"I'm looking for my mother." She sighed. "And Kyle. Did she come by here?"

He nodded, looking at her curiously. "Sure. She's in the meeting room with—"

She looked at him and groaned. "Not with Kyle?"

Dave hesitated. "Well, I don't know. I know she was meeting with Uncle Toshi. Whether Kyle decided to talk with them . . ." He shrugged.

"Thanks." Amy looked around. It was too late, but maybe she could stop her mother from causing more damage. Yes, there was the meeting room. She went to it and opened the door.

And faced not her mother nor the senior Mr. Nakagawa, but Kyle and a group of businessmen. She stopped, stared at Kyle's startled face, and backed out. "Sorry," she muttered, and felt her face grow hot.

Stupid! She hurried away. *Forget it.* It was a stupid idea, and it was clear she was barging in and not being very effective. She wasn't being businesslike. In fact, she was acting horribly unprofessionally. She'd go back out to the reception area, calm her nerves by reading the magazines there, and wait her turn . . . and hopefully melt into the furniture and disappear.

But she had wanted to see Kyle. She had wanted to see him so badly it hurt, and once again she hadn't thought. She didn't quite know if she wanted to marry him, if just the thought of him made her not think. It wasn't like her. She was used to thinking things through all the time.

"Amy!"

She turned. It was Kyle. She felt frozen in place, unable to decide whether to stay or leave. But by the time she decided to run it was too late. He had taken her hand and was leading her to his office. He shut the door, then turned and faced her.

"Your meeting," Amy protested. "I'm sorry . . . I didn't mean . . . It was stupid of me, very unprofessional—"

"The meeting's over," he said firmly. "Forget about it." He pulled her to him and kissed her. She sighed and put her arms around him, giving in to the kiss. "Good," he said, parting from her for a moment. "You still like it." He kissed her again.

"Oh, Kyle," Amy said, and felt tears bubbling up inside. "I'm so sorry."

He put his fingers to her lips. "Hush. Don't worry about it. My dad and Dave explained it all. You didn't know about it, and neither did I. They and your mother arranged it all. I swear, I've never met a more controlling set of people. We should skip a marriage ceremony and elope just to spite them."

Marriage. Amy looked up at him. "I don't know. I know I love you, but we haven't known each other that long."

He kissed her again. "Not a problem. I can wait. Meanwhile we can have lots of sex, and I'll feed you tons of chicken yakisoba."

Laughter bubbled up inside her along with the tears. "Chicken yakisoba. You think you can seduce me with chicken yakisoba?"

"Think? I know I can." He kissed her neck and moved his hands to her hips, pressing her close to him. "I've done it before." He moved from her a little, looking into her eyes. "I love you. It's just been a short time, but I know it. Crazy, huh? But if you can't think about marrying me, I'll wait."

She raised her hand and stroked his cheek. "Oh, Kyle, I've been thinking about it ever since I left. I think I want to. Yes, I want to. And I also want to get to know you better."

He sighed and kissed her again. "I can live with that," he said. His stomach growled, and he grinned. "It's about time for dinner, and I've skipped lunch. How about you come over to my place? I'll make you some chicken yakisoba."

Amy grinned and kissed him once more.

Mrs. Miyazaki peeped through the door of Kyle's office, and smiled. She closed the door quietly. *See?* She had fixed it. All she had to do was tell Amy she was going to come up to Washington, and do nothing. She knew her daughter. Amy would want to fix up her fix, and she would come back to Kyle; then everything would be good between them. And here it had come about. It was too bad that both of them would think they had returned to each other without her help. But this did not matter. It was better this way. Both of them were too stubborn, too used to having their own way. They were a good match; didn't she know it all along?

Mrs. Miyazaki moved away from the office and took the elevator down. She would return to her hotel room, and then after a few days of shopping in Seattle she would return to San Francisco. She had a wedding dress to make for Amy, and it would be the best one she had made so far. Nothing would be too good for her daughter; she would buy the best silk, the best lace. She sighed in satisfaction. Yes, she had done very well for her daughter. Very well.

And once Amy's wedding was all done . . . well, there were her customers, the rest of her children to deal with. Mrs. Miyazaki chuckled to herself. Yes, she was truly the Blind Date Empress of her neighborhood, and her life was very good. It was very good indeed.

A SIGNET ROMANCE SPECIAL EVENT ANTHOLOGY

LIVING LARGE

Rochelle Alers, Donna Hill, Brenda Jackson and Francis Ray

A voluptuously entertaining African-American fiction anthology about women who are livin' large—and lovin' larger!

Featuring all-new novellas by:

#1 Blackboard bestselling author Rochelle Alers, "one of the top 5 most popular African-American romance writers."

(Heart and Soul)

#1 Blackboard bestselling author Donna Hill, All-Time Favorite Fiction Author Award-winner *(Shades of Romance)*

#1 Blackboard bestselling author Brenda Jackson, winner of Viewer's Choice Best Multicultural *(Romantic Times)*

#1 Blackboard bestselling author, Francis Ray, whose stories "are written from the heart [and] definitely recommended."

(Eric Jerome Dickey)

0-451-20765-3

To order call: 1-800-788-6262

ONYX

Mary Jane Meier

"[A] heartwarming story of second chances and the healing power of love."
—Barbara Freethy

CATCH A DREAM

When rancher Zack Burkhart finds Meg Delaney stranded alone in Yellowstone, he offers her a place to stay. After Meg is dumped by her ex-fiance, Zack's Idaho ranch seems like a blessing—and the tall quiet rancher with tough hands and a soft touch makes Meg's heart sing.

Common sense tells her to return to Chicago and leave Zack to her fantasies.

But sometimes you have to throw your heart on a line—to catch a dream...

❑ 0-451-40975-2

To order call: 1-800-788-6262

O387/Meier